Sec

O

Heart Tattoo

Margaret Mc Cormack

First published in paperback by
Michael Terence Publishing in 2021
www.mtp.agency

ISBN 9781800942059

'Live! Live the wonderful life that is in you!
Let nothing be lost upon you.

Be always searching for new sensations. Be afraid of nothing.'

Oscar Wilde (Irish Author)

'Most of us only find our own voices after we've sounded like a lot of other people. But the one thing that you have, that nobody else has is 'You'.'

'Your voice, your mind, your story, your vision.

So write and draw and build and play and dance and live as only you can.'

'A book is a dream, you hold in your hand.'

Neil Gaiman (English Author)

Dear Readers,

This book is my dream, come true.

I hope you enjoy your journey through its pages, as much as I loved writing it.

I have included in my novel, my favourite uplifting, and cheerful word;

'Yippee!' (6 times), for my family and friends to find and enjoy.

I hope that you, my lovely readers, will also enjoy finding the cheerful word; 'Yippee!'

Many thanks for buying my novel.

This is book is dedicated to my wonderful family and friends.

- Love Margaret -

Chapter 1

Paul's footsteps faltered, as he approached the door of Siam College. He felt anxious and irritable, and he cleared his throat a number of times, to shake off his nerves. He took a few deep breaths to appear calm and composed, as he swung the door open, with attitude.

He knew, once again, he had been manipulated by his friend, Jayne Tierney, when he heard himself, foolishly agree, to attend 'Creative Writing Classes.'

As usual he was early, and of course there was no sign of Jayne. He wasn't at all surprised, Jayne was so laid back, she left everything to the last minute, yet somehow she always managed to get there, just in the nick of time.

Paul on the other hand, was always early for work, or meeting friends, he had a phobia about being late, and he wasn't pleased, when kept waiting.

Even though, Jayne knew this, she was frequently late for their 'rendezvous', and she just laughed, when he scolded her. She was such a good friend he always forgave her, but this time, he really wasn't impressed with her tardiness.

Paul dismissed his jumbled thoughts and forced himself to come back to the present moment, with a feeling of trepidation.

Unsure of what was causing his extreme anxiety, he sent Jayne a text; 'Please hurry, I have arrived at college.'

Paul now wondered why … he always gave in to Jayne's whims, like these silly creative writing classes, which he had absolutely no interest in attending. He was annoyed with himself for feeling so nervous and insecure; he was behaving like a baby. Normally he was quite calm; people said he had his late Mum's, quiet air of calmness.

Well, he certainly didn't seem to have that calmness this evening.

'What is wrong with me?'

'It's only a creative writing class. It's just a pastime, something to take my mind off Marissa, another failed relationship,' he mused.

As usual, Jayne's arrival was one of drama and excitement.

'I am really looking forward to the class, hope you are too Paul,' she said excitedly.

'Not really, you know well, I don't want to be here,' he muttered.

'Let's sit over there,' Jayne smiled, and nudged him, while ignoring his comment.

Suddenly Paul gasped.

'What's wrong?' Jayne asked.

'Nothing, I am just being foolish, I thought I saw Marissa rushing down the corridor.'

'You must be hallucinating,' Jayne giggled.

'It's not funny; she's been on my mind today, as it's her birthday.'

'Well, it's your fault it ended; I really don't know why you broke up with her.'

'It's probably just someone who looks like her,' Jayne said softly.

'You're probably right.'

'I am always right,' she laughed heartily.

Jayne and Paul knew each other for years, and they were totally at ease in each other's company. They were constantly in touch by text, and they met quite often for coffee, a glass of wine or a beer, depending on their mood. Neither of them were heavy drinkers, so they didn't suffer the dreadful hangover days, their friends often endured.

Paul was very popular with the ladies and his lustrous, jet black hair, added to his boyish looks and charm. He was actually unaware, and uninterested in how handsome he looked.

Jayne often teased him about his popularity.

'All my friends fancy you, all I ever hear is; 'Paul Rutlin is a fine thing!"

To hide his embarrassment, he'd smile and tease her.

'I suppose you fancy me too.'

'No way, I actually have good taste.'

'You are like, the brother I never had.'

Jayne had only one sister Imelda, who lived in Australia, so Paul had become her confidant, her friend, and her soul mate. They met during their first year in University, and they immediately became firm friends.

Some of Paul and Jayne's friends were convinced, they were in a relationship together, and they continually teased them.

But they both very firmly denied it, they didn't elaborate on their friendship, they just calmly said;

'No, we are not a couple, we are just wonderful friends.'

They didn't care, whether people believed them, or not.

They were inseparable, until Jayne took a year out, and travelled with her three friends to Australia. Paul sadly declined Jayne's very tempting invite to travel, as he was in his final year of gruelling accountancy exams. Jayne was disappointed but she totally understood.

'I have to continue my studies, and I'll also be busy working part-time for 'Winters & Son Solicitors', doing their book keeping and some training in the legal area of the firm,' he said.

'Don't let a wonderful trip to Australia and lots of fun stand in your way,' she teased.

'They also offered me a full time position, when I become a chartered accountant,' he explained, feeling quite torn between the superb job offer, or fun with Jayne and the girls.

When Jayne returned from her travels, they continued their friendship, as though they hadn't been separated by oceans and continents.

She had lots of exciting and funny stories for Paul, but she always emphasised; 'Even though I had an awesome time in Australia, I yearned for Ireland, and unlike Imelda, I could never settle, 'Down Under.'

Paul was secretly pleased Jayne was back home and part of his life again.

Paul couldn't seem to relax, and he even heard himself sighing, it wasn't like him to be so out of control of his feelings.

Jayne asked; 'Are you okay?'

'I don't feel good, I wish I hadn't come,' he said like a bold child.

'Don't worry you'll be fine, class is about to start,' Jayne pacified him.

It was his lack of control of the situation, and his strong negative feelings, which surprised and irritated him.

For some unknown reason, all day, he felt there was a heavy, black cloud hanging over him, weighing him down, and suffocating him. His gut feeling was, something bad was about to happen. He wasn't the premonitions type, but today there was something unusual happening, which was totally out of his control.

'Perhaps, it's because Marissa's birthday is today,' he pondered.

She was constantly on his mind. He recalled how much she loved her birthday, and he was tempted, many times, to text her, which unsettled him.

After all, he was the one who ended a perfectly good relationship, just because he couldn't handle commitment.

He had become a carbon copy of his Dad, who had abandoned him, when his Mum died, and that upset him and infuriated, even more. He certainly didn't want to be like his Dad, who had deserted him and sent him to live with his Gran.

Paul always had a fear of commitment, and he thought by staying with Marissa, the next step would lead to marriage. He knew he wasn't ready for commitment, and it wasn't fair to keep wasting Marissa's time. She deserved someone who could give her the family life, she wanted. Paul knew he needed to sort out his commitment issues, or he would end up, a lonely, bitter old man.

He now recalled how he panicked when Marissa had suggested that; 'they live together.'

He had instantly and cruelly ended their lovely relationship, because the commitment of living together was just too much, he felt he would suffocate.

He should have realised that was the next step in their relationship, but foolishly he had been content, to just float along.

He didn't have the worry of a biological clock ticking loudly; 'Tick Tock, Tick Tock.' He actually wasn't interested in having children any day soon, or maybe never.

Just like his Dad, 'Commitment' had always been a 'no go area' for him.

He had to remind himself, numerous times that day; 'Don't send Marissa a birthday text; it will give her mixed messages, which is unfair to her. It's best to leave it be.'

He had tried so hard to live his life without Marissa, and he thought he was cured, but instead, here he was, like a love sick guy.

'Why can't I stop thinking about her today?'

'What is wrong with me?' he asked himself rather irritably.

A few days previously, over a coffee, he had said to Jayne;

'It's Marissa's birthday on the first day of the creative writing class, and I have a bad feeling about those classes.'

She had laughed loudly.

'I don't mean to be rude Paul, but I think you are fabricating things, and using your law knowledge to find a;

'Get out clause,' for not going to the classes.'

'Don't try to fool me with your 'law tricks.'

'I have never known you to be afraid of anything new, so trust me, you'll enjoy the classes, and it will be a distraction.'

'I am not trying to fool you,' Paul said firmly.

'I am not usually superstitious, but for some unknown reason, I have a bad feeling about these classes.'

'Please don't worry, you'll be fine, I will be with you every step of the way,' Jayne coaxed.

'I'll go, but if I don't like the classes, I'll quit,' he said firmly.

'Well, that's fair enough, but I know you'll love the classes.'

'You'll probably be sad at the end of term.' Jayne said looking quite chuffed.

'Don't be silly, I certainly won't be sad when the term ends, if I last that long.'

'You know well, I am not comfortable in large groups, I prefer to socialise with my friends, not sure if you are included in the friend zone,' he said trying to lighten the mood.

During class, Jayne noticed an unusual look in Paul's tired eyes; she couldn't tell if it was worry, fear or a mixture of both. She actually felt bad for forcing him to attend the classes, but he was really missing Marissa, and she had hoped it would be a light-hearted distraction, not torture, as Paul seemed to think.

She should have realised how much he disliked group activities, from his grumpy attitude in the walking club, the previous year.

She had persuaded him to join the walking club, but he had only lasted two weeks. When she questioned him about his reasons for leaving the club, he said firmly;

'When you forced me to join, I realised immediately, that it wasn't for me, as I am a free spirit.'

'I really don't like the idea of other people deciding for me;

'What route I should take, or when I am entitled to break for refreshments etc., during my well earned free time.'

'My free time is exactly that; 'Free from the shackles that bind us to time, every single day, of our working life.'

'I need to 'roam free' and 'walk free' in the evenings and at weekends, and not adhere to the rules and regulations of a club,' Paul had strongly emphasised.

'But you are very sociable, and you are very good with people, I am surprised you don't enjoy socialising in groups,' Jayne said looking rather puzzled.

'I work with all types of people, every hour of every day, so I value 'my free time', and it's my time to be alone, or be with friends, and not with a group of strangers.'

'I really don't know why I hang around with you, 'Mr Loner',' Jayne said laughingly.

Paul smiled, as he recalled what his Gran said about people who went walking, hiking, or joined clubs or gyms.

'What are you smiling at?' Jayne asked.

'My Gran never understood why people found it necessary, to join walking or hiking clubs, or gyms.

She'd say; 'Well, if people did manual work in the house, or in their gardens, or on the farm, they wouldn't need to walk the roads and by-ways of Ireland.'

'Doing physical work indoors or outdoors is enough exercise for the body, and there's no need to roam the streets or go to gyms etc. Manual work keeps the whole body, 'fit as a fiddle', and it never killed anyone.'

'Gran would emphatically state; 'there's no need for frivolous exercise,' Paul laughed.

'Did your Gran really say that?'

'Or is that another one of your tactics, to brainwash me, to roam free?' Jayne smiled.

'Yes, Gran honestly believed clubs and gyms were 'frivolous places of exercise,' and who's to say she was wrong?'

'I always thought she was very modern, but that sounds very old fashioned,' Jayne said.

'Gran was an extremely hard worker, so I guess; she didn't see the need for 'frivolous exercise', as she called it.'

'When vacuuming, gardening or doing any physical work indoors or outdoors, you are using all your muscles,' she'd say.

'I saw her point of view, but I did tease her about her rigid views on 'frivolous exercise.'

'Well, I knew she loved swimming, so I would tease her about wasting time swimming, when she should be doing housework or gardening,' Paul said laughingly.

'What about swimming Gran?' I would smugly ask her.

'What was her answer, to that question?'

Gran would say with an impish smile; 'Ah that's different, that's a real sport given to us by God, and it's so good for the mind and body.'

'As you know, Gran always had the last word on things, she was so clever, so witty, and she always made me smile.'

'I really loved her too, she was so adorable, so kind and always optimistic, a lovable rogue,' said Jayne smiling.

'Yes, she was an amazing lady; she definitely saved my sanity and my life when Mum died.'

'I really miss her, but I know Mum and Gran are watching over me, some days, I can really feel their presence,' Paul said sadly.

During class Paul found his mind constantly wandering, thinking about his lovely Gran. He knew she would probably laugh at the situation, he now found himself in. She was always so positive, and she would look for the good in every situation.

'I am dammed if I can find the good in this situation, maybe Gran will give me a sign,' he hoped.

He now recalled the funny stories; his Mum told him; how his Gran and her friends had learnt to swim.

'Your Gran and her friends taught themselves to swim, by literally jumping off the river bank. They constantly practised paddling and kicking their feet, until eventually they became co-ordinated and able to swim,' she had explained.

'With lots of practice, especially on long hot summer days, they soon mastered their swimming strokes and techniques.'

'Your Gran actually thought your Dad to swim,' his Mum said proudly.

Paul's face clouded over, whenever he thought of his Dad, who had deserted him after his Mum died.

'What kind of a man would leave his only son behind, to live with his

Gran?' Even though Paul hadn't wanted to move from Dublin to Cork, his Dad should have understood, and not abandoned him. It was because of his lack of parents, he had been bullied in school and Paul felt it was his Dad's fault for not protecting him; thankfully his Gran had been an amazing parent.

Paul recalled how he never tired of hearing his Mum's stories, about his Gran's swimming adventures, and in particular the story of the 'clothes robberies.'

His Mum had said laughingly; 'Just as a joke, people often took the swimmers clothes, which were throw on the river bank. But your Gran and her friends certainly didn't find it funny, especially on the cold, frosty, winter days, when they discovered their clothes had disappeared.'

'They waited in the freezing cold, while someone went in search of the missing clothes. They laughed about it later, but not while they were freezing, and looking very foolish in their 'birthday suits.'

His Mum had always laughed, as she re-told him, how his Gran and friends devised a plan to save them, from the dreaded; 'birthday suit' experience.

'The game plan was; 'The last person to dive into the water, had to keep watch over their clothes.'

In later years, when he asked his Gran about her swimming escapades, a sad look would appear on her usually smiley face, and she'd say;

'We had the best of 'craic', swimming in the river and it cost us nothing.'

'The joy and the laughs we had, when competing to be the first person in the water, was never ending … each time was like the first time, when Freddy would yell;

'Last person in, has to mind the clothes.'

'We just went for it, like the wild things we were then.'

She would smile, lost in the memory of all her lovely friends, trying to avoid the dreaded; 'Last person in the river moment.'

'The last person in, had to return to the river bank, and mind everyone's clothes.

'Needless to say, there was a lot of arguing over who actually was the last person to dive in,' Gran said.

'Were you ever last?' Paul had asked.

'Never,' she replied smirking.

Paul tried to catch her out, but she always said she had escaped the 'last person in moment.'

He knew she was a strong swimmer, and he secretly hoped, that she was never last.

Unable to focus on what Hazel, their tutor was saying, and lost in his own thoughts, Paul now recalled how sad he was, when his Dad, allowed him leave home and live with his Gran, shortly after his Mum died.

His Dad hadn't really put up a fight to keep him, which had confirmed what Paul always thought;

'For some unknown reason, his Dad didn't seem able to love him.'

Paul had overheard his Gran say to her friend, that his Dad, had commitment issues, and he tended to run away from difficult situations.

Now years later Paul was annoyed to see that history was repeating itself, and like his Dad he also had commitment issues.

Paul was lucky, his Gran was absolutely wonderful; she was like a mother and father to him, he never wanted for anything, and she was always there to console him, the days he missed his Mum. Many a night he cried himself to sleep, listening to the soothing, comforting tones of his Gran, as she lay on the bed beside him. She always seemed to know when he was having a bad day, and missing his Mum so much, he felt his heart was breaking.

Paul's Gran had gently tried to explain to him, why his Dad couldn't look after him; 'Your Dad finds it difficult to deal with the death of Simon, and the death of your Mum, that's why he left Dublin, he cannot deal with or accept what has happened.'

'He does love you, but before he can take care of you, he needs to sort himself out,' she said gently.

'I miss Mum and my brother Simon too, but I didn't run away,' he had said angrily.

'Your Dad will return home soon, when he's feeling better,' she promised.

Sadly, that was the only promise his Gran hadn't kept, his Dad hadn't returned home.

As Paul grew older, he tried to emulate his Gran's positive attitude and in particular her, 'can do' attitude;

'If Anyone Can Do It,

I Can!' was her motto in life.

She constantly encouraged him to repeat that affirmation, which she composed, if he was struggling with difficult homework and in particular, when he was bullied in school.

Paul repeated the affirmation until he felt strong and confident again. His Gran would say with a knowing smile;

'My affirmation will make you confident and strong enough to achieve anything; you set your mind on.'

'How right she was.'

In college and throughout his working life, Paul found himself repeating his Gran's affirmation; *'If Anyone Can Do It, I Can!'*

He was always amazed at how strong and confident it made him feel.

Paul suddenly found himself thinking of his school days, which weren't always happy times. He had really missed not having a Mum or Dad, like the other children, as it made him a target for the bullies.

Life wasn't easy when you came from a different background, and people teased him, when his Gran collected him from school.

'Your Mum is very old,' they sneered.

Paul had explained to them numerous times, that his Mum had died of cancer, and it was actually his Gran who collected him. He had some bad memories of school, as some of his class mates teased him rather cruelly.

'You have no Mum or Dad, you are an orphan,' Donal Keily, often yelled in the playground, delighted to have a large audience for his bullying ways.

'I have a Dad.' he would shout.

'Well, why don't you live with your Dad then?'

'Why doesn't he collect you from school?'

'Why does your very old Mother always collect you?' he jeered.

'She's not my Mum, she's my Gran, my Mum is dead, I already told you,' he shouted back.

'Well, where's your Dad?'

'Is he dead too?' Donal mocked.

Unfortunately, no one had prepared him for those awkward questions, so he struggled to answer them.

He was too sad and ashamed to admit, that his Dad had abandoned him, and sent him to live with his Gran. If Donal ever found out the true story, he would bully him even more, so Paul was determined no one would ever know, of his Dad's desertion.

He never mentioned in school, how much he missed his Mum, and his brother Simon, who was killed by a drunk driver. He bore his secrets and scars bravely, unlike his cowardly Dad, who had deserted him, when his Mum died of cancer.

Donal constantly shouted, and bullied him in the school yard;

'You are an orphan!'

'Nobody wants you,' he sniggered, playing to his audience.

Finally, Paul could take no more abuse, and he retaliated with his fists.

'Fight, Fight!' the children had screamed.

Sometimes in his dreams, Paul could still hear the echoes of those dreadful chants.

Unfortunately, he got into trouble with the principal, Mr Fisher for fighting with Donal.

Mr Fisher spoke to his Gran;

'We cannot condone children fighting, so perhaps, you could explain to Paul; fighting is not the answer, when things don't go his way.'

'He must learn to control his temper.'

'I have also spoken to Donal, and to his parents, and we will monitor the situation.' Mr Fisher said kindly.

Paul recalled how angry his Gran was, upon hearing, he had actually hit Donal first.

'We need to talk,' she said rather sternly.

'I probably should have prepared you, for people like Donal Keily, who fear anyone who is different from them.'

'In future, you must learn to speak, rather than use physical force on Donal, or anyone who ever tries to bully you.'

'Often people bully, because they are insecure or jealous, so don't allow them to make you the victim. Please try to understand that you are 'Not,' the problem, they are the ones with the problem,' she said kindly.

Paul now recalled how his wonderful, kind Gran, held his hand and said;

'That boy, Donal appears to be insecure, and he's probably jealous because you have a different story to tell. He may be jealous because you get more attention than he does, because you live with, 'your Gran'.'

'Be patient with him, and he will come to accept you, and not feel threatened by you.' 'When he no longer feels threatened by you, he will leave you alone.'

'Do you understand what I am saying?'

'Yes, Gran,' he replied, knowing she would always protect him.

'When Donal is shouting and teasing you, just say;

'That's right Donal, whatever you say.'

'He'll get tired of teasing you.'

'But, do tell me if that doesn't work, and I will talk to Mr Fisher.'

'Promise me you'll try to be patient, and you won't hit Donal again.'

'I promise,' Paul had said, not wishing to upset his Gran again.

Paul had always trusted his Gran so he took her advice, and he endured weeks of harassing and bullying, and just, when he was about to ask her for help, things suddenly changed.

Donal got tired of bullying Paul, because he got no reaction, and thankfully he stopped harassing Paul, 'just like his Gran said.'

Paul's Gran always played a very important role throughout his life, and he hoped and prayed that today she would protect him.

'Paul, what's going on, are you okay?'

'You seemed in another world,' Jayne whispered.

'Sorry, I was just thinking of Gran; she would probably have a good laugh seeing me in a 'creative writing class'.'

'I know you idolised your Gran, and believe me, she would be happy that you are here.'

'Yes, I idolised her, and I miss her so much.'

'I always feel that she protects me, but I am not sure where she is today,' he said worriedly.'

'You are doing fine, she is right by your side,' Jayne said softly.

A few minutes later, Paul was distracted again, with thoughts of his Gran, and he begged her, to help him through the class. He missed her every day, but he was glad she hadn't suffered; she had died in her sleep, exiting the world quickly and quietly, exactly as she had wished.

He now recalled how the bond between him and his Gran grew stronger, as he grew older. She was so wise and so trendy; and she even encouraged and helped him save for his new house. She was sad the day he moved out, but as usual she quickly looked on the positive side and said;

'I am so happy for you Paul, you so deserve to have a place of your own, a place to call 'home'.'

'I know your Mum and Dad would be so proud of you. You are very independent, you are a great guy, and you have a bright future ahead of you,' she proudly said.

When he was younger Paul had often wondered how Mum's, and in his case his Gran, always seemed to know, when children were up to mischief. He remembered hearing the saying;

'Mums, have eyes in the back of their heads.'

'Well, so does Gran,' he believed.

No matter what he was up to when he was younger, Gran always seemed to know.

In particular, the time he couldn't concentrate on his Leaving Certificate study, and he sneaked over to Liam's house, while his Gran was enjoying her gardening.

Liam was a great pal, and even though he was an impish character, he had wise ways too. So when Paul arrived at his door, asking for study advice, he was willing to help.

Feeling frustrated Paul said; 'Liam, no matter what I do, I just can't seem to study, and I can't concentrate. When I recap on what I have read, all I remember are bits and pieces, all mumble-jumble.'

'I get so frustrated, because I am trying my utmost to study, and nothing is happening, just 'blankety blank.'

'Don't worry, we all have days like that,' Liam said wisely.

'What I'd suggest is; set some study targets, work solely on them, and then take short breaks as a reward.'

'Perhaps, on your breaks, watch some funny videos on 'YouTube', like I do.'

'That will perk you up, give you a good laugh, and help you to relax.'

'I guarantee you'll have no problem studying after the 'YouTube videos,' and things will actually sink into your large brain,' Liam laughed.

'Really, you think it's that easy. I am not so sure, but I am willing to try anything.'

'I really need to concentrate and revise, or I will definitely fail my exams.'

'Well, that certainly works for me, so try it. You will find your own special plan after a day or two.'

When Paul returned home, his Gran wasn't impressed.

'I thought you were studying for your exams,' she said rather crossly.

'I was Gran, I was studying with Liam.'

'Really?'

'Where are your books?'

'Oh no, I must have left my school bag in Liam's house,' Paul said anxiously.

'Would this be the bag you are talking about?' she asked, walking over to the couch, and holding up his school bag.'

Unfortunately, he had forgotten, he had thrown his bag behind the couch, after school.

He couldn't believe how his Gran had spotted his school bag, especially as she always claimed she had bad eyesight.

'Nothing wrong with your eyesight Gran,' he thought to himself.

'No need to go to 'Specsavers' optician, Gran.' he muttered.

'What did you say?' she asked in an angry tone.

'Nothing, Gran,' he said thinking; 'Not much wrong with your hearing either.'

Once again, Jayne interrupted his thoughts and whispered;

'Are you with us Paul?'

'Yes, I heard everything Hazel said,' he fibbed.

Paul tried again to concentrate, but he found himself constantly slipping back, into the land of reminiscing.

He recalled how his friend Liam told him stories, how his Mum caught him out on small, insignificant lies. She too seemed to have 'eyes in the back of her head.'

'I never did anything really bad, just small things, but Mum always caught me.'

'Like the time, I skived off school, and went to a movie. My neighbour, who was on a day off from work, spotted me going into the cinema.'

'How unlucky was that?' he asked Paul.

'Then another day, I decided not to go to school, 'Miss Busybody' sees me in the shop, and goes running telling tales to Mum.'

Paul laughed and said; 'Was that really her name, Miss Busybody?'

'Very funny, you know what I mean; she's one of those people, who are always watching everybody else.'

'She is always commenting on people's actions, and always causing trouble,' Liam said looking perplexed.

'You were so funny, you always got caught, I don't know why you kept trying to fool your parents.'

'Do you remember another time, you skived off from school, one lovely summer afternoon, you went fishing and you fell into the lake?' Paul laughed heartily.

'Your Mum nearly killed you, when she saw your wet clothes, and your dishevelled appearance.'

'Of course I remember, she was very upset, because I went to the lake alone.'

She ranted for days saying; 'If you got into difficulty, there was no one there to save you, from drowning.'

'Good God Mum, I was only fishing, not swimming for Ireland,' I joked, but she failed to see the funny side.

'She was right; you shouldn't have gone fishing alone, in case you had an accident and drowned.'

'Where I was fishing, the water was only up to my knees, I couldn't have drowned, you fool.'

'I tripped and I fell awkwardly, and that's why my clothes got wet.'

'You know, you shouldn't be fishing alone at the lake, anyway.'

'Give me a break, you're wrecking my head, you sound like my Mum.'

Liam had nudged Paul, and they both laughed at the absurdity of his antics.

Paul actually smiled thinking of his childhood memories, and his lovely friend Liam, who now lived in New York.

'Do I actually see a smile?'

'I knew you would enjoy Hazel's classes,' Jayne whispered smugly.

Not wanting to admit his lack of commitment to Hazel's tutoring, Paul kept smiling.

'Let Jayne think what she likes, if it keeps her happy and off my case, it's a victory for both of us,' he thought smugly.

Since his split with Marissa, Paul felt he had lost confidence. He felt so confused lately, and his mind was in a whirl, he didn't want to settle down and get married.

'But why then did he have this empty feeling?'

He was a free agent again; he should have been full of the joys of life, and not this sad, empty feeling, and missing Marissa, so much, it hurt.

He had really enjoyed the happiness, and the fun Marissa brought to his life.

She was like; 'A breath of fresh air and a joy to be with.'

'Why then, couldn't he settle down with Marissa, and have a family like most normal people?'

'What is wrong with me?'

It suddenly dawned on him, he wasn't like normal people. He definitely had a phobia about marriage, children, and about living with the same person for the rest of his life. He really didn't think he was husband material, and he felt panicky at the thoughts of ever becoming a Dad.

He was still trying to sort out his own life, maybe his Dad's abandonment, had actually affected him more than he realised.

'How could he ever protect and love a child, when he was so mixed up himself?' he pondered.

Knowing his phobia on the subject, Jayne often broached and even provoked him, on the topic of children, but he tried to avoid the subject, like a virus or a plague.

'For heaven's sake Paul, nobody is born with the knowledge of how to rare children.' 'There is no school for parenting.'

'Haven't you and I, and most of the world turned out well, considering our parents winged it. They had no helpful parenting books, or apps, or social media to refer to?'

'Sometimes too much knowledge is a bad thing; the mind gets more confused, with the reams of advice, and opinions from the so called 'experts',' Jayne said.

'No matter what you say, it won't change my mind.'

'The thoughts of being in charge of a tiny, defenceless baby, really scares me.'

'It just wouldn't be fair to Marissa, or to a baby, if I was permanently in their lives.'

'It just wouldn't work,' he emphasised heatedly.

'You're a smart man; you are well able to take care of a baby.'

'I am telling you, I wouldn't be, and more importantly, I have no interest in children.'

'It actually overwhelms me to think that, a tiny little person would depend on me, to make good choices for them.'

'Let's face it; my Dad didn't do a great job with me.'

'Where would I have ended up, if my Gran hadn't taken over, when Mum died?'

'I think I have my Dad's genes, not my Mum's where children are concerned.'

'My Dad and I are both hopeless cases in the children's arena.'

'My goodness Paul, maybe you are right.'

'An arena is for animals, not for children.'

'If you can't distinguish between children and animals, maybe it's best, you don't have children,' Jayne said jokingly.

Chapter 2

Marissa Moray was extremely annoyed, when her sister Rebecca phoned and said she had to work late.

'I can't believe you are not going to the 'Creative Writing Class'.'

'You forced me to spend my hard earned money, on something I had no interest in, and now you're not going'

'I was making the effort for you, as I have no inclination to be a writer,' Marissa sulked.

'It's just tonight, I can't go, I'll definitely go next week,' Rebecca said trying to console Marissa.

'Thanks for nothing.'

'I was forcing myself to go to support you, and now you expect me to go alone.'

'Please, don't be angry with me.'

'Believe me; I would rather go to a creative writing class, than face this large bundle of students' work,' Rebecca said.

'Okay, I'll go, but I am not happy at all about this.'

'You'll definitely owe me a coffee treat, next week,' Marissa said.

'No problem, I'll phone you later,' Rebecca said delighted, that Marissa was braving it alone.

'I better go, before I change my mind,' Marissa said anxiously.

Rebecca had been incredibly supportive to Marissa, when Paul, the love of her life, broke up with her. She felt she owed Rebecca a favour, and that's the only reason, she agreed to attend the 'creative writing classes.'

She really couldn't go back on her word now. If she didn't make the effort this week, it would be even more difficult next week, as she would have longer to procrastinate. Anyway, Rebecca was probably right, it would be a distraction, and it would definitely keep her mind off Paul.

She had really worked hard, trying to move on with her life, after her breakup with Paul. She was proud of herself, as thoughts of him no longer took over, every waking minute of her day.

Of course she still thought about him, but she had made good progress, she no longer thought about that part of her life, all day every day.

She only spoke about him when family or friends, inquired how she was feeling, but she quickly changed the subject, without appearing rude.

So, when Marissa very reluctantly walked into Siam College, and saw Paul in the distance, she felt like screaming and running.

He was talking to a very pretty lady and thankfully, he didn't see her. She ran to the ladies as fast as she could.

Marissa was shocked and very disappointed at how upset she felt. All her great efforts to accept the fact, Paul no longer wanted to be with her, just floated away. Suddenly she was back to the emotional wreck; she had been in the beginning of their break up.

'Why am I so upset?' she questioned.

'After all, Paul was only; 'talking to the lady' and he had every right to be at the class,' she consoled herself.

Perhaps, it was because he seemed so interested in chatting to the lady, and he was looking at her so attentively. It had reminded Marissa of the special way, he always looked at her.

Throughout their relationship, Paul had been a true gentleman; he had been devoted and faithful to Marissa. He was a great friend, a true soul mate and a romantic lover.

He didn't ogle, or chat up every good looking woman, like some of her ex-boyfriends. She knew he had issues with commitment, but nobody was perfect.

'Except herself, of course … joke!'

She hadn't realised how trapped commitment made Paul feel, until she asked him to move in with her. His reaction was crazy and so unexpected, and he had suddenly ended their relationship. She foolishly, hadn't seen that coming.

Marissa had been devastated and Rebecca had helped her through a very tough time. Weeks later, Rebecca said; 'It's so good to see you smile, you were like a weeping willow tree, your demeanour was so sad and droopy, but now you are looking strong, and willowy like an ash tree.'

'Wow, thanks for that analogy, I presume it's meant as a compliment, I am not sure how I feel, being compared to a tree,' Marissa smiled.

'You know how much I love trees and nature, so yes, it's totally meant as a compliment. I am so proud of you, you are my favourite tree like figure,' Rebecca giggled.

It was Marissa's birthday today, and she was feeling a bit more vulnerable than usual. Unexpectedly, seeing Paul on her special day most certainly didn't help her mood. She recalled how Paul had always pampered her, and made her feel very special on her birthday.

Marissa had told him; 'My birthday, is 'My Special day'.'

'It's the one day in the year, when all my family and friends, must be nice to me, whether they like it or not,' she laughed.

Marissa had always felt; 'A birthday was an important and momentous occasion, and must never be understated.'

She just loved the celebration of her birth, into this amazing, but sometimes crazy world. She wasn't too pleased that each birthday, she was aging, but she loved all the fun, and pampering on her special day. She always tried to accept the aging process gracefully, of course.

Reading some witty sayings about age, always managed to cheer her up;

'*Age is a case of mind over matter – if you don't mind, it doesn't matter.*'

She loved and never tired of reading these positive quotes about age, from 'Abraham Lincoln' and 'CS Lewis';

'In the end, it's not the years in your life that count; it's the life in your years.' Abraham Lincoln.

'You are never too old, to set another goal or to dream a new dream.'

C.S. Lewis.

Throughout her relationship with Paul, Marissa's birthday mornings, had always started with a 'cheerful birthday greeting text' from him.

She was surprised how sad she felt, when she didn't receive, the longed for 'birthday text.'

Paul had always sent a text, at exactly 12am on the morning of her birthday. She had foolishly thought he would still send her a birthday text. Obviously, in his eyes, they weren't even friends now, it made her realise, he had definitely severed all ties and moved on, which was a blow to her ego, and her confidence.

Her lovely family and friends had sent texts, and friends had phoned her, throughout her special day. Alas, not Paul, the one person she really wanted to hear from.

She now realised, no matter how hard she tried to move on, she still loved him, and she really missed him.

Marissa took a deep breath to return to the 'Now', as her 'Mindfulness Practice classes' had taught her. It suddenly dawned on her, the lady Paul was talking to was Patricia, whom they had previously met at the 'Mindfulness Practice classes', which she had dragged Paul to. Now that she realised it was Patricia, she felt a lot better, obviously they had only met in class.

She took a deep breath in through her nostrils, and let it out slowly after five seconds, she straightened her posture, which made her feel taller and braver. She concentrated on her birthday, to keep her mind off Paul.

She always got lots of birthday cards and presents, mostly because she drove her family mad, by sending lots of 'birthday reminder texts.' She usually sent 'the birthday reminder texts' months and weeks before her actual birthday. She enjoyed the fun of constantly reminding people of her special day.

As a teenager, she had discovered that most people forgot about 'birthdays', unintentionally. of course. They were so exhausted from the hustle and bustle of life, and birthdays became another task, to put on the long, long finger.

The last thing people needed was the chore of organising another birthday card, or choosing another present.

To add fun to birthdays, and to take the stress away from people having to remember her birthday, Marissa had devised the plan to send, 'birthday text reminders to family.'

She enjoyed sending the texts, and she felt most people actually enjoyed the fun too, even though they pretended otherwise. She simply loved her birthday, and she was determined every year, no matter how old she was, she would always celebrate and enjoy her birthday, Yippee! (1)

Suddenly Marissa felt she couldn't face Paul, she was feeling too vulnerable. She raced out of college, but only went a short distance when she thought;

'Why should I hide from Paul, I have done nothing wrong?'

'Isn't today, as good a day as any, to face him?'

'It's a small city, and I can't avoid him forever,' she thought.

Marissa now recalled how shocked she was, when Paul ended their relationship, she certainly hadn't expected it.

When she had asked him, what he thought of the idea, of them living together, she had foolishly presumed he'd be happy.

She would never forget his reply.

'Marissa, actually I think we should stop seeing each other, I feel I am wasting your time.'

'I don't want a serious relationship, and I feel you deserve someone who will offer you marriage and children.'

At first, she was so shocked she couldn't speak, but then she found her voice;

'Paul, what a crazy thing to say, I am not looking for a husband or children.'

'I thought you loved me, as much as I love you.'

'It's difficult trying to live in two places, so I thought we could live together instead.'

'I am so sorry Marissa, I just need my space.'

'I can't commit to our relationship any longer,' he blurted out.

Marissa had noticed Paul had a fear of getting hurt, and of getting too attached to anyone. It was probably because of his turbulent relationship with his Dad, who according to Paul had betrayed him.

Marissa knew she had been blessed with wonderful parents, and her lovely sister Rebecca.

But sadly when she asked Paul about his family, he explained; he hadn't seen his Dad in years, and his Mum and his brother Simon had died. He told her that his Dad had abandoned him when his Mum died, and sent him to live with his Gran, and now sadly his lovely Gran, had passed on.

Recently Marissa had honestly thought, he had overcome the fear of commitment, and that they were on the same page, as a couple.

'How wrong she was!'

She had been so happy with Paul, he was her soul mate, a total gem in her eyes, and a true gentleman and they seldom argued. They often laughed so much, the tears ran down their faces, and their sides ached from all the fun. They had the same wicked sense of humour, and they were extremely content in each other's company. They had a good circle of friends and they mixed well.

'So, what went wrong?'

That was the question she kept asking herself, especially at the beginning of their break up.

She forced herself back to reality and took a deep 'Mindfulness breath'. She uttered a sigh; she straightened her shoulders, and got ready to face Paul. She had learnt in Mindfulness class, that living in 'the now', and breathing mindfully kept the mind and body calm, she was determined she would be as friendly as possible, and show no signs of weakness.

She had no intention of letting Paul see, any chink of sadness in her armour. She would be the brave warrior, her family and friends thought she was.

She would act, like she never acted before.

The irony of it all, she would now use the affirmation he had taught her, and his Gran had taught him.

'If anyone can do it, I can!'

She would put it to the test now, and try to act as calm as possible. So far in her life it had worked, but this was her first really big test, and she was determined to succeed.

Like a ventriloquist, she repeated the motto under her breath; it made her feel strong and confident, as she walked towards the classroom;

'If anyone can do it, I can!'

Marissa quickly scanned the room, she spotted Patricia, and they smiled and waved at each other. Suddenly, Paul was beside her, and she nearly faltered, but thankfully the motto kicked in.

She heard herself speak very calmly, even though the butterflies in her tummy were doing extraordinary summersaults. Thank heavens, he couldn't see or hear the commotion, in her tummy, or see her poor broken heart.

Marissa had read on a 'breakup advice' website;

'A city becomes a battlefield, after a breakup.'

After her relationship ended, she had worried about the possibility of bumping into Paul. She had practiced lots of superficial things to say, if and when they met, as Dublin was a small city.

Of course she intended to act as calmly as possible, but unfortunately, things don't always happen as planned. She really hoped he couldn't hear the loud thumping of her heart.

She had finally said 'Goodbye' to the last chapter of her life with Paul, and she was determined not to reopen it, no matter how much her heart ached for Paul.

'That chapter is firmly closed, and it's staying shut, no matter what happens,' she reminded herself, rather firmly.

She must now shut down her feelings, to protect her poor broken heart. She knew only too well; 'Love could be so cruel at times.'

'Hi Paul, I never expected to see you at a 'Creative Writing class', but maybe you were dragged here, like I was,' she heard herself say, rather calmly.

'Hi Marissa, you're right, this is not my scene, Jayne forced me to come against my better judgement.'

'I foolishly promised her I would go, but if I don't like the classes, I'll be on my merry way.'

'Is Jayne here?'

'Yes, she went out for a glass of water.'

'I thought I spotted you earlier in the corridor.'

Marissa just smiled and pretended nothing; she didn't owe him any explanation for her earlier flight.

'Rebecca booked the classes for us, and then she had the nerve to tell me she couldn't make it tonight. I hope you enjoy the class.'

'I see a vacant seat over there, so I better go while it's free,' Marissa said sounding like she was totally in charge, of the most heart breaking situation.

'Talk to you later,' she heard Paul say, as she tried to walk away casually, even though her legs had turned to jelly, and her palms were sweating.

At least she had walked away with her dignity intact.

She was quite proud of herself.

No matter how heartbroken she felt, she was determined Paul must never know, how vulnerable she was. She took a few more deep breaths, and acted like 'a diva', calm and totally in control.

She felt she deserved a prestigious award, for her acting role of portraying, 'a happy, contented ex lover', while deep inside her heart was breaking. She thought her acting was definitely of 'Oscar' award standards.

She had no intention of talking to Paul later. She would leave the class as quickly as possible.

Jayne waved at Marissa as she took her seat beside Paul, and Marissa automatically smiled and waved. Marissa found it very difficult to concentrate on what Hazel, the lovely tutor was saying, but she forced herself to listen, and she tried not to look at Paul.

Unexpectedly, a silly thought came into Marissa's head; 'perhaps Rebecca knew Paul would be attending the classes.' She dismissed the thought as quickly as it came.

'How could she think such a terrible thing of her lovely sister?'

Her sister, who had been so kind and caring, throughout her recovery from the breakup.

Marissa always loved Rebecca's company, even though they were 'like chalk and cheese', they got along exceptionally well. Throughout the years, they were always there for each other, on the good and bad days.

Rebecca had been so supportive of Marissa, when Paul broke up with her. She would always be grateful for Rebecca's ability, to make even the darkest day, appear bright.

She really loved Rebecca's sense of humour and her impish ways. Rebecca was wild and witty; a good combination on any day of the week, but in particular on the cold, wet, dark winter's evenings.

After her split with Paul, Rebecca had phoned and sent texts to Marissa, every day for over a month. She had encouraged and persuaded her to come out from under the comfy duvet, and live life again.

Marissa now recalled, how grumpy and miserable she had been, especially during the first few weeks. She would be the first to confess, she was like a weasel, no matter what Rebecca said, she had snapped at her.

She had even said to Rebecca;

'How would you know, how I feel?'

'Your life is great, with your 'Mr Perfect'.'

'We can't all be lucky, and find the perfect man, like your 'Perfect Jim'.'

Marissa found it hard to believe, how cranky and cruel she felt, yet her wonderful sister continued to keep in touch. She kept texting, phoning, even though there must have been times, when Rebecca felt like letting her wallow in her own misery.

Thankfully, Rebecca understood, Marissa was just lashing out, because she was heartbroken, and she listened to her rants, and she didn't take it personal.

She stood by Marissa through the dark days, and they were many, especially in the beginning.

'I am so lucky to have such a wonderful caring sister, why am I thinking such bad things about her?'

'Of course, she didn't know Paul would be at the classes,' Marissa chided herself.

It was because of her sister's kindness, she had forced herself to go to the class. Rebecca was very arty, and she loved writing short stories and poems, while Marissa had no interest in creative writing, but she owed it to Rebecca, to support her for a change.

She had presumed that, using all her 'Mindfulness Practices', and having moved on with her life, she would be strong, when seeing Paul.

She definitely did deserve an 'Oscar' for her acting role, as she had handled it well, but alas, it was only on the outside. Unfortunately, inside she was a snivelling, weak bodied mess, whose legs and body had nearly failed her, when she spotted Paul.

Obviously, the wall she had built around herself wasn't half as strong as she thought.

A few years ago, she had been privileged to walk the 'Great Wall of China', or at least part of it, and she even had a plaque to prove it.

On the difficult days, she had used the image of the 'Great Wall' protecting her, like it protected the city.

She was shocked and disappointed how quickly her imaginary wall, had come crashing down, when she saw Paul.

All her feelings and emotions, had come to the fore, and she had used all her will power, to stop the tears from flowing.

'Does a broken heart ever fully mend?' she pondered.

At first, when Marissa was missing Paul and feeling so bad mentally and physically, she had conferred with her good friends, 'Google' and 'YouTube', to see what advice they could offer, to ease the dreadful, excruciating pain in her heart, her head, and her sick tummy.

Of course, this was mostly caused by too much crying, and not enough nutritious food, as she couldn't motivate herself to prepare dinners.

She was too busy wallowing in self pity, and the junk food aided the 'self pity process.'

She was a firm believer in 'Google' and 'YouTube', and thankfully, she found peoples' advice and comments quite helpful.

Rebecca had constantly reminded her, what she read on 'Google' or listened to on 'YouTube' was not the gospel, and not always true, but she was so desperate, she tried everything, apart from the 'happy pills.'

She felt 'happy pills' were only a temporary solution, and she needed a permanent fix, for sure.

Some of the information and advice she read, she already knew of course like;

'Everyone goes through heartbreak at some time in their lives.'

'At the time, it feels like the worst thing in the world. The signs of a broken heart are physical and mental, and knowing your heart is broken, is the first step you take, in order to mend it again.'

'Wow, she felt she could have written that piece herself.'

'Yet, it was very kind of people, taking time to share their pain and their advice, to help broken hearted people,' she thought.

When Marissa read the signs, which show your heart is breaking, she had all the symptoms and more;

> *'A list of the signs your heart is breaking;'*
>
> *'You can't stop crying.*
>
> *You can't sleep.*
>
> *You can't eat.*
>
> *Your chest hurts.*
>
> *You can't get the person out of your mind.*
>
> *You constantly try to figure out what went wrong.*
>
> *You get distracted easily.*
>
> *It's all you can talk about.*
>
> *You blame yourself.'*

Unfortunately, the article didn't have the answers to mending a broken heart.

Eventually, Marissa's research finally led her to the advice of 'the six steps to healing a broken heart.' She had tried so hard to take those six steps, especially on the numerous difficult, weepy, self pity days.

The 6 steps to 'Healing a Broken Heart:'

1. *Take heart, you will get through this.*
2. *Talk to people who care.*
3. *Allow yourself be human and feel the pain.*
4. *Take your broken heart to God, for healing.*
5. *Give yourself time to heal.*
6. *Learn lessons from the experience.*

Thankfully she had managed to keep her office life and her private life separate, so nobody in work knew Paul had deserted her.

In time she would mention it casually, as all her workmates kept their personal cards, close to their chest.

Marissa knew she wouldn't get much sympathy anyway, they were nice people, but they were all quite clinical. They definitely didn't wear their hearts on their sleeves, so she most certainly wouldn't either.

Chapter 3

Marissa took her 'Google' and 'YouTube' research advice on board, she worked extremely hard on the healing process of moving on, without Paul.

Each morning she used her 'Mindfulness Practices; 'Deep breathing, showering and dressing mindfully, eating mindfully, brushing her teeth mindfully and walking to work mindfully.'

It wasn't an easy task; 'Living in the moment and not allowing her sad thoughts intrude and distract her.'

Each day, she tried to live in the 'Now,' and feel grateful for being alive, which she had learnt in her lovely 'Mindfulness classes'.

She constantly reminded herself, how lucky she was; she had a wonderful family, great friends, a good job, and a good lifestyle.

But there was a limit to her acting skills and she most certainly wouldn't be joining 'Pharrell Williams' on his 'Happy, clappy, song' any day soon. Once a favourite song of her's and Paul's, 'Happy,' was now a gloomy reminder that Paul had dumped her.

Marissa came back to reality like a bolt of lightning, and she quickly scanned the room to check if anyone had noticed, she was in another world.

Phew! It looked like everyone was so engrossed in listening to Hazel, they hadn't noticed her distraction.

'It's time now to concentrate and try to enjoy the class,' she decided.

Hazel was so full of energy and ideas; she seemed to love nurturing their creative writing skills.

After a few minutes of listening intently to Hazel, Marissa actually felt interested, and was even enjoying the class, but she certainly wouldn't tell Rebecca that.

Marissa was seated quite close to the door, and as soon as class ended, she saw her escape route; she jumped up and moved swiftly out the door. She needed to protect herself from another onslaught of awkward networking, with Paul, Jayne or Patricia.

She walked briskly home feeling quite angry, that her birthday had nearly been ruined, thanks to Rebecca and Paul. She phoned Rebecca as soon as she reached the comfort of home.

'Thanks a million for forcing me to go, to those dreadful creative writing classes. I knew I shouldn't have gone, but of course you knew better, and you forced me to go,' she said angrily.

'Oh my goodness, Marissa!'

'Calm down please.'

'Take a deep breath, and tell me what happened, and why you're so upset.'

'Was the class really that bad?'

'The class wasn't great, because I couldn't concentrate, but worse still, Paul was there.'

'I got such a shock; I nearly had a heart attack.'

'I acted like, my life depended on it, I pretended I was happy to see him, and I showed no signs of heartbreak.'

'I definitely deserve an 'Oscar' for my performance, but it really upset me, and that's why I am angry.'

'If you hadn't forced me to go, I wouldn't have seen Paul, and I wouldn't be feeling so miserable now,' she sighed exhausted from her experience, and her rant.

'I am so sorry Marissa; I didn't think Paul was the creative writing type.'

'Perhaps he won't come back.'

'What?'

'Are you crazy?'

'You think I am going back next week, for more punishment?'

'You must be deluded, I am not going back.'

'Ah Marissa, don't fret so much, I promise faithfully, I'll be with you next week.'

'You must go, or Paul will think you are still pinning, and that you can't cope, seeing him in class.'

'I know you mean well, but I am not going back there. I have absolutely no interest in writing, and I certainly don't want to see Paul every week.'

'I don't need 'a weekly reminder' of how much I miss him.'

'Don't be so dramatic, I think, it's good for you to deal with your feelings, and by meeting Paul, it will help you heal quicker.'

'You have been dreading this day, now you have met him.'

'Well done, be proud of yourself, you have finally moved on,' Rebecca bravely said.

'Your next step is, to go again next week, and don't run away from the situation.'

'Oh my goodness sis, you are so good at manipulating, and brain washing people.' 'You should definitely give up the teaching and go into politics.'

'Well, as you know, one of my mottos is; 'Don't let anyone dull your sparkle.'

'So just go for it, and don't let other people affect your decisions in life, and things will always work out,' Rebecca said.

'Yes, you are so right; I won't let 'you' dictate what classes I should attend.'

'Marissa, you know well, that's not what I meant.'

'Don't let Paul's presence dictate to you, where you can go.'

'I know you'll enjoy the creative writing class, once you accept the fact, Paul will be there.'

'Anyway, who knows, he may not return,' Rebecca said firmly.

'What utter rubbish, what's going on in your head these days?'

'I was only going to class to support you, because you were so good to me, when Paul dumped me.'

'Have you forgotten, I have no interest and I'll never have, in creative writing?'

'Were you 'Not' listening to me?'

'I am sure you would scold your students, if they weren't listening to you.'

'I was listening, but I still think you would be amazing at creative writing.'

'I think you are a natural, you already have the talent, as you have a superb command of the English language.'

'Your stories are always so interesting, because you know how to embellish them.'

'A lot of my friends say you are a brilliant story teller.'

'You always have exciting things happening in your life, or in lives of people, you meet.'

'Okay, that's enough brain washing, thanks,' Marissa snapped.

'Honestly, Marissa, my friends and I, just don't seem to have an interesting life.'

'You are one of those people, who always has drama in their lives, and that's what storytelling or creative writing is all about.'

'Okay, that's enough, on that subject.'

'You are totally wrecking my head.'

'I'll attend the first term, and I'll make my decision after that,' Marissa said sharply.

'I appreciate that, it's fair enough,' Rebecca smiled.

'Have you got your good sense of humour back?' Rebecca asked softly.

'Yes, I haven't totally lost my sense of humour, even though it was a really tough day. After all, it's my birthday, so I won't allow anyone to ruin my special day.'

'Well, I heard a crazy hospital advertisement yesterday, and I thought of you, they said;

'They can fix broken hearts.'

'Unfortunately, I can't remember the name of the hospital, but I do know it's in America.'

'I can check it out if you like,' Rebecca laughed, knowing Marissa would see the funny side.

'Yes, find out how much it cost, and I'll start saving,' Marissa laughed.

They laughed until Marissa's tears began to flow again, but thankfully they were happy tears this time, Yippee! (2)

'I am so sorry, I've been really grumpy and self-centred lately,' Marissa said sincerely.

'That's a funny advertisement, but it's sad too, because my heart actually does feel broken!'

'But I am determined to work hard to mend it. No doubt with your great support, I will succeed,' she said firmly.

'When I spotted Paul in class, I realised how vulnerable I still am, and I felt quite distressed. That's why I was so angry and disappointed, but I'll put it behind me now, and start afresh.'

'We'll meet before next week's class, and devise a strategy to keep you strong and confident during class,' Rebecca promised.

'Thank heavens, I wore my lovely black trousers, and my pink flowery top, as I always feel confident wearing that outfit,' Marissa said.

'I am delighted, you wore that beautiful outfit.'

'You always look great, but you look like a model in that chic, classy outfit.'

'I hope it tore at Paul's heart strings … that's if he has a heart,' Rebecca said.

During the following week when Marissa thought about the classes, she felt stressed and irritable.

She dithered and dallied on class day.

'Marissa, please hurry, I hate being late for class,' Rebecca said anxiously.

'You, hate being late for anything, calm down, I am coming.'

It was on the tip of her tongue to say; you are so like Paul, you are 'a time freak', but thankfully she stopped herself, from opening that chapter again.

'I really don't want to go to those silly creative writing classes, anyway.'

'I know, you've told me numerous times.'

'You know, I'd prefer to go swimming, like we use.'

'Don't be so dramatic, I am not actually physically forcing you to go.'

'You might as well be, because over the last few days, you haven't stopped trying to brainwash me.'

'Trust me; you will learn to love the classes.'

'Rebecca, you are not listening, creative writing is not my type of class. I don't know how to write stories, off the cuff, like you do.'

'My office work is 'non-fiction', not 'fiction', as you seem to think.'

'Well, then you'll be happy to know, the classes are especially for people like you, absolute beginners.'

'Oh great, I feel so much better now, knowing it's for 'creative writing dummies', like me.'

'Please don't be annoyed with me, 'Hazel' is very patient tutor, and she has a superb reputation. She'll get your creative juices flowing; you'll be amazed at your creativity, by the end of term.'

'Attending the classes will also distract you, and help you get over your breakup.'

'Oh my Goodness!'

'Give me a break Rebecca, have you forgotten already?'

'Paul's in class.'

'It's not long since Paul and I split up, if you were in my shoes, you would still be hiding under the duvet, and you wouldn't ever leave the house.'

'Okay, point taken, but learning something new, will distract you and help with the healing process.'

'Tell me, how can a 'Creative Writing Course', with Paul sitting across from me, mend my broken heart?'

'Marissa, stop with the drama, please.'

'It will help you heal, and you'll thank me, just you wait and see.'

Rebecca suddenly screeched;

'I just realised, maybe this is an omen that you and Paul are meant for each other. The Universe is sending a message to you both.'

'Wow, wouldn't that be amazing?' Rebecca said excitedly.

'I know we are meant for each other, the Universe doesn't need to tell me, but the maybe the Universe should tell Paul.'

'Have you forgotten, he made it quite clear, he doesn't want to commit to a long term relationship, with me?' Marissa said crossly.

Later that evening, Marissa sadly, replayed her memory of the day, she had asked Paul; 'Should we move in together?'

Marissa was utterly exhausted from constantly travelling from Paul's house to her own pad. Some of her clothes and personal belongings were in both places, and at times it led to confusion, when looking for things.

It wasn't an easy life, and she was doing all the running, from Paul's, to her own pad.

After all, they were five years together, and they had a great relationship, so surely Paul would feel; 'that moving in together was the next step.'

At the time, she questioned; 'Why am I feeling so anxious, about suggesting to Paul that we live together?'

'Perhaps, it's because I feel, Paul may have a problem committing to our relationship, she pondered.

Marissa recalled, Paul often said laughingly, especially in the early days of their relationship; 'I am not the marrying type; I am the 'confirmed bachelor' type.'

At the time, she didn't dwell on it, she wasn't sure, if he was actually serious, about being 'a confirmed bachelor.'

'But what if he meant it and what if he never intends to marry, or even live with me?' she questioned.

'What would she do then?'

'How would she feel?'

'It's best not to think about that now,' she decided.

'I'll ask Paul if he can commit to us living together, if he says 'Yes', then I will be the happiest woman in Ireland.'

'If he says 'No', then I'll have to think about my future, and what I actually want out of life,' she contemplated.

She definitely wanted a family, now, she was in her thirty's; the silly, old biological clock had begun to tick faster and louder, 'Tick Tock, Tick Tock.'

'Guys are so lucky; they don't have to worry about the passing of time. They can even father children in their 70s or their 80s,' she contemplated.

'Men definitely have an easier life, no menstrual cycle, no pregnancy, no baby blues, no dreadful menopause, and most guys even age more gracefully than women,' she thought despondently.

Marissa decided to squash her negative thoughts, before she lost all courage, to ask Paul the dreaded, but exciting question.

She decided to rehearse; so she began writing and practising her question;

1. *'Paul, we are five years together now, would you like to move into my place, as it's a bigger house?'*

2. *'Paul, imagine, we know each other five years. I would love you to move into my place, or I can move into your house, what do you think?'*

3. *'Paul, where does time go?'*

'Can you believe, we are five years together? I would love us to move in together. What do you think?'

After much deliberation, Marissa decided she would go with her second choice of question, and hopefully she would get the right answer from Paul;

'Paul, imagine, we know each other five years. I would love you to move into my place, or I can move into your house, what do you think?'

Correct Answer: 'Yes, Marissa, of course I would love to live with you.'

That was the answer she had hoped for, and had secretly expected.

Marissa now fondly recalled, the first time she met Paul. It was a rather cute coincidence, they were both in a queue for the same rental apartment, and they had chatted like old friends, while waiting for the landlord to arrive.

They both really liked the apartment, but the landlord, chose Marissa.

The landlord had explained, he had interviewed numerous people, but he hadn't been happy with any of them. But as soon as he met Marissa he chose her, as he felt his property would be in good hands.

He apologised to Paul for making such a quick decision, and said;

'Marissa seems the perfect candidate, as she has all her papers in order, and she has glowing references and contact numbers, for her referees.

Marissa even had her referees on standby, and of course they highly recommended her when he phoned, which made his decision very easy.

Paul too had his paperwork in order, but unfortunately, he had no references with him, and that's what finally swayed the decision in Marissa's favour.

Marissa felt guilty, and just as Paul was about to leave, she asked him, would he like to go for a coffee.

'My treat, as a consolation prize,' she smiled.

They sat and talked for hours in the café, and when they could no longer justify, sitting there, they went for a walk.

'We'll be thrown out, if we don't move,' Marissa had giggled.

'Would you like to go for a walk along the canal?' Paul asked.

'Yes,' she happily replied, as she too wanted to prolong their time together.

Months later Paul told Marissa he was smitten by her, when they were chatting, while waiting on the landlord. He said he totally understood why the landlord had chosen her, as she had a lovely, warm, kind, and bubbly personality, and a definite air of honesty.

'You are so easy to talk to and you are a good listener. You appear to be very content in your own skin, you're intelligent and a very interesting person.'

'The type of person, you meet once in a lifetime,' he had said, sounding very happy.

'Why then had he deserted her after five years?' she still questioned.

It was the million dollar question, and one she may never get an answer to.

She needed to move on and finally accept that her relationship with Paul was now in the past. She took solace in the fact, that 'she had loved, and been loved,' and it was now part of her life-story.

Chapter 4

When Paul told Jayne, he had become part owner of 'Winters & Rutlin Solicitors', she was thrilled, but she couldn't resist teasing him.

'I can't believe Peter entrusted you, and Stephen to take over his brilliant company, when you freak out about marriage, and children,' Jayne said laughingly.

'You know well, that's a totally different responsibility,' Paul defended himself.

'You need to get over the fact that 'my name is now up in lights' as 'Winters & Rutlin Solicitors',' Paul laughed.

'I sacrificed and I worked hard for it, and I am so lucky to have been accepted by Peter and Stephen.'

Paul enjoyed worked as an accountant with Peter Winters, and his son Stephen at 'Winters & Son Solicitors.'

Peter, taught Stephen and Paul, all he knew on the law area, and he was a true gentleman who was exceptionally generous, with his knowledge and his time.

Paul was like the second son he never had, and he treated him with great respect. Indeed, it was like one big happy family, each of them looking out for each other. Peter's wife, Deirdre, was also part of the gang, and they all enjoyed socialising together.

Peter worked hard all his life, and he appreciated the success of his 'Solicitor business.' He was seriously thinking of retiring, and he was grooming Stephen and Paul to take over the reins.

He had recently told them of his future plans to retire.

'It's time to call it a day; my family and friends must come first in my life now.'

'It's time I let you young guys, take over the reins.'

'I am sixty-eight years old, and even though I feel very young at heart, my body and my brain are getting old and tired.'

'It's difficult, to work as fast and as furious as I use to. It's my time now to enjoy retirement, and let you young, clever guys take over the show,' he smiled.

'You are so right Dad, you worked extremely hard all your life, and now it's your time, to enjoy doing the things you love,' Stephen agreed.

'You certainly put your heart and soul into your thriving business, and I am happy you have decided to enjoy, the next chapter of your life,' Paul said.

Peter had always tried to prioritize his time, but keeping the business alive through good and bad times, often meant late nights, so family life frequently suffered. He realized it was the perfect time to leave, while he was still hale and hearty.

Now he and Deirdre had the ideal opportunity to travel more, and enjoy gardening, and other hobbies. He felt excited at the thoughts of the new chapter ahead.

He knew Stephen and Paul were both extremely capable of taking control and operating the company as well as he did. It was now time to put the succession plans in progress for moving the company forward.

Peter decided to discuss his plans with Stephen, who was a brilliant Solicitor, to see if he was willing to share the business with Paul.

Weeks of deliberating, had brought Peter to his decision, on the future of the business; he had lovingly set up from scratch. Of course he had discussed the plans with Deirdre, who had always taken an interest in the business. She was delighted that he intended including Paul in the company name, and business, if Stephen was agreeable. They both knew their wonderful son Stephen would be agreeable, as he loved Paul, like a brother.

Peter was pleased, with Stephen's reaction, when he explained in detail his plans, for the future of the company.

Stephen said; 'I have absolutely no problem sharing the company with

Paul, he's an excellent accountant, a dedicated co-worker, and he's like a brother to me.'

'Life wouldn't be the same, if we didn't continue to work together and share the company.'

'We have always worked as a team, and Paul deserves his share of the profits too,' he emphasised.

Peter hugged Stephen and said; 'I am so proud of you, you are a wonderful son. I knew you would understand and agree with my plans. We will start the process by changing the company name to; 'Winters & Rutlin Solicitors.'

'Are you sure you are in agreement with that decision?'

'Yes Dad, that sounds good to me, and I know Paul will be delighted with the news.' 'Of course, we'll be sad to see you retire, but it'll be a wonderful new chapter in your life, and in Mum's life too.'

'You both worked so hard, now it's time for you and Mum to relax and enjoy your travels and exploration of the world.'

'Thanks son, I am so proud of you.'

'Let's go to Paul's office, and we can both tell him the good news.'

Paul was delighted to hear of Peter's retirement plan. He felt truly honoured to have his name added to the company.

'Winters & Rutlin Solicitors.'

It sounded so good, when he was alone, he kept repeating the name, and he was very proud of himself.

'Wow! He knew his Gran and his Mum would be very proud of him too.'

His Gran would probably have jokingly said; 'Well Paul, at last your name is now, up in lights.'

'Sometimes when bad things happen in life, good things come along unexpectedly, which can change a person's life for the better,' Paul mused.

When the 'Winter family' realised Paul's Mum had died, and his Dad had abandoned him, and he lived with his Gran, they had generously

'A Pub with No Beer.'

'It's lonesome away
from your kindred and all
By the camp fire at night
where the wild dingoes call.
But there's nothing so lonesome
so morbid or drear
'Than to stand at the bar
of a pub with no beer.'

Paul now recalled the day; Stephen had admitted to his Dad that his sexual preference, was male. It was truly an eye-opening experience; Peter had dealt with Stephen's admission so calmly.

He treated Stephen with such respect, and it was lovely for Paul to witness. Even though, Peter did admit, he worried, that the path Stephen had chosen, would be tough, at times.

Paul presumed, Peter and Deirdre must have been upset when Stephen told them, he preferred men, as he was their only child. They probably worried, that Stephen may not have the privilege of having his own children.

Paul asked Stephen one night; 'Do you think you would like to have children?'

'Yes, I would love to have at least two children. So far I haven't met the right person,' he said, with a glint of devilment in his eyes.

'Well, actually Paul, on second thoughts, maybe I have met the right person, but unfortunately, they don't seem to feel the same way.'

'Don't panic, I am just joking,' he smiled.

Paul knew Stephen had feelings for him, but thankfully, Stephen accepted and respected that Paul's feelings for him were brotherly only.

Stephen often teased Paul. 'Maybe you are gay, and that's why you can't commit to a lasting relationship, with a woman.

'I have noticed, once a woman gets close to you, you run as fast as your lovely, long, legs will carry you.'

Stephen never hid the fact he fancied Paul, and he flirted with him, quite often.

'You are wasting your time and energy on me.'

'It will never happen.'

'Never, say Never', as the saying goes,' Stephen would laughingly reply.

'You're so wrong; I absolutely have no interest in men.'

'I love women, but I just don't like the idea of one man, and one woman living together forever.'

'It's a scary thought and I feel claustrophobic, when my relationships get too serious,' Paul admitted.

'Never, say Never,' Stephen repeated with a flirty look.

'Don't hold your breath, waiting for me to change my mind,' Paul laughed.

Paul recalled how difficult Stephen's Mum, Deirdre had found the situation; it took her a while to come to terms with Stephen's chosen path. Deirdre admitted to Paul, her world fell apart when her wonderful, bright, caring, sensitive son, told her, his sexual preference, was male.

'My son is brilliant and I love him, nothing has changed between us as a family, he is still the same person,' she said firmly.

'In my heart, my worry for him is, there are biased people, who will be only too willing to hurt Stephen, for who he is,' Deirdre said rather sadly.

'Stephen told me, at first he hated feeling the way he did about guys, and he would have given anything not to be gay. He even tried changing his friends, mixing with the more macho type and the straight guys. He tried dating a lot of girls, but in the end, he couldn't deny his true feelings. He told me he always knew he preferred guys,' Deirdre said.

'I am so scared of the prejudices and the discrimination he may have to endure,'

'I know things have definitely changed in Ireland, and people are more broad minded about sexual partners, but there's always the nasty ones, who can be so dangerous,' Deirdre said sadly.

'At first I thought, I won't tell anyone, it's nobody's' business, but thankfully, I came to my senses.'

'I realised my son deserves to live his life, the way he chooses,' she said firmly.

'I researched the subject, and I found websites for parents who have gay children, which certainly helped me, accept the path God has chosen for my lovely Stephen.'

'You and Peter are amazing parents,' Paul said emotionally.

'Thanks Paul, we will always accept Stephen's boyfriends, and not prejudge them.'

'An Irish mother made a great comment on a sexual preference website, which certainly helped me, become stronger and it gave me great hope for Stephen's future.'

'With no prejudice whatsoever, against homosexuality, I don't give a damn what gender people are attracted to, as long as they love, and treat each other with kindness,' she wrote.

'Isn't that a wonderful, compassionate statement?'

'Yes, that's an inspirational statement,' Paul agreed.

'Doing research from a parent's point of view was a smart decision. If everyone had a healthy attitude like you and that lady, the world would be safer and less narrow-minded,' Paul said.

'Another interesting point raised on the website forum was;

'People often have high expectations of their children, and what their lives should be like, people want and expect that;

'Normal', uncomplicated romantic love, between a man and a woman, followed by a happy marriage, which produces healthy children, who in turn have their own children. Then the children look after their silver-haired parents, as all good offspring should do.'

'My opinion is, all this is fine in theory, but in the real world, we have to accept people's choices. Everyone has the right to live their own special life, and not follow the herd, as is expected,' Deirdre said firmly.

'Deirdre, I know exactly how you feel, and I know it is a concern for you. I am always on the alert when Stephen and I are socialising, especially at weekends. Sometimes people have too much to drink, and their nastiness becomes visible.'

'But thankfully, I never had to protect Stephen, it was never physical abuse, just words, which Stephen just laughs at, and 'Throws them over his shoulder,' as he wisely says.

'He is an amazing guy. You must be very proud of him.'

'I am very proud to call him, my friend,' Paul smiled.

'Yes, Stephen is my pride and joy, and we can talk to each other about anything.' 'Thankfully he was able to talk to Peter and I about his sexual orientation, and preferences.'

'Wow! Deirdre, I am very impressed, you know the correct lingo.'

'You are an amazing modern lady, and you always manage to keep up to date with life.'

Deirdre said smiling; 'I'll never forget the day I told our neighbour Mrs Kearney, that Stephen's preference was for men.'

'I had planned to tell her first, as she is the most narrowed minded of our neighbours.'

'I hoped she would spread the news, in her usual way, like a wild, speedy forest fire.'

'That was a splendid idea; you are so brave and so amazing.'

'Would you believe it Paul?'

'For once Mrs Kearney was quiet; she was actually stuck for words.'

'When she eventually spoke she said; 'I always thought Stephen was a lovely guy.' 'Are you sure he is gay?'

'You know, young people often go through those phases, when they are experimenting.'

'It was at that moment, I knew I had to be strong, and show my support for Stephen.'

'I said very firmly, and with absolutely no hint of an apology.'

'Yes, Stephen is 'gay', and we love him just as much as we ever did.'

'I am so proud of him, he is true to himself, and believe me that takes a lot of courage.'

'I am sure you are aware, there's still a stigma about being gay in Ireland, even though people tend to deny it,' I said looking, Mrs Kearney straight in the eye.

'Wow, good for you Deirdre.'

'I am sure Mrs Kearney got the message,' Paul said.

'Yes, loud and clear, and that was my intention.'

'I thought it best, to put it out there but, in a diplomatic way.'

'I knew she wouldn't approve of Stephen's way of life, but I really emphasised that, I don't care what people think.'

'I was on a roll and I said to her; 'Peter and I will always stand by Stephen and love him for 'who he is', not for what people think he should be.'

'I am sure she ran home to phone her friend Laura, who also loves a good gossip. It'll be the latest gossip in the neighbourhood, by the end of the week or maybe the end of the day.'

'But who cares?' Deirdre said laughingly.

'Well, we definitely don't care what people think, we love Stephen for who he is.'

'You are probably right, it will be the talk of the place, until the next bit of gossip comes along,' Paul said.

'Thanks, Paul, for being such a good friend to Stephen, he is so lucky to have you by his side.'

'I've always appreciated that, you're like a brother to Stephen, and like a son to Peter and I.'

'We are lucky to have you in our lives.'

'I know Stephen and Peter would agree with me, but typical guys, I am sure they don't say it to you.'

'Well, maybe Stephen does, he is definitely more in touch with his feelings than Peter,' Deirdre said fondly.

'Don't give it another thought Deirdre.'

'We will always be there for each other; you are like the family I never had.'

'I consider myself the lucky one, to have you, Peter and Stephen in my life,' Paul said as he hugged her closely.

Chapter 5

Paul couldn't believe his eyes, when Marissa walked into class, as Jayne had convinced him; he had imagined seeing her earlier.

He was going to pretend, he hadn't seen her, but then his good manners took over and he walked over to her.

As if his nerves weren't tested enough, by being forced into attending the silly writing class, he now must deal with his ex-girlfriend discovering he hadn't a clue, how to write a short story etc.

'Could life get any more annoying and complicated?' he silently asked the Universe. 'Is there someone up there planning my demise?'

'What have I done to deserve this?' he wondered.

He would have laughed, if it had happened to his mate who was a real flirt, and spent his life avoiding women, he had unashamedly dumped.

'But no! Of course, it had to happen to me,' he thought.

Against his will, Jayne had persuaded him to join the writing classes; and he really hoped that she didn't know Marissa would be there. He would give her the benefit of the doubt, for the moment anyway.

It was inevitable that one day they would eventually bump into each other, but he didn't expect it to happen in a silly creative writing class.

He moved swiftly and made a bee line for Marissa, before she could escape.

'Hi Marissa, I didn't realise you were interested in creative writing.'

'Hi Paul, I never expected to see you at a creative writing class either, but maybe you were dragged here, like I was,' she said.

'You're right; Jayne forced me to come against my better judgement.'

'Rebecca booked the classes for us, and then she had the nerve to tell me she couldn't make it tonight. I hope you enjoy the class,' Marissa said.

Paul was relieved when they both laughed, and thankfully it seemed to clear, the rather tense air between them.

Paul wanted to say to Marissa; 'Please don't let my presence hinder you from coming to the classes, I don't think I'll continue to come, anyway.'

But unfortunately he couldn't get the words out, as he felt too emotional upon seeing her again.

Instead he said; 'At least we will have something to write about on our first day.' 'Who would have thought, we would both be forced into the same creative writing class, by our so called friend and family?' he said nervously.

'Oh dear! I hope Rebecca and Jayne didn't plan this.' Marissa said looking puzzled.

'I don't think they would be so devious, but then again you just never know what people are capable of,' Paul said.

'I will kill them if they did plan this,' he said pensively.

'Not if I get there first,' Marissa said furiously.

Paul knew he hadn't handled the situation too well, when Marissa said, she saw a free seat, and rushed off.

He had intended to rectify the damage at the end of class, but Marissa had hastily left.

Marissa recalled how she had tackled Rebecca, about what Paul had said.

'Did you know Paul was coming to the creative writing classes?'

'Did you and Jayne set us up?'

'Please tell the truth, I will eventually find out, anyway.'

'Paul seemed to think that maybe, you both planned it.'

Rebecca's face became flushed, as she said;

'I may have heard Jayne mention something, about herself and Paul joining the classes.'

'At first, I didn't give it a second thought, but the more I thought about it, the more sense it made, to get you to join the classes too.'

'Please Marissa don't be annoyed with me.'

'I know you both still love each other; I thought it was worth another try to get you and Paul back together.'

'Oh my God, I just can't believe you and Jayne.'

'I actually didn't say anything to Jayne, so don't blame her.'

'It was solely my decision, to persuade you to go to the classes; it seemed to make sense at the time.'

'Rebecca, I just can't believe, you planned that.'

'I just hope Paul doesn't think I am involved in this totally childish situation.'

'Please, tell me, you will forgive me for meddling?'

'I thought it was a shame to stand idly by, while one of the best relationships I have ever seen ends.'

'I can't believe you put me in such an awkward situation,' Marissa said furiously.

'I feel really bad now, but in hindsight, I would probably do the same all over again.'

'You and Paul are soul mates,' Rebecca said firmly.

'Believe me, not everybody is that lucky, to meet their soul mate.'

'Tell Paul that, not me, he's the one, who couldn't commit to the relationship,' Marissa said angrily.

'If you are lucky to find your soul mate, you should seize the opportunity with both hands, it only ever happens to a few people in life,' Rebecca retaliated.

'A widow in work recently told me, she found her soul mate, and they were very happily married until the day he died. They had forty years of happiness and that's some achievement. She told me that they knew each other's thoughts, before they ever said them out loud,' Rebecca said trying to justify herself.

'You and Paul remind me of that couple, you are definitely soul mates.'

'Even if, Paul is my soul mate, if he's not willing to commit to our relationship, then it makes no difference. I can't push him into something he's not willing to be part of,' Marissa said heatedly.

'Well, I think you and Paul are two special people, who have found their Mr & Mrs Right … and it would be a shame to reject; 'Manna from Heaven.'

'How many people think they go to bed with 'Mr Right.' and they wake up and realise it's definitely 'Mr Wrong?' Rebecca questioned Marissa.

'What on earth are you talking about?'

'What do you mean by 'Manna from Heaven?'

'It means an unexpected gain or a gift; 'It's a reference to the Biblical story of food, which God miraculously provided, to the Israelites as they wandered in the wilderness.'

'Oh for goodness sake, I know what 'Manna from Heaven' means, I just don't understand the relevance to Paul and I.'

'You and Paul were miraculously given a rare gift of being 'soul mates' from the Universe or from the Gods.'

'You were meant to be together, seize that wonderful opportunity, with both hands, that's my advice.'

'Well, I didn't ask you for your advice, thank you very much.'

'It seems we are both attending class against our will, so your plan will backfire anyway,' Marissa said heatedly.

'I know you meant well, but remember faith plays a big part in life and in 'God's plan' and the 'Universal plan', and that may not be the same as 'Paul's plan', or 'My plan', or even 'Rebecca's plan',' Marissa said angrily.

'Sorry, I was just trying to help,' Rebecca said heatedly.

'You shouldn't meddle in other people's lives.'

'Sort your own life out first, and then you can attempt to sort mine out.'

'I won't mention your meddling to Paul, even though I think he probably guessed that you and Jayne are responsible, for this embarrassing situation.'

'Honestly, Jayne didn't know.'

'I'll force myself to attend a few more classes, but I am adamant, if I feel totally uncomfortable, I won't return.'

'Anyway, Paul said he feels the same as me, creative writing is for not for him.' 'Please promise me; 'No more meddling in my life.'

'I promise.' Rebecca said quietly.

'You better help me with this short story assignment, to make amends for forcing me to class,' Marissa said firmly.

'No problem, call to my pad after work tomorrow, and we can tackle our masterpieces, with the aid of a bottle of red wine,' Rebecca promised, trying to make amends to Marissa.

During the weekend Marissa couldn't get Paul out of her mind, no matter what she did, flashes of their great time together kept appearing. She thought a brisk walk in Phoenix Park, would help her focus on the peace and beauty of nature.

At stressful times like this, Marissa really missed her jogging; she had always found it very therapeutic. But unfortunately a year ago, she had injured her ankles, while training on hard ground. Her poor little ankles had ungraciously given in, and now she walked instead of jogging. To console herself she used the motto;

'Why run, when you can walk?'

She loved a brisk walk in Phoenix Park, which in her eyes, was the most wonderful, peaceful place on earth. Even though, there was continuous traffic, she didn't notice it, as she used her earphones, while listening to her favourite classical music. She loved music, and she revelled in the beauty of the park and the elegant, sprightly herds of deer.

She really wished she could still jog, as it was a speedy way of taking her mind off her troubles.

Memories of her very last running session during the 'Mini-Marathon' came to the fore. She had foolishly run most of the Mini-Marathon, even though she hadn't trained; as she had originally planned to walk it, because her ankles were still weak.

On that day, she was feeling very energetic, and she automatically started following the runners, and suddenly she realised she had foolishly run most of the min-marathon. She had felt euphoric when running, obviously the endorphins had kicked in, and she was in a really happy place, so she just kept on running.

She actually didn't feel any aches or pains, or even any tiredness during the mini-marathon. She had truly felt rejuvenated and excited during the run.

Unfortunately, that evening it was a different story, her ankles began to swell and she was in terrible pain. She put ice on them and it helped a bit, but sadly, the damage was done.

The next morning she could hardly walk. She was so annoyed with herself, as it was the second time she had injured her ankles so badly, and she was now paying the price.

Marissa phoned her physiotherapist who recommended ice, a gentle massage and gentle stretches of the ankles, for a few days. She scolded Marissa for jogging when she hadn't trained, and she also recommended a number of physiotherapy sessions, to speed up the healing process.

Once again, it seemed Marissa had 'Achilles tendinitis', which caused pain and stiffness in the area of the tendons, and she found walking very painful, especially in the mornings.

'Would she ever learn?' she pondered.

She loved jogging, and was difficult to give it up, but her ankles couldn't take any more running. She thought she had reconciled herself to brisk walks, so she was quite baffled, and annoyed with herself for running the mini-marathon that day.

Marissa's family and her friends were not impressed with her for jogging, and now because of her foolishness, she was house bound for a few days.

She decided to put her 'invalid time' to good use. To cheer herself up, she checked out the story of the bravery of her idol, 'Terry Fox'.

He was her sport idol, who had died far too young; she had great admiration for him and his wonderful achievements. He was so courageous and full of positivity, he was her role model.

Paul was also a fan of 'Terry Fox', and they had often discussed his amazing courage.

'Fox' had completed marathons while in incredible pain, and amazingly with only one leg, as his other leg had been amputated, due to cancer.

Not that Marissa ever intended to run again, however, to stop the negativity and her 'self-pity party', she refreshed her memory of the courageous, most fascinating man.'

Marissa read aloud for her own benefit; to brainwash herself into the positivity mode. 'Terrance Stanley Fox', (Terry Fox), (1958-1981), was a Canadian athlete, a humanitarian, and a remarkable cancer research activist.'

'In 1980, after his leg was amputated due to bone cancer, he embarked on an east to west; 'Marathon of Hope' across Canada, to raise money and awareness for cancer research.'

Terry Fox's courage and determination never ceased to astonish her, and his achievements gave her strength in mind and body.

'At twenty two years of age he ran from St. John's, Newfoundland, to Thunder Bay, Ontario, covering 5,373 km in 143 days, but unfortunately he was forced to halt his 'Marathon of Hope', when the cancer invaded his lungs.'

Marissa was really fascinated by 'Terry Fox's' iron will and determination in one so young, she thought he was so wise and courageous; he most certainly was one of a kind.

Marissa continued reading; 'In 1980, after 'Terry Fox' commenced his 'Marathon of Hope', the Star newspaper assigned a reporter to follow him weekly, in a wonderful feature called; 'Running with Terry'.

The reporter was 'Leslie Scrivener', a Star feature writer, who wrote the unambiguous book on the young amputee, it was named;

'Terry Fox: His Story'.

'Fox' said he was so touched by the pain and suffering he witnessed from numerous cancer patients during his chemotherapy, he decided to run the 'Marathon of Hope' to raise money, and awareness for cancer research.'

'He started his marathon training with a special prosthetic leg, made specifically for running.'

'When he ran, Terry was like; 'A moving picture of dedication, determination and unrelenting courage.'

Marissa loved that description of 'Terry', who had the courage and the drive to run and raise money for cancer research for people he never even knew.

Marissa felt it was a testament to this brave and courageous man that, millions of people throughout the world still participate annually in the 'Terry Fox Run.'

'Terry Fox' was an amazing person, who died young, but he left an inspiring legacy which will continue for many years to come,' she proudly read.'

Marissa said out loud, hoping her neighbours wouldn't hear her, and think she had lost her sanity;

'Well, 'Terry Fox', you are definitely my inspiration in life, and it's thanks to your courage and dedication, people still run marathons for charities, and in particular for cancer research.'

'I will try to be brave like you, and stop feeling sorry for myself. I will deal with my injuries and I'll continue to complete women's mini marathons for cancer research too. I know I will never be as brave as you 'Terry Fox', because in future I will definitely walk, rather than run the mini-marathons,' she mused.

While she was recovering Marissa wondered; 'Why do we always struggle to stay in a positive mood?'

'Why are the majority of our moods so negative?'

'Perhaps, God made a mistake and put too many negative vibes in our genes.'

'Or did he deliberately make life more of a challenge for us?' she pondered.

danger, let's go talk to the lifeguards,' Paul kindly said.

'Maybe I am on high alert because during the week, I actually heard the 'Irish Water Safety', (IWS), issue a warning regarding unsupervised children in pools, lakes, rivers and at the beach,' Marissa explained.

'The IWS actually emphasised how important it was for children to be supervised at all times, in the water, because they can drown so quickly and silently.'

'You are right, it's better to be safe, than sorry, we'll ask the lifeguards to check it out,' Paul said.

They walked quickly to the lifeguards hut, and they asked to speak to the Supervisor, and they pointed to the boys' on the rocks. They were amazed and delighted, at how quickly the supervisor reacted; he looked through his binoculars and spotted the boys, and set up a rescue plan immediately.

The supervisor, then calmly and very quickly issued instructions to two lifeguards, who went running in the boys' direction. At that stage, Marissa and Paul noticed the tide was coming in quite rapidly, and the boys were now surrounded by water on all sides, and the tide was coming in fast and furious.

'Marissa and Paul were in awe of the lifeguards as they appeared so calm, so efficient, and confident. They could see them scampering along the rocks, trying to reach the boys.

They also noticed that the boys' hands were high in the air, and they appeared to be holding something. The lifeguards were trying to persuade the boys to use both hands, in order to balance themselves, while moving along the rocks.

They later discovered, the boys were protecting their mobile phones from getting wet, and they hadn't noticed the tide come swiftly in, around the rocks. At the lifeguards' suggestion, they reluctantly put their mobile phones in their pockets during the rescue. Miraculously, the phones weren't damaged, and of course the boys were delighted.

When they were finally safely on shore, the boys told their story.

They said, they were shouting and calling out to people, to rescue them, as the they didn't want to get their phones wet. The youngest boy was nearly in tears, as he said;

'Nobody helped us, even though we were shouting for help.'

'Thank you so much for rescuing us,' he said excitedly.

The fact that the tide was coming in, and they could have actually drowned, obviously didn't register with the boys. The innocence of it all, they were more concerned about saving their phones, than saving themselves, Marissa and Paul realised.

Paul didn't even want to take credit for the rescue, even though he was involved in it too. He actually said to the boys; 'thankfully, my friend Marissa, realised you were in trouble, and she sent the lifeguards out to rescue you.'

The older boy pretended, he wasn't scared or upset, but it was obvious he was. He mumbled; 'Thanks.'

Marissa recalled how some of the lifeguards had scratches on their feet, from the rocks. When they thanked the lifeguards for acting so promptly and calml, they just smiled and said; 'It was a pleasure, we are here to keep the beach as safe as possible, and it is so rewarding when we save people.'

'It's also thanks to people like you, who are observant and caring.'

'You make our job rewarding, and you help make the beach a safer place for everyone.'

The head lifeguard further explained; 'We are continually patrolling the beach, and we observe the beach, for any unsafe situations, which may arise. But we also need the public and parents to be vigilant too, so we can respond immediately to any hazardous situations, and rescue people when necessary.'

'We constantly remind parents that children, like those two young boys, should not be left alone on the beach, it is their duty as parents to supervise them at all times.'

They brought the boys into the lifeguard hut, and they proceeded to contact their parents.

Chapter 6

Marissa was so disappointed, all her hard work on moving forward, after her break up with Paul, seemed lost now. She couldn't stop thinking about him and their life together. She suddenly got a flash back to when she actually thought she was pregnant, and how she was a little disappointed, when it was a false alarm.

She remembered how worried she was about her nausea feelings, for what seemed a lifetime, but it was only, two agonizing, really long, slow weeks.

She had taken four pregnancy tests, which thankfully had shown negative, but she still couldn't rest easy until she got her period.

Thankfully, a miracle happened, her period came, and for once in her life she wanted to jump for joy, at its appearance, but surprisingly part of her was disappointed too.

She now recalled the day she thought she was pregnant. She was feeling poorly with flu like symptoms, she decided a visit to the hairdresser would take her mind of her flu.

Mentally and physically she just didn't feel good, and she hoped a new hair cut would cheer her up, which it usually did.

She decided to go to 'Miguel', who had been recommended to her, she had to wait a while, as he was busy with a customer.

All of a sudden she began to feel ill, possibly a combination of tablets and the cough bottle she was taking, for her flu symptoms, she presumed.

She tried some deep breathing 'Mindfulness Practices', but she still felt quite queasy, and she was disappointed her deep breathing exercises, just didn't seem to be working. She tried her utmost to convince herself to stay, but she was feeling so ill and miserable, she just wanted to go home and lie down.

Just when she was about to leave, Miguel called her name, thanks, to her persistent 'Mindfulness techniques' of breathing deeply, she managed to survive the hair wash, but it was quite an ordeal.

She began to feel faint again, so she asked Miguel for a glass of water.

'It's too late to turn back now, with my wet hair, I must soldier on,' she mused.

Her tummy felt very nauseous and her head felt dizzy, and a glimpse of herself in the mirror, didn't paint an encouraging picture either. Her face was ashen and she looked as ill as she felt, even her makeup couldn't hide her illness.

Once again, she felt faint while 'Miguel' was cutting her hair, and she asked him, for a break, explaining she felt ill. He very kindly understood, and thankfully he gave her some space.

She put her hands on her lap and put her head down, as low as possible, and she rested for a few minutes, hoping the dizziness would pass. After what felt like ten minutes, she felt a little stronger.

She went to the bathroom, and let the cold water flow over the pulses on both hands, until she could no longer bear it. She eventually felt a little stronger, so she returned to Miguel.

Miguel, seemed to understand how ill she was, and thankfully he didn't keep chatting to her. For once she was grateful that Miguel's English wasn't the best, so he wasn't one for the continuous idle chatter. He was only in his mid-twenties, but he seemed to have wisdom beyond his years, he kept an eye on her, and he calmly replenished her glass of water, a number of times. The waves of nausea kept occurring, and she tried to roll with them, and not panic.

Marissa remembered that suddenly out of the blue, this awful, scary thought popped into her head.

'What if I am pregnant?'

She and Paul had always taken precautions, but she knew sometimes couples were unlucky and were doomed, when their precautions failed. She knew if she was pregnant, there was no way, she could tell Paul. He most certainly wouldn't be jumping for joy, and with his commitment issues, he would definitely feel trapped.

Marissa treasured her time with Paul and she most certainly didn't relish the patter of tiny feet, just yet. She knew children weren't on Paul's wish list, at all. She thought; 'Now is not the time to think about pregnancy, it will only make me feel worse, if that's possible.'

She tried to smile as Miguel, finished her blow dry, for a change she didn't care what her hair looked like.

'Thanks, that's lovely,' she said, as Miguel, showed her the back of her hair in the mirror. She just wanted to run out into the fresh air, and make the nausea, and the scary pregnancy thoughts go away.

She was being silly, it probably was the medication, and the overpowering smells of the hair dye etc. which made her feel so ill.

'Nothing to be worrying about,' she tried to convince herself.

Deep down Marissa was relieved when she finally discovered she wasn't pregnant, but surprisingly she was somewhat disappointed too.

By going through the pregnancy scare, it made her realise that, she would actually like to have children.

Marissa now felt that perhaps after all her destiny was never meant to be with Paul, he didn't want children, and she knew that someday, she would like to be a Mum.

Marissa really missed Paul, but thankfully Rebecca was always by her side, on the good and the bad days.

They always enjoyed each other company, and Rebecca was full of positivity and wisdom.

Her motto was; 'Treat each day as an adventure, treat the bad parts of the day the same as the good parts, and life will run more smoothly.'

'In time, you will notice the negatives parts, will be easier to deal with, if you just treat them as adventures,' Rebecca advised.

Marissa felt very lucky to have such an amazing sister, so full of wisdom, and yet she was full of fun too. She always saw; 'The glass half full.' so life was a thrilling adventure in her company.

She never seemed to sit still, going from one adventure to the next. Her face was always alight with mischief, and life was never boring when she was around.

Even though Marissa was still angry with Rebecca for dragging her to the classes, knowing Paul might be there, she smiled when she thought of the fun Rebecca brought to her life.

Like Rebecca's 'special jeans' phase; the wide leg jeans, which she worn, for years. Then as fashion changed, she was eventually persuaded to acknowledge, the jeans were far too wide.

One evening she decided to cut the legs of her special jeans to make them narrower, and she then proceeded to sew them by hand.

When Marissa and her friends saw what Rebecca was up to, they chorused while still in shock; 'You can't wear those jeans out, they'll rip, they need to be sewn by machine, not by hand.'

'Don't be silly, they'll be fine.'

'You know I don't have a sewing machine, and I can't afford to get them done professionally,' she said with an impish smile.

A few days later Rebecca arrived home from work and her jeans were ripped along both legs, but she wasn't the least bit embarrassed.

When Marissa asked; 'What happened?'

'They ripped, don't look so worried, nobody got hurt or died and it taught me a lesson, I am definitely not a good seamstress,' she laughed heartily.

'Thankfully they didn't totally rip or it would have been indecent exposure,' Marissa smiled.

Another time, Rebecca bought a beautiful, brightly coloured dress in the sales, and it kept sliding up her body, as she walked, to the local pub. It was way above her knees, and her underwear was nearly showing, by the time they reached the pub, which was only a five minute walk.

She acted so cool, as she fixed her dress before entering the pub, she laughed; 'Now, I know why it was reduced so much, there obviously is a flaw in the material.'

'Well, at least we had another adventure on the way to the pub, and we had a good laugh,' Marissa mused.

After that night, Rebecca left the dress in the bottom of her wardrobe, intending to exchange it, but she totally forgot about it.

When she found it a few months later, she decided she couldn't possibly leave it back, but Marissa tried to persuade her to exchange it.

'I can't possibly do that, I have it for months, and unfortunately it got buried in the bottom of the wardrobe. I totally forgot about it,' Rebecca said.

They had some good laughs, while trying to compose a plausible story, to tell the posh sales assistant, for the delay in returning the dress.

'We could try the sales jargon technique too, by telling an embellished story to 'Ms Snooty', in her expensive boutique,' Marissa said laughing heartily.

'We can't tell Ms Snotty that I left the dress in the bottom of the wardrobe and forgot all about it,' Rebecca said.

Ms Snotty, would probably say; 'Such bad standards, leaving our beautiful, one of a kind dress, in the bottom of your wardrobe.'

'Don't you realise how exquisite and unique our fashion is?'

'That's why it's so popular with everyone,' Ms Snooty would possibly say.

'Well, you should inform her; 'Your exquisite fashion is actually faulty, as the dress moves up the body, when walking, and you may be liable for indecent exposure law suits,' Marissa said laughingly.

'That's brilliant Marissa, but I am sure she wouldn't believe me, she would probably blame my body and say it's faulty.'

'You are so right, she would never admit liability.'

She would probably say; 'In all my years working in retail, nobody has ever complained about our exquisite and unique fashion.'

'Don't you know?'

'Style is a way to say; 'Who you are, without having to speak,' Rebecca said in a very posh accent.

'Ah that's brilliant and so witty, where did get that quote about style?'

'It's so funny and it would be so typical of Ms Snotty,' Marissa giggled.

'I actually read it in a magazine, and it's a great marketing ploy. I memorised it, as I thought, it would come in handy some day.'

'See how right I was,' Rebecca laughed.

Rebecca had a really hearty laugh. When she laughed everyone else laughed, whether they knew the joke or not. She had such an infectious laugh; it was amazing and so cheerful.

You could never be angry with her for long, as she was such fun, and she would laugh it off, and you would find yourself doing the same.

Marissa always tried to surround herself with positive people, and she loved that Rebecca and Paul were full of life and full of positivity, and like her they enjoyed positive affirmations.

One of Marissa's favourite affirmations, which helped her start the day so positively and so cheerfully was;

'Hope, is what I like for breakfast every morning.'

She had typed up the affirmation and framed it, in a cute, silver heart shaped frame, and it sat stately on her kitchen table. She read it every morning as she ate her breakfast. She really believed in it, and she felt surrounded by hope and positivity. At the start of each day, and it provided her with an amazing, wonderful feel good factor.

Marissa had another great affirmation which she had shared with friends and family. They said they also used it on the difficult days, and it made them strong and helped them through many troubles in their lives.

'I am Powerful and Loving and I have Nothing to Fear.'

Good powerful words which made Marissa feel strong and determined to face the day.

Now unfortunately, affirmations even made her think of Paul, they had so much in common and she still found it difficult to understand, why he threw all away.

When he discovered she was interested in affirmations, he had very kindly given her one his Gran composed. She had to admit, Paul was a very kind and a very generous person.

When she was doing something new or dealing with a difficult situation, she repeated his Gran's affirmation.

'If Anyone Can Do It,

I Can.'

It made her feel stronger, and she could visualise herself in control of a difficult situation, or a new work project, in the office.

Thinking of projects Marissa recalled the time she painted Paul's house. Just like her Dad, Marissa loved painting and decorating. She discovered she had the same quirky characteristics as her Dad.

She acted the same as her Dad, when she completed any tasks, but in particular painting and decorating, she would stand back, and admire her masterpiece. When she was painting Paul's house, on her breaks, she would stand back and admire her handiwork.

Just like her Dad, she got tremendous joy out of decorating and refreshing the house, both inside and out.

She always felt, 'A lick of paint made even the oldest and drabbest things, look cheerful and new again.'

"Leonardo de Vinci', eat your heart out,' she'd say with a smile, when her painting and decorating masterpieces were completed.

Her Mum often joked with Marissa and her Dad, about their love of painting and decorating.

'If I stood long enough, the two of you would paint me, so I better keep moving,' she'd tease.

When Paul bought his second hand house, it needed a lot of indoor painting and decorating, as it looked old fashioned and jaded. Paul had moaned about it so much, Marissa had offered to paint it, but on condition they would choose the colours together.

Paul agreed to Marissa's request, as he wanted the job done as quickly as possible. He knew Marissa would do a good job, as he saw the wonderful, professional painting and decorating she and her Dad did, in their family home.

Marissa now recalled on her first day of painting at Paul's house, she foolishly had eaten a large lunch, with her friend Audrey.

As she arrived at Paul's house she felt heavy and sluggish. She knew climbing the ladder would be a chore, after eating so much. She explained to Paul, she had eaten too much, and that she would be a slow starter, but in time she would speed up.

Paul told her not to worry, he felt privileged she had agreed to decorate his pad. But then he laughingly said; 'Hopefully you wouldn't break the ladder.'

They both had a good laugh as they had a wicked sense of humour. She really missed the fun and laughter with Paul.

She forced herself back into a positive mode, and she smiled to herself, when she thought of Audrey's brother Rory, who had a fixation on people's weight.

He often commented on people, in particular TV personalities and presenters saying;

'I think they have put on weight, they look 'Fah!'

He had a problem with pronouncing words ending in 't', and Marissa and her friends, tried to stay serious, when he said the word, 'Fah!'

Sometimes, when a few too many drinks were taken and they were giggly, they would mimic him, when he was at the bar, but not in a bad way, of course. They would fall around the place laughing, and usually they were still laughing, upon his return.

He would ask, 'What are you laughing about?'

Trying not to laugh hysterically they replied;

'Nothing really, we just noticed a lot of people in the area are getting 'Fah',' and he would agree with them.

Thankfully, he didn't seem to notice they were emphasising the word, 'Fah,' and giggling, or if he did notice, he never gave them the satisfaction.

Paul was thrilled when Marissa finished painting his house, as it looked so modern and cheerful, and even his very fussy friends admired her work, and her artistic talent.

Marissa was proud of her work and very happy when Paul said;

'Wow! I am amazed at the standard of your work, it is so professional. I think it's as good as the professional painters and decorators.'

'You have set a very high standard, and you completed the work with minimum fuss.' 'I am thrilled with the results, my lovely home is like 'a five star villa',' he said proudly.

Marissa replied jokingly; ''Leonardo de Vinci', eat your heart out,' and they had a good laugh.

It was sad those days were now over, but Marissa was now more determined than ever, to hide her feelings from Paul, and keep moving forward in life.

But 'surprise, surprise', a few weeks later during the creative writing class tea break, Paul asked Marissa if she would like to go for a coffee.

She was in total shock, but she heard herself say calmly, even though she had butterflies in her tummy; 'I can't make it this evening, as I am meeting Audrey.'

She was surprised and delighted at how quickly the lie tripped off her lips. After all she had been through, she didn't intend to rush back into Paul's arms, and she knew at all costs she must protect herself.

'Maybe, next week would suit you?' he said hopefully.

'Maybe, excuse me, I must go to the bathroom, before class starts,' she said, to give herself time, to digest, what had just happened.

On the way home from class she discussed Paul's coffee invite with Rebecca, and she wasn't at all surprised when Rebecca starting jumping for joy and said;

'OMG! I told you; 'You and Paul are definitely soul mates.'

'That's superb news; I can't believe I didn't see Paul talking to you.'

'You were too busy chatting to Patricia.'

'I don't think I can put myself through this again,' Marissa said looking rather sad.

'Don't be silly, it will all work out this time, it's so obvious Paul loves you.'

'Now, you think your clairvoyant, when did that happen?' Marissa asked.

'I was always clairvoyant, Rebecca said laughing heartily.

'Please Marissa; you must give Paul a second chance.'

'I don't know if I can do that, maybe he just wants friendship.'

'Believe me, he doesn't,' Rebecca laughed and nudged Marissa.

Marissa found herself laughing too; Rebecca always made her see the funny side of things.

'Sleep on it, at least you have a week to make your decision, before the next class.'

The following week, Paul asked Marissa again; 'Would you like to go for a coffee?' and she actually said; 'Yes.'

They had a lovely evening together, and it was amazing how easily they clicked again, it was so natural, they immediately picked up where they had left off.

'Maybe, Rebecca was right, maybe we are soul mates, time will tell.' Marissa thought.

Chapter 7

Susan felt exhausted and extremely cranky. She really wasn't in the mood to go to the 'creative writing classes.' If only she hadn't promised her friend Tara (Fallon), that she would go.

Tara had forcibly convinced her, it would be a great way to relax and de-stress, after a tough day in court. Susan wished she hadn't succumbed to Tara's persuasive powers. But when Tara set her mind on something, it was difficult to divert her, and lately she was a lady on 'a creative writing mission.'

'It'll be as good as a tonic,' Tara said.

Definitely the type of tonic Susan felt she could do without. In the end, Susan had agreed to go; more for a peaceful life, than any aspiration of becoming a writer.

Now, all she wanted to do was to curl up on the settee, with a bottle of her favourite chilled South African wine, and watch reality television.

'I certainly don't need two hours of taxing my brain, and feeling embarrassed, when the creative juices refuse to flow,' she thought.

Oh how she wished for a lovely, lazy, relaxing evening watching TV, after her hard day's work. Instead, here she was preparing to attend, writing classes, she had absolutely no interest in. If only she had the courage to skip the class, stay at home, and relax after her exhausting day in court.

She deliberately took the scenic route, to delay the inevitable pain of the creative writing class. She didn't care if she was late; she really wished she hadn't given in to Tara's pleading. An evening by the fire, under the duvet watching TV was much more her style, than an evening trying to write silly, short stories.

She had been so tempted to phone Tara to cancel, but she really didn't like cancelling arrangements, especially at the last minute.

She thought it best to take the experts' advice;

'*Feel the fear and do it anyway.*'

Maybe by shedding her formal, 'John Rocha' suit and after a quick shower, she would feel refreshed, and ready to learn, how to write the novel that Tara expected, (what a joke!).

Susan always wore expensive suits to court. It gave her the confidence to shine in a man's world. She was well known and respected in the legal profession, and she was a highly recommended, family law solicitor. She worked hard and she had the ability to empathise with her clients while also remaining professional.

Unlike most of her colleagues, she often recommended a peaceful way forward, where possible, with the solicitors and barristers of the adverse party.

Unfortunately, she realised that, the legal profession still shone, more brightly for men than women.

She was; 'A no nonsense person', but she was a very sincere and determined person, which helped her excel and added to her good reputation.

Judges and barristers were amazed at the confidence of this fiery, petite, 5ft lady, with beautiful, big blue eyes.

Susan worked for 'McHale & Co Solicitors', and she was their Family Law representative. She represented clients in court on contentious cases pertaining to divorce and domestic violence.

Make no mistake; even though she was cute and petite, people saw her steely side too, when making a point of law, whilst fighting for her client's rights.

Susan's big blue eyes would dance in her head, when she was excited about proving her client's entitlement. She left no stone unturned when she took on a client; her detailed research was the reason, she worked from dawn to dusk.

During her career, Susan had lost, only one case, at the beginning of her career. Her client had lied through his teeth, and unfortunately she hadn't completed a thorough research. She believed she was a good judge of character, but alas not in the case of 'John Munroe vs. Mary Munroe.'

She had learnt her lesson, and thankfully she never repeated that mistake again, she was now known for her thoroughness and fairness in court.

During her training Susan's tutors had informed the students that;

'People sometimes forget that basically a marriage is a contract between two people, and by ending the contract there will of course be significant legal consequences.'

They were also informed that; 'The Family Law Acts' set out the rights, duties, powers and liabilities of spouses and children, and provides for enforcement of those rights, and liabilities as well, as the dissolution of marriage.'

The tutors also emphasised that solicitors, must recognise the psychological and emotional trauma of the people involved in the family law conflict, and their greed when property and money was involved.

The important advice which Susan unfortunately forgot during the case of;

'John Munroe vs. Mary Munroe;'

'Always be aware and always remember there are two sides to every story.'

'Always research thoroughly, look at both sides of the case, and never take a short cut, or never presume anything.'

'The distress and worry, the hurt and pain, which is present in most family law disputes, is often soul destroying. People can turn into demons, and the love they once had for their partner, can become a very strong hatred,' this was vigorously emphasised in lectures.

It was on Susan's second case, in which she failed her client, because she didn't adhere to the most important advice, her tutors had given.

Looking back now, she realised, having won her first case so easily, she probably had acted, too smug and over confident, on her second case.

She completed her research, but unfortunately, she didn't do enough research into her client, 'John Munroe's' background. She was taken in by his charm, and regrettably, she took him at face value. She actually believed his stories, he was so convincing and he seemed so willing to do the right thing by his wife.

She forgot the significance of the basic marriage contract, and the things people often do, to get what they covet materially, when a marriage ends unharmoniously.

Some days she wondered, 'Why had she chosen, Family Law?'

She knew only too clearly, 'Relationships, marriages and families were great, when things were running smoothly, but a total disaster; 'When love turned to hate.'

In numerous, Family Law cases, she had witnessed, where greed and vengeance became the norm, when the marriage had turned from good to bad.

During her Law Degree lectures they had constantly discussed the topic;

'If married couples realised how complicated their lives would become, when they chose the Court route, would 60% of the couples have swallowed their pride, and tried to make a go of their marriage, or tried mediation, instead of the courts?'

'It is one of those million dollar questions, discuss.'

There had been many interesting discussions on the complicated issue of marriage and relationships, and when 'love turned to hate.'

Susan's view on the topic was that her clients should try 'Mediation', and if at all possible try to make their marriage work.

She had suggested that parents take time out and discuss the situation calmly, and certainly not rush to Court while still angry.

Susan didn't wish to put herself out of a job, but when she noticed there was still a spark of love, or a ray of hope between couples; she always encouraged them to try, 'Mediation' first, especially where children were involved.

'If you can meet halfway with the aid of 'Mediation', and not take the Court route, life would be smoother for you both,' she often advised couples.

She explained the 'Mediation process' to the couples, in a quiet, calm manner, hoping they might follow the peaceful, less angry, less expensive route.

She informed clients that; 'The Mediators were skilled communicators who would work with them, and assist them in resolving their dispute, and if they were willing to reach an agreement on their issues, they could then take the 'Mediated Agreement' to their own Lawyers, and they would then act independently for each of them.

She explained to the couples, in layman's terms, 'Lawyers will advise on the 'Mediated Agreement', and shape it into a legally binding contract, for you both.'

Sometimes her mediation advice fell on deaf ears, but sometimes it worked its magic.

The couples would calm down and agree to try mediation. Or sometimes they even surprised themselves, and opted to actually consider reconciliation.

When Susan managed to get matters agreed through mediation, she would feel a great sense of achievement. She had a passion for helping people and fostering relationships, and she loved a happy reconciliation.

Susan strove to keep the children out of the couple's disputes, by keeping the discussions and decisions on the children's welfare as a separate, calmer issue.

She worked extremely hard with her clients, and she was determined to keep the children out of the legal disputes, for their future wellbeing.

She had seen too many children scarred by legal separation and by the divorce process. She always hoped and prayed the couples with children would find love again and stay together.

'You are a hopeless romantic,' her friends teased.

She had quite a number of mediation success stories. She mistakenly told her friends and they were forever teasing her.

'You are definitely, in the wrong job. You should have been a marriage counsellor,' Tara often teased her.

Susan tried to explain to Tara, why she pushed the 'mediation agreement' on her clients.

'Sometimes, in divorce proceedings, married couples don't realise, their lives will become public. I make it clear to them; they have the option of the 'mediation process,' before the court process. I remind them, that any faults they have, or any mistakes they made, they will now be aired and exaggerated in court, in order to defame the other person's character.'

'I inform my clients that the 'mediation process' provides a forum and an atmosphere in which both parties can work together, to explore options for resolutions.'

'You are so thoughtful,' Tara said admiringly.

'Unfortunately, human nature can turn from 'Love to Hate' very quickly indeed,' Susan said sadly.

'As I already said, you are definitely in the wrong job.' Tara laughed.

'No, I am definitely in the right job, I can make a difference, by saving clients from making the wrong decisions in anger; just because some solicitors encourage them to defame their wife or husband, and make a profit from the situation.'

'Thankfully, I am a quite a good judge of people now.'

With all my experience in 'Family Law', I know when people should stay together and when it's time for them to go their separate ways. If I can save some marriages, then I feel I have done a good days work.'

'The clients are so lucky to have you by their side,' Tara said proudly.

'I rest my case,' Susan said laughingly.

In the Family Courts, Susan saw everything; from small deceptions about income to complete fabrication of the truth, and some horrendous stories of abuse. Some people enjoyed manipulating the truth, and manipulating their spouse's also. They seemed to experience a great sense of power in trying to fool the court, and defame their spouse during the process. It was sad to see how often 'Love turned to hate.'

That was the situation in the case of 'John Munroe vs. Mary Munroe. Unfortunately, Susan had discovered too late in the proceedings that John had deceived and manipulated her and the court.

He had shown no respect for the court, he was a 'Con Artist', and she found out the hard way.

'I definitely learnt my lesson,' she told her law colleagues, after losing the case.

'It took this case to remind me of the 'Golden Rules', which our tutors laid particular emphasis on; 'Never assume the person is telling the truth.'

'Always, complete your research thoroughly, and always seek corroborating evidence.'

'Always remember, people fabricate events, and use the courts to get revenge or money, when things are not going their way.'

'You need to remember they are not acting like an average person. Their lack of empathy can turn them into perjurers, and sometimes into violent people, when things are not going their way.'

Of course she had forgotten the 'Golden Rules', and she had paid the price.

'Solicitor Paul Donnelly', had painted the real picture, of hidden accounts, mistresses etc. and unfortunately, a most damaging picture of her client, 'John Munroe.'

Thankfully, 'Munroe' hadn't succeeded in totally fooling the court, even if he had fooled her. At least, the lesson she learnt in the 'Munroe case' hadn't been a lesson in vain. Since that case, she always made certain, to complete a thorough research of her clients, she now dug deep, until there was nowhere else to go for information.

Susan worked hard but she liked to let her hair down too, especially when socialising with her family and friends.

She was very like her Mum, Alma; full of positivity and full of life.

Susan lived life to the full, and her positivity allowed her see the glass; 'Half Full', rather than 'Half Empty', unlike some of her less positive friends.

She was feeling very tired after her hard day's work, but she knew she couldn't let Tara down; she'd go to the creative writing class. She felt it might indeed be payback time, for Tara's amazing support and friendship. Tara was a superb friend, she had always been there throughout Susan's dramatic life, in particular the days she missed her Dad.

Not that Tara did kind things for people, with the expectation of being paid back, she was naturally very kind, and a very thoughtful person. That kindness and thoughtfulness was hard to find, and Susan really appreciated Tara's friendship and kindness.

Most recently Tara had actually saved Susan from a debilitating illness, which unfortunately, was caused by an allergy to her beautiful, impish, pet canary called, 'Rashers.'

Susan had been feeling quite ill for a number of years. In the last year, she found it difficult, to climb the stairs, or even walk up a small incline, and the ordinary day to day house chores, had become a heavy burden.

Recently, when Tara heard Susan really struggling with her breathing, she said;

'Let's 'Google' all your symptoms, and see what shows up.'

Susan was very sceptical, as she had been prodded and tested over the last few years to no avail. The Doctors, Consultants, and Alternative Therapy Gurus, kept telling her, the results were clear and that she appeared to be in good health.

She realised that they were saying, 'not very discreetly;'

'There is nothing wrong with you; it's all in your mind.'

On one occasion, a Doctor had the audacity to say to her;

'Your results are so good, if you were a horse, you could run in Cheltenham.'

That comment really upset her, as she was feeling quite ill, and her friend who very kindly recommended, that particular Doctor, was rather shocked at his comment.

Susan was feeling so ill; the last thing she needed was, to be compared to a horse, and told that her illness was all in her mind, when she knew it wasn't.

She promptly replied to the Doctor; 'If you lived in my body you wouldn't say that.'

He had half heartily apologised, but she knew his diagnosis, as he dismissed her was; 'It's all in your mind.'

Thank heavens for her amazing friend Tara, who acknowledged and believed that she was struggling with her health, most days.

'Don't worry, we won't give up, let's do our own research,' Tara said.

Susan knew she was lucky to have such a wonderful, caring friend.

'Let's do some research now,' Tara said.

'Really?'

'There's no time like the present,' Tara smiled.

After a few hours of researching on 'Google', Susan spotted something which gave her goose bumps, and shocked her.

'Tara, please stop there, let's look at this article;

'Bird Fancier's Lung Disease.'

'I actually have goose bumps.'

'Omg! I think we may have actually found what's causing my illness.'

They began to read in unison, and they looked at each other in amazement, while reading the article;

'Bird Fancier's Lung Disease, (BFL), also called bird-breeder's lung and pigeon-breeder's lung disease is a type of hypersensitivity pneumonitis (HP).'

'The symptoms can be a dry cough, shortness of breath, chest tightness, fever, chills, or tiredness.'

'It's triggered by exposure to avian proteins present in the dry dust of bird droppings, and sometimes in the feathers of a variety of birds.'

They continued to read the article, and Susan, felt enormous relief, at long last, she understood why she was feeling so ill. She felt a weight had been lifted off her shoulders, and she felt vindicated.

But Susan also felt very sad, as she continued to read the advice on healing her ailments; 'BFL symptoms should improve, dramatically, in the absence of such allergens.

'Therefore, it is advisable to remove all birds, bird cages, bird food, sandpaper etc. from the person's home.'

Tears came into Susan's eyes, and she actually felt heartbroken. She realised, she had to find a new home, for her beautiful canary.

People often laughed when she told them, she had a special bond with her canary, but when they saw the interaction, between Susan and 'Rashers', they actually believed her.

One of her friends said; 'I didn't realise how clever canaries are, they sing so sweetly and they are so cute and clever.'

'Now I understand why you rave about 'Rashers' so much.'

Susan and Tara continued to read the article;

'It is also advisable to wash all soft furnishings, walls, ceilings and furniture, and to avoid any future exposure to birds, or bird droppings or any items containing feathers.'

'In extreme cases, some people may be advised to evacuate their homes permanently, and discard all possessions that have been exposed to avian proteins.'

Tara, couldn't help laughing; 'OMG, you will have to leave home because of little 'Rashers.'

'It's not funny, if you felt as ill as I do some days, you wouldn't be laughing.'

'It's also upsetting for me to discover that, to improve my health I must give away, my beautiful cheerful 'Rashers.'

'He has given me such joy in life, and now I'll have to live without his cheerful presence.'

'It's just not fair.'

'I am so disappointed and so annoyed.'

'Sorry I laughed,' Tara said sadly.

'Maybe, you should get a second opinion, before you jump to any conclusion.'

'You know, I have been to four different consultants, and I have tried 'Acupuncture', 'Reiki', and other alternative remedies, to no avail.'

'Now, it's time I took control of my own health, and cured myself, as the medical profession were unable to help me.'

'Regrettably, I have all the symptoms mentioned in that article, so I do have 'BFL disease'.'

'In hindsight, I probably should have known that anything with feathers or fur would affect me. After all, I am allergic to most things in life like; wool, or anything that is not one hundred percent cotton.'

'I am also allergic to perfumes, most moisturising creams, most costume jewellery, I could go on and on, but I won't bore you anymore.'

'Please don't,' Tara smiled.

'We should put you in a manmade one hundred percent cotton 'bubble' to protect you from us mortals, and all our dangerous material possessions.'

'Shhh … Tara!'

'Let me read this in peace please, it's fascinating but rather scary too.'

'I definitely have all the symptoms of 'Bird Fancier Lung Disease', (BFL), which are listed here;

'A dry choking cough,

Shortness of breath,

Chest tightness,

Fever and Chills, and most certainly the last symptom;

Tiredness.'

'Isn't it rather scary, the damage, a tiny, cute bird, can do to a person's body?'

'Yes, it's scary that such a small, happy little bird can cause such extreme allergies,' Tara replied sadly.

'I am so grateful to you, for helping me discover this information.'

'I am also sad; I'll no longer be able to keep 'Rashers.'

'I will certainly continue to research further, but it does seem that, I have BFL and I'll have to find a suitable home, for my beautiful, clever, sweet 'Rashers.'

'I am really sorry; I can't take 'Rashers.'

'I am always out and about, and I just wouldn't have the time, or patience to look after him,' Tara said rather sadly.

'Don't worry; I'll talk to the Manager of my local pet shop and the Animal Welfare Veterinary Clinic. I am sure they'll know someone who wants my sweet, beautiful 'Rashers,' Susan said tearfully.

A few weeks later, Susan reported to Tara, her vet had found a good home for 'Rashers.'

Susan lovingly recalled the laughs Tara and herself had when picking a name for her canary. At first they had chosen some crazy names, before they finally settled on 'Rashers.'

As the canary was a beautiful, vibrant, deep yellow colour, she was actually considering the name, 'Yellow Belly, ' but Susan changed her mind, a few days later, when Tara said;

'I think 'Rashers' would be a lovely name for your canary, he looks so mischievous.'

'No way,' Susan replied.

'We can't call my cute canary that silly name.'

'People will mock and joke about eating him in their 'full Irish breakfast.''

'No, girl, I don't mean that type of rashers.'

'I mean 'Rashers Tierney', from Strumpet City.'

'Oh, pray tell me more, my genius friend.'

'I am not quite sure who 'Rashers Tierney' is.'

'Well, I'll try my best to educate you, but it will not be an easy task.'

'You are so witty; less of the wit, just refresh my memory of 'Rashers Tierney',' Susan asked.

'Well, 'Rashers Tierney' was a mischievous, character in 'Strumpet City', which was a best-selling novel by, 'James Plunkett'.'

'The novel was set in Dublin between 1907 and 1914, and it was adapted for Television by, 'Hugh Leonard'.'

'Strumpet City' represented pivotal events in the history of Dublin city, and it dealt with the mass lockout of trade unionists by employers in 1913.'

'The movie had a most wonderful, popular cast of characters, not least, the mischievous character of 'Rashers Tierney.'

'Thanks for that enlightening interpretation of Strumpet City.'

'I still can't totally recall 'Rashers Tierney.'

'Do you remember the wonderful actor 'David Kelly?'

'Yes, of course, I have heard of 'David Kelly', and of 'Strumpet City'.'

'I have it on DVD, but unfortunately I never got time to watch it,' Susan said.

'Well, 'David Kelly', brilliantly portrayed, the mischievous character, 'Rashers Tierney'.'

'Well, your lovely, mischievous canary's actions remind me of the mischievous 'Rashers Tierney.'

'Your canary looks so impish, and he is always watching us.'

'He certainly acts like he is up to some mischief, just like 'Rashers Tierney', who was always up to some mischief or other. He was a great Dublin character whom everyone knew and loved. He did lots of odd jobs for people for money and for drink, which unfortunately he became too fond of. He had a lovely dog 'Rusty', who was his faithful companion.

'Thanks, Tara.'

'I applaud your great knowledge of 'Strumpet City', and your keen interest in the history of Dublin.'

'Well, what do you think of the name 'Rashers' for your canary?' Tara asked laughingly.

'Now that you have explained, so eloquently, who 'Rashers Tierney' was, I do like the idea of naming my beautiful, mischievous canary, after such an impish character.'

'It will be a talking point at my dinner parties, as people will think I mean, 'ordinary edible rashers', therefore I will try to explain as eloquently as you did, who 'Rashers' is actually named after.'

'You will also need to know for your dinner parties that 'Strumpet City' is a great, sweeping Irish historical novel of the 20th century and in 2013, it was named;

'*One City One Book*' at the Dublin festival, which is led by Dublin City Council, and they encourage Dubliners' to read, a book associated with Dublin, during the month of April, every year.'

'I'll lend you my book to read, and I know you will really enjoy it,' Tara said happily.

'Thanks, I would love to read the book, to refresh my memory on the famous, 'Rashers Tierney.'

Chapter 8

When Susan eventually reached 'Siam College', she was feeling rather tired and cranky and even a little anxious. The first person she saw was Tara, who was sitting smugly at a table with a number of people, and thankfully, a spare seat beside her.

She plonked herself on the seat beside Tara, with attitude.

As per usual, Tara just smiled and greeted her warmly. That's what she loved about Tara; she was always so calm and content. Nothing seemed to faze her, and God knows she had been dealt a tough hand in life.

Tara's Mum had struggled with lung cancer for years, and unfortunately, she had lost the battle and died a few months ago.

While Susan and all her friends were out socialising, poor Tara had spent most of her young life helping her Dad, care for her sick Mum at home. Susan was amazed at Tara's patience, her kindness and her maturity.

Susan knew there was no way; she would have coped, as well as Tara did, she had the patience of a saint.

When Susan and friends questioned Tara, about her superb nursing skills, and her kindness and devotion to her Mum, Tara always said;

'It's not too difficult; Mum is a brilliant patient and a pleasure to be with.'

'She's like an angel, and she never complains, even when she is in severe pain.' 'She is a true warrior, and I hope if I am ever ill, I'll be as brave as my Mum.'

Tara's grandmother and her great-grandmother had also died of lung cancer. Susan hoped, against hope, it would skip the next generation. She loved and relied so much on Tara, she felt she wouldn't cope well, if anything bad happened to her.

'Well, maybe not today,' she mused.

After all, it was Tara who had forced her to come to the creative writing class, totally against her will.

She would certainly think of some small punishment for Tara, for dragging her to the classes. Maybe, she would insist on Tara applying her make-up, for the next few months.'

Tara was a gem at changing Susan's serious solicitor image into, 'an elegant swan.'

Susan always felt more confident when Tara did her makeup; she managed to bring out the best in her features, without making her look false.

She could mix it up so well, she gave Susan a very glamorous look for a night on the town, and a very professional look when attending important meetings.

Susan was always so grateful to Tara; 'I really love the way you do my makeup.'

'Well, I am lucky; I have a very good canvas to work on.' Tara would emphasise.

Susan, smiled to herself; 'Yes, I'll get my revenge, by making Tara apply my makeup for my next meeting, and for my nights out.'

Tara asked; 'What are you smiling at?'

'What are you plotting?'

'Don't worry, you'll soon find out,' Susan said smugly.

In December, Susan couldn't believe, she was still trudging along to the classes with Tara, but still unwillingly of course. The classes began in September, and Susan was surprised she was still attending them, but due to Tara's amazing persuasive powers, and their great friendship, she had agreed to continue to the end of term.

'In January you may even decide, you want to return to classes,' Tara said coaxingly.

'Don't hold your breath on that happening,' Susan said firmly.

The only consolation Susan felt was, it was snug and warm in the classroom, while the winter elements of wind and rain battled fiercely outside.

Susan wasn't into the outdoor life, during wintertime, she had no interest in walking on wet, cold winter days, and she most certainly wasn't the camping type, like Tara.

Poor Tara continuously tried to persuade her to go for long walks in the winter, and she even tried to persuade her go camping, but to no avail.

'I know, if you gave it a try, you would love walking on the dry, crisp winter's days.

It really is something special, and it is so good for the mind and the body,' Tara coaxed, in her best brainwashing voice.

'You would also enjoy camping, all year round, if you just gave it a chance.'

'It's great fun and it's a wonderful experience, seeing nature and being with nature at its best, in the spring and summer seasons, and then seeing the many changes of autumn and winter.'

'I believe you, but no matter what you say, camping is certainly not my idea of fun.'

'You are missing out on life, by not trying it.'

'It's all right, don't worry, I don't feel I am missing anything.'

'I am lucky; I do have a great life, thanks.'

'Camping is just not part of my life, you must accept that,' Susan emphasised.

'Just think about the long hot summer days, when nature is bursting with all types of life, and when it's full of colour and activity. In particular, the spectacular types of flowers in bloom, and all the beautiful colours on display, in the parks and forests.'

'Camping costs very little, and yet it brings such joy to people.'

'I do love the forests and the parks in the spring and summer time, and I also go for walks in autumn and winter, but unlike you I choose to walk during the dry, warm days, not the miserable wet, frosty, snowy days,' Susan said emphatically.

'If you went camping, you would see the insects flit from flower to flower, and the bees busy foraging for nectar and pollen. Nature is so busy, and you would see lots of varieties of flowers, plants and fruits.'

'I see all that happening anyway, I don't need to sleep in a tent with nature to observe it.'

'But you'll see far more of nature, when camping.'

'You see the laid back atmosphere and easiness of nature in summer, you can see birds nesting and raising their young.'

'It's an exciting time of the year as everything is coming to life, and you see the circle of nature at its best, especially when camping.'

'Oh my goodness Tara, you are certainly selling it well.'

'You should work for 'Bord Fáilte.'

'You might succeed in brain washing the tourists, or even some Irish people, but please don't waste your energy on me.'

'I am a lover of hotels and their luxurious, warm accommodation, not a lover of freezing in nature on a camp site,' Susan stressed.

'You haven't experienced the new camp sites, they are so incredible nowadays.'

'It's so exciting to go camping on the crisp, dry days, but it's really fun on the wet days too.'

'Tara, you're not listening to me.'

'I will spell it out for you again.'

'CAMPING IS NOT FOR ME!'

'Do you not remember, the weekend in summer, I went camping, and it rained non-stop?'

'It was the most miserable cold weekend of my life, and yet it was supposed to be the long hot, sunny days of summer.'

'Our clothes were saturated, and we spent most of the time struggling to stop the tent blowing away.'

'Believe me, we didn't get time to look at nature, nature was busy wrecking our tent, and trying to kill us in the process.'

'The wind was howling and the trees were actually creaking and bending with the force. Just when we thought it couldn't get any worse, the thunder and lightning came roaring and flashing.'

'We decided to pack up what we could salvage, and we battled the wind, the rain, thunder and lightning, until we reached the safety of our car.

We drove to the nearest town, and thankfully we were lucky to get accommodation, safe from your friend, nature, which was definitely trying to mutilate or kill us.'

'We soaked in a luxurious, beautiful bubble bath, compliments of the manager as he felt really sorry for us, when he saw our dishevelled, horrific camping look.

'Well, okay, I surrender, maybe camping is not for you,' Tara acknowledged.

'But you should go for walks during winter, even in the rain.'

'The quietness and the darkness of winter, isn't sad and dreary, it can be very calming, enchanting, and fascinating to observe.'

'Tara, please don't expect me to venture out in wind and rain, after a hard day's work, that would totally stress me, not calm me.'

'Just accept, it's never going to happen,' Susan said vehemently.

'I go to the gym for exercise and to de-stress, and that's sufficient exercise for my sanity.'

'Most days, exercise is a chore for me, but I do it for my sanity.'

'I go for walks with you in the summer time, so be happy with that, and let me do my own thing in the winter.'

'I am not a fanatic walker, like you are, and I don't intend to become one.'

'You are so fanatical about walking; remember you even went out during 'Storm Desmond, how over the top is that?' Susan asked irritably.

'To this day, I still can't believe you actually went for a walk during that storm.'

'That was so dangerous and so careless of you.'

'What if of a tree fell on you, or you were hit by flying debris?'

'I certainly don't think it was clever of you to go walking, when 'Met Éireann' and 'An Garda Síochána' had advised people to stay indoors, and not make unnecessary journeys.'

'That included walking, my dear friend.'

'I understand what you are saying, and I did regret that decision.'

'I love my walks and it helps me stay sane. It was only one stormy evening, that I went walking,' Tara said softly.

'Believe me, I haven't attempted to go walking again, in stormy weather, as it was such hard work fighting the wind and the rain, and it was quite scary.'

'If you like, you can inform 'Met Éireann' and 'An Garda Síochána' that I have learnt my lesson, and I won't battle through storms in the future,' Tara said laughingly.

'You must remember, if people don't listen to the experts' advice, and they make unnecessary journeys, they put the Emergency services at risk, trying to rescue careless people during storms.'

'I know, I have learnt my lesson, Yippee!' (3)

'You were so lucky you weren't injured.'

'Even the meteorologist in 'Met Éireann' said it was the first time, he had issued a status red warning for rainfall, since the coding of weather warnings began.'

'He also warned, there would be strong winds with gusts of 100 to 120km/h throughout the storm period.'

'I was shocked that you didn't heed the severe storm warnings.'

'The strong winds could have swept you off your feet, and you could have been killed, you were so lucky nothing happened to you.' Susan said angrily.

'Calm down, I won't be attempting that again, I promise you.'

'I have learnt my lesson, 'Honestly.'

Susan returned her focus to the reality of the classroom, and she suddenly realised all eyes were on her. Tara nudged her and said;

'Hazel asked, if you would like to read your short story.'

Susan had been sitting absent-mindedly, with a rather haughty attitude, while she had been doodling and thinking back on her camping escapade and on 'Storm Desmond', etc. Perhaps, Hazel had noticed her lack of class participation.

'Oh my God!' Susan muttered.

The dreaded moment had come, and she was now the centre of attention. Her plan had been to nod and smile in class, without actually getting involved in writing silly, short stories which bored her.

She had been daydreaming and doodling, and drawing her favourite shapes; hearts, diamonds, stars and all types of geometrical shapes. She was tired after her busy day in work, and totally disinterested in compiling a short story on any subject, that Hazel requested.

Now she was under pressure, to read a short story she was supposed to have written, the stress of it all. Thankfully her determination and her legal ability to think quickly, kicked in to rescue her from total embarrassment.

She recalled a short story she had recently read in a magazine, and she decided to pretend she wrote it, she just hoped nobody else had read the story.

She looked at her notebook and she brazenly began pretending to read from it.

'Caroline's first evening in University,' she said in a strong, determined voice.

Out of the corner of her eye she could see Tara, looking at her in disbelief. Tara could see doodling only, on the page she was 'pretending to read.'

She quickly flicked back a page, where she had previously taken some notes during class, to pacify Tara.

She boldly continued reading; 'Caroline's daughter, Nicole was excited

'I can't believe you took the credit for that short story.'

'I know you didn't write it, and I am sure other people in the class knew that too. Maybe even Hazel knew, and she was playing mind games with you.'

'Oh for goodness sake Tara, it's only a short story. No one was hurt or killed in the reading of it.'

'What else could I do?'

'I couldn't say, I had been doodling, so instead, I improvised.'

'I actually think it was very clever of me. Don't you?'

'No, I don't.'

'Promise me you won't do that again, and you'll make more of an effort in class.'

'Ah, sorry Tara, I didn't mean anything bad, I was just saving myself from embarrassment.'

'I'll make an effort next week.'

'I want you to make an effort every week.'

'Yes, tutor,' Susan said playfully, and they both laughed. Tara was so good natured, she couldn't remain angry, with Susan.

Chapter 9

Patricia was really excited about the 'Creative Writing Classes', and she walked briskly to 'Siam College.' All day long, she had been looking forward to the classes and now finally she had arrived. Hopefully she would become the budding writer she had always dreamed about.

As she entered the college, the first person she noticed was Paul. He stood out in the crowd with his tall, dark, handsome good looks. Paul smiled at Patricia and she was annoyed with herself, for automatically smiling back.

'What was she thinking; she was here to become a famous writer not to socialise?'

She took a seat beside two ladies, to let Paul know his smile meant nothing to her, and to keep her mind focused on her dream of 'becoming a writer.'

She was a firm believer in working hard, and all her life she worked diligently for what she had achieved.

'You reap what you sow', was a favourite motto of hers.

She now recalled the great advice of 'Albert Einstein'.

'If you want to live a happy life, tie it to a goal, not to people or things.'

This advice from 'Einstein' made Patricia even more determined to reach for her goals, and become a successful author.

Paul was disappointed when the blonde girl, who had such a beautiful smile, sat in the far corner of the room. He felt the warmth of her smile, when she initially entered the room, then suddenly her smile changed to a really cold, steely stare.

He was no fool; he knew, she had definitely given him, the brush off. If the rest of the evening continued like that, he certainly, wouldn't be coming back, for more punishment.

He hoped she didn't think he fancied her. He had automatically smiled, because he thought he knew her, her face seemed familiar.

He felt he had met her before, but he couldn't actually recall where, perhaps he would remember later.

When she had snubbed him, he felt like saying;

'Don't worry dear, you are safe, I am just out of a long relationship, and I have no intention of starting another.'

'That would stop her in her tracks, and she might even apologise, for her cold stare,' he thought.

To distract herself from looking at the handsome guy, Patricia opened her handbag to switch off her mobile phone.

She kept rummaging in her bag, and she soon discovered she didn't have her mobile. She felt very panicky, her phone was like an extension of her hand, she never went anywhere without it.

She must have left it in the office; hopefully nobody would need to contact her urgently.

She did some 'Mindfulness Practices' to distract and to ground herself, while waiting for class to start. Thank heavens; she had completed the 'Mindfulness Course', it made her calmer and less dramatic, in awkward situations, as lately her life seemed to be full of drama.

But she wasn't complaining, because the more drama in her life the more stories she wrote.

Within a few minutes of 'breathing mindfully', she felt calm again.

'Mindfulness' was like a door opening to a world of peace and calmness, where she felt in control of her life again.

She had discovered through 'Mindfulness Practice classes' that 'Mindfulness' is the basic human ability to be wholly present, to be aware of where we are and what we're doing, and not feel overcome, by what's going on around us.'

Having 'Mindfulness' in her life gave her confidence to do things, she had dreamed of like; travelling all over the world, all types of sports and now creative writing. Things she procrastinated about, she no longer put on the 'long, long finger' for tomorrow or the next day. Now, she just got on with things, no matter how difficult they were.

The 'creative writing class' was part of a new chapter, and there was no room for any man in this chapter. She gave Paul another cold stare, to get her point across. After all it was her life, and at present she hadn't time for the complications of romance.

She stopped thinking about her mobile, and she suddenly found herself getting totally immersed in the 'creative writing class.' This was her idea of heaven, her place of peace and creativity where she was totally true to herself. She liked the tutor Hazel, and she was very impressed with her style of teaching.

Patricia had attended numerous types of classes over the years and some of the tutors hadn't been great, whereas, Hazel was so enthusiastic and so full of life.

She seemed so organised, and she presented them with a copy of her plans for each term, and Patricia happily noticed, she had lots of 'Assignments' for them.

When Hazel explained the details of the course, it was obvious; she had devised a specific plan, which would encourage their 'creative juices' to flourish.

That's exactly why Patricia had joined her creative writing class, she knew she had the talent to write; she just needed direction and encouragement.

Patricia had always dreamed of writing a novel, and hopefully now was her time. What an achievement it would be, and it would certainly stop the doubters and the sceptics in their tracks. But, even better, it would make her family and friends so proud of her, for persevering with her love of writing, thus making her dream come true.

Patricia took notes when Hazel said; 'Please keep in mind during your day to day living; stories come from the life you live, and the life you see all around you.'

'Always try to be observant; always carry a pen and a notebook with you, so you can jot down your thoughts and ideas. Record anything new and exciting, you see on your daily travels.'

'Those nuggets of life you see and collect on your travels will improve your writing skills, thus enabling you to write an incredible short story and perhaps, even a novel.'

'Who knows?'

To quote one of my favourite authors and a wise man, 'Neil Gaiman' an English author;

'The imagination is a muscle. If it is not exercised, it atrophies or shrinks.'

Hazel explained; 'In order to keep our writing skills and our imagination alive, we must exercise our creative muscles all the time.'

Since a child, Patricia had always written stories, now she loved the arts with a passion, and she even looked quite arty.

She worked as a medical receptionist for the local doctor, Dr O'Connor, as she needed the money to live and to support her dream of writing a novel.

She was very lucky, she loved her work, and Dr O'Connor was an excellent doctor. He was pleasure to work for and a total gentleman, what more could she ask for?

Absolutely nothing, she was very happy in her job.

She was extremely lucky to get the job, under the unusual circumstances, which occurred around her interview.

On the day of her interview, she was running late, she was rushing so fast, she tripped on the uneven footpath and fell heavily. She cut her knees and laddered her tights, but thankfully she didn't do any permanent damage, nothing was broken.

Unfortunately or maybe luckily, she didn't have time to change her tights, so she went directly to the interview. She was rather flushed, her tights were torn and dirty, and she looked an utter mess.

As soon as she explained the situation to Dr O'Connor, he was very understanding. He even took a look at her knees and recommended a special cream, to speed the healing process, and stop any scaring.

Her friend Sarah said in jest; 'In future, when I go for an interview, I must ladder my tights, pretend I tripped and fell, and I'll probably get the job.'

Patricia replied; 'I really must have looked a sight, when I arrived at the interview. I must have looked more like a patient than an interviewee.

I really appreciated Dr O'Connor's faith in me, in offering me the job, under the crazy circumstances. We work really well together, we are a good team, and he certainly made a wise decision.'

'He must have been impressed by your modesty too,' Sarah teased.

'Well, I am just telling it, as it is,' Patricia laughed.

Patricia was always cheerful and she loved meeting people, even the most cantankerous patients, left with a smile. She had lots of arty friends, so she always had interesting stories to tell.

She was so excited the day of the creative writing class that she had to use all her will power, to concentrate on work.

She realised she had a permanent smile on her face, when people commented; 'You must be in love, you are smiling nonstop today, and there seems to be an extra spring in your step.'

Having mixed up two patients charts, Mrs Murphy, had teased her;

'You must have a hot date tonight, as your mind seems to be elsewhere.'

Mrs Murphy didn't realise Patricia had a dream, that one day she would write a bestselling novel!

Only her close friends were aware of her dream. She smiled to herself when she thought of the attitude of some patients, if they knew about her dream.

Mrs Flanagan, a rather serious lady, would probably say with a hint of sarcasm; 'What a silly idea.'

'I do hope you aren't taken some of the prescription drugs?'

Mrs Reilly, forever the moaner, would probably give one of her cranky looks, and say; 'Whatever will you be thinking of next?'

'I suppose you have your eye on the President's job?'

Having dabbled before in writing Patricia, felt the creative writing classes, would be so exciting and interesting, and just like second nature to her. Her creative juices would flow non-stop, like a graceful but speedy waterfall.

'All the cynics will be shocked, but they will have to eat their words of 'hostility and discouragement' when I am famous,' she mused.

Having washed the odour of her medical life, and the aura of the begrudgers in the shower, she felt ready to take on the writing world.

Patricia sang her favourite 'Katy Perry' song, 'Firework', as she dressed for success in the writing world.

> *'Baby you're a firework*
> *Come on let your colours burst.'*

'Well, that's exactly what I will do,' Patricia vowed. Once I journey through my creative writing classes, the fireworks and the colour of words, and ideas will go off with a very loud bang,' Yippee! (4).

People near and far will be in awe. 'I will eventually write the novel, I have always dreamed about,' she smiled.

Patricia felt quietly confident in life; she was the type of girl who liked to maintain high quality standards, by having a good professional image and a good social image. Unfortunately, she was also a minx, who hit the snooze button in the mornings, which usually left her hurriedly preparing for work. Yet she always managed to look smart, neat and professional, on the receptionist desk.

Patricia loved fashion and people always commented on her outfits.

Men seemed to find her very attractive, yet she had no steady boyfriend.

'You are just too fussy,' her friend Freya (Casey), frequently said.

'I have so much to do, I don't have time for a serious relationship at the moment,' she defended herself.

She had lots of ideas about things she wanted to achieve, and she was always in a hurry to tick things off her imaginary; 'To do list.'

Like the numerous times she had said to her Mum, Helen; 'See Paris and Die.'

'One day I will go to Paris, I love the thoughts of visiting that beautiful, cultural, romantic city, before I die.'

Her Mum just smiled, but Patricia presumed she was probably thinking;

'What will my wild daughter do next?'

As usual, Patricia was just joking, she did intend to go to Paris one day, but it wasn't at the top of her 'To do list.'

She didn't realise her Mum, had taken her seriously, and she was actually plotting with Freya their trip to Paris.

'Helen phoned me today, and asked me to book five days in 'Paris' for the three of us, and she wants to pay,' Freya announced.

'Pardon, what do you mean, who is going to Paris?'

'Who is Helen?'

'Your Mum, of course.'

Patricia thought Freya was just telling fibs, as they were inclined to tease each other, they both had a good sense of humour.

She soon realised Freya was not playing games with her.

When Patricia got over the shock, she laughed and said;

'Oh my Goodness!'

'I do hope Mum doesn't think I am going to die soon, I was joking with her recently, about Paris.'

'Just for a laugh, I kept repeating to her, that famous saying;

'See Pairs and Die.'

'I do hope the 'Universe' is not plotting my death, phew!'

'I don't think you need to worry Patricia, only the good die young, you'll be around for a long time yet,' Freya said flippantly.

'If only the good die young, then we will both live to a ripe old age,' Patricia retaliated, and they both laughed heartily.

After lots of discussions, Patricia finally accepted her Mum's unexpected invitation to Paris, but she agreed to go on condition, they all paid their own way.

Freya then booked the five day trip, to beautiful, romantic Paris.

Patricia offered to do research, and to compile information packs for them, on all the historic places in Paris.

A few weeks later, they met for coffee, and they were very impressed when Patricia presented them with A4 wallets, in beautiful, cheerful pink, yellow and purple colours, full of historic information and pictures of beautiful Paris.

Helen and Freya got excited when Patricia mentioned that; 'A leisurely hop-on, hop-off River Seine boat cruise, was a spectacular way to see the beautiful sights of Paris.'

Helen asked; 'Can you really hop-on, hop-off the boat like on the buses?'

'Yes Mum, you can hop-on and hop-off the boat, to visit the sights along the Seine, it's like a water taxi.'

'Well, that's amazing, well done on your excellent research. I look forward to that particular trip.'

The Paris trip had now suddenly become a reality, and they were all excited at the prospect of seeing the splendid sights of wonderful Paris. Helen and Freya hugged Patricia, and thanked her, for her superb information packs, which would certainly refresh their knowledge of Paris.

They chatted and browsed through the interesting information;

'The name 'Paris' was derived from its early inhabitants, the 'Celtic Parisii tribe'.

'Paris, is often referred to as, 'The City of Light', (La Ville Lumière), because of its leading role during the, 'Age of Enlightenment', and more factually because Paris was one of the first European cities, to adopt 'gas street lighting'.'

Patricia's Mum began to read aloud some of the information;

'Paris the capital of France is the world's most visited city. Paris is very proud of its many monuments from the iconic *'Eiffel Tower'*, to the splendid *'Notre-Dame Cathedral'*, and of course the majestic *'Arc de Triomphe'*.

Patricia and Freya giggled when Helen read;

'Paris is called, the *'City of Love',* for its amazing sights, and its romantic French language, and also its popularity as a honeymoon destination.'

'It is so cute to have a *'City of Love','* Freya, ever the romantic, said smiling happily.

A few weeks later, they arrived in Paris, full of excitement and thrilled to be spending time together, in the 'City of Love'.

On their guided tour they were thrilled to see, the most famous building in the world, the 'Eiffel Tower' standing stately above the city, it was everything they expected and more.

With the aid of Patricia's notes and the guides amazing knowledge, they soon learned a lot about the 'Eiffel Tower', and beautiful, romantic Paris, for example;

'The 'Eiffel Tower' was designed by 'Alexandre Gustave Eiffel' in 1889, and it's the world's greatest engineering accomplishment. It's a huge, wrought iron, skeleton tower which stands majestically in Paris, for the entire world to see and admire.

The guide informed the tour group that; 'The exquisite, 'Champs-Elysées' is one of the most iconic Paris boulevards.'

'Who hasn't dreamed of strolling, glamorously along its tree-lined streets towards the towering 'Arc de Triomphe'?' he asked smiling.

They all looked at each other and smiled and nodded, and even the guys in the group were impressed.

Patricia now recalled the fun and the crazy, most unusual things that happened to them in Paris.

On their return home, they told their adventurous stories of 'Paris' to family and friends; everyone was amazed and laughed at all their crazy adventures.

To this day, Patricia and Freya enjoy telling their crazy; 'Paris adventure stories' to new acquaintances, and friends who still want to hear about their bizarre experiences in Paris.

Basically their extraordinary Paris adventures in a nutshell are;

'Patricia got hit by a bus, Helen got food poison, and Freya and Patricia ended up in a brothel, all in the space of five days'

The story goes; on the second day of their trip, after a few hours of shopping, they went for a coffee. Helen stayed at the beautiful outdoor cafe, to relax and watch the world go by, and Patricia and Freya returned to the shopping area, where unfortunately, disaster struck.

A bus drove onto the footpath and it hit Patricia's right arm. To this day, they still laugh at what Patricia said to Freya, immediately after the accident;

'I think I was hit by a bus.'

Patricia continually defends herself by explaining;

'I was obviously, in shock, and it all happened so quickly.'

'My reaction was calm at first, until the reality of the situation, and the pain in my arm registered in my brain.

'I knew Freya hadn't seen what happened and I didn't want to alarm her.'

'Hence, my ridiculous statement;

'I think, I was hit by a bus.'

Apparently, it was the young, bus driver's first day, and he misjudged the footpath, as he pulled up to the bus stop.

After the accident, a man ran up to Patricia, saying;

'I am a witness, I saw the whole thing, the bus driver drove onto the footpath, and I saw the bus hit your arm.'

Patricia calmly said to the man;

'Many thanks, but I am all right, I have no broken bones.'

Freya tried to persuade Patricia to go to hospital, but she was adamant, she had no broken bones.

'I am okay, it's just my arm and my ego that's bruised.

Patricia very kindly said to the bus driver;

'I am fine, and there is no need to report the incident.'

The poor pale faced, shocked driver, was delighted to hear Patricia wasn't taking action against him, or the company. He thanked her profusely in his broken English.

As she left the scene, Patricia said to Freya;

'Please don't tell Mum, as she would be very upset and worried.'

'I am all right; my arm is bruised not broken. I know I'll be very sore tomorrow, but I'll live.'

'Your arm will be very painful tomorrow, my poor petal,' Freya said as she hugged Patricia.

'We'll go to the chemist, and get some painkillers and cream to heal the bruising,' Freya said.

'I'll wear long sleeves tomorrow, to hide the evidence from Mum,' Patricia said, smiling bravely.

'Good plan, but please don't be too brave.'

'If you feel ill during the night, let me know, and I'll take you to hospital.'

'Thanks, Freya, you're a true friend.'

The next day Patricia's arm was quite sore and very badly bruised. The colours of the bruising were amazing; 'Red, yellow, brown, and some dark blue patches, and dark purple and black patches also.'

Like a child, Freya would ask discreetly, when Helen wasn't around.

'Can I see the colours of your arm today; it's fascinating, it's like a cute rainbow.'

'It certainly doesn't feel like a cute rainbow.'

'Sorry, is it sore?'

'Yes, it's very painful, especially at night.'

'When we get home you must promise me, you'll go for an x-ray?'

'Don't worry, I will.'

Thankfully, they managed to keep the accident a secret from Helen, even though, one day she commented to Patricia.

'Are you not too warm in that long sleeve top?' she queried, looking puzzled.

'No, Mum, I don't feel too warm,' Patricia replied trying to appear cool, even though her body was on fire.

On their return home, Freya persuaded Patricia to have an x-ray.

Patricia's x-ray showed severe soft tissue bruising, and thankfully no broken bones.

The next drama in Paris, was the day after Patricia's accident, poor Helen got food poison. They had dressed up in their chic dresses, and they went to a lovely restaurant in the centre of Paris, close to their hotel.

Helen had spotted the classy restaurant the previous day and the manager said there was a cancellation, and they were delighted as they got a table by the window.

They enjoyed watching the world go by, while they ate and chatted.

Patricia and Freya had steak for their main course, and Helen had chicken. The food was nicely presented, and it tasted delicious and fresh, so they thought.

Unfortunately, during the night Helen woke up suddenly, feeling quite ill. She managed to make it to the bathroom, where the dreadful vomiting, and diarrhoea began. Thankfully, the contaminated chicken she had eaten, disappeared down the toilet bowel, she felt very weak, but a little better.

She sipped some water and then curled up in her lovely warm bed, while the two ladies slept soundly in the next room, unaware of the food poison drama.

The following morning Helen was feeling quite weak, and she was unable to eat breakfast. The girls were upset when they discovered Helen got food poison, and they were rather annoyed with the restaurant, as it was quite expensive.

Helen persuaded them not to tackle the manager, and not to fuss, as she was on the mend. Later in the day she managed some tea and toast, and thankfully, she felt a lot better by evening.

The next incident happened the night before they left Paris to return home, Patricia and Freya went for a drink. Helen decided to relax in the hotel, as she was still feeling a bit weak from her food poisoning drama.

Patricia and Freya went to a wine bar close to their hotel. They ordered two glasses of full bodied, French red wine, and they chatted and relaxed.

Suddenly they noticed people who came into the bar, disappeared through beaded curtains. Patricia nudged Freya discreetly, and they both smiled knowingly at each other.

They soon became aware that the waitress and people at the bar were actually scrutinising them. In their innocence, they thought, it was because they were tourists, but later they realised they were under severe scrutiny.

They finished their drinks as quickly as possible, as they knew, they were definitely being watched and discussed at the bar. When they got outside, they fell around the place laughing, they weren't sure whether the people in the bar, thought they were clients, or undercover cops.

But they both said in unison;

'It's a brothel? Isn't it?'

The wine bar appeared to be a front for the brothel industry.

'I really wanted to know what was happening, but I also wanted to leave, in case they invited us to take part, in whatever was going down, behind the beaded curtains, excuse the pun,' Patricia roared laughing.

'You couldn't make up a story like that, even if you tried,' Freya said laughing so much, tears streamed down her face.

'Patricia, there's never a dull moment with you, that's why I love your company so much.'

'When you are not being; 'Hit by a bus, you are drinking wine in a brothel, or your sleeping, while your poor Mum's head is hanging over the toilet bowel.'

There's definitely never a boring minute in your brilliant, crazy company,' Freya said laughing heartily.

'Yes, we certainly had an action packed, eventful five days, 'dans le beau Paris', 'in beautiful Paris',' Patricia giggled.

Chapter 10

Hazel Griffin was always excited on the first day of tutoring her 'Creative Writing Class.' It was exciting and amazing, the feeling of camaraderie she always felt with her students.

Their talent knew no bounds, and they took on board her advice and encouragement, and their imaginations ran riot. Even the most unlikely student, became a keen writer by the end of the course. She had a great rapport with people, and she always got the best out of her students.

Hazel fondly recalled Robert from last year's class, and his wife Emma, a former student, who sadly died the previous year.

After Emma died, Robert joined the writing class because Emma had always been so enthusiastic about Hazel's classes, and she had even tried to persuade him to join.

He now felt she would be proud of him for joining the classes.

But in her usual witty way, she would probably say;

'Now that I have gone, you decided to join the writing classes, pity you didn't do it when I was alive.'

Over the year Robert had blossomed, and his writing had flourished, and his enjoyment was delightful for all to see.

Each week students read their short stories to the class, and Robert's stories were so captivating and fascinating, that the silence in the room was surreal. No coughing or shuffling, or yawning, his fellow students were mesmerized by his exciting thrillers.

'Whodunit stories?'

He had become a master of crime and thriller stories, and a great storyteller.

He was a total gentleman, and he was so unassuming, and everyone in the class warmed to him.

Hazel was pleased that Robert still kept in touch by e-mail, and he often asked her opinion on his short stories.

She was delighted to see that some of his short stories were published in crime magazines. Hazel felt so proud of all her students, but in particular the ones who continued to write and be published.

Her students were like her children, she couldn't do enough for them, and she was always willing to give advice. The amazing thing was the job had landed at her feet, without any planning or choosing it as a career. When her daughter Clara had left the nest, she had felt so lonely.

It was the loneliness which led her to attend the 'Creative Writing Classes.' Now years later, no longer the student, but the tutor, and she really loved teaching and nurturing her students.

She herself had learnt so much from her wonderful tutor, 'Grace Daly', while attending evening 'Creative Writing Classes' in Dublin.'

Grace was one of the finest teachers she had ever known, and she had numerous novels and poems published, and she had written numerous plays also.

Grace had such a lovely way with words; you could easily picture yourself, in the situation which was unfolding in her books etc.

Hazel was inspired by Grace, and she was fascinated how easily she unveiled the creative, and the emotional side of her students.

Grace taught her pupils from the heart, and she succeeded in enlightening and educating them, and in addition encouraging them to love literature and writing.

Grace gave her heart and soul to the job, and she was very sad when she had to retire.

Grace had insisted that Hazel apply for the position and she was delighted when the College appointed her, as there were over 100 applicants. Hazel was rather pleased when the interview panel said that her 'First-Class Honours' 'Bachelor of Education Degree (B. Ed)', would be an asset to 'Siam College'.

During class, Hazel asked her students to read their short stories or poems and she encouraged feedback, but she always emphasised;

'That positive criticism was as important as negative criticism.'

It was delightful to see their creativity at work, and to observe their amazing talent. She was impressed with the valiant creative effort of each student on the topics, and assignments she chose for them.

Hazel completed in-depth research before the term began, and it most definitely was worth it. She scoured magazines, newspapers and websites to get ideas and plots for her students' assignments.

She made copies for her students' of clever stories with intriguing plots and impressive, memorable characters. Her research facilitated students' in developing a plot for their short stories, and it also helped them create their lovely characters who became relatable people.

Hazel was constantly surprised, how much she also learnt during the year, from her students' inspiring stories.

Like every path in life, she felt there was always something to learn along the way, even as a tutor.

She was a diligent teacher, and she acknowledged and appreciated that her students had completed a hard day's work, before they came to class.

She informed them that; 'Some days you will struggle and 'the creative juices', just won't flow. I would encourage you to ask for assistance if you are struggling, we can all help each other, by sharing ideas.'

'Even the best of writers can have, *'Writer's block',*' Hazel said smiling.

On the first day of the creative writing classes, Hazel decided to share the history of creative writing and some of the basics on how to write a good short story, a poem or a novel.

Hazel addressed the class; 'Tonight we will examine the; '*The History of 'Creative Writing*';

Originally, throughout the world, stories were passed from generation to generation through 'oral storytelling' traditions.

As most of you will know; 'Ireland is famous for the 'Art of Storytelling.'

'The Seanachaí and Scéalaí', were the traditional bearers and storytellers. They passed the old stories down through generations.'

'It's amazing that even today in the twenty first century, there has been a revival of the ancient 'art of storytelling' in Ireland,' she said proudly.

'Storytellers of Ireland/Aos Scéal Éireann' is an Irish voluntary storytelling organisation which was founded in 2003, and is still going strong throughout the country.'

'Eamon Kelly' is a classic example of the Irish storyteller or 'Seanachaí, and years ago, he presented a brilliant storytelling programme, 'The Rambling House' on RTE1.'

'He was born in Glenfesk, Co Kerry, in 1914 and he is best remembered for bringing the art of storytelling to the people of Ireland, through RTE radio, and TV in the '50s and '60s.'

'Perhaps, you could check him out on 'YouTube' before your next class,' Hazel suggested.

'He was an extraordinary storyteller, and that's what writing is really all about.

It's about telling a story whether it's fiction or non-fiction, the writer is actually painting a story with words,' Hazel explained.

'Storytelling is one of the one of the most important traditions we have in Ireland. Every story can educate, relax and often amuse the reader and the audience. Stories can do so much, they can teach us to love, to understand people, to forgive others, to be just and honest, and to even strive for a better life.

The playwright, 'John B. Keane', once said of 'Eamon Kelly';

'He can take a word or phrase, and swing it in front of you like a hypnotist's pendulum, so that he captivates you; it's a magician's art.'

'Yes, Sarah, did you want to say something?' Hazel asked.

'Yes, my Gran was a great fan of 'Eamon Kelly.'

'She introduced me to 'Eamon Kelly's' story about 'The White Cat.'

'I actually found it on 'YouTube'. It was wonderful to witness 'Kelly's' unique storytelling ability.

'Kelly' states in his story that; 'Drinks lubricates the talking machine.'

'I think, that's an amazing description of our voice box, a 'talking machine', as 'Kelly' called it, and he said the drink helps to move the talking machine.'

'Thank you very much, Sarah, that's excellent storytelling on your part.'

'Perhaps, we could all look at 'The White Cat' on 'YouTube' during the week, and we can discuss it next week.

John who was of the older generation said;

'I've seen it on 'YouTube', and it's very good, I am also a great fan of 'Kelly's'.'

'He has a marvellous flare for storytelling, his sharp wit and voice inflections keep you interested throughout the story.'

'Thanks John.'

Hazel continued with the history of storytelling;

'It wasn't until later years, with the invention of the written word, people started writing stories.'

'This is where the history of 'Creative Writing' really began, when storytellers started writing their stories, instead of telling and retelling them.'

'The written language, gave storytellers the ability to keep a record of their stories, and by using a drafting process, they could actually improve their stories.'

Hazel continued to explain; 'The art of writing was a mysterious discipline for a long time, at first, only the monks and the rich and educated classes were taught how to write, with inks and quills which were expensive, and paper which was hard to get.'

'Eventually people like us, were given the freedom to write and tell their stories.'

'So please use and enjoy the remarkable gift of writing, which you have been given, not everyone has this wonderful gift,' Hazel emphasised.

'Always remember, a good storyteller has the ability to captivate their audience.'

Some of the best authors and storytellers are people like;

'William Shakespeare', 'Charles Dickens', 'Anton Chekov', 'Stephen King', 'Oprah Winfrey' and 'Virginia Woolf', and of course my favourites; 'Maeve Binchy', 'John Grisham' and **'Neil Gaiman'.**

'If you are not familiar with any of these wonderful authors, I suggest you 'Google' them, or borrow one of their books from your local library.'

It is important to remember when you are creating your work of fiction;

'For stories to live, they need the hearts, ears and minds of the listeners and the readers.'

'*Without the listener and the reader there is no story.*'

'Lawrence Clark Powell' once said these very wise words;

'*Write to be understood, speak to be heard, read to grow.*'

'Does anyone know who he is?' Hazel asked.

'Yes,' said Noel.

'I am a librarian, and I have read a lot of his work, and 'Powell' was also a librarian. He was a literary critic, a bibliographer and an author of over one hundred books. He made significant contributions to the literature of the library profession, and we are very grateful to him.'

'He was born in Washington, D.C. in 1906 and he died in 2001, in California, where he and his family had moved to. He was a legendary librarian and author.'

'He was dean of**,** (UCLA), 'University of California, Los Angeles' libraries, and under his directorship he almost 'quadrupled the size' of the library collection to over 1.5 million volumes.'

'Thanks to Powell's dedication and love of reading and writing, UCLA libraries went from a regional resource, to students nationwide,' Noel said proudly.

'Noel, thanks very much for that enlightening information, we certainly are privileged to have your librarian knowledge in our class.'

'We may call upon you during the year to assist us in research on books, DVD's etc., if you are agreeable.'

'It will be my pleasure, to help in any way I can,' Noel said beaming.

'Folks, I can't emphasise enough, how important reading and libraries are for the creative writer, and the blossoming novelist … which I hope and believe most of you will become,' Hazel said encouragingly.

Hazel further explained; 'Words are so powerful; they can take your breath away.'

'In Ireland, we have some of the greatest inspirational sayings and mottos, in particular these wonderful quotes from 'Oscar Wilde;'

'The old believe everything, the middle-aged suspect everything, the young know everything.'

'Keep 'Love', in your heart. A life without 'Love,' is like a sunless garden when the flowers are dead.'

'Experience is simply the name we give our mistakes.'

'If one cannot enjoy reading a book over and over again, there is no use in reading it at all.'

And the last 'Oscar Wilde' quote which unfortunately is true to life, but it's such a witty quote. It may take you a little time, to understand what he's actually saying.

'Some cause happiness wherever they go; others whenever they go.'

'I'll actually explain what he's saying, in those rather witty words;

'There are people in this world, who bring happiness wherever they go, but there are people who don't spread happiness when they visit, therefore people are happier when they leave.'

Hazel noticed Noel had his hand up.

'Yes, Noel.'

'By using my 'Mindfulness' muscle, I feel more in control of what life throws at me.'

'What exactly is 'Mindfulness'?'

'What do you mean using your Mindfulness Muscle?' Freya questioned.

'Well, our lovely lecturer Lucy informed us;

'Mindfulness is a very old technique, and it's linked to Buddhism, and it has become increasingly popular nowadays, as it helps to de-stress the mind and the body.'

"Mindfulness' means really living life, moment by moment, aware of our thoughts, and feelings, and the environment. When we practice mindfulness, our thoughts tune into the now, rather than rehashing the past, or imagining the future.'

'Mindfulness' is like a muscle, the more we use it, the more we benefit from it, as it reduces stress, and it gives us more control over our lives.'

'Don't get me wrong, my life isn't perfect because of 'Mindfulness', but I have a more balanced life.'

'I now accept life is not perfect, and it's okay to have good days and bad days,' she explained to Freya.

'It teaches us to appreciate the good times, and to handle the bad times, without going off the rails altogether,' Patricia emphasised.

'You have sold me on it, I will definitely check it out and maybe even give it a try soon,' Freya said.

'I think it's a simple practice, but it's a miraculous one, but you must practice it daily to benefit,' Patricia smiled.

Patricia recalled how she had always strived to do everything perfectly.

It was such a relief when she discovered through, 'Mindfulness;

'That everything doesn't have to be perfect.'

'What an amazing discovery, as throughout her life, she had been foolishly influenced by people who had always preached;

'If you are doing a job, do it well, or don't do it at all.'

Unfortunately, that silly phrase, had put so much pressure on her, she had always aimed for perfection, even on the smallest of tasks, phew!

Now through her new 'Mindfulness' friend, she gave herself permission;

'To do things, to the best of her ability, and not seek total perfection.'

'Perfection' had been a heavy weight to carry throughout her life. 'Praise the Lord, Alleluia', the burden was now lifted from her shoulders.

She was thrilled, to have discovered the website on 'Mindfulness', as it had enhanced her life so much. Since she began her journey, on the 'Mindfulness,' path, she had become a very content, self assured person.

In class, Lucy had asked them:

'Do you get something wrong every day?'

'Yes,' the class chorused, rather honestly.

'If you do get things wrong and acknowledge it, that's what we call in 'Mindfulness';

'*Bombu Nature*',' Lucy explained.'

'I think it's a witty way of saying, we are not perfect and we never will be, but that's okay.'

'This Buddhist concept means, we never get things completely right, instead we often make a mess of things, because we are only human.'

'*Bombu nature*', means we need to accept that; 'We can never achieve the highest levels of excellence, we can never be those sparkly, perfect human beings, we pretend to be.'

'Hands up anyone who honestly feels, they don't get something wrong every day.' Lucy said with a smile.

Maeve raised her hand, and most of the students looked at her in shock.

'Sorry, I didn't raise my hand, because I am perfect,' she smiled.

'I wanted to say; 'I spent most of my life trying to be the perfect version of me, which was exhausting.'

'Now, thankfully, I can finally relax knowing, it's okay not to be perfect.'

'I love the idea of '*Bombu nature.*'

Like Maeve, Patricia had definitely taken the '*Bombu nature*' on board, which wasn't an easy task, after years of striving to be 'Ms Perfect'.

When she finally accepted her '*Bombu nature*', she no longer judged herself, against a standard of excellence, she couldn't possibly meet.

She also found that through 'Mindfulness;' 'You can learn to laugh at yourself, instead of condemning yourself.'

'You even learn to laugh at other people's failings, instead of condemning them.'

Patricia now recalled how Lucy had made a good point about the 'chattering voice in our heads,' and she asked the class some important questions;

'Folks, isn't it time we gave our heads a break, by simply just taking time to breath in and out?'

'We all happily chorused; 'Yes.'

'By just noticing the; '*In-breath' and the 'Out breath',* it brings you back to the present moment, and it stops all that 'chatter in our heads'.'

'So why would you not practice 'Mindfulness, especially when research has shown how it de-stresses the mind and the body?' Lucy questioned.

She explained to them, how much 'Mindfulness' had changed her life, and made living easier and happier.

Patricia came back to reality, and she was surprised to see Marissa enter the classroom. They nodded and waved to each other. Then it suddenly dawned on her, where she had met the overfriendly guy.

'Oh my goodness!'

'The overfriendly guy was actually Marissa's ex-boyfriend Paul.'

'This is like a soap opera,' she mused.

'There undoubtedly would be no shortage of material for her debut novel. Of course, she would need to change the people's names, and professions, in case of libel.'

She couldn't wait to phone Freya and tell her, the weird situation which was unfolding before her eyes.

Patricia had met Marissa and Paul at the 'Mindfulness' classes, and Marissa and Patricia had kept in touch, and met for lunch at least once a month.

A few weeks ago, Marissa told Patricia that Paul had broken up with her.

She had explained, rather sadly that, she had asked Paul, about them maybe moving in together.

Poor Marissa was shocked and horrified when his answer was to immediately break up with her. She told Patricia she was devastated but she was trying her best, to accept his decision, and move on with her life.

Marissa had known he was afraid of commitment, but unfortunately, she hadn't realised how scared he was, she had rocked the boat, and now she was paying the price.

'I am so sorry to hear that, Marissa.'

'Maybe, it is all for the best, Patricia, as Paul seems to be stuck in a rut and I want to move on, and perhaps have a family at some stage, she said sadly.

'What's going on now?'

'Was this a planned meeting between Paul and Marissa?' Patricia pondered.

'No, definitely not,' she decided, as she examined their body language.

Patricia was a good judge of character, and she most certainly felt the tension between them.

During the break, Patricia shamelessly took on the role of detective. She made a beeline for Marissa and caught up with her on the corridor, heading to the ladies.

'Hi Marissa, I didn't expect to see you here.'

'Unfortunately, it's not my scene, but I agreed to try the classes, to pacify Rebecca.'

'Is Rebecca here too?'

'No, she's working late; she let me down at the last minute.'

'How are things with you?'

'All was well, until I stepped into the classroom, and saw Paul.'

'You didn't know he was coming?'

'Goodness no, if I did, I wouldn't be here, it's so awkward and so embarrassing.'

'Sorry to hear that,' Patricia said genuinely.

'I'll be okay, but I am not sure about Rebecca.'

'I'll kill her when I see her, it's all her fault, I came here,' she laughed rather falsely.

'I'll call you during the week, and maybe we can meet for a coffee,' Marissa said.

'Yes, that would be lovely,' Patricia replied.

Patricia felt she was being dismissed, so she dashed off to the ladies.

When she got home, Patricia phoned Freya.

'You will never guess who was at the class,' Patricia said.

'Prince Charming?'

'No, I told you, I am not interested, my writing class is about fulfilling my novel dream, nothing else.'

'Okay, how boring.'

'Well, who was there, that makes you so excited?'

'Marissa and her ex-boyfriend Paul.'

'Am I supposed to get excited too?'

'Who are they?'

'Remember, I met them at the 'Mindfulness classes.'

'I often meet Marissa for coffee.'

'Still not getting excited, am I missing something?' Freya asked calmly.

'That's not the full story; the weird thing is Marissa didn't realise Paul would be there. She was quite upset, and the body language was tension at its highest.'

'They are no longer together. Isn't life full of coincidences?'

'Of all the classes in Dublin, they both end up in the same creative writing class, by default.'

'Marissa's sister dragged her there, and Paul's friend dragged him to class.'

'It would make for a great story,' Patricia said excitedly.

'Oh you are so callous; think how upset they must be,'

'You, and your silly writing, it'll get you into trouble some day,' Freya said.

'O course, I wouldn't use their names or personalities, but it would be an amazing short story with a twist.'

'What do you mean?'

'Imagine if it was actually planned by Marissa's sister Rebecca and Paul's friend Jayne.'

'You really are letting your imagination run riot. I hope you get lots of writing assignments, to keep you out of trouble.'

'Me too,' but you must admit that was an exciting first class.' Patricia laughed heartily.

After class, Paul suddenly remembered, where he met the girl, who had snubbed him in class. It was at the 'Mindfulness classes' he had attended with Marissa in Dublin.

As usual, Marissa had tried to drag him on her new adventure, of two weeks of 'Mindfulness Classes.' He was adamant; he wasn't interested in spending his precious time, trapped in a class with, 'meditation nerds.'

When Marissa realised she couldn't persuade Paul to go for the entire two weeks, she gracefully accepted, his offer of attending Saturday only.

Paul wasn't really aware of what 'Mindfulness Practice' classes were, but Marissa was so into it, he decided it might be worth checking out. He had checked on 'YouTube', and he was actually intrigued by it.

Marissa introduced him to lots of good 'Mindfulness' websites.

Paul was amazed at the generosity of people, as the websites were free.

'I use 'Mindfulness' in my everyday life, Marissa said;

'*Mindfully going up or down stairs or steps - Brushing my teeth, Mindfully Showering, - Eating, - Driving, - and Vacuuming Mindfully.'*

'So basically, you are saying, every action we do, should be taken 'Mindfully',' Paul queried.

'Yes, by 'Mindfully' doing things, you are living in the now, and not automatically doing things, 'on autopilot'.'

'I am more aware of my actions and I appreciate life, far more than I use to,' Marissa said.

''Mindfulness practice' is a calm and peaceful way of living,' Marissa explained.

Paul surprised himself, and actually enjoyed the Saturday 'Mindfulness' class. He actually agreed with Marissa that; "Mindfulness' brought a soothing, tranquil feeling, to the mind and the body.'

In general, Paul was calm, but when driving in rush hour traffic, he would get angry with careless drivers, who totally ignored the rules of the road.

He bought a 'Mindfulness CD' for his car journeys and he had discovered by;

'Taking a deep breath, in through his nose, and exhaling slowly through his mouth" it calmed his reaction to crazy drivers.

Instead of shouting at people, who couldn't hear him anyway; he practiced 'Mindfulness' and remained quite calm.

At least it was one less stressful situation in life, and rush hour traffic didn't bother him as much.

He knew it would take discipline and practice, to include it in his daily life, like Marissa did, but he was willing to try.

Paul remembered, at the end of the class, Marissa had briefly introduced him to the lady, who snubbed him. He was amused, to see the two ladies chatting so enthusiastically about 'Mindfulness' and he had to interrupt Marissa, to remind her, her parking time was almost up.

Mystery solved, he now knew where he met the lady, but he couldn't actually remember her name. He most certainly wouldn't approach her, or talk to her again, as she had suddenly turned into an ice queen.

Perhaps, she knew he had broken up with Marissa and she wasn't impressed. He didn't really care what she thought; after all, his personal life was his own business.

parenting, since Helen died.

Patricia had always felt that women made more sacrifices in their relationship than men did. She had often said to her Mum;

'When I die, I would like to come back as a man.'

Her Mum, had looked at her rather strangely and said quietly, in case anyone overheard.

'Why my love, would you want to do that?'

She would answer emphatically;

'It's a Man's world Mum.'

Be careful what you wish for, her Mum would say with a smile;

'We all need each other.'

As the 'Godfather of Soul' himself said; 'We definitely need Men, Women and Children in the world for it to make sense. The world would mean nothing if women and children had no existence at all.'

Patricia threw her eyes up to heaven, when her Mum talked about, the 'Godfather of Soul,' 'James Brown'.

Her Mum explained to her that 'James Brown' was an American singer, songwriter. Sometimes her Dad would join in the chat, but thankfully, unlike her Mum, he didn't attempt to sing.

Patricia nearly lost the will to live, when her Mum began to sing her favourite 'James Brown' song.

'Sure, her Mum had a good voice, but who wants to listen to their Mum singing?' It was so embarrassing.

'Mum I'll 'Google' the words, please stop singing,' she pleaded.

When Patricia listened to 'James Brown' singing 'Man's World,' on 'YouTube' she was quite surprised, how the words affected her.

She actually felt quite emotional, but of course, she didn't admit that to her Mum.

When her Mum was out, she often played 'Man's World', and she would sing loudly along.

Patricia was surprised to read that; 'Man's World' was actually recorded, like a sermon, and 'James Brown' had developed the passionate ballad from some lyrics which 'Betty Newsome' wrote.

It was said that Ms Newsome's words were actually derived from the Bible, and her observations of her former boyfriends, including the 'Godfather of Soul' himself, 'James Brown'.

'This is a man's world, this is a man's world
But it wouldn't be nothing,
Nothing without a woman or a girl.'

Her Mum explained, the song was written in 1966, and during that time, men were the bread winners, in most families, and the 'Godfather of Soul' was saying;

'Man is nothing without a woman or a child.'

Helen further explained, that 'The Godfather of Soul' was saying to families that; 'Men are hard-nosed and always out working and striving in life, but women soften their edges and make them into better people. So the world needs women and children too, to make it a balanced place. 'Let's hear it for the girls."

'Basically he was trying to say that; 'Men, Women and Children, all need each other',' her Mum emphasised.

Most of Patricia's friends and work mates, didn't really believe she was serious about her view on, 'It is a Man's World.'

They just smiled and humoured her when she said; 'If there's reincarnation after death, I want to return as 'a Man', as it's a less complicated life.'

They believed, she was just being her usual eccentric self, as some of her ideas were quite different, than the normal persons,' (whatever normal was!).

Lately, Patricia noticed for some unknown reason, she was making that statement quite often, to random people.

She would firmly say; "It's a Man's World,' and when I die, I am definitely coming back as a man.'

Some of the reactions she got were really funny, people didn't know, how to deal with such a brash statement. Other people just pretended they didn't hear, but she would boldly repeat it, just to get a reaction.

She certainly wasn't convinced by her Mum's favourite song; 'That men believed a life without a woman, or a child would mean;' 'Nothing to them.'

Unfortunately, she knew of married couples, where the man still lived a nice single lifestyle, and his wife and children were his accessories.

Those men liked the idea of marriage and children, but without the drama or reality of family life.

They wanted it all; the beautiful wife and children, yet the lifestyle of a single man, burying themselves in work, in the golf course, and the pub.

Those men lived a married life, but they still had the perks of a single life.

Hence, Patricia decided when she died, and was waiting at the pearly gates, she would immediately put in her request.

'Please may I return to earth as a 'Man' next time?'

Her friends just laughed when she told them her request.

Her Mum teased her; 'You should request to return as; 'A Tall, Dark and Handsome Man,' and they laughed heartily, Patricia really missed those fun times with her Mum.

Chapter 13

Patricia now recalled her first day back from her wonderful holiday in South Africa, she had forced herself to unpack, and do all her washing.

The Universe had constantly teased and reminded her of her travels around South Africa. She was drawn back to holiday mode, numerous times, when she noticed planes flying over her house, sounding so loud.

They seemed much closer than usual, so close, she actually checked in case they had landed in her back garden, wishful thinking on her part, of course!

The sight of the planes made her thoughts return to her heavenly holiday in South Africa, and she thought about the superb time she had with her Dad.

Suddenly it now became clear to Patricia, she would write her short story assignment on spectacular South Africa, and her fantastic holiday with Conor.

Patricia had been overjoyed when Hazel handed the class, the short story assignment, to complete, over the next two weeks;

'Write about a memorable holiday with a special person, be they real or imaginary, approximately 3,500 words.'

Hazel said happily; 'Holidays always put people in good humour, and I know your imagination will flourish on such a lovely, cheerful, exciting topic.'

'Please, make your story as interesting as you can, so it connects, captivates and even charms the reader.'

'Writing is a skill, which anyone can learn if they are motivated and determined to write. You must practice and keep writing in order to become a good author, and a good communicator with the readers.'

'This Assignment will give you the platform to let your imagination run riot,' Hazel encouraged them.

A few hours later, Patricia was rather pleased, she had settled into her holiday story assignment, and there was no stopping her.

She tried to type as fast as her thoughts were flowing, but the creative juices were like the 'Niagara Falls'. They were thundering, pounding and flowing strongly and speedily along in her imagination.

Recently, she read about the speed and the volume of the 'Niagara Falls,' and the speed which her thoughts and fingers were moving at, now reminded her of the speedy, majestic 'Niagara Falls.'

A holiday to Canada was definitely top of her, 'to do list' for the future.

She found herself writing parts of words, just to get her memories onto her laptop, she intended to edit them, as soon as the creative juices calmed, as no doubt they would.

Patricia was so excited when Hazel asked the class to complete the, 'Holiday Short Story Assignment.'

She felt they were kindred spirits, as she loved to travel too. She couldn't have asked for a more suitable topic, after all, everyone knew, travel was most certainly her favourite pastime in life.

She had travelled to Europe with friends, but her most memorable holiday was definitely with her Dad, Conor, when they went to spectacular 'South Africa.'

As her thoughts drifted back to the holiday she felt a warm glow.

My goodness, she had some marvellous stories to tell, 3,500 words would be so easy, as she could probably write a book on South Africa.

'Well, maybe someday I will,' she thought happily.

She tried to calm down, but the truth was she couldn't wait to tell her stories. She had her notes from the trip, so she would have no problem reaching the target, Hazel set.

It was like going back in time; the memories just kept flooding back. She even remembered the year they travelled to South Africa, without having to confer with her journal. Yes, it was 2007, a great year and to date, it still was her most memorable holiday.

After her Mum died, she had been surprised when her Dad said he wanted tick things off the 'bucket list' before his time ran out too.

'I want to go to South Africa,' he said firmly.

Patricia recalled, she was quite puzzled about the 'bucket list' until her Dad explained.

'Your Mum and I compiled a 'bucket list' of experiences and achievements, we hoped to accomplish, before we kicked the bucket and died,' he said sadly.

'Little did we know, Helen's time was near the end, or we would have begun our adventures immediately, but as usual in life, we put the 'bucket list' aside, and I only came across it recently.'

'I have decided as a tribute to Helen, I am going to experience all the things we both planned to do.'

'Top of our list was a trip to South Africa, so I would love if you would join me; I know Helen would be delighted with my decision.'

'Many thanks Dad, I would be thrilled to accompany you to South Africa, on your first 'bucket list' experience,' Patricia said excitedly.

'What else is on your list?'

'I'll show you the list someday soon, but things are still a bit raw for me at the moment.'

'No problem, I totally understand, we will browse it together, whenever you are ready.'

Patricia realised how lucky she was to get the opportunity to travel abroad as often as she did. She had vowed to the 'Universe' she would always travel and broaden her mind and her horizons.

Her Dad had explained that years ago it was very difficult to afford travel to Europe, or anywhere in the world, unlike nowadays, where travel was so accessible and affordable.

He quoted a lovely description of travel by 'Wilbur Wright' (who invented the first successful airplane, with the help of his brother 'Orville').

'The desire to travel is an idea handed down to us, by our ancestors who looked enviously on the birds.'

However a few days later, Patricia was shocked to discover, Conor had been in touch with, 'Munroe Travel Company', and he had provisionally booked the trip to South Africa.

'It's the trip of a lifetime, for you and me.'

They were his exact words to Patricia, when he phoned her, with the news.

There was no time for second thoughts or mulling it over it, which Patricia had intended doing. It was all done and dusted, before she had time to think too deeply, about spending two weeks holidays with her Dad.

Now the trip to South Africa was a 'fait accompli.' Patricia couldn't really refuse to go, under the circumstances.

'Can my holiday buddy Lauree, come too?' she asked.

'Well, I actually thought it would be nice for you and I go on the trip,' Conor said.

'That's no problem Dad, I understand, and I am sure Lauree will too, as she is very easy going.'

'You are lucky; you have lovely, fun loving, and thoughtful friends.'

Patricia knew Lauree would understand her decision to accept her Dad's holiday offer, as it was a trip of a lifetime. She loved her holidays with Lauree, so she would promise her; she could choose their next trip.

Lauree's, Mum had chosen her unusual name because of its meaning;

'Honour and Victory.'

She wanted Lauree to become a strong, independent lady, and she hoped, by bestowing the name 'Lauree' on her, it would bring honour and victory to her life, no matter what road she travelled.

At first, it was the bane of Lauree's life, nobody knew how to pronounce or spell it properly. Then she saw the advantages of it, and she began to treasure it.

'You can always change your name,' Patricia advised her.

'Well, I guess, I have got used to it, and I actually love the drama around it.'

'It's always a talking point with people, who don't know me, and it makes me appear so interesting,' she laughed heartily.

For years Patricia and Lauree, went on holidays together, and they always had great fun. She would miss her friend's company, but she couldn't turn down the opportunity of such a wonderful trip with Conor.

He had promised lots of truly amazing adventures, including game hunting in 'Kruger National Park', where they would be up close with the 'Big 5' animals.

She knew Laurre would be happy for her, going on such a wonderful trip to South Africa, with her Dad.

Patricia recalled rather fondly, the many sun holidays she had with Lauree, she was the type of person who lit up a room, and people would automatically smile when she smiled.

Her laugh was the hearties, sexiest, infectious laugh, which captured the imagination of all ages, males and females, who had the pleasure of hearing it. Patricia often found herself joining in her friend's laughter, even when she didn't know, what the joke was.

Lauree's laughter was so infectious, even strangers often joined in the laughter, and sometimes strangers joined their company for 'the craic', and by the end of the evening, they would no longer be strangers.

Lauree was the type of person, if you only met her once, you would never forget her. She had the warmest personality and the biggest, blue eyes, you could ever imagine. Her eyes became larger, the more excited she was. With her big blue eyes, and her beautiful, dark, shiny hair, she was always the 'belle of the ball.'

Irish guys, and foreign guys just loved her, because of her flirty ways, which were totally natural and part of her lovely, bubbly, vivacious personality. The men were like, 'bees to the honey', so enthralled by her girlie, flirty ways.

She could flirt so well and so ladylike, with very little effort, it just came so naturally to her.

Patricia often asked her; 'How do you get away with that bold flirting?'

Lauree would say in all innocence;

'Was I really flirting?'

'I didn't realise I was.'

'Well, you have been flirting with all the guys, and they just love it.'

'If I tried flirting, they would just ignore me and walk away.'

'You definitely have the best flirting techniques I have ever come across,' Patricia said in admiration.

Patricia fondly remembered, at the end of the night, guys would stand in line waiting, and hoping to be chosen by Lauree.

She would walk off into the sunset alone, and surprisingly when they met her again, they would talk to her; amazingly, they bore no grudges, because they really enjoyed her bubbly company and her flirting.

Lauree was a total sun worshiper, while Patricia liked the sun, but couldn't cope with the intense rays, for long periods. She would take breaks to cool down, hiding under the parasol, or in the swimming pool.

Lauree really adored the days of intense heat; 'The hotter the better,' she would say.

If a cloud appeared in the sky, Patricia would be thrilled to get a reprieve from the intense heat, while Lauree wouldn't be a bit impressed.

Patricia would pretend she was upset too, but she really wanted to dance for joy and sing from the rooftops; 'Please bring on those clouds, the more the merrier.'

Lauree usually guessed when Patricia was delighted with the 'cloudy sky', and they would tease each other.

Patricia would certainly miss the fun with Lauree, but she needed to seize the opportunity with both hands, as invites to South Africa, didn't come often.

Lauree was quite surprised when Patricia told her about the 'fait accompli' trip to South Africa with her Dad.

'I hope you won't kill each other,' she said laughing heartily.

'What is this 'fait accompli' you are talking about?'

'I have heard of it before, but I forget what it means, 'Ms Clever Buddy'.'

'The phrase, 'Fait accompli', is actually French, and it literally means;

'An accomplished fact'.'

'It's used by people in everyday life, but particularly in legal situations, for instance; 'It's often said the jury was influenced, by the media coverage of the crime, and thus the verdict of 'guilty' was issued, 'fait accompli.'

'Oh my goodness, let's hope there won't be any crime committed on your holidays in South Africa,' Lauree joked.

'It's not funny; I am trying to get use to the idea of spending two weeks alone with my Dad. On the positive side, we won't be totally alone; we'll be joining an Irish group, in wonderful Cape Town.

Conor will just have to accept, I am an adult now, and he can't be babying or protecting me on this holiday,' Patricia said rather firmly.

'That's it girl, go with that attitude, and you and Conor will be okay.'

'I know you'll have a superb time in spectacular South Africa, and you'll always have the memories, of time spent with your Dad.'

Patricia and Lauree were such good friends; they were always honest with each other, without causing any friction.

'I know, you are right, it probably will be the best holiday ever, but I am still surprised at how quickly Dad booked the trip.'

'One minute he was asking me, if I would like to go, then a few days later, he told me he had booked it.'

'I hadn't the heart to tell him that, I hadn't actually confirmed I was going.'

'But, I must admit, I am excited and I do have a good feeling about the trip.' Patricia said calmly.

'Trust Conor, he obviously went with his, 'gut instinct.'

'He knew your Mum would be so proud of you both, holidaying together.

'I am sure it will be a trip of a lifetime for you and your Dad,' Lauree said happily.

Chapter 14

As the holidays drew nearer, Patricia did her own research on South Africa, even though they had received lots of information from their travel agent.

She was so excited to learn about the 'Big Five' game animals;

'The 'African Lion, African Elephant, Cape Buffalo, African Leopard, and White/Black Rhinoceros.'

She discovered the term 'Big Five' was invented by big game hunters and it actually referred to *'The five most difficult animals in Africa, to hunt on foot'.*

When the day of their trip to spectacular South Africa finally dawned, Patricia didn't hit the snooze button, she didn't mind getting out of her warm bed, because she was off on her holidays. Whereas, when she was working, the snooze button often got pressed and put in motion.

Patricia came back to reality again, and continued writing her memorable holiday story assignment;

When my Dad/Conor, and I discovered we had a 3am start it didn't bother us at all, we couldn't wait to get on the road. The taxi arrived and we set off for Dublin Airport for our flight to Amsterdam, we were very excited but also a little nervous.

It was a hectic morning as we had to ensure, we were in time for our connecting flight from Amsterdam to Cape Town. We met the guide and the rest of our Irish holiday group, when we arrived in Cape Town, exhausted but happy.

Conor had been on trips to Europe, but he had never been on a long haul flight. It was lovely to see his excitement and fascination, when I showed him, how to watch movies on the plane.'

'I gave him a list of my holiday tips and tips from websites;

'How to survive comfortably on a long haul flight.'

The tips were on; 'How to prevent boredom, dehydration, sleep deprivation, deep-vein thrombosis etc. I didn't want to scare Dad, but I explained, he must prepare himself mentally and physically for the long haul flight, to his dream destination of 'South Africa.'

We brought magazines, books, puzzle books, a pack of cards, water and of course my 'Berlitz pocket guide' book on South Africa.

'Are you always so well prepared for your trips?' my Dad inquired.

'I always do my homework before I go on a holidays. If I have a good knowledge of the countries customs and traditions, I can mix well, and feel comfortable with the people.'

'I am so proud of you,' he said with a catch in his voice.

'We are like the scouts, we are well prepared,' I giggled.

'I reminded him to drink plenty of water, so he wouldn't become dehydrated.'

'I also encouraged him to walk up and down the plane, and I showed him numerous leg exercises, to prevent clots or thrombosis, and to prevent the body from aching due to poor circulation.'

'My Dad smiled patiently, as I explained how important it was to keep moving on long haul flights. I showed him how to do some in-seat exercises, such as circling ankles and stretching arms, and I reminded him to be careful of his fellow passengers. We had a good laugh when I said; 'Be careful doing your exercise, don't give anyone a black eye or don't elbow anyone.'

Patricia now fondly recalled on the first night of their trip, when they had arrived safely in Cape Town, her Dad hugged her and said;

'Thank you so much for organising things, and making me feel so comfortable on the flights, you are amazing.'

It was a very special moment for Patricia, as Conor was not really the demonstrative type.

I brought a travel journal with me, as I always enjoyed recording my holiday adventures. Throughout the trip the 'Munroe Travel Company' brought us to numerous fabulous, historic places, and it was important for me to write, every gem of wisdom, our guide Mamello gave us.

There was so much to remember, it was best to write it all down, when Mamello was talking on the coach. I sighed longingly, as Mamello told us, South Africa averages up to nine hours of sunshine a day, regardless of the seasons!

'Wouldn't it be lovely, if we had the same amount of sunshine in Ireland?' I thought. But then I cheered up, when I realised the Irish weather wasn't too extreme, and therefore there were no drought seasons, which unfortunately happen quite often in South Africa.

I still fondly remember the day we went to the spectacular, 'Table Mountain.'

It was such a tremendous day, the sun was shining brightly. We all commented on, the lovely warm heat of the sun on our faces, as the cable car took us to the flat-topped summit.

Mamello, informed us;

'The 'clouds' often hover over the mountain like a 'Tablecloth' and that's why it's called 'Table Mountain'.'

We were so lucky, on the day of our trip; there was no 'tablecloth/clouds' over 'Table Mountain', the sun shone brightly, so the walks and views from the summit were breath-taking. The spectacular views stretched all the way to 'False Bay', 'Robben Island', and the 'Devil's Peak'.

The journey up to 'Table Mountain' took only over five minutes, and we were thrilled when the cable car rotated through 360 degrees, allowing us to clearly see, all the breathtaking views.

When we reached the summit of 'Table Mountain' Mamello said;

'Take lots of photographs, as we are very lucky today with the crisp, cloudless, beautiful blue sky, when the mountain is covered in a 'tablecloth' or blanket of dark, black clouds, the photographs can look sad and morose. Unfortunately, yesterday was like that, we are very lucky today, so take full advantage of the sunny views.'

The following day, we went by coach to some local vineyards and of course our group, being Irish, really enjoyed the wine tasting.

'I have never seen an Irish person, who doesn't enjoy a wine tasting excursion,' Conor said smiling.

Mamello proudly informed us that; 'Cape Town is the largest winemaking region in South Africa, and wine tourism is a big business.'

'The estates are quite large, and every winery offers accommodation, fine dining, casual bistros and elaborate tastings, which in the more established regions are not free, but not expensive either,' he explained.

'But most importantly, there is a young generation of winemakers who are producing better and better wines, which we are very proud of,' he said.

We also visited the 'Cape of Good Hope' where the Portuguese explorer 'Bartholomew Dias' first established trading routes between Africa and Asia as early as the fifteenth century. At the end of the tour on that particular day, we were all exhausted, but very happy from the wine tasting.

We thoroughly enjoyed the night our group was treated to an evening's entertainment of music and dance by a large local group. We absolutely loved the African music and the wonderful dancers.

They were incredible, the singers and dancers had such a natural gift for rhythm, harmony and song. They played 'Zulu' musical instruments and I'll never forget the laughs, when they literally dragged some of us up to dance.

The booming sounds of the drums were wonderful and we danced like crazy Irish folk.

Mamello told us, the drums were made from double-ended cowhide.

Some of the dancers wore rattles on their ankles and some of them had hand rattles and reed pipes. The combination of all the unusual instruments created, mystical tones, harmonic perfection, and a music that brought total peace, and tranquillity to us all.

As the group continued to play and dance, it was like a magical symphony, glorious tones and rhythms and melodies, which touched all our hearts, a sweet taste of heavenly music, just like total perfection.

Well, that's the way I saw it, and felt the magical music, and I hadn't even consumed any of their delicious, opulent wines at that stage.

Conor and I smiled at each other during the performance, and we both did 'a thumbs up sign', while feeling a total sense of peace and contentment.

During the performances, the South African men and women stamped their feet and clapped and roared, and when I closed my eyes, the sound of music was so enchanting, it gave the impression there was a full orchestra playing.

It was a most wonderful night, which I'll always treasure.

Patricia now felt she was on a roll, writing her holiday assignment. It brought back such happy memories, of time spent with her Dad. They were both been quite sad when it was all over, and they promised each other, they would travel to Canada or India next. Time had passed, and they hadn't fulfilled the promises, but Patricia still lived in hope, that one day they would.

Her mobile beeped, and she was just about to check it, but she changed her mind. She had already decided, when she was writing, there would be 'No, interruptions', after all, she was hoping to be a professional writer someday, so she needed to be disciplined. Anyway, she didn't want to return to reality just yet; she wanted to stay with her happy memories of South Africa.

Patricia always preached to her friends; 'Don't be a slave to your mobile phones.'

Her friends just smiled, nodded but continued texting, checking emails etc. Their phones were a major part of their lives, and they couldn't seem to survive without them. Sometimes, Patricia found it exhausting, just watching them on their phones, and getting no feedback from them.

'I will never be like that,' she vowed.

'You will get the phone bug, some day, everybody does eventually,' Freya said firmly.

'I won't allow myself to become a slave to technology, life is too short to have my head stuck in the phone all day,' she replied, rather crossly.

'Well, I use to think that too, until I was bitten by the bug.'

'Now, like everyone else, I am hooked, I just can't manage a mobile phone free day. I even get upset when I forget my phone, which thankfully doesn't happen too often.'

'I actually feel happy, when you or my other friends, forget their phones, as we are meant to be enjoying girlie time together, not phone time together,' Patricia said.

'Oh dear, we definitely are on our 'anti mobile phone soapbox,' today phew!' Freya said.

'What is a soapbox?' Patricia asked looking puzzled.

'Ah, now I hope you see why it's important to have your phone on standby, in particular for information you may need on a subject. If you just 'Google' 'soapbox' on your phone, you'll actually find the meaning.'

'Wouldn't it make more sense, if you just told me what it means?'

'Then we can have a normal chat, without having to refer to 'Ms or Mr Google' all the time?' Patricia whinged.

'Wow, there's no doubt about it, you are definitely still on the 'soapbox."

'Please, no more drama, just tell me what it means.'

'Okay, I'll try to explain the term 'soapbox', even though I know the 'Google' definition would be better.'

'Fadó Fadó', 'Long Ago', when a speaker, wanted to make a point, they stood on crates to elevate themselves. The crates were originally used for shipments of soap, and that's why they were called a 'soapbox.'

'See, you are better than any phone or any 'Google',' Patricia said. She laughed and hugged Freya.

'Do you remember the day I left my mobile phone, in the ladies toilet of the restaurant?' Freya asked Patricia.

'Dear God, I most certainly do. You were like a mad woman, screaming;'

'My mobile phone, my mobile … I have lost my mobile.'

'You scared me with your screaming, I actually thought someone had died.'

'At first, I couldn't make out what you were shouting about, and when I knew, I couldn't help laughing, such hysteria and drama, over a mere mobile phone.'

'You don't understand, it is a huge part of my life, I have all my friends' numbers, and important contact numbers, my emails, my appointments and my calendar details are there. Basically, my whole life in a nutshell on my mobile phone,' Freya said in a very haughty, high pitched voice.

'Calm down Freya, all ended well, and you got your mobile back.'

'I know, but it was very traumatic at the time.'

'Do you remember, I tried to contact the very honest lady, who left my phone at reception, because she saved my sanity that day?'

'Remember, I even asked the girl on reception if she could get me the lady's name or number, to reward her for her honesty.'

'The receptionist didn't have the lady's name or number, but she very kindly, gave me some wise advice.'

'Her advice was to 'pay it forward', by sending; 'love and kindness' to the lady.'

'She explained that even though, I didn't know the lady's name, she would still receive the 'love and kindness' I was sending her.

'You can pay the lady's act of honesty and kindness forward, and she will feel the 'love and kindness', and she will then pay it forward,' she said.

'All that week, I sent the lady, lots of 'love and kindness' through the universe, and I actually felt that she had received it and paid it forward.'

'Hopefully you will be impressed, as losing my mobile phone taught me two lessons in life;

1 To be more careful of my mobile phone as it means the world to me.

2 To always try and 'pay kindness and love forward', as much as possible in life.

'Maybe, unlike me, you won't become attached to your mobile phone, but don't rule it out, it could happen to you one day.' Freya said with a glint in her eye.

'Okay, I get the message; I am just getting off my, 'anti-mobile phone soapbox' now,' Patricia smiled.

The sound of her mobile notification brought Patricia back to reality, and she was annoyed that her stupid mobile had distracted her from her writing; she would certainly never admit that to Freya.

As she settled down to her assignment, Patricia could hardly keep up with her thoughts, as her fingers hit the keys at full speed; she loved writing, that's where she was happiest.

She recalled more exciting memories of the holiday, and their lovely, efficient, patient guide 'Mamello', whose kindness and incredible knowledge made the trip so wonderful.

At first, Conor and I had mixed emotions, when we discovered our beautiful luxury lodge, was actually in the grounds of 'Kruger National Park'. Neither Conor or I had noticed that, when reading our information schedule.

'You will all be up close and personal, with some of the monkeys, snakes and birds etc.,' Mamello told us with a smile.

Mamello was very kind, and he didn't wish to scare us, he emphasised that the lodge area was a safe place, but obey the list of rules, stay inside the complex, and when walking, stay on the path.

Conor and I looked at each and smiled, there was no fear either of us would divert off the path. We both liked animals, but we weren't the type to pet strangers' dogs, or cats etc.

Mamello, explained to our group, that his name meant; 'Patience.'

'I think, my parents gave me that name, as a reminder, to always be patient with people, and with life.'

'If you have any problems with my lack of patience during the trip, please, feel free to remind me of, 'the meaning of my name',' he said light-heartedly.

Throughout the trip, Conor and I found 'Mamello.' truly lived up to his name. He was so patient with our group, and we all enjoyed, his wicked sense of humour.

'You must have been Irish, in your previous life, you have that great 'Irish sense of humour,' Dad laughed heartily.

'I take that as a compliment, as I love the Irish humour. I have lots of Irish tour groups every year, we always have great chats on history and lots of 'craic', as you would say. I really appreciate the Irish people's interest in the history, customs and the culture of my country,' Mamello said proudly.

Mamello also informed us that; 'South Africa is fondly known as, the 'Rainbow Nation', and it offers an assortment of unique cultures, and it has a very rich history, for all to enjoy.'

Patricia felt the excitement butterflies, begin to tingle in her tummy, as she began writing about their most spectacular three day 'Safari' in the incredible 'Kruger National Park'.

When Mamello informed us we would be exploring some of the magnificent, two million hectares of 'Kruger National Park' in an open top, four-wheel drive jeep, we were so excited we were grinning from ear to ear.

He told us, it was one of the most famous, national parks in the world, and the oldest and the largest park in South Africa.

We also learnt that in 1898 the motion for the development of 'Kruger National Park' was actually implemented, and the credit for this was attributed to 'President Paul Kruger', who established the original park.

Kruger's vision was of a protected wilderness reserve, which would last forever, and thankfully that's exactly what happened.

Mamello then introduced us to our ranger, who was the incredible

'Lebona', who was known for his love of animals in 'Kruger National Park' and his love of bush life.

Mamello said; 'Lebona, always ensures his clients see all the animals, up close and personal, and his love for animals and the park is totally infectious. As you are all extremely interested, and excited about the game viewing Safari trip, I made sure you got the best ranger, so hopefully you will get to see the 'Big 5' game animals.'

Even if Mamello was only trying to 'butter us up', we didn't care, as by the end of the Safari trip, we loved 'Lebona', he ensured we saw every animal we wanted to see, including the 'Big 5' animals of course. Yippee! (5).

We were like children; we were so excited, knowing we would be so close to all wonderful the animals.

Lebona proudly explained to us, the park was home to approximately one hundred and forty seven mammal species, and over five hundred bird species.

'Of course, it's home to the 'Big Five' game animals, which are the; '*Lion, Elephant, Buffalo, Rhinoceros and Leopard*', and we will see all those incredible creatures in their natural habitat,' he said very proudly.

He most certainly didn't renege on his promise; we enjoyed the most spectacular Safari trip.

Lebona informed us that we had a 6am start, which caused some people to gasp. My Dad and I just smiled at each other, as Kruger National Park was the highlight of our trip, we didn't care what time we had to arise.

We just knew it would be worth the very early start to see all the animals and in particular the 'Big 5.'

When Lebona explained the temperatures would be cooler, and the animals would be most active early morning, then thankfully, people understood the reason for the early start.

Lebona informed us that traditionally, the 'Big 5' were the five most dangerous animals to hunt on foot in Africa.

'The *buffalo, elephant, rhino, lion, and leopard,* represent the top five animals that people hope to see on safari, and I am going to make sure you see them all,' he stated very proudly.

In fact, we saw all the 'Big 5', thanks to Lebona's incredible talent for spotting animals in the bush, and he seemed to have a wonderful knack for 'being in the right place at the right time.'

He explained in detail to us about the habits of the 'Big 5' game animals;

'The *buffalos* may not look fast, but they can be totally unpredictable, often giving no warning before they charge. They are extremely large animals, and they can be six to seven feet long, and five to six feet tall, and weigh up to 2,000 pounds, and their tail may be three feet long, which they use to swat at irritating bugs.'

We all had a great laugh when one of the very skinny guys in our group said; 'Holy God, I don't think my heart would take it, if a buffalo charged at me.'

Lebona smiled and continued when the laughter died down;

'My favourites are the *elephants,* as they can look graceful despite their size, and I enjoy watching their interactions with each another. Like us humans they have their own personalities, and 'don't forget'; that 'they don't ever forget',' he said laughing loudly at his own joke.

'If you do them wrong, they will remember and they will also charge at you.'

Florence said; 'My goodness! Lebona please don't tell us anymore stories about animals charging at us, or you will have to bring me back to the lodge.'

'Sorry, all the animals here are beautiful creatures, and they are here for you to see and enjoy, but it's also my duty to remind people, that they are wild animals and they will charge at you, if you don't treat them with the respect they deserve,' he explained.

'Another animal that may surprise you is the *rhinoceros* means, which means 'nose horn', and it's often shortened to 'rhino', but because of their huge bodies, their strong horns and armour like skin, they have no natural predators. Believe it or not they get frightened easily, and their instinct is to charge at whatever scares them.'

'Oh my goodness! not again,' Florence whispered, looking rather scared.

'Another interesting fact is that rhinos haven't good eyesight, they mainly rely on their strong sense of smell.'

'Don't worry Florence they won't see you,' Peter said laughingly.

'Hopefully they won't smell my expensive Marc Jacobs perfume,' Florence said trying to see the funny side of things.

Patricia had noticed that Florence looked like a rich, classy lady, and now with the mention of the expensive perfume; she knew she had guessed right.

Poor Lebona, continued to try to educate us on the 'Big 5' like Mamello he had great patience with us, as we were all a bit giddy, with the excitement of Safari.

'Lions are very social animals, and they live in groups, called prides. A pride consists of up to three males, a dozen related females, and their young,' he said.

'The size of the pride is determined on the availability of food and water. The female lions are the hunters and they usually hunt at night. Their prey includes antelopes, buffaloes, zebras, young elephants, rhinos, hippos, wild hogs, crocodiles and giraffes and they even steal food from other animals. The lions are the laziest of the big cats, and they can sleep up to 20 hours a day,' he smiled.

'But folks, don't be fooled by them, if they charge at you, it is vital to stand your ground, and retreat very slowly, but continue to face the lion while clapping your hands, shouting and waving your arms around to make yourself look bigger. Most charges are mock charges, so you will usually be fine, and always remember, to hold your ground.'

'Never run or turn your back on a lion,' he emphasised.

'But don't worry; this is just background information, you will be staying in the jeep during our 'Safari',' he kindly said.

'My Dad and I smiled at each other, when we heard Florence say under her breath; 'I think we all know not to run, or turn our backs on any animals.'

'Of all the 'Big 5 animals', the leopard is definitely the most elusive, and sadly sometimes people don't get to see them on safari, because leopards are largely nocturnal and spotting them isn't easy.'

'But folks, the good news is that, there has been a sighting of a leopard, so I'll do my utmost to ensure that we see the leopard,' Lebona promised.

My Dad and I were thrilled with Lebona's promise of possibly seeing a leopard.

I actually felt goose bumps on my arms, and shivers down my spine with excitement.

We were rather surprised how crisp and cold it was at 6am, thankfully Mamello had warned us to layer up. We had a quick cup of tea and some sandwiches for breakfast which we ate, while standing, as time was of the essence.

We laughed when Lebona gave us big heavy coats, but we were so grateful for them, during the first two hours of our game hunting. Then little by little we removed the layers, as the day got hotter, so hot, we were eventually down to our t-shirts and shorts. We had a good laugh as hour by hour we all stripped and de-layered along the Safari route.

Dad asked Lebona; 'Did you always work as a ranger in 'Kruger National Park?'

Lebona proudly said; 'I am based in Kruger National Park, and I absolutely love it, no two days are the same, but I also work in other Safari's when needed.'

'I love my job, as I have the privilege and the honour to work in the most natural, unspoilt, beautiful Safari's in the world. In my eyes, my office actually is Africa!'

'It's peaceful, safe and huge, but like everything in life you must treat it with respect, and you must also be vigilant.'

'On our trip, we will see and experience something new and thrilling, every single day, and if we are all willing, we will learn something new every day about the animals and Africa. So please enjoy the Safari,' he said so proudly.

Lebona was so right, to this day I still bore the pants off anyone who will listen, to my repetitive story of the time; my Dad and I went 'Game viewing in South Africa.'

I am still trying to paint; 'My wonderful experience of the flamboyant presence of the animals, in particular the '*Big 5*' and the miracle of the vast landscape of the wild bush,' which we experienced, thanks to Lebona, our amazing, expert ranger.

Before I actually did my research on our Safari trip, I foolishly thought all the animals would be in full view for us to see, not hidden in the bush etc. playing hide and seek with us. My Dad had a good laugh when I told him, my innocent thoughts of the Safari trip.

It was amazing, we actually had to keep our eyes peeled, to spot the game, and we were rewarded at some of the rivers and the watering holes, when we spotted rhinoceros and hippopotamus.

Lebona explained to us that; 'The rivers running through the park, were crucial for the survival of all the wild, and the scenic, flat plains made it ideal for spotting animals of all sizes.'

We were amazed to learn that hundreds of different types of mammals make their home in 'Kruger National Park', and there are diverse bird species; such as vultures, eagles and storks. The beautiful mountains, the bush plains and the tropical forests were all part of the spectacular landscape, we witnessed.

To this day, when I close my eyes, I can still see the beautiful, magical scenery and all the spectacular animals.

Lebona, told us that it was official, there was definitely a 'Leopard' sighting in the area, and he intended to spend the day searching for him, as it could be months, before a leopard would be spotted again.

We were all thrilled to hear this good news, and soooo excited at the prospect of seeing a leopard in the flesh.

After hours of travelling in Kruger Park, with not another animal, or jeep in sight, we suddenly spotted the leopard; 'It was the most astonishing, wonderful, exciting experience of my life.'

It's so difficult to explain in words the wonderful vision of the majestic leopard, we felt so privileged to be in his magnificent company.

Lebona, stopped to allow us take lots of photographs, as the leopard crossed the road, just a few feet in front of the jeep.

My Dad and I were so thrilled, we had the biggest smiles on our faces … feeling the danger and the wonder of being so close to the magnificent, stately leopard.

It was a most marvellous sight, seeing the leopard walk slow and stately across the road, within touching distance of us.

The leopard just looked at us and the jeep, with a totally disinterested superior stare, as he walked slowly and regally along. He was so haughty and so impressive looking.

I will never ever forget that magnificent sighting of the leopard, and thankfully I have lots of photographs to reminisce over. Conor and I still talk about the leopard, and we still get excited. It most certainly was a once in a lifetime magical experience.

Even Lebona was excited when he saw the leopard, even though he was ten years on the job, you would think it was his first day. He explained that it was three months since they had spotted a leopard, and sometimes it could be longer.

The jeeps were linked by Radio, so word could spread quickly when rare animals were sighted.

Lebona was so kind to us, he didn't radio the other rangers' immediately, and he helped us get our spectacular photographs, of the graceful, sleek leopard. He explained that the leopard would hear the sound of the other jeeps in the far distance, and he would instantly run off.

To this day my Dad and I still wonder at the kindness and braveness, or foolishness of Lebona as he took photographs with all our cameras, while standing quite close to the leopard.

We were all so delighted with our sighting of the leopard and the amazing photographs, that we found it difficult to concentrate on Lebona's information on leopards.

But I do recall that 'Leopards' live in a wide variety of habitats, and they have a preference for trees, which play a role in a leopard's feeding practices. They are solitary creatures, and they only spend time with others, when mating or raising their young. They are also nocturnal and their nights are spent hunting instead of sleeping.

John said while smiling at us all; 'I can certainly relate to the leopard, being nocturnal myself.'

'I am more alert at night time, than during the day, but I am lucky I have the ideal job, as I do night time security,' he laughed.

'Yes, like leopards, some people are more alert at night, and your night security sound likes the perfect job for you,' Lebona laughed.

Fortunately or maybe unfortunately for some of us, Lebona decided to educate us further on the eating habits of leopards;

'Leopards are sleek predators and they can get within five meters of their prey, without being spotted, before launching a deadly attack. They are classed as South Africa's most successful predator.'

'Leopards ambush their prey, pouncing before they have a chance to react, they break their prey's neck, and then suffocate it. Afterwards, they carry their food to an isolated location, usually up a tree, and they feed on the carcass over the course of a few days. They are very clever, they know the rotting carcass will attract other potential prey, and the height of the tree keeps the food safe, from hyenas and lions,' he said calmly.

I could see the pale faces of some of the ladies in the group, as Lebona, described how leopards kill their prey. I felt a bit queasy myself, but I knew for survival, unfortunately that's the reality of what happens in the wild.

It was lovely to see Lebona's enthusiasm for all the animals in the Safari Park, and Lebona laughed heartily when one of the guys in our group said;

'You are like 'Tarzan', you're so into nature and you adore the animals.'

Patricia took a short break for a quick snack, and once fed, she continued typing speedily, to keep up with the boundless flow of the creative juices. She was so eager to share her experience of the trip to the 'Niall Mellon Townships', and she vowed that one day she would return as a volunteer.

When we received our itinerary from the travel agents, Conor and I were delighted to discover, the 'Niall Mellon Townships' was part of our tour.'

We visited a township in 'Imizamo, Cape Town', and we were amazed and in awe of the work the Irish volunteers did.

We went on a tour of the 'Shanty towns', and there we saw the contrast of the old homes and the new houses 'Niall Mellon', and his superb Irish volunteers had built.

Conor and I felt quite sad, to see the very poor conditions the families lived in, but we were extremely surprised, at how happy and content the people were.

It was quite humbling; to experience their friendliness, and cheerfulness under the difficult circumstances they lived in.

Mamello had discreetly explained on the coach; 'The shanty towns or squatter areas are settlements made of plywood, corrugated metal, sheets of plastic and cardboard boxes and they are usually found on the periphery of cities.'

We were shocked and ashamed to hear that a typical 'shanty town' often lacks; 'Proper sanitation, no electricity, no safe water supply, and it lacks hygienic streets or other basic human necessities, and because they are built so close together, fires can spread very quickly.'

I felt sad and embarrassed as a white person, when Mamello explained; 'The term 'township', usually referred to the urban living areas which, from the late nineteen century until the end of 'Apartheid', were actually reserved for non-whites, black Africans, coloured people and Indians.'

I was amazed, Mamello wasn't bitter about the whole degrading situation. I know in my heart and soul, if I walked in his shoes, I would be extremely angry about the obvious racism which existed then, and sadly still does to this day.

It made me realise how lucky I am, with my good job, and my privileged sanitary, hygienic lifestyle and everything I need, at my fingertips.

Our trip to South Africa was an amazing experience, and the good and the bad experiences on the trip, actually helped change my outlook on life quite a lot.

Since that day in the shanty towns, my Dad and I have made a huge effort;

'Not to sweat the small stuff,' basically, not to moan about small silly things in life.

We are learning to appreciate and be grateful for the wonderful life we have in Ireland, in comparison to the very difficult life, the people in the shanty towns lead. They are amazing people, always smiling and they don't seem to care about material wealth like we do.

I deliberately took lots of photographs, of the smiling faces of the children and their parents, to remind me, how happy they were, with so little.

Yet, we Westerners, who have so much more in life, seem to smile far less.

I vowed that one day, I would return with the 'Niall Mellon Trust', as a volunteer painter and decorator. I know I will fulfil that dream, someday soon.

Mamello said to us with deep gratitude. In his voice;

We are so grateful to 'Niall Mellon' for his 'Building Blitz'. We also thank the amazing Irish volunteers, and of course the Irish people for supporting the volunteers financially, and making an extraordinary difference to thousands of lives here in South Africa.'

Mamello said proudly; 'We are now embarking on the next chapter which is; 'To educate thousands of disadvantaged children across South

Africa over the next few years.'

As the wonderful 'Nelson Mandela' once said;

'*Education is the most powerful weapon which you can use to change the world*,' he proudly quoted.

Patricia now felt she was born to be a writer, and her trip to South Africa with her Dad had been so amazing, it was lovely to now share her memorable holiday story, with the creative writing class.

She felt a great love for the diversity of 'Cape Town', where the rich and the poor lived side by side.

She began typing again frantically as she still had so much to tell about her wonderful memorable holiday with her Dad in South Africa;

Mamello said he was one of the lucky ones, he was from the better-off area of Cape Town, and he was grateful for his good life.

He explained to us; 'People fondly call 'Cape Town', the '*Mother City*'.

'It's one of the most popular tourist destinations in the world and boasts five, of the top ten attractions, in South Africa. These include; 'Table Mountain', the 'V&A Waterfront', 'Robben Island', 'Kirstenbosch National Botanical Gardens', and 'Cape Point'.'

It was obvious to our group, Mamello was very proud of 'Cape Town', and he was pleased to hear, how much we loved it too.

Chapter 15

Patricia couldn't wait to finish work and become engrossed in writing her short story of their amazing, but scary trip to 'Robben Island.

It was her first day to finish early; she had been working overtime all week, clearing a backlog of medical files. There definitely was a spring in her step as she walked home, while thinking of the next part of her memorable holiday story.

She had prepared her dinner the previous evening, she heated it in the microwave, and she wolfed it down as quickly as possible.

'Not very ladylike at all,' she mused.

However, time was precious and she wanted to share her wonderful holiday experiences with Hazel and her fellow students.

She began her story about 'Robben Island;'

On the coach to the ferry for 'Robben Island' Mamello informed us that 'Nelson Mandela' really admired 'Martin Luther King' and he often recalled his inspirational speech of 'I have a dream'.

Mandela maintained that King's dream of equality was also the dream of South Africans.

Mamello asked us; 'When did 'Martin Luther King' receive the 'Nobel Peace Prize?'

He was rather pleased when, most of our group said, in unison, '1964.'

'Do you know how many times he used his famous phrase; *'I have a dream'* in his speech?' he asked.

Peter who seemed very interested in history answered; 'Eight times.'

'Yes, excellent, that's correct.'

'One of the things he said in his speech, which I think is inspirational was;

'I have a dream that my four little children will one day, live in a nation, where they will not be judged by the colour of their skin, but by the content of their character.'

'What amazing, inspirational words!' Mamello proudly said.

'In 1968, 'Martin Luther King' gave his final speech, which proved to be an uncanny, visionary speech,' Mamello said.

'He proudly told his supporters, at the Mason Temple in Memphis;'

'I've Been to the Mountaintop.'

'I've seen the Promised Land. I may not get there with you. But I want you to know tonight that we, as a people, will get to the Promised Land.'

Mamello said rather sadly; 'Would you believe, the very next day, while standing on the balcony of his room at the Lorraine Motel, Memphis, Tennessee, he was struck by a sniper's bullet?'

''Martin Luther King' and 'Nelson Mandela' will always be remembered for their inspirational speeches, and their amazing efforts to make the world a better place, for all races black or white,' Mamello said very proudly.

Mamello was delighted when we all automatically clapped, at the bravery of 'Martin Luther King' and 'Nelson Mandela.'

The boat trip to 'Robben Island' unfortunately reminded Patricia of the severe seasickness she suffered in Tenerife.

Over the years, she had been on lots of boat trips around Europe, and she had never been seasick. Yet on that famous day, on the three-hour boat trip in Tenerife, she actually thought, she was going to die, and be buried at sea.

Lauree had been very kind, and her calmness, and her encouraging words, helped Patricia believe, her sickness would eventually end.

'We very close to the shore, and you'll be back on dry land shortly,' Lauree had promised.

'Really, are we that close to shore?' Patricia asked weakly, but rather hopefully.

'Yes, look there's the shore, we're nearly there.'

Patricia had foolishly persuaded Lauree, to opt for the three hour boat trip, rather than two hours, of dolphin and whale watching.

'What a bad decision on my part,' Patricia thought, as she hung over the side of the boat.'

About half way through the trip, when she stood up to take a photograph, of the beautiful school of whales, she knew she was in trouble.

She begun to feel extremely queasy, as the angry waves smacked against the side of the boat, and the motion sickness completely took over her whole body.

She felt nauseous, quite dizzy and woozy, and suddenly the hot and cold sweats started.

Oh my goodness! She had to put up a brave fight to survive the seasickness. She had to keep telling herself; 'I am not going to die at sea.'

'I'll soon be on dry land shortly,' she kept repeating in her mind.'

Unfortunately, they began serving dinner on the boat, and that definitely was the final straw, for poor Patricia.

She said to Lauree; 'Sorry, I have to turn my back to you, I can't look at people eating, it's making my stomach more nauseous.'

She got some comfort, and she didn't feel like a total wimp, when she noticed other people of all ages, sick too.

Later, when Patricia was safe on dry land, she said to Lauree;

'Wasn't it weird, the way I was able to control my mind and body, at times?'

'In particular, when the crew called out;

'There's a pod of dolphins to the right, or there's a school of whales to the left.'

'It was crazy, and weird, that I actually managed to force myself to raise my head and take photographs. Yet, once I had taken the photographs, I then collapsed like a rag doll, feeling utterly miserable again, with my head resting on the boat.'

'It's amazing how the mind can control the body, even for short periods,' they both agreed smiling.

At first, Patricia didn't understand, why a crew member had offered them small black bags as they boarded the boat, thanks heavens she took the black bag. Later when the sea sickness hit, she realised the significance of the black bags.

Unfortunately, she had to use hers a number of times, before she eventually disembarked. She recalled, it took a few of hours on dry land, before she felt like her normal self again.

Unfortunately, on the trip to 'Robben Island', she was seasick once again and she felt utterly miserable. The only consolation was most of the passengers on the boat were really ashen, and they looked as ill, as she and Conor felt.

Laptop at the ready, Patricia continued her 'Robben Island' story. She thought, 'even if I am over the assignment word quota, I'll have a record of my adventures and I can compile my short story from that.'

On the way to 'Robben Island', the sea was so choppy the boat was tossed around like a toy, and we could hear the loud crashing of the angry waves against the side of the boat. The waves looked like an avalanche of water, under dark and moody clouds, which were threatening to sink the boat and drown us all.

The poor seagulls were like flashes of white dust, being tossed around in the scary, dark stormy sky, as they too struggled bravely against the storm.

The waves were getting stronger and angrier by the minute; they appeared to be violent and unforgiving. I wondered we would survive this monstrous storm, or would we all perish at sea.

Maybe this time, I wouldn't survive and I would be buried in a foreign land. The only consolation I felt was, it would be nice to die, while still on holidays.

We saw some people, bless themselves, they were praying, for a safe landing on shore, like Conor and I, and they were possibly promising lots of changes, if they were allowed survive.

Thankfully the return journey wasn't too bad as the storm was abating, but unfortunately the storm had delayed the ferry.

To this day, I can still picture the look of fear on people faces, when they discovered the ferry to 'Cape Town' was delayed.

We all felt the same crazy fear.

The fear of never getting off 'Robben Island' and becoming a prisoner like poor 'Nelson Mandela' and all the other prisoners, the guide had spoken about. People were actually pacing up and down the jetty, looking anxiously into the distance, hoping to see the ferry.

Patricia recalled how one of the ladies in the group commented on Conor's 'Heart Tattoo', while waiting on the ferry. Perhaps she was trying to distract herself, from the worry of the delayed ferry.

Patricia listened again to Conor's tale of the 'Heart Tattoo', even years later, she never tired of hearing Conor's story, about his 'Heart Tattoo'.

When she was very young Patricia would constantly plead; 'Dad, please tell me the story of your 'Heart Tattoo.'

Conor would try to divert Patricia's attention to other things, but to no avail, and he found himself repeating the story quite often. Patricia seemed to be the only one, who still referred to his 'Heart Tattoo', and still enjoyed his tattoo tale.

Conor had explained to Patricia; "The Heart' is an amazing part of the 'body and the soul', and that's why I chose, and why I love my 'Heart Tattoo', which I got as a teenager.'

He explained the meaning behind the '*Heart Tattoo'*.

'The heart is a symbol of love, but it has other meanings too, some people believe the heart is the location of the human soul.'

Patricia loved when he further explained;

'Every second of every day, something incredible happens to us all; the heart works day and night constantly pumping blood into our lungs, where it loads up oxygen and then it pumps the blood around the rest of the body.'

'If this finely tuned amazing busy heart stopped, we would be dead in seconds,' he whispered quietly.

Patricia fondly recalled, how her Dad would ask her to put her hand on her heart, and he would then put his hand on his heart and he would ask;

'Do you feel the life and soul of your body there?'

'Yes,' she would smile in wonder, as she felt her heart beats … thump, thump, thump.'

Her Dad told her that; 'In many religions, the heart had 'a mystical importance', and that Christians believed it to be the place of all emotions, 'especially love', and other religions saw the heart as the 'spiritual centre'.'

Patricia really loved Conor's image of the heart tattoo, and she always smiled, when on her travels, she saw someone with a 'heart tattoo.' It reminded her of her Dad and his 'heart tattoo' story, and she felt tempted to ask the person;

'What's the significance of your heart tattoo?'

But her sensible side made her refrain, as people loved their space on trains and buses, and they certainly wouldn't encourage a conversation, especially about their personal tattoos. So Patricia let the temptation to intrude on their private tattoo stories, pass swiftly by.

Patricia came back to reality and continued her 'Robben Island' story;

Nearly an hour late, the ferry eventually arrived and people ran speedily towards it.

Mamello knowingly smiled and said; 'Please don't panic, sorry for the delay, the ferry will be leaving shortly and I promise, no one will be left behind.'

We believed Mamello, but we were taking no chances, after Bandile's stories, we all rushed to the ferry, to ensure we wouldn't be left behind.

While waiting to board the ferry, I remember thinking of a wonderful quote of Mandela's; 'To be free is not merely to cast off one's chains, but to live in a way, that respects and enhances the freedom of others.'

I still get the shivers, when I think of 'Bandile', who was our guide on 'Robben Island'.

He really scared us all, when he told us in detail, the life story of 'Nelson Mandela', and the other prisoners.

His story telling was so eloquent and so dramatic, and it caused us to panic, when the ferry was late.

For dramatic effect he had even pointed at me and other people in different tour groups. He singled us out because we had; '*Blue eyes and blonde hair.*'

(When I returned home, I was sorely tempted to die my hair black, after that dramatic escapade).

Bandile had dramatically explained to us that; 'Portions of food were divided in relation to the colour of the prisoners' skin.'

He asked all the tour groups, to form a circle in the main prison area.

He then said; 'The larger portions of food went to the 'blue eyed, pale skin prisoners.' That's when he pointed at us accusingly, for effect only thankfully, but we felt the hostility from other people in the circle, who looked at us rather strangely.

He continued his story, knowing well that his dramatic actions were taking their toll on all of us; he was really enjoying the drama, and our fear.

'Then smaller portions of food went to the prisoners with a 'darker shade of skin', and he pointed out the darker people in the circle.

'Then the prisoners with the 'darkest skin' got the smallest portion,' and lastly he pointed at them rather sadly, for effect.

It was strange to see that his story actually divided the group, but thankfully we all got over it, and smiled at each other, in the end.

In the heart of the main prison we saw 'Mandela's' tiny cell.

Bandile told us; 'It was from that small cell, that 'Mandela' ran the island like a University; he was amazing, he educated his fellow prisoners and even some of the white guards.

'What an incredible man!' Patricia wrote.

Bandile showed us the limestone quarry where 'Mandela' and his fellow prisoners, broke rocks. The prisoners weren't allowed dark glasses, so many of them suffered permanent eye damage, from the glare of the white lime.

It was sad to hear that 'Mandela' couldn't tolerate any bright lights or flash photography, because his eyes were so badly damaged.

I was amazed to learn that; 'Mandela' was imprisoned for 27 years for his opposition to 'Apartheid', yet, when he was released from prison in 1990, he expressed no bitterness or anger towards his tormentors. That forgiveness and kindness made me admire Mandela even more.

'Mandela' was one of the few leaders capable of inspiring confidence in South Africa, and throughout the world, and his spirit and goodness will always live on in South Africa,' Bandile said with pride.

We certainly all agreed with Bandile that 'Mandela' was a wonderful and inspiring man.

As we left his cell, we found ourselves giving 'Mandela' another round of applause, and we hoped he felt the good vibes, and the love.

We were further amazed, when Bandile informed us, that he also was a prisoner on 'Robben Island' for four years for 'terrorist' offences in the 1980's, as he was a member of the ANC (African National Congress).

He explained to us the ANC had led the struggle against racism and oppression, often organising mass resistance, and taking up the armed struggle against '*Apartheid*.'

In his autobiography, '*Long Walk to Freedom*', 'Mandela' stated; 'I could walk the length of my cell in three paces, and when I lay down, I could feel the wall with my feet, and my head grazed the concrete at the other side.'

My Dad and I had often discussed those terrible stories and facts, of life on 'Robben Island', it made us realise how lucky we were in Ireland.

Patricia made a quick cup of coffee, and raced back to her laptop, she wanted to keep on writing while her South African stories were fresh on her mind.

Patricia continued; 'Our trip to 'Robben Island' was an amazing, profound experience, and it's carved in my memory, forever.'

Bandile was so knowledgeable and he reminded us that during apartheid, people in South Africa, were divided into *'four racial groups and kept apart by law.'*

To this day, I still find it extremely difficult to comprehend how people could treat each other so cruelly.

He explained that the 'apartheid system' was used to deny many rights, of mainly black people, the laws actually allowed white people, keep black people out of certain areas.

It was quite upsetting when Bandile reminded us that laws were made so black people couldn't own land in white areas, and they weren't even allowed vote, and people of different races couldn't marry.

Even as I write this part of my short story on South Africa, it still upsets me to think, how cruel people can be to each other, just because of the colour of their skin.

Hopefully one day we will all accept and respect each other, no matter what colour our skin is, or no matter what our beliefs are.

After hearing so many sad stories, it was wonderful for us to hear the incredible stories of 'Mandela's' courage and the courage of all the prisoners.

We were thrilled when Bandile, reminded us that in 1993, 'Mandela' was awarded the 'Nobel Peace Prize', which he shared with former South African president, 'F.W. de Klerk'.

Bandile spoke proudly and knowledgably to us, about how those two very brave, courageous men, worked tirelessly together, to successfully end the country's apartheid system of racial segregation.

Thankfully, Bandile had more good news for us, he told us, 'Robben Island' now has approximately one hundred and fifty residents, including many children, and it is a safe place to grow up.

Bandile explained that, 'Robben Island' was declared a 'World Heritage

Site' because the buildings on the island are a reminder of its sad history, but the buildings also show the power of the human spirit, and freedom and victory of democracy, over oppression.

'Robben Island' had a huge impact on my Dad and I, as the stories, and the history of the place, was incredible.

My Dad said; 'It was bravery at its best, that a black man, 'Mandela' and a white man, 'F.W. de Klerk', actually worked side by side, for the cause of freedom from oppression of black people, in South Africa.

We thought they were both extremely brave and wonderful people, putting their lives on the line, for the rights of others.

I remember feeling very emotional and I replied to my Dad; 'It was great that, the world acknowledged how wonderful 'Mandela' and 'F.W. de Klerk' were, by awarding them the highest honour, the 'Nobel Peace Prize'.'

I was also amazed how much I actually enjoyed the food in South Africa; it was so tasty and so fresh. Conor and I would always scrutinize the menu for something plain for me, as I was unable to eat spicy food.

Actually, I couldn't believe how much I loved the food.

'It's because it's fresh, and it's not imported,' Conor told me.

I was so happy there were a great variety of delicious dishes, which suited my non- spicy palate.

Our group also thought the food was delicious and so many choices; the delicious fresh African dishes, the blending, tantalizing European cuisine, and the spicy curries of India.

To this day, I feel there was something wonderful and very special about South Africa; 'Its' wonderful, brave people, its haunting music, its beautiful rhythm, and of course the incredible animals.'

South Africa took my breath away, and stole my heart forever. It unquestionably was an amazing, and an enriching experience with my Dad, and a most memorable holiday.

Chapter 16

Patricia offered to babysit Freya's two children when her widowed Dad, was ill with a bad flu. She suddenly found herself embellishing and exaggerating stories for them, about her trip to South Africa, just to keep them entertained.

Freya's children, Emma and Kevin, never tired of Patricia's exciting stories of South Africa.

'Please, Patricia, please tell us again; 'the story of the herd of elephants in Kanger Park, who 'nearly stumpeeded' you all, and nearly overturned the jeep,' Emma pleaded, full of excitement.

'It's 'Kruger Park' and 'stampeded',' Patricia kindly spelt the words for Emma.

'All right, but it's the last time I am telling you that story, you must know it off by heart now.'

'I love that story; I'll never get tired of it,' Emma said.

Patricia smiled and once more, began her elephant story.

'Lebona was sitting very relaxed in the jeep, allowing us time to take photographs. We were busy taking our best shots, and we didn't realise how close the elephants had come, until a lady started shouting, in a panicky voice;

'Lebona move the jeep, move quickly, the elephants are getting dangerously close to us.'

'Lebona took one look at the elephants, and the lady, and he tried to start the engine, but nothing happened. Then all of sudden another herd of elephants on the rampage, came crashing through the trees, trumpeting loudly, their ears were flapping, and they looked really angry and ready to kill us all. We were shocked and amazed at how fast they were stampeding toward us.'

'We tried to remain calm but as they came closer, we felt really scared.'

'Lebona said in a very quiet voice; 'Relax and keep quiet, we will be alright.'

Then all of a sudden, one of the elephants went to charge at the jeep, and just at the last minute he stopped, and stood in front of the jeep, just glaring at us.'

'You could hear a pin drop in the jeep; we were all shocked into silence.'

'Then a lady broke the silence and said; 'Please go Lebona.'

'Lebona whispered we can't go yet; 'Please stay calm and stay very quiet.' Patricia whispered these words, enjoying the look of excitement on Emma and Kevin's faces.

'After a few minutes, which seemed like an hour, the elephant ran off into the trees and we began our escape. Thankfully, after a few attempts, the engine spluttered and worked, and Lebona drove off speedily.'

'The elephants could have trampled you all,' Emma always said, in a very high pitch, excited voice.

'Lebona said we were in no danger,' Patricia said trying to calm Emma down.

'But you said, Lebona drove off quickly,' Kevin said worriedly.

'Well, the good news was, we got excellent photographs of the elephants, and I lived to tell the tale,' Patricia said laughingly, tickling Emma and Kevin, to lighten the atmosphere.

Even though they knew the story well, they still sat close to Patricia for comfort, and they laughed nervously, at the danger.

'More stories please,' they pleaded.

Patricia dramatically threw her eyes up to heaven.

'Okay, but you must go to bed shortly.'

'Tell us again about Nora and the Zebra's,' Emma pleaded.

'I can't believe you want to hear that story again … here goes.'

'The zebras were Nora's favourite animals and she was really excited when she spotted them. She asked Lebona to stop the jeep, as we approached a very relaxed group of zebras.'

'Do you remember the three names, for a group of zebras?'

Emma shouted excitedly and Kevin said calmly; 'A herd, a dazzle or a zeal of zebras.'

'My favourite one is 'a dazzle',' Emma said excitedly.

'I like them all,' Kevin said in his quiet, relaxed manner.

The two children were like chalk and cheese, yet they got on well together.

'Lebona foolishly asked Nora if she would like a close up of the zebras. He took her camera, jumped out of the jeep, and went quite close to the zebras. He noticed we were all looking enviously at Nora, so he offered to take photographs for us all.'

'He spent ages taking the photographs, and in our excitement, we forgot that poor Lebona could have been attacked by any of the animals, while he was out of the jeep,' Patricia said.

'Please tell us more stories about the animals you saw,' they cried in unison.

'Well, okay, just a few more stories and then you must go to bed, or I will never be allowed babysit again.'

'I really loved the giraffes, they were so elegant, and so tall. They are the tallest creatures in the world, they can reach nearly six meters, in height and they eat up to 34kg of leaves and shoots each day, which they pluck with their tongues from very high trees and their tongues are nearly 45cm long.'

'Can you remember what a group of giraffes are called?' Patricia asked.

'A tower of giraffes,' Emma shouted before Kevin got a chance to reply.

'I love giraffes too, and I hope to see them some day,' she said.

'I know you'll both get to visit South Africa some day, and see all the wonderful animals,' Patricia said.

'It was lovely to see all the elegant giraffes, but later in the trip, we were cheeky when Lebona pointed out another tower of giraffes.'

'It's okay thanks, we have enough photographs of the giraffes.'

'I think he understood, we didn't mean any disrespect to him, or to the giraffes,' Patricia smiled.

'I know he forgave us, when he saw how excited we were, at the prospect of seeing a leopard.'

'Please tell us the story of the leopard,' they said excitedly.

'Lebona told us that a 'Leopard' had been spotted in the park, and he planned to spend the day in search of him, as it could be months before the sighting of a leopard again.'

Emma and Kevin would huddle closer together, as they loved the excitement. and the danger of the leopard story.

'After hours of travelling in 'Kruger Park' we spotted the leopard and we were thrilled. There wasn't another jeep or animal in sight, and it was the most astonishing, wonderful, exciting experience.' Patricia said in hushed tones.

'Lebona' allowed us take lots of photographs as the leopard crossed the road, a few feet in front of the jeep.'

Emma and Kevin would squeal with excitement, when Patricia produced the superb photographs of the stately leopard.

'Oh Wow, he's beautiful!' they chorused.

'We were all delighted, and we had the biggest smiles on our faces … my goodness, it was thrilling being so close to the leopard.'

'It was a most amazing sight, seeing the leopard walk stately and slowly across the road, before our very eyes.'

'The leopard, just looked at us and at the jeep, with a totally disinterested stare, as he walked slowly by. The leopard was so haughty and so impressive looking; I will never forget that vision.'

'But it's mostly thanks to Lebona's bravery for getting out of the jeep and taking the close up photographs of the leopard, that I will never forget that wonderful day.'

'It was a truly beautiful sighting, and I'll always treasure the memory of that beautiful leopard,' Patricia said looking at the photographs, with

He pacified them and nodded and agreed, when they suggested counselling.

'Yes, thanks, I find counselling great,' he lied.

They didn't need to know his business.

He had tried counselling before, when Simon died, it hadn't worked then, and it most certainly wouldn't work now.

After a few counselling sessions, Conor realised he just couldn't sit there with Kate and the counsellor, and pretend he was healing, when he wasn't.

He was extremely angry about Simon's death, and that was the reality of his life, counselling didn't take his pain away, whereas Kate found the counselling, very helpful.

To put his horrendous past behind him, after Kate's death, he had moved from Dublin to Cork, for a fresh start. Paul didn't need him, or want him around, and he had settled in with well his Gran.

As promised his Mum, kept in touch with him, by mobile phone and letters and she even sent photographs of Paul.

She was truly an amazing woman, and throughout Paul's life she sent Conor details of his achievements, of which there were many.

Conor was shocked when his Mum told him, Paul was studying Accountancy, but he was quite pleased that Paul was following in his footsteps.

Conor dozed for a short time and dreamt of Kate, and when he awoke he fondly remembered his first business trip to Cork, when Kate was still alive.

He had taken the train, to enable him to work on his clients' accounts, and also to have some time to relax, before his meeting.

He had left Dublin on the 7am train, on a very wet, dirty grey, windy morning; he couldn't believe his eyes when he arrived in Cork, to a beautiful, warm, sunny day. There wasn't a dark cloud in the sky, which was a bright, happy, sunny shade of blue.

It never ceased to amaze him that the weather in Ireland, could vary so much, from county to county.

The fast lilting accents of the Cork people, he met on the train and in the city, was so foreign to him, he thought he had been transported abroad.

He now recalled the fun they had, when he phoned Kate, and told her about the beautiful weather in Cork.

'The weather is brilliant here, and the accents are so different to the Dublin accent, I feel like I am abroad,' he laughed.

They both had a wicked sense of humour, and Kate replied;

'In future, that's where we'll go on holidays. We won't need to ever travel abroad again for the sun, when it's there in abundance in Cork.'

'We'll also enjoy a lovely cosmopolitan feeling, listening to the cheerful, lilting voices of the Cork people.'

'What more could we want?' Kate said laughingly.

'Let's not get too carried away with the idea of holidaying in Cork, I think we should still have our holidays abroad,' he had laughed heartily.

Conor knew if Kate had lived, he wouldn't have made such a mess of his life, she had always kept him grounded. In his line of business he mixed with a lot of wealthy people, who were full of their own importance, and sometimes he acted the same way. If Kate thought he was getting 'too big for his boots,' she would calmly make a comment to ground him, and he gracefully accepted and understood her motives.

Conor continued to toss and turn, and he tried to go back to sleep, but his mind kept going over everything; he sadly recalled his desertion of Alma and Susan.

Now, looking back it seemed such a cruel thing to do, but at the time he was suffocating and he needed space.

He had lied to Alma, he told her he had important clients to meet in Dublin, and it would probably take a few weeks.

Alma was such a lady; she didn't question it, and she even offered to pack.

She was such a kind, honest person; she never suspected anything, which made his escape so easy.

Conor recalled how his escape plan had automatically happened, as he felt overwhelmed when their unplanned baby arrived, the night feeds and the crying was incessant, and head wrecking.

He was exhausted from pretending that he was happy with baby Susan's arrival, when all he wanted to do was to run away, as fast as he could.

Even though poor Alma had dealt efficiently and bravely, with all the feeding, napping changing and crying, Conor needed to escape, from the drama of it all.

Here he was again, on the same dreadful, nightmare path.

'Would he ever learn?'

Well, it certainly didn't look like he would.

'Where will it all end?' he thought.

Alma had been worried when he couldn't sleep at night, but thankfully she didn't realise it was his guilty conscience, as all he thought about was Kate and wanting to escape his marriage.

Lately, he was constantly thinking about Kate, so much, it was debilitating and painful for him.

When things got on top of him, he would ask himself;

'What would Kate do?'

She had always been the calm one in their relationship, and she was wise beyond her years. She loved people and she was superb in all types of company.

She treated everyone the same, no matter how little they had, or how rich they were, and she brought the best out in people, especially him.

Conor knew Kate would be annoyed and totally disgusted with him, for hurting and ruining the lives of so many people, but in his defence, it was unintentional.

Kate knew his virtues and his faults; in fact she knew him inside out, warts and all, and he was amazed, that she still loved and respected him so much as a person.

Well, now he had totally lost the plot, and made an utter mess of his life and the lives of his families. He knew, Kate would expect him to sort things out, and be truthful with Paul, Alma, Susan, and Patricia, and hopefully Helen would forgive him too.

Kate had always hated lies, so why had he become so deceitful?

'Was it my way of rebelling at her for dying?' he wondered.

Kate use to say; 'I have no idea why people lie, because the truth will always triumph in the end.'

'Lies can cause so much pain and anger, and they can ruin peoples' relationships and their lives.'

'I'll never understand why people waste their time and energy on lies,' Kate said numerous times, when people's foolish lies were discovered.

He knew Kate would have been disappointed and disgusted that his life had become, 'a life of secrets and lies.'

'What is wrong with me?' Conor sighed with frustration.

'Why had he ruined Alma and Susan's life with his deceit and lies?'

'Why hadn't he been honest with them?'

They possibly would have understood that, he couldn't stay with them any longer, because he missed Kate too much.

He had made a mess of their lives and his own just because he couldn't face up to his responsibilities and he took the cowardly, escape route.

Suddenly an escape plan formed in his head, and all he could think about day and night was returning to Dublin, without Alma and Susan.

Unfortunately, that's exactly what he did, he packed his bags and left, knowing that he was ending his marriage, and closing down his business in Cork.

During his time in Cork, he had really missed Dublin; after all it was where his roots were for generations, he was proud to be a 'True Dub.'

Within a year of returning to Dublin, he had built another layer of secrets and lies to add to his deceitful life. It was no surprise that the nightmares were constant, and his lack of sleep was beginning to take its toll.

A friend had introduced Conor to Helen, who later became his third wife. He had met her briefly a few years previously, and he found her very easy to talk to. They spent quality time together, and he was enjoying the relaxed easy pace of their relationship, until Helen dropped the bombshell.

Conor now clearly remembered, the day Helen told him she was pregnant.

He was so shocked, his head was in a spin and he felt like screaming; 'No.'

He had acted like he was a seasoned 'Oscar' winner, and pretended he was happy with the baby news, while all he wanted to do was run away, as fast as he could.

Helen was so excited about her pregnancy, and he hadn't the courage to tell her how upset and angry he was.

What a mess he had made of his life again, it had become so complicated, he was reeling with the shock of the news.

They had been careful, and he had always ensured they took extra precautions, as he most certainly didn't want a child, and he thought Helen felt the same.

'Why hadn't he been honest with her, why had he hidden the truth of his previous failed marriage so well?'

'What is wrong with me?'

'Will I ever learn?'

'Will I always keep making mistakes?'

'Will I be forever running away from life?' he questioned himself.

He tried to make sense of it all, but nothing seemed clear, his life was one big mess, and he had the nightmares to prove it.

At least, he had told Helen, about Kate and Simon's death, and he told her that Paul was living with his Gran, but thankfully she didn't question that crazy situation any further.

She had been so trusting; it was quite easy for him to omit the full truth.

Of course, he had conveniently omitted to tell her, he had been married a second time and divorced. He didn't tell her, how he had selfishly abandoned his wife Alma, and his daughter Susan.

No point on dwelling on that now, he had to deal with the dreadful situation, he now found himself in.

'What is wrong with him?' he questioned feeling frustrated.

He kept making mistake after mistake, and baby after baby, and now his nightmares were punishment for all his secrets and lies.

Conor had prayed to Kate for guidance, the night he discovered Helen was pregnant. He awoke suddenly during the night and thanks to Kate, he suddenly knew the right thing to do was, to ask Helen to marry him.

He was surprised that he actually was happy when Helen said;

'Yes.'

She then surprised him and said;

'I would like to get married in Rome; I don't really want a fuss, maybe just the two of us.'

'What do you think?'

Conor couldn't believe his luck, that's exactly what he wanted, he certainly didn't want any fuss.'

Conor and Helen didn't tell their friends about their wedding, until they returned from Rome.

When they returned Conor said; 'You wouldn't believe what happened to us in Rome, it was like a crazy, weird comedy.'

Some of them retaliated and said;

'Well, that serves you right for not inviting us to your wedding.'

Conor ignored the comments and continued his story;

'The night before our wedding, the church was broken into.'

'We arrived at the church around 10.30am for our 11am wedding, and two men were hammering in the church, as they were repairing the damage done by the burglars, the previous day.'

'Fr Rosewood, told the builders to continue their work, and they were still hammering while the four of us walked up the aisle.'

'As it was early, we presumed it was a rehearsal, until we reached the altar, and Fr Rosewood began the marriage ceremony.'

'We all just looked at each and smiled.'

We had met with Fr Rosewood the previous night, and he hadn't mentioned that we would be married with another couple, or that we would have to do a reading, and he boldly stood on the altar and asked;

'Who's doing the reading?'

Helen and I were shocked, so we said nothing, hoping Fr Rosewood, would get the message. He just stood there silently waiting, so in the end, I actually had to do the reading,' Conor told them.

Ross and Jason laughed heartily and said; 'See what happens when you don't invite your friends to your wedding.'

'It wasn't funny, there was cellotape on the pages of the readings, and they weren't even stuck together properly. I tried my best to decipher the cellotape readings, but I had to improvise where necessary.'

'I muffled some parts, and even made up names for the difficult biblical names. I wasn't impressed with Fr Rosewood, for putting us in such an awkward position, on our wedding day.'

'I am sure you loved the attention,' Ross said laughing heartily.

'No I Didn't,' Conor said firmly.

Conor recalled the friendly banter about their wedding fiasco and how their friends said it was more like a black comedy, than a white wedding.

'Helen had booked our wedding by phone, with a young Irish priest who then disappeared back to Ireland, and left old Fr Rosewood in charge, he proudly told us he was eighty two years of age.'

'He even invited himself to lunch with us, and ran off without paying, of course. He took our hard earned cash, and decided to make up his own rules.'

'So instead of being married alone, as we had requested, we were married with another couple, total strangers, of course. But we were lucky; they were a really wonderful, fun loving couple and we became friends.

At that stage of Conor's story, Jason was laughing so heartily the tears were streaming down his face.

Conor said; 'It's not funny, you would also be annoyed in that crazy situation, but fair play to us all, we made the best of it.'

'If you got married in Ireland, like the rest of us, that wouldn't have happened. We know, how to organise and celebrate weddings here,' Ross said firmly.

'It gets worse, Helen booked the photographer through our travel agent, and we couldn't believe, he hadn't a word of English. The photographer, literally kept pushing me around.'

'I remember saying to Helen;

'Do you understand Italian?'

'You seemed to know when the photographer wanted us to go right or left, I was always in the wrong place, and he just kept pushing me around.'

Helen laughed, and said;

'I don't have a word of Italian, but women have good instincts.'

'When we collected the photograph album a few days later, we just laughed. The photographs were quite dark, and they were lob sided, and they weren't even mounted in the album. We paid a lot of money for the album, which was very unprofessional, and we would have done a better job ourselves.'

Conor had surprised himself and said proudly; 'Thankfully, Helen wasn't a 'Bride Zilla.' She was very chilled, on the day and that's one of the many reasons I love and admire her.'

'Well said, Conor,' Ross and Jason chorused, looking rather surprised.

Helen had smiled lovingly at him.

Conor loved Helen's sense of humour, she always laughed when he told the crazy wedding stories. He had really hoped their marriage would work out, as he was tired of running. He did love Helen, and thankfully she seemed to have melted some of the amour, around his broken heart.

Conor now recalled the evening of their wedding, he drank too much, as he was trying to forget the baby situation.

He recalled how Helen had touched her tummy lovingly and said;

'I better not drink, now that junior is on the way.'

That was the only black cloud over him on the day, and he went into total shock when he realised, he was now married, and there was a baby on the way.

'What was he thinking?'

'How had he got himself into another crazy situation?'

'Would he succeed in making this marriage work?'

He certainly didn't have a good track record, but he was more determined to make it work this time.

He hadn't looked after his son Paul, and his daughter Susan, and yet he had the audacity and stupidity to bring another child into the world. He took a big gulp of his pint of Italian beer and thought;

'Don't worry, and don't think about it now, just work hard and make this a successful marriage.'

Conor was wide awake now, sleep just wasn't happening, as his mind was too alert. He recalled what Helen lovingly said on their wedding day;

'I am so happy, this is the day, I dreamed about; marrying a kind, caring, handsome man and having a baby.'

'I couldn't ask for anything more. I am a lucky lady.'

Conor knew, he couldn't burst her happiness bubble, and he vowed to himself to make their marriage work. But the Universe had other plans and his lovely Helen had died suddenly of a heart attack, Conor felt that was his punishment for his secrets and lies.

What a legacy to leave to the world, a dead child (Simon), a dead wife Kate, a deserted son Paul, and a divorced wife Alma and a deserted daughter Susan, and now a dead wife Helen.

Thankfully due to his daughter Patricia's persistence in keeping in touch, she was still in his life.

'Would his nightmares ever end?'

He jumped out of the bed, before any more dark thoughts surrounded him.

Chapter 18

Paul wasn't impressed when Hazel asked the class to write a short story assignment of 3,500 words. So many words, that didn't seem like a short story to him, she would be lucky to get 1,000 words from him.

He was procrastinating for days and then, it suddenly hit him like a bolt out of the blue. He would write about his holiday in Canada with Connor.

It had been a memorable holiday, but he didn't consider Conor to be a special person, but then Hazel had said the assignment could be fiction and non-fiction. The irony of it all was, it could be therapeutic for him, as experts believed writing about negative issues was a form of therapy.

Paul had been forced into going on holidays with his Dad, Conor.

It came as a total shock, and he recalled how angry he was with his late Mum, for planning it.

He never fully admitted it to anyone; especially to Conor or his Gran, but he actually did have a most wonderful time on the holiday, in Canada.

He eventually forgave his Mum for putting him in such close proximity with his Dad. She was always a peacemaker, and Paul knew, she planned it for all the right reasons, as she was the kindest person he had ever known.

Perhaps, he could now use his holiday experience for his assignment, and exaggerate parts, where necessary. He knew he would enjoy reminiscing on beautiful Canada, and his wonderful experiences there. After all, he surprisingly did have a great time with his Dad, on the trip.

It might even help him lose some of the anger he had always felt towards his Dad. After all, they did say, writing about stressful things, was part of the healing process and very therapeutic too.

He decided to begin his short story, and keep it positive, as nobody in class would be interested in an angry, depressing, short story.

He would now concentrate solely on beautiful Canada, and the bonding which occurred during the holiday.

He certainly wouldn't mention that when they landed in Dublin Airport, the 'Father and Son,' bonding disappeared into thin air, never to happen again.

Paul now recalled how he and Conor, had finally bonded on the boat cruise to the 'Niagara Falls.'

It was such a special day for them, as they both felt a real closeness while standing together in the boat, with the gentle spray of the falls on their faces, and the amazing 'Niagara Falls' within touching distance.

Paul began writing his short story assignment on his laptop; hoping that the seventeen words in the title, could be included in the word count.

'Write about a memorable holiday with a special person, be they real or imaginary, approximately 3,500 words.'

He was surprised how fast the memories of his holiday were returning, in particular the trip on the 'Niagara Falls.'

His short story begun;

My Dad and I went on a memorable holiday to Canada, which is a most beautiful country, and the people are warm and friendly, and very relaxed.

Lucas, our lovely Canadian tour guide introduced himself to our Irish group of twenty five, at the airport in Toronto.

My Dad and I settled into our lovely hotel. Then the following day we went by coach to 'Niagara Falls', and we were full of anticipation and excitement while waiting in line to board the boat, 'Maid of the Mist'.

There were lots of witty Irish comments and laughter, when we were handed, 'pink plastic ponchos' to protect us from the spray of the

'Niagara Falls.'

We most certainly looked ridiculous, in our ponchos, but then so did all the other tourists.

We were surrounded by a wall of water on all sides, and we were astonished at the power of nature, which had created such a spectacular masterpiece.

The pure sound of the crashing 'Niagara Falls' was like the 'a raging thunder', but of course, it was more exciting than fearful.

Conor and I agreed, that the 'Niagara Falls' was absolutely stunning, a memory we will both treasure and hold forever.

I thanked my Dad for inviting me on the trip.

He surprised me by saying;

'Your most welcome son, I wish we had visited more places together.'

'We can still do it Dad; we can spend more leisure time together in future.'

'Yes indeed, son,' my Dad said softly.

On the coach, Lucas our excellent guide said proudly to us;

'You can't actually fully comprehend the power of 'The Niagara Falls' until you are standing in the boat right in front of the falls, and you will sense the vast power when you are '*Face to face*' with one of the breath-taking, natural wonders of the world.'

'You'll feel the mist spray lightly on your face, you will hear the loud rumble of the water, and you will experience the close proximity of the most powerful waterfall in the world.'

'It's just magical, a true wonder of nature. My advice is that, everyone should see the 'Niagara Falls' before they visit the next world,' he smiled.

The group commented to each other; 'Please don't mention death,' and laughed heartily.

Paul continued writing speedily; his thoughts were full of happy memories of 'Niagara Falls;

We were standing only a few feet away from the falls, and we witnessed millions of litres of water rush over the brink, every second at 'Niagara Falls!'

It was an experience my Dad and I will never forget, words failed us, and we watched in awe, the impressive power of the water and nature at its best.

Everyone on the boat stood quietly, and admired the miracle of the 'Niagara Falls.'

Paul suddenly stopped writing as he recalled how shocked he was, when his Dad asked him to go on the trip to Canada.

In the text Conor sent to Paul, he said, the trip to Canada is partly business, and mostly pleasure.

At the time Paul didn't realise, it actually was Kate's dying wish for them to holiday in Canada, and Conor certainly wasn't going to tell him.

Conor had found the travel agents vouchers after Kate died.

Her note said;

'Dear Conor, it is my dying wish that you and Paul use these vouchers to bond on a holiday of a lifetime in Canada. Please, please enjoy!

Love Kate.

Kate knew Conor had always wanted to see the 'Niagara Falls', and she knew he wouldn't deny her this last wish.

On the trip, Conor had been tempted to tell Paul the story behind the holiday invite, but Kate had asked him not to, and he didn't want to fail her again.

Paul had been rather surprised that Conor was actually enjoying all the trips to the touristy places in Canada, as his memories of his Dad were that he worked nonstop.

Paul was never quite sure what companies his Dad worked in, as he was always told in muffled tones by his Mum;

'Your Dad is working 'Freelance' as an Accountant for a number of companies.'

'I never want to be an Accountant, because I don't wish to work as hard as Dad does,' Paul had said grumpily.

Years later, Paul's Gran teased him when he chose 'Accountancy' as a career.'

'The mathematical part of your brain is hereditary; it's in your genes, whether you like it or not. I am very lucky to have two mathematical geniuses in my family.'

'I guess I'll always have money in the bank, with two smart Accountants in charge of my finances,' his Gran said smugly.

'I didn't become an accountant, just because Dad is,' Paul said rather sharply.

To keep the peace, his Gran said;

'I know love; it's in the genes, you really had no choice.'

'You're so right Gran.'

'I love dealing with figures and finance, and it has nothing to do with Dad.'

'I know,' his Gran said gently.

Paul realised his Gran only agreed with him, to keep the peace. It was obvious, he followed in his Dad's footsteps, whether he liked it or not, and he had inherited the 'mathematical genes.'

'Life can be so predictable in ways, and yet so complicated,' he pondered.

Paul had told his friend Stephen about his Dad's surprise invitation to Canada.

'Of course, you must go, it's a chance of a lifetime,' Stephen said.

'If my Dad offered me, an all expenses paid holiday to Canada, I would say;

'Bring it on Dad, when are we leaving?' Stephen laughed heartily.

'It's different for you; you and your Dad have a wonderful

relationship.'

'I am wary of the invite, and I am quite anxious about spending two weeks with my Dad.'

'As you know, my Dad, has never really been around, I don't actually know him.'

'He doesn't really know me either, or seem to even like me.'

'Well, isn't it time you got to know one another?'

'Life is short, take the opportunity, and get to know your Dad before it's too late, he won't live forever.'

'Gosh! Stephen, you are full of good cheer today.'

'My Dad won't be 'kicking the bucket' for a long time yet.'

'None of us know when it's our last day on earth.'

'Look, at your lovely Mum who died so young,' Stephen said.

'Wow, what was in your cereal bowl this morning?'

'It certainly wasn't filled with a happiness cereal,' Paul said emphatically.

'I am just giving my opinion, you did ask me.'

'Let Conor make up for lost time, he let your Gran raise you, so he owes you big time. I am sure he must feel guilty, and maybe he's trying to make up for lost time.'

'Don't analyse it too much, just go on the trip and savour every second, that's my advice to you and it's free,' Stephen smiled.

'I know, you're probably right, opportunities like this fabulous trip to Canada, don't come often. I'll sleep on it and I'll make my decision tomorrow.'

'That sounds like a good idea.'

'Whatever you decide tomorrow, I will respect your decision,' Stephen said.

'Thanks, that means a lot to me,' Paul replied.

Next morning as Paul pulled the bedroom curtains, he finalised his decision on the trip. He would accept his Dad's holiday offer, and he would make the most of their trip together.

After a hearty breakfast, he sent Conor a text, and he was amazed at the prompt reply.

'That's good news; I'll book the holiday today.'

'Let me know, how much I owe you,' Paul texted.

'It's all settled, so no worries.'

Paul wasn't sure what Conor's text meant, so he gave him a quick call.

'Don't worry; it's been taken care of Conor said elusively.'

'Thanks, but I want to pay my own way, we'll talk about it later.' Paul said not wanting to cause a fuss.

'No worries, it's a business trip and I can bring another person.'

As Paul was thinking about the holiday, all the minute amazing details of the trip came flooding back. He jumped up from his chair, made a quick coffee, grabbed his laptop, and started typing as fast as he could.

All his lovely memories came flooding back, at a speed, not unlike the speed of the 'Niagara Rapids.'

He was surprised when a few minutes later; he had written two A4 pages about wonderful Canada. He kept going while the momentum was there, afraid he would hit the famous '*writers block*', so he continued letting the superb memories flow, whilst catching his speedy thoughts, and writing them as fast as he could.

I can clearly recall how excited my Dad was at 'Niagara Falls',' he said, it was the highlight of the holiday for him, and he was grinning from ear to ear.

It seems he had always dreamed of seeing 'Niagara Falls', and it was on 'his bucket list' for a long time. He said he loved watching 'YouTube' videos which showed the speed, the velocity and the magic of the 'Falls'.

The more Paul concentrated on writing his short story, the more excited and happy, he felt, and he was grateful for the lovely memories of the time spent with his Dad Conor, at the awesome 'Niagara Falls.'

When our group was finally on the coach, Lucas informed us, he had leaflets on the history of 'Niagara Falls.

He asked us, for our undivided attention, so he could give us some nuggets of information about 'The Falls.'

It was truly amazing, everyone was so interested to hear about 'Niagara Falls', our group of twenty-five people; suddenly fell silent, as Lucas began to speak;

"'Niagara Falls' has an extensive history, dating back hundreds of years.

They were first discovered by the French explorer, 'Father Louis Hennepin' in 1678 and the 'Niagara USA region' soon became a French stronghold. They built forts at the mouth of the 'Niagara River', which is now the modern day 'Old Fort Niagara'.'

'Just in case some of you don't know; 'Niagara Falls' is the collective name for three waterfalls, from the largest to the smallest; 'Horseshoe Falls', 'American Falls', and 'Bridal Veil Falls'.

'People from all over the world, are inspired and are in awe of the power and beauty of the magnificent 'Niagara Falls',' he said so proudly.

'Have you heard of the 'Ice Bridge'?' Lucas asked.

Most people in the group knew of the 'Ice Bridge', but a few people didn't, including me.

Lucas eloquently explained; 'This incredible volume of water at the 'Niagara Falls' never stops flowing but years ago, the falling water and the mist created ice formations along the banks of the falls and the river, and this resulted in mounds of ice, which were often as thick as fifty feet.'

'During a long cold winter, the ice would completely stretch across the river and form what was known as the '*Ice Bridge*'.'

Conor and I looked at each other, nodded and smiled; we both seemed to love learning about the incredible history, and the customs of countries.

Lucas continued educating us; 'The 'Ice Bridge', sometimes extended for several miles down-river, until it reached the lower rapids. Although the ice bridges appeared safe, they actually broke apart very quickly, and lives were often lost.'

'Thankfully, nowadays the flow of water over the falls is closely monitored, and ice bridges are now a thing of the past.

'What if an 'Ice Bridge' did form?'

'What precautions are in place?' a lady asked.

'If by chance an ice bridge did actually form, it's totally illegal now, to venture out on an ice bridge,' Lucas replied.

I was surprised when my Dad asked Lucas;

'What causes the 'green colour' of the 'Niagara River'?'

I was hoping, Conor didn't think the green colour had anything to do with Ireland, and I was so relieved when he didn't mention, or joke about the beautiful, rich green colour of Ireland.'

It was actually Lucas, who said smiling;

'The Niagara River' is most definitely a beautiful, rich green colour, like the lovely rich green, of your wonderful Irish countryside.'

Lucas then said to Conor; 'That's a very good question, I'll try to answer it to the best of my knowledge.'

I actually felt quite proud of my Dad for asking the question.

'The striking, beautiful rich green colour of the 'Niagara River' is caused by the erosive power of water. It is estimated that sixty tons of dissolved minerals are swept over 'Niagara Falls' every minute.'

'The green colour comes from the dissolved 'salts' and 'rock flour', (very finely ground rock), which is picked up from the limestone bed, and the green colour also comes from the shales and sandstones under the limestone cap at the Falls.'

Our group were delighted with Lucas, he was so knowledgeable, and he was so willing, and proud to share information about his country.

Lucas continued; 'I am sure you are aware, 'Niagara Falls' has been a destination for daredevils, world explorers, and honeymooners, throughout the years.

'Annie Taylor' was an incredible daredevil who survived a trip over the 'Niagara Falls'.'

''Taylor' was a sixty-three-year-old schoolteacher, who decided a trip over the 'Niagara Falls' was her way to fame and fortune. In 1901, assistants strapped her, along with her cat, into a special harness in a barrel.'

'A small boat towed the barrel into the main stream of the 'Niagara River', and the barrel was set loose. The rapids first slammed it one way, then the other, then came the drop, and a wrenching thump, so violent that 'Taylor' thought she had hit the rocks.'

''Taylor' was very lucky, as the barrel had been tossed close enough to the Canadian shore where it was then hooked and dragged onto the rocks, and thankfully Taylor was rescued.'

''Taylor' was totally dazed, but triumphant and being the first person to conquer and survive the mighty, 'Niagara Falls'. She found the fame, she had sought.'

The women in our group really enjoyed Lucas's story.

I couldn't help smiling when I heard some of the ladies say;

'Girl Power!'

My Dad was on a roll and he asked Lucas, to tell us about 'Nik Wallenda' and he informed us that;

'In 2012, the 'Niagara Parks Commission', (NPC), approved an application by 'Nik Wallenda' to walk a tightrope across 'Niagara Falls', which stretched between Canada and USA, and he actually succeeded.'

'Wallenda had to fight clouds of swirling mist which were blowing from every direction, straight into his face. He's such an amazing daredevil that he actually ran on the last part of the wire, to the finish line,' Lucas said proudly.

'People muttered; 'Oh my goodness, he was either brave or crazy.'

'Well, in recognition of the role, 'daredevil performances', and 'stunting' played in the history and promotion of the 'Niagara Falls, the 'NPC', ruled it would consider proposals, once every twenty years by stunting professionals, as a tribute to the daredevils, who made

'Niagara Falls' a top global tourism destination,' Lucas said proudly.

My Dad asked; 'Lucas, would you ever consider doing a daredevil performance on the tightrope over 'The Falls?'

'No way, I am far too cowardly,' he laughed heartily.

Our next trip was to the stunning town of 'Niagara on the Lake.'

There was breathtaking scenery and we took lots of photographs of the spectacular views and the horse driven carriages, prancing throughout the village.

Lucas told us that; "Niagara on the Lake' was home to the first provincial parliament of Canada in 1792, and the first lieutenant governor was 'Sir John Graves Simcoe', and amazingly, it was also home to the 'Shaw Theatre Festival'.'

Some of the group were unaware of the 'George Bernard Shaw' connection to the town, so Lucas informed us;

'During the 'Shaw Theatre Festival', which runs from April to November every year, there are a series of theatrical productions, and plays which feature the works of 'George Bernard Shaw' and his contemporaries.'

'The plays are lovingly and artfully brought to the stage, by an excellent team of Canadian directors, actors, and designers, showcasing their incredible talent to the world.'

Lucas further explained; 'The Shaw Festival' has become a major Canadian cultural symbol, a real gem in my country's rich, cultural heritage.'

'You'll be proud to know that the festival was inspired, by the wit and the passion of 'George Bernard Shaw', from Dublin, Ireland,' he said smiling at us.

Conor and I were amazed and so proud to see the 'Shaw Theatre' in such a beautiful setting.

I didn't really know much about 'George Bernard Shaw', and later Conor, gave me an update on the story of the incredible man.

We were both extremely proud that an Irish man, was so well known in

Canada, so far away from, 'little old Ireland.

I was quite surprised Conor knew so much about the life of 'Shaw.'

While Lucas allowed us time to relax on the coach, Dad very kindly proceeded to give me a synopsis of 'Shaw's' life;

"Shaw,' was born in Dublin in 1856, and in 1876 he moved to London, where he wrote regularly, but sadly like most writers, he struggled financially. He became a theatre critic in 1895 and he also began writing plays.'

'One of his famous plays was; '*Pygmalion',* which was made into a film twice. The screenplay he wrote for the first version, won him an Oscar.'

"Shaw's' play, '*Pygmalion,* was modified numerous times, but the most famous is the musical, 'My Fair Lady'.'

I was happy to tell Conor that I had actually seen and enjoyed 'My Fair Lady'.

"Shaw' wrote more than 60 plays, and he won many awards, among them the 'Nobel Prize for Literature' in 1925,' Conor said very proudly.

'Wow, Dad, I never knew that he won the 'Nobel Prize for Literature', he was a very intelligent, amazing man.'

'He most certainly was, he is celebrated in Canada, and all over the world, we should be very proud of him,' my Dad replied.

'He was actually raised in 'genteel poverty' and it was his mother's career as a professional singer, which influenced his love of literature, music, and art.'

I asked Conor; 'What is genteel poverty?'

'Years ago, that phrase was used to describe people who were;

'Trying to keep the style of a high social class, but unfortunately they had very little money.'

'It seems a very clever way to move up the social ladder,' I said.

'Yes, why not try to better yourself, using whatever tactics you can,' Conor laughed.

'It's fascinating that such a small country, can produce such talented writers, artists and of course, some of the world's best musicians and singers too,' Conor said.

Lucas overheard Conor trying to educating me on 'Shaw's life', and he too asked Conor some questions about 'Shaw'. He was delighted with the information Conor gave him, as he intended to pass his knowledge on, to the next Irish group. My Dad was really pleased, and I felt very proud of him.

We also visited the beautiful cities of Toronto, Montréal, and Québec.

We were fascinated by 'Toronto's Underground Path System', which is over 30km (19 miles) in length and it's used by over 300,000 people daily. It's spectacular and mind-blowing, and it connects over seventy buildings, walkways, tunnels and shopping areas. As the winters can be very cold, the underground path system is used for walking exercise also.

Conor and I thought the underground system would be a great invention for Ireland, in particular on those dark, rainy winter days.

In Montréal we explored the wonderful city, which is set on an island in the 'Saint Lawrence River' and named after 'Mt. Royal', the triple-peaked hill at the heart of the city. There is a large French influence in the city and many people speak French and English.

We also visited the magnificent, peaceful 'Notre-Dame Basilica', which is a place of Catholic worship and it is also used for grand events; celebrity weddings, state funerals, and for the visit of dignitaries, including Pope Jean-Paul II in 1984.

Throughout the years, thousands of tourists have entered its magnificent doors to take photographs of its rose windows and flying buttresses.

We also strolled through the beautiful Botanical Gardens, of Montréal, which is considered to have the world's most prestigious collections of plant life and it also features the 'Insectarium', a natural history museum of living and dead different species of insects, from all over the world.

Later Lucas gave us free time, to experience the shops and my Dad and I browsed for a short time, and we bought some nice unusual gifts for friends. Then we took some precious time out, to relax and enjoy a coffee while watching the world go by.

Lucas spotted us at the café and he joined us. We were having a nice relaxing chat, and I was rather surprised when Lucas asked Conor what his red 'Heart Tattoo' represented.'

I was interested to hear my Dad's reply, as I had never asked or queried the significance of his heart tattoo.

'As a teenager, I decided to get the 'Heart Tattoo' and thankfully I have never regretted my decision,' Conor explained.

'I was always fascinated by the power of the heart, both physically and emotionally, and to me; it's a symbol of 'Love'.'

'When I look at my 'Heart Tattoo', I get a sense of peace and love,' Conor said proudly.

'It must be nice to wear the symbol of 'Love' with honour,' Lucas said.

Conor, muttered; 'Yes.'

Paul thought that perhaps Conor may have felt some guilt when talking about love and honour, as he had shown a total lack of love or honour to Paul.

Paul continued writing, furiously, he wouldn't think about his relationship with his Dad now, or it would spoil his wonderful memories of Canada. Nobody in class would be interested in his sob story anyway.

Conor and I both agreed that our favourite city was definitely Quebec.

It was known as the 'Crown Jewel' of French Canada, and it was one of the oldest and most magnificent settlements.

Lucas was only too delighted to furnish us with lots of information on Quebec, he explained that;

'The Old Town of Quebec' is a 'UNESCO World Heritage site' and it has beautiful ancient, narrow cobblestone streets, with really cute, seventeen and eighteen century houses, and magnificent soaring church spires, with the splendid 'Château Frontenac' towering above it all.'

Quebec's was so exquisite and so classy and it's compact size made it ideal for walking, there were lots of classic bistros, sidewalk cafés, and daintily manicured, really stylish squares. It was like something you would see in a classy movie, and the people were remarkable too.

During our free time, Dad and I enjoyed, sitting outside the cafés; sipping a delicious coffee, while watching people stroll by, looking so elegant, and so calm. Some people spoke in English, but most people spoke in their beautiful French dulcet tones.

We both felt the magic and the warmth of Québec city, and its happy, easy going people, who enjoy entertaining the tourists.

Throughout the summer festivals; 'Musicians, acrobats and actors in period costume take to the streets, and their beautiful voices fill the air with songs, and the colours of the fireworks displays transported us to another world.'

Even two serious accountants like Conor and I, really appreciated the street theatre, and the spectacular fireworks.

'We love our festivals and in the colder months of January and February, 'Québec's Winter Carnival' is the biggest, and the most colourful winter festival,' Lucas said.

'The 'Fall', (our Autumn), and 'Spring', bring beautiful, colourful foliage, to breathtaking Québec. It's a beautiful city throughout all seasons,' Lucas proudly informed us.

Paul now smiled to himself, when he recalled, how shocked Jayne was, when she discovered he had based his short story assignment, on his Canadian trip with Conor.

'I can't believe you wrote about your holiday with your Dad.'

'You don't really like him, and you never have anything good to say about him.'

'I am really quite baffled,' Jayne said.

'Good God!' there's no pleasing you.'

'You should be delighted, I am making an effort to complete the assignment, especially as I have no interest in writing.'

'It was your silly idea, to drag me to the writing classes,' Paul said sullenly.

'I am confused and I'm just wondering, what were you thinking, when you made that decision?'

'Is it because writing is supposed to be therapeutic?' Jayne asked in wonder.

'I honestly don't know why I chose to write about my trip to Canada with Conor, it just felt right at the time. After all, Hazel emphasised that our holiday story, could be based on a real, or an imaginary person, so I went for the real one.'

'Of course, I thought of Dad, as he's always been the bane of my life, but surprisingly we did have a good holiday in beautiful Canada.'

'While writing my short story it made me understand, it hasn't been all bad. I also realised, there must be something good about Dad, for Mum to have loved him so much.'

'It was very therapeutic writing about my holiday with Dad, and I don't seem to dislike him, as much now.'

'I am not saying, it's a miracle cure, but I can see we are similar in ways, some good values, and some not so good.'

'Well, I am really astonished, maybe it is a miracle,' Jayne teased.

'The experts say, writing can be very therapeutic, it helps people heal, and it appears, you are now living proof of that theory,' Jayne smiled.

'Ah, don't get too excited, Conor and I actually haven't been in touch since our trip.'

'Surprisingly, Conor and I actually put our differences aside while on holiday.'

'We actually had more things in common than I realised.'

'Like what?' Jayne asked.

'For instance my fear of commitment, I think it stems from my bad relationship with my Dad.'

'Well, I am really happy something good has come out of your trip, and I am also glad I persuaded you to attend the classes.'

'We should go for a coffee to celebrate, Paul, you are buying, as it was me who influenced you to write, so it's payback time,' Jayne laughed.

'I am even hopeful, that someday soon, you and Conor can be friends.'

'No worries, I will buy you a coffee, but don't hold your breath on Conor and I becoming friends,' Paul said gruffly.

Chapter 19

Susan felt quite panicky when Hazel said their assignment was to write a short story;

'Write about a memorable holiday with a special person, be they real or imaginary, approximately 3,500 words.'

On their way home from class, Tara tried to calm her down.

'Why don't you write about your wonderful trip to 'India' with your Dad,' she suggested.

'Yes, I actually loved India and surprisingly Conor and I did get along, maybe I'll think about your suggestion.'

Now Susan reluctantly sat at her desk in her home office, feeling frustrated and lacking in ideas. She really wasn't in the mood to start her short story, but if she didn't attempt it tonight, her deadline would be tight, as she had a busy work schedule.

Perhaps, if she looked at her notes on India, maybe 'the creative juices' that Hazel always spoke about would start flowing. She read a few pages of her notes, on the wonderful time spent with Conor in awesome India, and in particular their incredible trip to the 'Taj Mahal.'

Now her fingers hovered over her laptop, but unfortunately nothing was happening, just 'blankety blank, blank, blank.'

Well, at least she had 17 words and 109 charcaters and spaces, if she was allowed to include the title of the assignment.

'Perhaps, I should refresh my memory further by reading through my book on the 'Taj Mahal', and my 'Berlitz' book on 'India', she decided.

'Maybe the creative juices will start to flow then.'

'They say, 'Miracles do happen',' Susan pondered.

Susan's heart skipped a beat, as she began reading her book on the magnificent 'Taj Mahal', which had been her main reason for going to

India.

The 'Taj Mahal' had definitely lived up to and even surpassed her expectations.

The memories of the day at the 'Taj Mahal' still brought peace and joy to her life, it was such a spiritual place. She certainly understood why it was chosen, as one of the 'Seven Wonders of the World.'

Now, looking at the professional photographs taken by the Travel Agent's photographer, she felt a lovely sense of peace and calmness.

'Perhaps, I will succeed in writing a good short story on 'India, because it's such an incredible place, and it was a special, healing time for my Dad and I,' she reflected.

Susan had mentioned to her Mum, that she would love to go to India, but unfortunately none of her friends were interested, as they were nervous of the 'Delhi belly bug.'

She had always believed that, life was full of coincidences, and when she received the letter that particular day, she knew her trip to India, would happen.

She totally understood her friends' fears of the 'Delhi belly bug,' especially when she researched the 'Travellers' Guide to India,' and read;

'Delhi belly', or traveller's tummy, can actually affect an estimated ten million people each year, and over half of the people affected are international tourists.'

'It causes cramps, vomiting and diarrhoea, and it's commonly caught after eating contaminated food or water. Unfortunately, due to the poverty in India, there are hygiene and sanitation problems, which can contaminate the food and water.'

Susan now recalled the day she got the letter, from her Dad, inviting her to India. She couldn't believe her eyes, so she read the letter, a number of times.

In the letter Conor explained that his friend from Cork, Greg Dugnan, had been in touch, and had updated him on Susan's life, and what a coincidence, Greg was also a neighbour of Alma and Susan.

What an amazing coincidence, it seems in conversation Conor told Greg that he was going to India.

Greg had explained to Conor, that Susan's Indian friend, 'Saloni', had given Susan a great love for India.

'Susan constantly talks about going to India, someday soon.'

'Wouldn't it be a good, kind deed, to offer her a free holiday to atone, for the way you deserted her and Alma?' Greg asked Conor.

'I know it's none of my business, but you do owe your lovely daughter for deserting her, and a holiday to India would be a wonderful treat.'

Needless to say, Conor didn't tell Susan the full story in his letter, he took the credit for the holiday, and he didn't mention that it was Greg's idea. More secrets and lies, what's new?

Conor was really shocked when Greg tracked him down in Dublin, but he was more shocked at Greg's aggressive tone, and he tried to defend himself.

'You don't know how bad things were for me after Susan was born, I felt trapped.'

'I knew, I had made a mistake by marrying Alma, while I was still in love with Kate, RIP. I realised I had married on the rebound, and because Alma was pregnant.'

'I believe you send them money, but that's material things.'

'You could do a good deed now, and redeem yourself a little, by treating Susan to her dream holiday to India.'

'How do you know she wants to go to India?' Conor asked.

'My daughter is Susan's best friend, that's how my wife and I put the pieces of the puzzle together, and tracked you down.'

'We didn't tell Alma or Susan, so it's up to you to do the right thing, but I must warn you, if you don't invite Susan to India, we'll give Alma your new phone number.'

'Just remember, it's a very small country and it's a small world too.'

'I really don't understand, how you thought, your secrets and lies wouldn't be discovered,' Greg said angrily.

'I didn't plan it, circumstances just happened,' Conor said defensively.

'That's a very lame excuse, for such a clever man, you made very selfish decisions.

'You missed out on your beautiful daughter's life, she is an amazing girl, and we all love her,' Greg said.

Conor said gruffly; 'I have to go now, I have a meeting to attend.'

Just before he hung up, he heard Greg say;

'That's right, as usual, run away.'

Conor was shaking as he slammed the phone down. Thankfully, he hadn't any meeting; he just used it as an excuse. He realised everything Greg said was right, and that's why he was so angry.

Greg had told Conor, that Susan wanted to go to India, but unfortunately her friends didn't want to go, because of the 'Delhi belly bug.'

He didn't need Greg or anyone to tell him that, he had made a mess of things.

His life was full of back tracking, secrets and lies, it was exhausting, and the crazy thing was, he wasn't even happy.

At least, he had always looked after Alma and Susan financially, and ever Christmas he sent extra money, even though he didn't make it obvious, he knew Alma would know.

Every Christmas a substantial amount of money appeared in the post, in an unsigned Christmas card, and Alma knew it was from Conor. She said to her friend;

'I know its conscience money, but I don't care.'

'I want Susan to have a good quality of life and I tell her, the money is from her Dad. At least, it makes her happy that her Dad remembers her, even if it's only once a year. I remind her the money is for her education, but I also organised 'a treat day' for us, and we enjoy ourselves shopping and eating out, and we so deserve it.'

Alma didn't want to waste time on resentment, even though she found it hard to forgive Conor for absconding. At first, her pride made her want to give the money to charity, but then she decided to use it, and made a good life for Susan.

Conor had covered his tracks well, there was no address on the card, and weirdly, the post mark was always blurred either from the rain, or the post office stamp.

Susan's initial reaction was to refuse, the weird invitation to India from her Dad.

Then she thought; 'Why not accept it?'

'I deserve this, my Dad owes me big time, for the way he treated Mum and I.'

Susan decided she would use her Dad's estrangement to begin her short story. She smiled to herself, when she thought how surprised he would be, to know she was writing about their trip to India.

Susan's short story assignment began;

I was in total shock, when I received a letter from Conor, my long lost Dad, and even more surprised to discover that, he was inviting me on a trip to India.

Tears came to my eyes, as I read the letter, I just couldn't believe that my estranged Dad, wanted to bring me to India, a country that I absolutely loved.

I discussed the letter with my Mum and my friends, and they all came to the same conclusion; that I should accept the invite, as I wouldn't get that opportunity again.

They agreed with me, it would be rather strange at first, but they said I would be fine, as I had good social skills. They believed I would find a way to forgive my Dad, and thus enjoy my dream holiday in India.

I was rather chuffed with their very kind remarks, but then realised it was also part of their brainwashing process, to encourage me to accept the invite to India.

After the initial awkward meeting at the airport, I was rather amazed at how well my Dad and I got along. I found Conor very knowledgeable and very open. Suddenly, all the anger and all the years of missing him, seemed to melt away, and I found myself warming to him. It was then I realized that; 'Blood was obviously thicker than water', as the motto implied.

Susan now recalled the good chats; they had about their travels abroad. Conor had explained to her, that years ago it was very difficult for people to afford to travel to Europe or anywhere in the world. He stressed how lucky people were now, to have the funds to enjoy travel so effortlessly.

Conor had excitedly explained to Susan that;

'Wilbur and Orville Wright' made the first successful flight in history of a self-propelled, heavier-than-air aircraft. Orville piloted the gasoline powered, propeller driven biplane, which stayed aloft for twelve seconds and covered one hundred and twenty feet, on its inaugural flight.'

'How amazing and incredible is that?' he asked Susan.

'Wow! That sure is amazing,' she replied in awe of the two brothers who invented the airplane.

Susan said; 'I personally think, the airplane is one of the best inventions in life, and I will always be grateful to the 'Wright brothers' for their superb efforts in getting us airborne.'

Susan forced herself to return to her assignment, and she jotted down points, as she read through her notes. She felt like she was reliving the wonderful, exciting, wild, yet very spiritual experience of India. She couldn't wait to share her story with Hazel and the class.

Suddenly the memories of her most memorable holiday, with her Dad in India came flooding back. She began typing frantically on her laptop, with the excitement of India running through her mind, and her fingers. She was now determined to keep writing while the miracle of 'the creative juices' was now flowing.

Our lovely guide, called 'Prasham', met my Dad and I, and the other people in our group, at Cape Town airport.

Prasham informed us, he was from Delhi, and he wanted to share the wonders of beautiful, wild India, with the world, so he became a tour guide. On the coach he proceeded to give us some nuggets of information on 'Delhi;'

'Delhi' is the capital city of India, and it's the home of executive, legislative, and judiciary branches of the Government of India.'

We listened intently, as he explained that there were six districts in Delhi, some rich and some poor, but unfortunately his family were from the poorer area of the north district.

'But we don't moan about things like that in India, we just do the best we can, and we don't take life too seriously,' he said smiling.

'I think that's a lovely way to live,' a lady in the group said.

'Thank you,' Prasham replied politely.

'Well, I was lucky, my Mum and Dad sacrificed a lot to educate my sister and I, we are both working as tour guides, and we now repay our parents kindness.

'It was lovely to hear Prasham speak so proudly of his parents and India.

'Delhi is one of the oldest existing cities in the world, and people say that Delhi has been built and destroyed approximately eleven times,' he said proudly.

'Isn't Delhi an amazing city, and so resilient?' he asked.

'It is indeed,' we chorused, amazed at its resilience.

'I think this is a good description of India,' Prasham said reading from his notes;

'Mother India, with her 1.3 billion inhabitants, can astonish, inspire, and enlighten and frighten you, all at once. It's certainly not for the faint hearted because of her chaotic madness, and her countless challenges of noise and scents; the crazy traffic, the beeping horns etc. and the smells of incense, spices and unfortunately even some quite bad odours.'

Jake, a guy in our group said to Prasham; 'That's an amazing description, and so true to life. I also read that you must keep an open mind in India, as it plays with all your senses and your emotions.'

'Yes, India can be exhausting, and it can even overwhelm some tourists. It's just like a massive fireworks explosion full of dazzling colours, of saris worn by Indian women, and the bursts of marigold flowers and the spectacular sunrise and sunsets and of course, the lumbering cows,' Prasham said smiling.

'India is a really difficult country to describe in words, you must experience it for yourself, but I know you will love the joy, the spirituality and wonderment of it all. It's a great test for the mind and the body, so much happening around you, all at once.'

'But I know that Irish people are strong and fearless, and 'Mother India' will not scare you or overwhelm you. I have heard you are called the 'Fighting Irish'. So you won't be running home scared,' he laughed heartily.

Dad said; 'Prasham, you know too much about us already, we definitely don't go down without a fight,' he said adding to the banter.

We were all amazed at how witty Prasham was, and he seemed to have the same sense of humour as us.

We laughed when my Dad said; 'I think you were Irish in your previous life, as you totally get our wicked sense of humour, while lots of other nationalities don't always appreciate our dry wit. Therefore, we must act in a more subdued way, in their company, for fear of insulting them unintentionally.'

'It's a relief that we can be ourselves in 'India', and have the fun or '*craic*' as we say in Ireland,' Conor said happily.

'Ah yes, I know that word, '*craic*', and I love using it. It sounds so full of fun, and that's what life should be all about. We should all enjoy each other's company, as life is short,' Prasham said in his excellent English.

'Someday soon, I hope to go to Ireland and experience, the 'craic', and have lots of fun while seeing your beautiful, small country,' he laughed.

'You probably will be surprised, how small a country Ireland is in comparison to India. We are only a dot on the map of the world, but don't be fooled by us, after all we are the 'Fighting Irish' and we will live in your memory forever, as we are strong, witty, dynamic people.' Jake said rather proudly.

'Well said Jake,' we all chorused and clapped.

Jake was rather pleased with himself. He was one of those outgoing, kind cheerful people, who always had a witty word to say. I noticed, he was also very helpful to the older people in our group. Clever, Prasham had spotted that too and he often gave Jake, chores as he knew Jake loved to get involved.

We had a great laugh on our trip to beautiful 'Agra' when Prasham handed Jake, his tour guide banner, which of course, was the Irish flag.

Prasham said; 'Now you can be the tour guide, while I get our tickets for the 'Taj Mahal' tour. I will meet you at the entrance in five minutes. People will probably take photographs and wander off, so don't forget to count the group at the entrance, to ensure you have all your clients,' he said smiling.

Jake was beaming from ear to ear, and he was thrilled with the responsibly of taking care of us all. He was certainly kept busy, as people wandered off taking photographs, but thankfully nobody got lost. Prasham told him, he passed the tour guide test.

An older gentleman in the group, asked Prasham;

'Where did you learn your excellent English?'

'I actually, learnt 'English' and 'Hindi' in school.'

'What are the different languages in India?' he asked.

'There are many languages spoken in India, actually there are over twenty two official languages spoken throughout the country, including Hindi and English.'

Prasham told us that, the British colonial legacy had resulted in English being the primary language for Government, Business, and Education. He explained, he learnt Hindi and English in school, because they were the two official languages.

Chapter 20

Susan decided to refresh her memory of the romantic story of the 'Taj Mahal' mausoleum, so she began reading the beautiful picture book, she purchased in India.

Later, with her mind full of information and love stories, she continued writing, and she was surprised when the words just flowed onto the page.

She wrote; We all recognizes the 'Taj Mahal' as one of the most beautiful and most romantic buildings in the world. The mausoleum is a glorious structure, built of white marble, and symbolizes purity, love and pain, like no other architecture does.

The 'Taj Mahal' was built in Agra, India, and it has many stories around it. It is an ivory, white-marble masterpiece and it's truly breathtaking and unforgettable.

Here are a few wonderful descriptions of the 'Taj Mahal'; Nobel Laureate, poet, 'Rabindranath Tagore' called the 'Taj Mahal';

'A tear drop on the cheek of eternity.'

'Rudyard Kipling' said it was;

'The embodiment of all things pure.'

Its creator, 'Emperor Shah Jahan' said;

'It made the sun and the moon shed tears from their eyes.'

I love the wonderful romantic, but unfortunately sad story of the 'Taj Mahal', which was built by 'Emperor Shah Jahan', as a memorial for his wife, 'Mumtaz Mahal', who sadly died, giving birth to their fourteenth child in 1631.

It was said that the death of the Emperor's wife 'Mumtaz', left the emperor so heartbroken; his hair turned grey, virtually overnight.

Susan continued dipping into her 'Berlitz' book on India, and her holiday notes, and writing from them. It gave her a warm glow thinking of the love and time, which went into building the 'Taj Mahal'.

It's been recorded, that the construction of the 'Taj Mahal', mausoleum began the year after the 'Mumtaz', died. Although the main building is thought to have been built in eight years, the whole complex wasn't completed until 1653.

Sadly, not long after it was finished 'Shah Jahan' was overthrown by his son 'Aurangzeb' and imprisoned in 'Agra Fort' where, for the rest of his days, he could only gaze out at his 'Taj Mahal' creation, through a window.

'Oh my goodness, how sad and cruel is that?' Susan wrote.

I was pleased to hear that following his death in 1666, 'Shah Jahan' was actually buried in the 'Taj Mahal' alongside his beloved wife 'Mumtaz'.

Prasham proudly said, that every year, tourists pass through the majestic gates of the 'Taj Mahal', to catch a once in a lifetime glimpse of what is considered the most beautiful building in the world, and very few leave disappointed.

I couldn't believe that anyone in their right mind wouldn't fall in love, with the incredible, awe-inspiring, majestic 'Taj Mahal'.

I said to Conor; 'If I ever hear of anyone in our group, who doesn't appreciate the beauty and splendour of the 'Taj Mahal', I will definitely recommend that, they go to 'Specsavers' and get their eyes tested.'

'I totally agree with you,' Conor said laughingly.

'Thankfully the 'Taj Mahal', tour didn't disappoint anyone in our group, so I didn't need to recommend 'Specsavers!'

It's difficult to put into words the splendour of the 'Taj Mahal', mausoleum, but when it's right there in front of you, it really doesn't disappoint, because it's truly magnificent and breathtaking and peaceful.

'A building, like no other, made for 'Love and Homage', is a great description of the the 'Taj Mahal'.

We saw local people dressed in their finery, decked out in their most beautiful colourful Saris, and tourists all dressed up too, and the 'Taj Mahal', comes to life even more, with the fusion of all the spectacular colours, and yet there is amazing peace and tranquillity.

One of the many fascinating things we saw, was the spectacular changing colours of the 'Taj Mahal' from the soft dreaminess of pink at dawn, to the dazzling whiteness at midday, and the enchanting golden colour at night, and its cold splendour in the moonlight.

Prasham gave us lots of time for our photo shoot, and we even got a chance to take everyone's favourite comedy shot.'

I must admit, I was a bit embarrassed, as I didn't know about the comedy shot, where you put one hand on your hip, and stretch your other arm out, and hold your fingers like you are about to pick up the 'Taj Mahal' like a teapot.

Prasham told us we would see lots of people pretending to hold the dome of the 'Taj Mahal', as if they were about to break into the nursery rhyme; 'I'm a Little Teapot'.

I actually felt that he wasn't impressed with people disrespecting his adorable 'Taj Mahal.'

When I got my photographs developed, I was delighted with the cute comedy shot, Conor took of me, and it was then I understood why people posed for the 'teapot photograph.'

Susan continued writing, and she was amazed at how happy she felt reminiscing on her wonderful trip, with Conor.

I can still recall the wonder of the 'Taj Mahal'. It was a very spiritual experience for my Dad and I. We were surprised at how much it touched us; it most certainly, had a good effect on our mind and body.

As we were leaving the awesome, beautiful, 'Taj Mahal', we both automatically said; 'Thanks, 'Taj Mahal', for a great visit.'

Conor and I smiled at each other, when we heard other people in our group, repeat what we had said.

Back on the coach, everyone was chatting excitedly, and everyone seemed moved by the spectacular, beautiful building which represented; 'Love and Homage', to a woman, from her loving husband.

We all felt their love, and it was undeniably a wonderful, once in a lifetime experience for us all.

Susan now happily recalled how lucky she was, to get some precious time alone, at the 'Taj Mahal.' Even though there were thousands of people there, she managed to find a space to herself, where she could meditate, and send peace, health, love and happiness, to her family and friends, as she had promised.

Susan took a break from writing, but she continued to read her book, which had many interesting facts and myths about the 'Taj Mahal'.

'The 'Taj Mahal', India's most iconic marble mausoleum and tomb was inspired by 'Love'.'

'It was built with a blend of Indian, Persian and Islamic styles of architecture.

The architect of the majestic building was 'Ahmed Lahauri', and he had over 20,000 people working on the building; including labourers, stonecutters, painters, embroidery artists, calligraphers, and many others.'

Susan remembered the fun they had guessing when Prasham asked;

'How were the stones and materials transported for the construction of the mausoleum?'

People made lots of guesses, but Prasham kept shaking his head, and saying 'No.' Eventually a lady said; 'Please Prasham, do tell us, and put us out of our misery.'

'Well, the elephants were employed to do the task, and amazingly, there were more than one thousand of the majestic creatures used.'

Susan pitied the poor elephants, and she hoped they were paid in kindness, with lots of pampering by their owners.

Susan was excited as she began writing some amazing facts from her holiday notes. At first, when people saw Susan writing notes on the coach, they looked at her suspiciously, but then the teasing began, when they discovered she was just acting like, a nerdy tourist.

'Be careful what you say Susan is taking notes, and you may hear from her solicitor, if you are not careful,' they laughed heartily.

'Look she's writing at full speed, I wonder which of us, she is writing about today,' they laughed.

Well, thankfully she didn't let them intimidate her, so she had lots of interesting facts for her assignment such as;

'The majestic 'Taj Mahal', is constructed of an ivory white marble and it's surrounded on three sides by red stone walls. The Emperor had the best quality marble brought from Rajasthan, Afghanistan, Tibet and China, and it's believed that over twenty eight, different types of precious and semi-precious stones, including the striking *'Lapis Lazuli'*, were inlaid into the marble.'

I remembered, as most ladies did; "The *'Lapis Lazuli'* is one of the most sought after precious stones, and its deep, celestial blue colour is 'the symbol of royalty and honour, Gods and power, spirit and vision', and it's also a universal 'symbol of wisdom and truth'.'

I considered the *'Lapis Lazuli',* a symbol of extreme wealth, as was the 'Taj Mahal', and I wondered where the Emperor got the money to build such an exquisite emblem of love, and of course Prasham had the answers.

Prasham explained that; 'The funds for the construction of the 'Taj Mahal' were provided by the 'Royal Treasury of the Emperor.' and the 'Treasury of the Government of Agra Province', and the 'Taj Mahal' was completed at an estimated cost of around 32 million rupees, but nowadays it would probably cost, approximately 60-70 billion rupees.'

I am a hopeless romantic, and I live in hope that someday, a nice rich guy, like the 'Emperor', will show his undying love for me, by building me a 'Taj Mahal', but preferably while I am still alive.

'A girl can dream, can't she?' Susan smiled as she asked this rhetorical question, in her assignment.

I wasn't surprised when Prasham informed us that;

'The 'Taj Mahal' structure is perfectly symmetrical, except for the two tombs, unfortunately, for some reason known to man only, the male tomb had to be larger than the female tomb,' Prasham said smiling, trying to keep harmony in our group, which was predominantly female.

But then he went ruined it all, by saying;

'The changing colours of the 'Taj Mahal', were said to be equivalent to the moods of a woman, 'Mumtaz Mahal', to be specific.'

Needless to say, some of the guys added their cheeky comments about women's mood swings, which was not appreciated by us ladies, who are seldom moody.

It was interesting to learn that, in India people have many types of jobs. In the case of the 'Taj Mahal', there are men who, for a small tip, will actually clear people away, so that tourists can take good photographs, without strangers lurking in the background.

When we were taking photographs at the *'Lady Diana bench'*, all the ladies tipped the Indian guys, so we could get a good, clear photo on the bench.

We tried to replicate the same elegant, but lonely looking pose, but of course, no matter how hard we tried, none of us succeeded in looking as good, as *'Lady Diana.'*

Prasham explained to us that; 'It actually wasn't unusual for VIP's to be photographed sitting alone on the bench.'

I was rather surprised when he said; 'Believe it or not, 'Prince Charles' had been photographed, sitting alone on the bench, twelve years previously.'

'But of course, the photograph of 'Lady Diana' hinted at loneliness and isolation, and therefore it took on a greater significance, when the royal couple separated,' he explained.

A lady in our group, Lucy said; 'I also read the story, that Prince Charles had his photograph taken in front of the 'Taj Mahal' years before Lady Diana. I suppose we love the romantic idea, of the unrequited love of a beautiful, young lady, sitting all alone at the 'Taj Mahal'.'

Prasham said to us; 'That beautiful, but defining image, of the Princess sitting all alone outside the 'Taj Mahal' on a bench, which would later be renamed in her honour, has been remembered, as an iconic moment in India, and in the history of the royal family,' Prasham said.

Lucy, a lady in our group felt ill with 'Delhi Belly', but thankfully she was fine the next day, as she had medication which worked a treat, and Prasham gave her good advice also.

He informed us; 'It's the luck of the draw,' whether you get 'Delhi Belly', or not, but it's essential to take as many precautions as possible with hygiene.'

Prasham further explained; 'Tourists often become ill from eating and drinking foods and beverages, which may have no impact, on Indian people.'

He explained this was due to immunity which develops with the locals who are in constant, repeated exposure to 'pathogenic organisms.'

Conor asked; 'What are 'pathogenic organisms?'

'It's; '*An organism capable of causing disease to its host. A human pathogen is capable of causing illness in humans.'*

'The extent and duration of exposure necessary to acquire immunity, hasn't been determined; it can vary with each individual organism,' he explained.

'Oh my goodness, that's too much information,' one of the ladies in the group said, looking worried.

'I think you're right, we don't need to dwell on the negative side of India.'

'We have lots of positives in my country, in particular we have amazing history and customs, we also have a wide range of superb colours, and we know how to enjoy ourselves, and not take ourselves too seriously.'

'I can guarantee you all; we will have lots of fun on this trip.' Prasham said proudly.

'We will hold you to that,' Dad said smiling.

Susan surprised herself, as she continued to type at an extremely fast speed;

Our guide Prasham, was really superb, he was very patient, and very respectful to all ages. At times, there was so much happening on the trip, Conor and I would recap on the day, while we relaxed in the hotel.

We saw large crowds of Indian people on the roads, in cars, dangerously perched on top of buses and trains, and bulging out of tiny auto-rickshaws.

Some days, we spotted, families of four or five on motor scooters, clinging to each other, and we even saw a large class of students on a bullock cart. We saw many hazardous situations, which a 'Health and Safety Officer', in Ireland would definitely frown on.

I actually asked Prasham; 'Are there many accidents and what about the 'Health and Safety Legislation?'

Prasham laughed and said; 'Buses do topple over, rooftop passengers on trains do occasionally get swept off the top, by an overhanging cable. I know it must be astonishing to see, but people here accept the risk, for the free ride.'

'In India poverty is borne with a kind of social resignation, and the jostling and elbowing of people for space, may be alien to people in the Western world, but it's a natural way of life in India,' Prasham said in resignation.

One evening while we were relaxing, I noticed my Dad's lovely tattoo, and I asked him why he chose to get a 'Heart Tattoo.'

'As a teenager I decided to get a 'Heart Tattoo, as it's a symbol of 'Love', and thankfully I have never regretted my decision,' he replied.

'I was always fascinated by the power of the heart physically and emotionally. It keeps us alive physically and mentally it allows us to love people.'

I then noticed my Dad swiftly changed the subject.

'Have you any Tattoo's?'

'No, but I think, someday I'll get a butterfly tattoo,' I replied.

'I longed to ask my Dad;

'Why did you leave Mum and I, if you believe in the heart and love so much?'

'Why did you marry Mum, if you didn't love her?'

'Why did you abandon us?'

'Where was your 'Heart Tattoo', symbol of love then?'

But I knew it wasn't the time or place to ask those questions, I would ask him on my return to Ireland.

Now that my Dad was back in my life; I had no intention of letting him escape again, I was determined to keep in touch, whether he liked it or not.

My Mum Alma had explained that he had married on the rebound after his wife Kate died, so I tried to bear no grudges, as he had deserted me, and divorced Mum, because he couldn't deal with his own pain.

Chapter 21

Susan now recalled how fascinated they all were, upon seeing the great respect for cows in India.

She wrote speedily;

My Dad and I will always treasure our wonderful memories of India, but in particular the scenes of cows lazing on the road, while all the traffic circled around them, it was just incredible, and yet delightful to see.

When our coach got stuck in a massive traffic jam, we soon discovered that; 'The cows most certainly have the right of way everywhere in India.'

It was so funny to see; the cows sitting stately on the road while our coach and all the traffic circled around them. They seemed to know, they were sacred animals, and they loved the attention.

Prasham informed us that the cow was actually a symbol of wealth in India, since ancient times.

Kevin laughingly said; 'Road frontage, is a symbol of our wealth.'

Prasham looked puzzled and asked; 'What does that mean?'

'To own land with access to a main road, is often a measure of eligibility for marriage, and it can be banded about in country areas, or even in some famous night clubs in Dublin,' Kevin said laughing heartily.

'It's a bit of 'craic', and it breaks the ice when people say to each other;

'Have ya got road frontage?'

'So land is more important, than cows in Ireland,' Prasham queried.

'Yes, well spotted, we treat the land with the same respect, you treat your cows.'

Prasham explained to us; 'The holy 'Hindu' scriptures, the 'Vedas', contained verses, which emphasise, 'it is a sin to kill cows and eat their meat.' There is also an emphasis on cows being offered protection, and to this day many Indian states prohibit the slaughter of cows.'

'Oh my goodness! I would never survive in India as I couldn't live without my steaks.' Kevin said in shock.

Sharp witted Jake said, with laughter in his voice;

'Don't worry Kevin, they'll never pass that law in Ireland, we just wouldn't allow it, we love our meat too much. People would be protesting on the streets, and the Government would be lynched by, the meat loving mob.'

'I hope you are right,' Kevin said, looking worried.

'Well, I suggest we don't tell anyone about that particular Indian custom, we have plenty of other stories to tell,' Jake laughed.

Prasham further elaborated; 'In 'Hindu' religion, the cow is sacred, and deeply respected. Hindus do not actually worship the cows, but they are definitely held in very high esteem.'

'Some Hindus rely heavily on cows for dairy products, and for tilling the fields, and the dung is used as a source of fuel and fertilizer. So, in India the cow is actually seen as a 'caretaker' or a 'maternal figure.'

Jake laughed heartily, and he said to Prasham;

'Wow that gives me a new respect for 'dung'. I knew it was used as a fertilizer, but not as a fuel. In future, I'll try not to complain about the odour, when the cows are urinating and pooping,' he laughed heartily.

To change the subject from dung and cows, I asked Prasham about the dress code, for men and women tourists in India.

I had noticed his clothes were always immaculate, and he always dressed extremely trendy. He had the brightest of smiles, I had ever seen. His whole face lit up when he smiled, which sent out happy rays, which made us all smile, and he was so clever and so knowledge for such a young guide.

Prasham very kindly explained to us that, there was 'a reserved dress code' in India; 'While it's acceptable to wear Western clothes to most places, it's essential to wear them in a manner which is respectful, to the very modest Indian culture.'

'Would you believe most Indians are actually too polite, to tell you, to your face, if you are inappropriately dressed?' he said.

'Indian people are pleased to see tourists wear Indian clothes, they feel, it shows the person's appreciation of their culture,' he explained.

We all commented on how kind and polite the Indian people were.

I said to Prasham; 'I think, the fact that tourists are asked, to wear long dresses or long trousers in the temples, its India's polite way of saying;

'Please dress respectfully while in our temples.'

I thought it was a clever way, and extremely polite way of dealing with the dress code in the temples.

We were all interested in the trips to the temples, not because we were 'Holy Mary's' or 'Holy Paddy's', but because of the beliefs of the Indian people. They believed going to the temples bestowed a positive mind on a person, and therefore a positive energy, which then leads to 'a healthy mind and soul.'

'It is an important practice to take off your footwear, when entering temples; to prevent people bringing in dirt or grime, to the cleansed and sanctified temples,' Prasham explained.

As Susan continued writing her short story, at a speed she couldn't ever have predicted, she felt transported back to the breathtaking, wild, very diverse and unique culture of India, and in particular their dazzling, colourful unique fashion.

We saw Indian women dressed in amazing colours, the ladies loved 'The *Sari*', which arguably in my eyes is, the most beautiful style of dress in the world. It is worn so elegantly by women, throughout India. It is wrapped in different ways around the body according to their local customs.

Prasham told us; 'The *Sari,* is comfortable and easy to wear once you get used to wearing it.'

The Irish wit came to the fore once more, when Jake asked; 'How do you know it's comfortable?'

'Do you often wear a 'Sari?'

'No I don't,' Prasham laughed heartily.

'I did my research, and I asked my sister and her friends,' he laughingly replied. Prasham continued on the tourist's code of fashion; 'Whether, you are male or female, one rule covers all visitors to India; 'Don't leave the hotel with your arms or legs extremely bare.'

'You'll naturally get attention as a foreigner in India, as full-on staring is common and accepted on Indian streets, but you get less negative attention, if you remain covered up.'

'For most locations and seasons in India, thin, loose linen or cotton pants and button-down shirts will keep you comfortable in hot, humid weather and help you blend in,' he said.

Prasham explained: 'When we visit the temples and other religious sites on our tour, there will be signs advising visitors to dress in a specific way, before we can enter the temple. Some of the religious institutions require visitors and tourists;

'To cover your heads, and remove shoes, and cover your legs and arms, as a mark of respect, especially in the temples.'

'So please bear that in mind when we visit the temples,' Prasham said.

My Dad and I had a good laugh at our first Temple, when young Heather, unfortunately, didn't heed Prasham's advice on the dress code.

When we arrived at the Temple, Heather was wearing a short dress, and a 'Pujari', (Hindu priest), spotted her inappropriate dress code, and he handed her a really long, dark green dress to wear, which was about three sizes too big.

Heather told us unfortunately, she didn't have time to read the list of things to bring, and she only packed short dresses and shorts. She always looked so cute and trendy in them, but in her new rather large garment, she looked like a poor orphan, from the 19th century.

Dad and I enjoyed the banter, when some of our group caught a glimpse of Heather, in her new finery. The Irish wit began to flow, and we fell around the place laughing, at some of the comments, but thankfully we all managed to be respectful, as we entered the temple. It was one of those special moments, where everyone in our group had a good laugh, and even Heather, joined in the banter, and gave as good as she got.

Sean, one of the quieter guys, surprised us and said; 'Heather, I see you're in your nightgown, I didn't realise its bedtime, is my watch slow?'

'It must be. My watch says 2 a.m. definitely bed time, that's why I am wearing my nightgown,' she said laughingly.

'Maybe we should all request one of those lovely fashionable gowns,' he laughed.

'Yes I would recommend it, it's very cool and comfortable,' Heather promptly replied.

After the banter, we settled down and thoroughly enjoyed the unique architecture and splendour of the temple, and the exquisite detailed work on the doorways, pillars and on the ceilings.

Later, when returning to the hotel by coach, I asked Prasham about the 'Bindi', tradition.

'A bindi', meaning point, drop, or small particle, is a red dot worn on the centre of the forehead, commonly by Hindu women,' he kindly explained.

'If a woman wears a red 'bindi', it shows that she is married, and it signifies; 'True love and prosperity'.

'Widows in India don't normally wear a 'bindi', but in Southern India, they are allowed to wear a black **'bindi' to show their loss.** However, nowadays, young girls are allowed wear a 'bindi' of any colour,' he explained.

'There is also a spiritual role for the 'bindi', would you like to hear about it?' Prasham asked us.

Before anyone could reply, I said; 'Yes please, I have always been fascinated by the 'bindi' tradition.'

'In the Spiritual view, the 'bindi' plays the most important role in 'Hindu' culture.

But the red 'bindi' actually has multiple meanings which are all simultaneously valid. One interpretation of the 'bindi' is that; it is a cosmetic mark used to enhance beauty, and another is that the 'bindi' was created as a means to worship one's intellect, therefore, it was actually used by both men and women,' Prasham explained.

'Well, the worship of the intellect was to ensure that thoughts, speech, habits, actions, and a person's character became pure. It was believed, a strong intellect would help a person make noble decisions in life, assist them in being courageous and to have good thoughts.'

'The belief was by wearing the 'bindi', a strong individual, a strong family and a strong society could be formed.'

'Also the colour 'Red', represents '*honour, love and prosperity*', therefore the red 'bindi' was worn to symbolise those facets of life too,' Prasham explained proudly.

I really loved the Indian tradition at our hotel, where we were greeted on return from our trips, by a guy or a girl in traditional Indian costume. We noticed one girl in particular, she was absolutely, beautiful, and she always wore stunning coloured saris, and a red 'Bindi on her forehead.

There was a beautiful air of peace and tranquillity about her. She greeted everyone, with her hands joined, her head bowed and she spoke rather gently saying; '*Namaste.*'

We asked Prasham to explain the origin of the Indian greeting, and he was delighted to oblige.

'The traditional Indian form of greeting is the '*Namaste*', which literally means, '*I bow to the divine in you*',' he proudly said.

He specified that '*Namaste*' is used for all greetings; saying hello, saying goodbye, and also for seeking forgiveness, and for all occasion's day or night.

Prasham then passed around a photograph of a beautiful Indian lady, to demonstrate the proper way to do the hand greetings.

'It's a very graceful gesture, and a very warm, and welcoming greeting,' he said.

We all made a great effort to do the *'Namaste'* greeting properly.

Prasham kindly explained; 'You just put your hands together in the 'pranamasana gesture' for added respect, which is; 'The palms press together in front of the heart's centre', while allowing the shoulders to roll down the back, and the elbows rest at your rib cage.'

He watched our efforts and said; 'That's what I love about the Irish tourists; you are always willing to get involved, and you always try new customs, new food, and new ideas.'

I noticed everyone was smiling, and it made me realise, everyone, young and old likes to be praised.

Our group ranged in age from early twenties to late seventies, and it was fascinating to see how well we all mixed. Conor and I were amazed at the agility and stamina of the seniors.

We overheard six seniors, chatting in the lift, and we discovered that most evenings they met, for a 'Gin and Tonic', before dinner and then another after dinner. They felt it kept the 'Delhi belly bug' away!

Amazingly, nobody in that senior group had been ill during the trip, while some younger people had suffered a very mild does of 'Delhi belly.

When chatting to them later in the trip, we discovered the couples had actually travelled the world together, having met on a holiday ten years previously. In my eyes they were certainly a great advertisement, for enjoying life, and growing old gracefully.

They were so knowledgeable about India and the world in general, and it was exciting and fascinating in their company. They got involved in all the fun of the holiday, and they even went on the rickshaws, and the elephant rides.

One of the ladies, named Rose (her name really suited her, she was like a rose flower, so elegant and graceful), said excitedly to our group; 'The joy of travel is, you never know what will happen, from one day to the next, we make sure we enjoy every second, and we always have a wonderful time.'

'I know, I probably won't have the privilege or the money to return to this beautiful country again. But that's okay, as I'll always have the most wonderful memories of this wild, exciting, wonderful country with its amazing, beautiful people.'

'You never know in life. Rose, you may come back again someday, and you might even retire to this amazing, exquisite, country of India,' Jake said.

'Did you see the movies; 'The Best Exotic Marigold Hotel' & 'The Second Best Exotic Marigold Hotel?' Jake asked Rose.

'No, unfortunately I didn't, but I will.'

'What are the movies about; I know they are based in India?'

'They are about seven elderly British men and women, who for a variety of reasons, reply to an online advertisement and travel to Jaipur, India, where they find a rather run down retirement hotel. The hotel is managed by a very young, exuberant, and very optimistic host.'

'That sounds good; I'll check it out on my return home.'

'Well, the story shows how India affects all of them in different ways; enchanting some, and making some of them re-examine their lives.'

'I won't spoil it for you, perhaps, you may wish to follow in their footsteps after you see the movie,' Jake laughed.

'I think retirement in India, would be a very exciting end to the last chapter in anyone's life. There would never be a dull moment; life would be full of colour, full of action and fun.' Jake smiled.

'I agree, life would certainly never be dull here,' Rose said smiling.

As soon as Susan began to reminisce on their 'Rickshaw' adventures, she smiled happily. The creative juices started flowing so fast, she could hardly keep up with her thoughts. She was surprised at the speed her fingers were moving, it was like they had a life of their own.

She happily recalled the fun they had on the rickshaws, and how competitive they all were, when trying to reach their destination.

When Prasham asked; 'Who wants to go on the 'Rickshaws?'

All hands went up straight away, without any hesitation, even the oldest in our group was excited, and brave enough to try the rickshaws.

Conor and I shared the 'Rickshaw' and we were partly shocked, and amused when we realised, there was absolutely no protocol on the roads. It was survival of the bravest and the boldest every time.

Our driver inched his way into the chaotic intersections, continually beeping his horn and cutting off buses, motorcyclists, other rickshaws, and overcrowded jeeps, where passengers were literally hanging on for dear life.

Wow, vehicles were constantly swerving to avoid each other. It was so chaotic; it was hard to believe that it was real life, and not part of a stunt movie.

Our wild, brilliant driver took on the buses and the cows, with such braveness or madness; I wasn't sure which it was. The cows continued to sit lazily, calmly and stately, in the middle of the road, while all the traffic chaos bustled around them.

Glancing over our shoulders, we could you see 'Tuk, Tuk Rickshaws' and buses rapidly approaching at full speed, but our driver fought a brave fight, and continued on regardless of our safety or the rules of the road.

He was determined we would be the winners, in our group, even if it meant being dead on time, (excuse the pun).

Thankfully, we made it safely, to our destination, to discover, we were actually second, not first, but we didn't mind. I noticed, everyone was talking excitedly and laughing rather nervously, after the crazy experience, but luckily we were all in one piece.

Prasham explained to us; 'The Rickshaws first began as two or three-wheeled passenger carts, called a 'Pulled Rickshaw', and they were generally pulled by one man with just one passenger.'

'Then over time, 'cycle rickshaws', also known as 'pedicabs', and 'auto rickshaws', and 'electric rickshaws', were invented. The 'Auto Rickshaw' is often called the 'Tuk Tuk', by the Indian drivers.

'A lady asked; 'Why is it called a 'Tuk Tuk'?'

Prasham patiently explained; 'It was named for the sound it makes, from its two-cycle engines, and because of its small capacity.'

'But don't be fooled by it, it can go at a good speed, and it is great for cruising around the markets and the narrow streets. As you've now seen, the flow of traffic rarely stops, and the drivers are experts at manoeuvring the 'Tuk Tuk', in all types of heavy traffic.'

'The Rickshaws', are great for short distances, or places which are too far to walk, but too short to take a bus or a taxi. The cycle rickshaws are the best to use in 'Old Delhi', when visiting the intricate *'galis',* (walkways), and you get to experience the different smells, some spicy and some which can be a bit overpowering, but that's our India. You also get to appreciate the amazing sounds and sights of the city by rickshaw,' he proudly explained.

Conor and I thoroughly enjoyed the cycle-rickshaw ride around the bustling streets and the bazaars. We were all in healthy competition with each other, and at the end of our journey, we were all very gracious, and we decided, 'we were all winners.'

We all declared, we hadn't laughed as much, or as loudly in ages.

Even though, young and old rickshaw drivers cycled for hours every day, in exceptional heat, they continually smiled and enjoy the fun with the tourists. They manoeuvre their rickshaws around people, cars, buses, taxies, motorcyclists, other rickshaws, and cows, like professionals.

I thought they were amazing, wild guys, but astonishingly safe drivers, as surprisingly we saw no accidents, during our holiday in India.

I must include the beautifully painted 'Elephants', in my short story, as they play a large role in India's history and culture. They are held in high esteem by the people of India. They are beautiful animals, they are kept very clean and they are decorated in gorgeous, bright cheerful colours.

When we booked our holiday my Dad and I said, we would participate in all the trips and get involved in the Indian culture. It was a dream come true for both of us, seeing the exquisite sights of 'Amber Fort', by elephant.

The elephants were such wonderful docile animals, and they were beautifully decorated and painted in traditional patterns of exquisite, bright colours.

Lucy questioned Prasham about the treatment of the elephants;

'Some people think, the elephants in India are treated cruelly by their owners. Do you think that's true?'

Thankfully, Prasham informed us, the conditions and treatment of the elephants had greatly improved, especially in recent times, as the 'Rajasthan', government now conducts regular checks, to ensure the safety and the welfare of the elephants.

He explained that originally the elephants carried a driver and four passengers, and were worked all day, but thankfully nowadays, the elephants are limited to five trips per day, and they only carry a driver and two passengers.

'Elephants were used for the transport of Kings, and are still considered to be a symbol of royalty today,' Prasham boasted.

'I am so pleased to hear they are considered to be a symbol of royalty. I would hate to think they are not treated with the kindness and respect they deserve,' Lucy said.

On the coach Prasham explained that for decades elephants were used to bring tourists to popular destinations, and it was a major part of the Indian custom.

He had informed us that an elephant would carry two of us on his back, and on a very scenic route to 'Amber Fort', which was an opulent palace, high on a hill, seven miles outside 'Jaipur', 'Rajasthan's' capital city.

When we saw the hill the elephants had to climb, with two of us on their backs, we were surprised, but Prasham assured us the elephants, wouldn't be in any distress.

Lucy said sadly; 'I wish I hadn't eaten such a big breakfast.'

Jake forever the optimist and always full of fun said; 'I am sure you could walk up the hill, if you like.'

'Thanks Jake, I'll walk if you do.'

'Well, I am okay to ride the elephant; I didn't have a big breakfast,' he laughed.

'Very funny,' Lucy smiled.

Conor and I were very excited, as we had never been on an elephant ride. Our elephant was so docile; he walked up the steep hill, slowly and stately, with not a care in the world. As it was exceptionally hot, the driver very kindly gave us beautiful coloured umbrellas, which added to the drama of the elephant ride.

I was very grateful to the elephant for the lift, as it was a very steep hill. We could see for miles and miles, beautiful scenery and the majestic 'Amber Fort.'

We noticed Lucy seemed to enjoy the elephant ride too.

It still gives me a warm glow, and it brings a smile to my face, when I think about that amazing elephant ride. We all enjoyed it so much; we talked about it for days.

Prasham proudly explained; 'The magnificent 'Amber Fort' overlooks the 'Maota Lake' which provides a beautiful, serene setting. It was mainly a fortification, which is obvious by its location, by its high walls, its multiple gates and the surrounding fortifications.'

Susan continued writing excitedly;

Inside the Amber Fort, we saw amazing palaces, such as the 'Sheesh Mahal', (Palace of Mirrors), which was breathtakingly beautiful. The walls and the ceilings of the Palace were inlaid with thousands of small mirrors; it was truly a spectacular sight. There were exquisite courtyards and gardens which gave 'Amber Fort,' more of a feeling of a palace, rather than a fortress.

We learnt from Prasham, the 'Hindu and Mughal' traditions influenced the design of the very impressive, remarkable 'Amber Fort'.

Another amazing trip, we took, was to 'Jaipur'' also known as the 'Pink City of India', and it's famous for its forts, museums, palaces, gardens and festivals.

People often say it's; 'Pink in colour and pink in vibrancy.'

The splendid atmosphere of 'Jaipur' brought joy and delight to us, as we walked through the city, and the delicate 'pink colour' of the city oozed a romantic charm, which captivated all our hearts. Even the guys who acted macho, they too, looked at the city in awe, and total appreciation of its beauty.

In my estimation; 'Jaipur' is certainly one of the most beautiful and charming cities of India. It is difficult to put into words, but I will try to describe the abundant charm the city has, which fascinated us all.

The city has an abundance of culture, unique architecture, wonderful traditions, art, jewellery, textiles and it definitely charmed us all.

It's a city which still manages to hold its roots and values, even after modernisation, which is unusual nowadays.

'Jaipur' was named the 'Pink City' because of the terracotta pink colour of the stone, which was exclusively used for the construction of all buildings. The pink colour historically represents hospitality, and a welcoming in India.

In 1876, The Prince of Wales, Albert Edward VII, visited India and surprisingly, the 'Maharaja of Jaipur' painted the whole city pink, to welcome his guest.

Conor and I were fascinated by this, as we both remarked that normally the colour 'Pink' represents female life, rather than male life.

Prasham enlightened us further by telling us that the 'Maharaja of

Jaipur' also constructed an exquisite concert hall which he named; 'The Albert Hall', in honour of 'Prince Albert'. The Albert Hall stands proudly and stately, amidst the carefully laid out grounds of the beautiful 'Ram Niwas' public gardens.'

Some people, mise/me, included, were totally unaware of the existence of the 'Albert Hall' in India, we all knew of its existence in England.

Of course, my clever Dad knew, well he said he did, anyway. I wasn't a hundred percent sure, he was telling the truth.

It was fascinating to hear that, the tradition of the 'Pink City' was still being adhered to, as the residents of 'Jaipur' are compelled by law to maintain the colour pink in all future constructions.

Susan was delighted at the speed she was writing, and she was pleased that her exciting memories of India were still so vivid.

She couldn't believe she had written so many pages, she realised she would need to edit later or she would be well over the word quota.

'Maybe, I have the potential to be a budding writer, after all,' she thought.

'You just never know, life is full of twists and turns.'

'Well, perhaps I am getting a bit carried away, I don't love writing that much' she mused.

It would be interesting to see what Hazel thought of her short story assignment.

Susan continued her story;

The following day we went to 'Agra Fort' and Prasham informed us that; 'Agra Fort' was marked by invasions and battles. The red stone fortified fort was built using a combination of 'Hindu and Islamic architectural styles,' and it was comprised of several structures. It was original constructed in red sandstone, and white marble was added later, when it was transformed into a palace by 'Shah Jahan'.'

Jake wittingly commented that 'Shah Jahan' loved his marble, and grandeur.

'No small trinkets for him, he certainly knew how to splash the cash,' he said laughingly.

Prasham excitedly informed us of the beautiful; 'Diwali Festival of Light', which takes place in Jaipur, the, 'Pink City'.

'The ancient 'Hindu festival' is celebrated in autumn every year, and it spiritually signifies *'the victory of light over darkness'*.'

He explained; 'There are special activities for tourists, which include fireworks, flower work decoration, and cultural folk dances, to celebrate *'The victory of light over darkness.'*

Conor suggested; 'We should have a 'Festival of Light' in Ireland, during and after, our dark, harsh winters,' people smiled and nodded in total agreement.

'We could celebrate that we have survived another dark, wet, cold, long, dreary winter and rejoice that spring, is on the way,' Conor said smiling.

'That's a great idea, we should certainly celebrate; 'The v*ictory of light over darkness'*, an end to dark winter nights and a beginning to bright spring days,' Jake agreed.

Susan happily recalled Prasham's description of the 'Deepawali', or 'Diwali Festival', and she was excited, as she continued writing and showing off her knowledge of the festival.

'Diwali festival', is the biggest and the brightest of all 'Hindu', festivals. During 'Diwali', lights illuminate every part of India, and the lovely scent of incense sticks hang in the air, mingled with the sounds of fire-crackers, combined with joy, love, togetherness and of course 'hope' and it all helps to light up the soul,' Prasham told us proudly.

'Diwali,' is actually celebrated around the world. Outside India, it is more than a 'Hindu' festival, it's also a celebration of South-Asian identities.'

'I informed Prasham that, my friends and I had the pleasure of going to the wonderful celebrations of the 'Indian Diwali Festival of Light' in Dublin.

Our next trip was to 'Jodhpur', the second largest city in Rajasthan, which is sometimes referred to as the 'Blue City', due to the brightly painted houses around the 'Mehrangarh Fort'.

'In 2014, it was named as the 'Lonely Planet's most extraordinary place to stay',' Prasham said rather proudly.

Witty John, asked; 'What's this phobia about painting cities in different colours?'

'It does sound like a cheerful idea, once depressing black isn't used as the colour theme,' he said laughingly.

Needless to say, it started a lot of witty conversations, but Prasham enjoyed the banter. He knew people weren't being disrespectful; they were just having a laugh.

In Jodhpur, we visited the 'Mehrangarh Fort', which is an imposing structure sitting on a hill, which was seen in the film 'The Dark Knight Rises.'

We will also went to 'Jaswant Thada', a beautiful monument built entirely out of white marble.

John interrupted again laughing; 'There you go again, with your colour schemes.'

'Yes, we do love our colours, and that's evident in our beautiful coloured Saris, and our magnificent, coloured buildings,' Prasham smiled.

We also visited 'Udaipur', which is known as the 'city of the lakes'.

This beautiful city has also been described as the 'Venice of the East', and its centrepiece is the impressive 'Lake Palace' which sits in the middle of 'Lake Pichola'.

We all enjoyed a tranquil, majestic boat cruise on the beautiful, serene lake.

Prasham informed us that, the holy city of 'Varanasi' reigns supreme, with its ancient 'funeral ghats', where Hindus pay their last respects to the dead, beside the sacred 'Ganges River'.

'People come from all over India, to pray, to collect sacred water, to bathe, and to attend to their dead,' Prasham said respectfully.

I noticed most people in our group went rather quiet. I realised, we are not as open or as comfortable dealing, or talking about death, unlike the Indian people, who speak about it freely. They have a healthier outlook on death; unlike us, they don't see it as a sad occasion, they see it as part of life's cycle.

Conor and I were really pleased with our hotels, which were very impressive, and astonishingly clean and bright. They actually were an oasis of calm, a complete change from the fast pace of traffic and the mayhem surrounding them.

One particular evening, Conor and I had a good laugh during dinner. The majority of our group had ordered an Indian curry, not realising the difference between Irish spicy food, and Indian spicy food.

After a few mouthfuls of the curry, they were sweating profusely, because it was so spicy. They drank lots of water as the tears rolled down their faces, from the heat of the curry, the waiters were kept busy replenishing the bottled water, because once the bottles were placed on the table, they were emptied immediately.

The following day Prasham made an announcement on the coach; 'Folks, I would like to remind you, whether you like mild or spicy food, the hotels cater for all palates. Just check the menu and ask the waiter, for a dish which will delight your taste buds Indian style, but remember to say; 'Not too Spicy.'

'I believe last night's curry was extremely spicy, obviously not suitable for Westerners,' Prasham said with a wicked smile.

We felt he purposely didn't warn people, as he wanted to observe their reaction to the Indian curry.

Chapter 22

Hazel felt quite emotional reading Susan's short story on India, it reminded her of her family holiday to India, with her husband Jim and daughter Clara.

It was bitter sweet thinking of her last family holiday, she was well aware; she had a touch of 'the empty nest syndrome.'

India had been her last holiday with Clara, as she was all grown up now, she had left the family unit, and was in the big, bad world phew!

Hazel's poor heart was broken, as Clara left for the exciting world of University, she knew she had to let go of the strings, but by golly it was a tough ask.

While reading Susan's short story, Hazel clearly recalled the sounds and smells of awesome India. It was the most exciting, crazy, wild holiday, they had enjoyed as a family, India was so different, and there wasn't a dull moment.

Hazel now recalled the crazy, noisy traffic, all moving together in the same direction, with no traffic lights to assist them, it was a spectacular free for all.

It was amazing and mind blowing to see, the cars, buses, cyclists, motorcyclists, and rickshaws fighting for the rite of passage, all at the same time.

Amazingly they all seemed to succeed in completing their journeys, with no mishaps, but there were definitely some close calls. Yet throughout their holiday they didn't witness any accidents. The noises and the mayhem on the streets was more fascinating than annoying.

Hazel and Jim were in agreement that, the Indian people could teach Westerns a thing or two about life. They were extraordinary people and it was astonishing to observe them as they travelled, they had attitude, which was hard to describe. It was an art in itself, the way they weaved around each other in traffic bedlam, and still got safely to their destination, with horns blowing, yet there were no angry voices raised.

Hazel recalled how hygienic Indian people looked, they came out of, what looked like hovels, and yet they were immaculately dressed. The ladies were dressed in beautiful coloured 'Saris', and the men dressed in whiter than white shirts, and trousers or long white robes.

The one custom in India, Hazel frowned upon and couldn't understand was, when people squatted on the streets. Thankfully, she did lots of research before they travelled, and she was prepared for that unusual, unhygienic custom.

Hazel recalled she had dressed elegantly, for the trip to the 'Taj Mahal.' She knew it was a once in a lifetime experience, and she wanted to look well for the professional photographs, their guide had promised.

Jim and Clara teased her, when they saw her beautiful royal blue and white top, and her royal blue trousers, navy shoes and her dark shades. She looked the part, and people in the group teased her, as she boarded the coach.

Some of the ladies were actually disappointed and rather annoyed because they hadn't dressed up, especially when they saw Hazel's lovely, nicely posed professional photographs on the 'Lady Diana bench' at the 'Taj Mahal'.

Hazel explained to them, that she had dressed up, because she loved and admired 'Lady Diana' and she had always wished to replicate her photograph, at the 'Taj Mahal'.

'I was so lucky to get this wonderful opportunity, and I was determined to make the most of it,' she said smiling, trying to ease their disappointment.

Hazel recalled how professional their photographer had been, he had treated it like a photo shoot, he put everyone at ease and made them all feel special.

He knew it was a once in a lifetime chance for them, as they probably wouldn't get the opportunity to return to India.

He made it an exciting, extra special photo shoot for them all, and Hazel and her family, never tired of looking at the beautiful photographs of them on the 'Lady Diana' bench.

Secretly Hazel's favourite, was the photograph of herself, posing on the 'Lady Diana bench.'

Hazel now recalled her own experiences in India, in particular the intense heat, as they travelled around India, but luckily the air conditioning on the coach was excellent, and they managed to survive the burning temperatures.

Of course, the Indians always looked so cool in their beautiful colours, and their layers of material, while most of the Westerners looked quite hassled and they were perspiring, in far less layers.

Hazel remembered how surprised their group was, when a very elegant and cool looking Indian lady, wearing a beautiful, colourful sari, asked to take a photograph of them, (they looked so uncool, just sweaty Westerners, struggling with the heat). They were quite pleased she wanted a photograph, but they didn't dare ask the reason, just in case they would be disappointed with her reply. They preferred to think, it was because they were all 'so beautiful and exotically white.'

Hazel was happy to read that Susan also liked and bought the Indian spices. She was pleased the guide still organised the selling of spices on the coach, as it had been a delightful experience.

The sisters who sold the spices had informed Hazel and the group that; 'India was the Land of Spices', and according to the ancient principles of Indian medicine, the myriad spices, actually improve a person's health,' they explained sweetly.

'The combination of the spices stimulates the appetite and aids the digestive system, for example;

'Turmeric has strong anti-inflammatory properties which help ease the condition of rheumatoid arthritis and it's very good for skin ailments.'

'Ginger is good for the liver and rheumatism.'

'Cloves help the kidneys, and they relieve fever, and also they help to stimulate the heart.'

'Coriander fights constipation and insomnia.'

'Cardamom is one of the most versatile spices, it helps in the battle against; headaches, bad breath, throaty coughs and haemorrhoids,' the sisters confidently explained.

Hazel and the group were quite surprised that the young girls were so interested in healthy living, and they were extremely interest in other people's health.

They patiently answered health issue questions, as best they could, and they were a very good advertisement for their spices, as they looked so healthy and happy.

They were very lady like and had stunning Indian features, and they wore beautiful, cheerful coloured saris, and they had fluent English. They explained they were part of a family business, and they took a large number of spice orders, which were then delivered to the hotel.

Hazel was delighted to read that Susan had similar views on India, and the same love and appreciation for it. Like Susan, Hazel's view on India was;

'India was hectic, noisy, smelly and absolutely beautiful all at once.'

Hazel felt to appreciate and enjoy India; 'You must go with an open mind, in order to understand its goodness and its craziness, because it offers a unique experience which no other country has, it can excite and shock you, and you'll never forget the unbelievable, contrasting sights you see.'

Hazel and Susan both found, the Indian people to be very welcoming, and they both enjoyed their experience of the wonderful Indian culture and history, and in particular the 'Taj Mahal.'

Chapter 23

Hazel had read at least eight short story assignments, submitted by her diligent students, and she was delighted with the excellent standard of writing.

But one thing really bothered her; she had noticed three of the short stories, seemed quite similar. In all her years of teaching creative writing classes, she had never come across this type of situation.

At first she thought, maybe it was a coincidence, but she soon realised it was too weird and similar, to be a coincidence; three students writing about their Dad named, 'Conor', who had a 'Heart Tattoo.'

Hazel was totally mystified; three people had based their main character, on their Dad, 'Conor. But even more astonishing, in each story, the guy, 'Conor', had a 'Heart Tattoo'.

She decided to recheck the three students' assignments. She had been so engrossed in Susan's story on India; she needed to recheck whether the man with the 'Heart Tattoo' in her story, was named Conor.

'Wouldn't it be an awesome story, if there were three people in her class, who were actually unaware, they had the same Dad?'

'Now, I am really letting my imagination run away with me,' she mused, smiling to herself.

She shuffled through the papers and eventually she found the three similar stories. She looked at the name of each student, and she was even more confused, they had the same surname 'Rutlin', and yet they didn't appear to know, or acknowledge each other in class.

'Maybe they are actually related, and they don't realise it. Wow, wouldn't that be an extraordinary, but daunting non-fiction story,' she thought.

'Could it be possible, that Conor is; Paul, Patricia and Susan's Dad?'

she wondered, feeling quite puzzled.

Maybe she was hallucinating, it was quite possible, as she was feeling rather tired after reading so many short story, non-stop for a few hours.

Maybe, there was a logical reason to it all. She needed to take a break now, and think about it rationally.

While she had been reading the assignments, she definitely heard her crazy, cuckoo clock, striking at least three times, announcing loudly the passing of at least three hours.

One day, she would get rid of that clock; she had a love-hate relationship with it. She had taken it as a souvenir when they sold the family home, after her parents died, and it brought back some lovely memories, and some sad memories.

Her husband Jim laughed when she took the cuckoo clock.

'I can't believe you took the clock as a keepsake, you never really liked it.'

'What's that all about?' he asked, looking quite puzzled.

'I took it because it's the one thing, which reminds me of family life in the kitchen. In the middle of any family drama, and believe me there were many, the cuckoo would always appear,' she explained.

'The cuckoo always seemed to mock us, and the drama would stop, even if it was just for a few minutes, while the cuckoo popped in and out, and sang his calming song, 'cuckoo, cuckoo.'

My Mum always said; 'That poor cuckoo clock, always tries to keep the peace, and some days, that's a difficult job in this house.'

Hazel decided to read the three short stories again, and unfortunately her suspicions were confirmed;

In each of the three stories; there was a Dad, named 'Conor', with a 'Heart Tattoo'. She felt shocked with her discovery and yet the writer in her was quite excited.

She decided she would talk to Jim, about the three similar stories, as soon as he returned from his GAA training.

She had re-checked the three assignments, a number of times, and she most certainly wasn't hallucinating.

During the week and at weekends, Jim trained the local teenagers' in GAA football, he was a total fanatic on Gaelic football, and subsequently Hazel had become a GAA fan by default. 'It's either that or become a GAA widow,' she laughingly told Grace.

She had a niggling feeling that, possibly this man Conor was leading, 'a triple secret life,' and her three students were unaware of it.

'What on earth would she do, if Jim confirmed her fears that Conor was probably Paul, Susan and Patricia's Dad?'

She loved a good story, but she didn't really need a dramatic true story in her class, or in her life. She would prefer 'Fiction' to 'Non-fiction', in this case.

She decided, she would discuss her suspicions with Jim and her friend Grace, and ask their opinion on the three similar short stories.

She spoke to Jim first, and she asked him to read the three short stories.

Always, the cool dude, Jim calmly listened, took the assignments and went to the living room to read them. When he had finished the three stories, he returned to the kitchen, and confirmed her suspicions.

'I don't think there is any doubt, that your three students are talking about the same man Conor, who is their Dad, and he has a 'Heart Tattoo.'

'That's so weird,' he said shaking his head.

'Could they possibly be estranged from each other?' he asked.

'I think with all my experience of people, I would know if they were just ignoring each other. I have examined their body language, and I am 99% sure, they don't know each other, at all.'

'They don't acknowledge or even look curiously at each other, they definitely act like total strangers, which I feel they are. If they are related, then I think they will be as shocked, as we are.'

'Their Dad, Conor, will be in for a big surprise, as he's definitely a man with many secrets, which surround his 'Heart Tattoo',' Hazel said emphatically.

'I most certainly wouldn't like to be in his shoes, when his three secret families, decide to confront him,' Jim said.

A few days later, they asked Grace over for dinner, and they explained the situation. She read the three stories, and they tried to wait patiently, until she gave her comments.

'Wow, that's amazing; it most certainly is the same man in the three stories, there are too many coincidences; I am 99% sure that Conor must be Paul, Patricia, and Susan's Dad.'

Even though Hazel, Jim and Grace came to the same conclusion; they felt more evidence was needed, before Hazel spoke to the three students. They came up with the idea of Hazel asking the class to do another assignment, using the same character/person from the first assignment.

This would help Hazel decide what to do next, and if necessary, she would have further evidence, to show the three students.

At times, Hazel found it difficult to concentrate in class, as she secretly scrutinised the features of the three students, for familiar hereditary family signs.

She hadn't spotted it before, but they all had lovely sparkly eyes and they were well educated, and quite meticulous and precise in their ways.

They had an affluent air, and they all dressed very well, more designer fashion than high street style.

Hazel now wondered did Conor secretly help in their education, as they all spoke posh like private school type, and a single parent possibly couldn't afford a private school.

Hazel informed her students;

'For your next assignment I would like you all to write a short story of approximately 2,000 words.'

'Using the character you wrote about in your holiday assignment, write a short story based on that person and develop the character

as much as possible!'

Robert asked; 'The person I wrote about was totally fictional, will I just elaborate more on that type of character?'

'Yes, that's exactly what I want.'

'This is an exercise to build on your main character, from your holiday assignment.

Make your character even more interesting; show their good and bad qualities, the vulnerable and flawed side, and elaborate on any physical traits, or body art they have. Draw upon your own experiences of people, to develop the character.'

'Thanks, for all the great work on your first assignment, I am look forward to reading your next assignment.'

Hazel thought; 'Little do they know, why I am asking them to complete this assignment, it will be so interesting to see what Patricia, Susan and Paul write.'

'We will now examine the importance of good strong characters in your short stories, and hopefully in your future novels.'

'At the risk of boring you all, I have some wonderful, descriptive quotes from my favourite book and movie, '*The Shawshank Redemption*', which demonstrates how important strong, imposing, and interesting characters are in a novel or a short story.'

'For those of you who may not know, the movie or the book; 'It's a 1994 American movie, written and directed by 'Frank Darabont', and based on the 1982 'Stephen King' novella 'Rita Hayworth and The Shawshank Redemption'.

'The story is based on a banker 'Andy Dufresne', who is sentenced to life in 'Shawshank State Penitentiary' for the murder of his wife and her lover, despite his innocence,' (Tim Robbins is the superb actor who plays the part).

'During his time in prison, 'Andy Dufresne' became friends with a fellow prisoner, 'Ellis Redding', nicknamed 'Red', (Morgan Freeman is the superb actor who plays the part).

'Red' is a contraband smuggler in the prison, and he helps 'Andy' set up of a money laundering operation, which is led by the prison warden, 'Samuel Norton', (Bob Gunton is the superb actor who plays the part).

'Here are some copies of excellent, humorous parts from the movie. We will examine these wonderful quotes from 'Stephen King', which show an enjoyable, witty way to use words.'

'The first quote is from; 'Warden Norton' as he emphasises his rules to the new prisoners;

'I believe in two things; 'Discipline and the Bible', here in prison you will receive both. Put your trust in the Lord. 'Your ass belongs to me. Welcome to Shawshank Prison.'

'This quote shows, you can have great fun with language, and yet make a strong statement, to portray your message.'

'Here we see 'King' use some more witty language, when the warden discovered, Andy had escaped from prison, and the guards hadn't a clue how he escaped.'

Warden Norton said: 'Lord! It's a miracle!'

'Man up and vanished like a fart in the wind!'

Hazel enjoyed how much fun the class had, with the witty quotes. Some of the students' even made up their own jokes. Hazel realised how lucky she was, her students always participated, and enjoyed playing with words.

One of her male students said; 'Hazel, what about this for an obvious, witty, smelly description;

'The aroma of his flatulence was so strong, people began to faint.'

The rest of the students roared laughing, and Hazel couldn't help laughing too.

'Yes, that's the idea, use wit and humour to tell your story, it always works,' Hazel smirked.

'On a more serious note, words and language, can describe a situation so dramatically, for example, here is 'King's' brilliant description of how 'Red' feels, when 'Andy' escapes from prison.

Red; 'I have to remind myself that some birds aren't meant to be caged.'

He compares 'Andy' to a caged bird, who you know, should be set free, yet part of you is sad, when they escape.'

'This is my favourite description from 'King', because it's only one sentence, and yet it totally describes the length 'Andy' went through, to reach his freedom.'

'Andy Dufresne, the man who crawled through five hundred yards of shit, and came out clean the other end.'

Once again we see how powerful, witty words describe 'Andy's' escape, as he had crawled through a sewage system to freedom, but it was worth it in the end.

'Another superb quote from 'King' is; *'Get Busy Living or Get Busy Dying.'*

These words of 'Andy Dufresne' have been quoted all over the world, because they are inspirational, powerful and encouraging words.'

'This motto; '*Get Busy Living or Get Busy Dying*', is often used to motivate people, especially people who are going through a tough time, the words remind people that life is worth living, no matter how difficult the circumstances.'

'When people talk about great books or movies, '*The Shawshank Redemption*' is always mentioned, because it is a genuine, feel good factor movie.'

'There are undercurrents of hope and freedom, in the story, as we see there's a better life in store for someone like 'Andy', who was wrongfully convicted.'

Hazel noticed Josephine's hand slightly raised, she loved when her students participated in class.

'Josephine, do you want to say something?' she asked.

'Yes please, I actually know that quote very well,' and I use it to motivate myself, on the days I am feeling lazy and unmotivated.'

'I remind myself to; '*Get Busy Living or Get Busy Dying,* and thankfully it works every time, it stops my procrastinating, and I get on with life.'

'Yes Josephine, they are powerful, motivational words which can have wonderful results, if we heed them,' Hazel agreed.

'We see that the characters in the 'Shawshank Redemption' are well rounded and very interesting, for instance; 'We have the cynical, 'Red', the innocent 'Andy', and the crooked warden, 'Norton'.'

'Please, ensure the characters in your next assignment are even stronger and more interesting than before, so the reader can relate to them, perhaps, they may even have tattoos or distinctive physical features.'

Hazel was really trying to encourage her three students to elaborate more on Conor's personality and his heart tattoo, to help her decide, if it was the same man.

'I would suggest that, you check in your local library, for 'The Shawshank Redemption' book or movie, and you will enjoy the witty pun on words.'

'It will give you taste of excellent writing, because 'King' tells the story in a magnificent way, with lots of humour and puns on words, and he shows the tough side of prison life so well, and so dramatically, but there are lots of sprinkles of hope too.'

'It's a serious subject, but because of the wit, it takes the darkness from the situation, and it makes you curious and interested to know, what happens next.'

Hazel continued; 'The superb description by 'King' and the music from the movie, never ceases to captivate me, and it still gives me goose bumps!'

'Watch out for the power of the melodious opera music, and the deep satisfaction, 'Andy' gets from sharing it, at his own peril, with his fellow prisoners, it's truly magnificent. It's just a single scene, an opera song floating in the air, but it has an incredible charming effect on the prisoners' minds and souls.'

'The opera scene embodies the spirit of the film's story of hope, when 'Andy' locks himself in the prison office, and plays a record of 'Duettino – 'Sull'aria', a duet from one of Mozart's most popular operas; 'The Marriage of Figaro'.

'Andy' plays the music over the loudspeakers, to spread hope, and freedom to his fellow prisoner, thus creating a sense of peace, and exhilaration in the prison yard.'

'Red' says; *'For the briefest moment every last man in Shawshank Prison, felt free.'*

'What an amazing description of how the music affected the prisoners, it was so beautiful it touched their hearts, and for a short time, it gave them a glimpse of freedom and the good in the world.'

Hazel decided she would try not think or worry about her discovery until she had further evidence, by giving her students this assignment, she would discover more about the man 'Conor', and if her instinct was right, she would contact her three students.

She dragged her thoughts back to reality and began telling the students about her favourite writers.

Hazel's favourite authors were; 'Maeve Binchy', an Irish author, 'Neil Gaiman', an English author, and 'John Grisham', an American author.

She constantly referred to their style of writing and their books, in her creative writing classes.

She always emphasised that; 'You don't need to use big words, or complicated scripts to be a good writer. Using simple words, making the story interesting, exciting and believable can actually create the best books.'

'Binchy', 'Gaiman' and 'Grisham,' brought many hours of joy to

Hazel's life; she constantly read and re-read their works, even though they were works of 'Fiction', she thought they were full of gems of wisdom, and wit, and true to life in many ways.

An amazing quote from 'Neil Gaiman' Hazel used quite often in her classes was;

'A book is a dream, you hold in your hand.'

She told her students; 'I love that description, as every author, dreams of becoming a writer, and when they finally hold their book in their hands, 'it's a dream come true'.'

'You too can dream and be successful, and I know, that one day you'll hold your book/dream in your hand, it takes lots of hard work, research and months or maybe years of dedication, but it's all worth it in the end, when your dream finally comes true.'

Hazel also told her class about a great quote from Maeve Binchy, in which she said;

'I have always believed, life is too short for rows, and disagreements. Even if I think I'm right, I prefer to apologize and remain friends, rather than win and be an enemy.'

'I know I am biased, where 'Maeve Binchy' is concerned, but I do think that's an amazing insight into living a good, kind life.'

'If we could all be as amiable as Maeve, wouldn't life be so peaceful and less exhausting, don't you think?' Hazel asked her students.

Clodagh who appeared to be one of life's rebels said, with attitude;

'I think life would be very boring, if we all acted that way, there would be no room for debates in life, and it would be impossible to get what we want in life. It's like turning the other cheek, just to be friends with someone, who probably doesn't even appreciate your friendship.'

'I know if someone hit me on the cheek, I most certainly wouldn't turn my other cheek, and they would need to run really fast, as I would be hot on their heels,' Clodagh said looking ready and willing to do battle.

Attempting to keep the peace Hazel tried to explain what she thought,

'Maeve Binchy' was actually saying.

'I think 'Binchy' meant when you realise you definitely won't win the argument, it's wiser to give in gracefully, than to lose a friend.'

'It doesn't actually mean that you always have to be a 'Yes Woman', or a 'Yes Man' when you know it's a losing battle, just give in gracefully, and peace will be restored.'

Clodagh quickly responded; 'You also have to protect yourself, and not become a doormat for people. People will try to manipulate you, if they get the chance.'

'I take your point, Clodagh.'

Hazel tried not to smile; she just couldn't picture Clodagh, ever allowing anyone, to make a doormat of her, it certainly would take a very brave person to attempt, to take on Clodagh.

Hazel passed around some handouts on her favourite authors;

'For anyone who is not familiar with 'Maeve Binchy', I will give you a brief history of her life.'

'Maeve Binchy' was born in 1940 in Co Dublin and sadly she died in 2012. She was a wonderful Irish novelist, a playwright, a short story writer, a columnist, and an orator.'

'She was best known for her sensitive and witty portrayal, of life in Ireland, and she wrote with honesty, and she had a wonderful flair for words, which portrayed happiness and sadness in her novels. Her clever way with words made her a wonderful storyteller.'

'When asked who influenced her as a writer?' Maeve said;

'I write exactly as I speak, so therefore I wouldn't say any writer influenced me at all.'

'I admired that honest, fascinating reply. Maeve always came across as a very self-confident person, who believed in her own abilities, her strengths and powers. She didn't seem burdened at all by self doubt, or low self-esteem, which a lot of writers and artists seem to suffer from,' Hazel commented.

'When asked if she had any regrets Maeve said;'

'Happiness is in our own hearts. I have no regrets on anything in the past; I'm totally cheerful and happy. I think that a lot of your attitude is not in the circumstances you find yourself in, but in the circumstances you make for yourself.'

'That's an amazing legacy to leave to the world; 'Joy and happiness, and no regrets',' Hazel said proudly.

'Not many of us can say; we have no regrets and yet it's a very healthy way, of looking at life. Maeve was an incredible author and an awe-inspiring person, and she is sadly missed, but we are lucky, we still have the pleasure and the memories of her wonderful books and movies, and her amazing wisdom and kindness.'

'We will now discuss the wonderful author 'Neil Gaiman.'

'Has anyone heard of him?' Hazel asked.

Hazel was delighted and surprised to see, nearly half the class had their hands up.

'Well, for those of you who don't know him, I'll summarise his life and his works, and I hope you too will become a 'Gaiman fan.'

'Neil Gaiman' was born in the United Kingdom in 1960, and he now lives in America.'

'As a child he discovered his love of books, devouring the works of 'C.S. Lewis'. He has dedicated most of his life to writing, creating favourites like the comic book series, '*The Sandman*' and also many wonderful novels.

'Would you believe; 'Gaiman' spent much of his childhood in libraries?' Hazel said.

'I can relate to that story,' Ben said. My parents were so busy running their own business; they hadn't time to look after me, and they couldn't afford a child minder, so they shipped me off to the local library.'

'I feel privileged because I had such an amazing childhood, surrounded by wonderful books, which inspired me to become a librarian, a job I absolutely love. Throughout my life, I have met the most remarkable people, and I still meet fascinating people every day, in our library.'

'That sounds like an incredible life, surrounded by books, and meeting interesting, intellectual people. No doubt, you'll have lots of wonderful material for your short stories, and novels in the future. With such a rich background, you are blessed, and I look forward to reading your interesting stories, you will certainly identify with 'Gaiman's' life story,' Hazel said smiling.

'Thanks for the notes you gave us on 'Gaiman, I haven't actually read his life story. I would love to meet him some day, and share our unique childhood stories. I have never met anyone, with a similar adolescence to mine,' Ben said.

'I know you will enjoy 'Gaiman's' story, and I am sure you will see lots of similarities, for instance 'Gaiman' said;

'I had the kind of parents who could be persuaded to drop me off in the library, on their way to work during summer holidays, and the kind of librarians who did not mind a small, unaccompanied boy, heading into their children's library every morning.'

'Gaiman's story is quite fascinating, he found himself giving advice to people who were graduating from higher education, yet he hadn't graduated himself, as he had found school life stifling.'

'Gaiman's' philosophy on writing well is; 'Find your own unique voice, develop original ideas, and inject life into your characters.'

'He emphasised how important it was to develop and study your characters, and make them exciting and interesting, like real people, which the reader can then relate to.'

Hazel didn't want to overload her students with too many facts about her favourite authors, so she suggested a short break.

'After break, we will discuss another of my favourite authors, the most wonderful legal guru, 'John Grisham.' This writer is a total gem, for anyone who is interested in thrillers and the law.'

After break, Hazel informed her students; 'Grisham's books are full of exciting twists and turns, a total joy for the avid reader. When we have studied his works, I will be amazed if anyone has the audacity to tell me, they don't enjoy the thrill of 'Grisham's' writing and his exhilarating, superb storytelling.'

'For those of you who haven't read 'Grisham', shame on you, I am just joking, as you may have already guessed, I am extremely biased.'

'I really enjoy stories about the law, but even if I didn't, 'Grisham's' writing is so easy to understand and his stories flow so magnificently, you want to rush from chapter to chapter, yet you want to prolong the enjoyment, and the excitement. You'll want to savour each intricate twist and turn he creates so splendidly.'

'Please indulge me, while I tell you a little about the life of 'John Grisham.' He is an American novelist, attorney, politician and an activist, he is best known for his popular legal thrillers. He was born in Jonesboro, Arkansas, USA, in 1955.'

'I am sure most of you, have seen some of 'Grisham's' brilliant movies, for example;

'A Time to Kill, The Rainmaker, The Firm, The Pelican Brief, The Client, The Chamber, Runaway Jury and many more, too numerous to mention.'

'When Grisham was asked; 'why did you leave your legal profession, and start writing?'

'He explained that during a trial in 1984, he heard the horrific details of a young girl, who had survived a rape. This prompted him to start writing a novel which examined the issues of rape, focusing on the actions of a fictional father, and an attorney, and the book was, *'A Time to Kill.'*

A famous quote by 'Grisham' is;

'There's always such a rush to judgment, it makes a fair trial, hard to get.'

'Did anyone see the movie, *'A Time to Kill'* or read the novel?'

'I read the novel first, then I saw the movie, and I really appreciated how well 'Grisham' dealt with that sensitive issue,' Patricia said.

Hazel noticed, before Patricia got a chance to talk further on the movie, Clodagh interrupted.

'I saw the movie too and even though it was sad, it was an excellent movie,' said Clodagh.'

'Can you recall what it was about?' Hazel asked her.

'Yes, it was so skilfully told, I don't think I'll ever forget it.'

'The movie begins with the rape of a ten year old black girl, and at the court hearing, the father of the child kills the two rapists, and a deputy is accidently shot and crippled.'

'A white lawyer takes on the case, defending the father of the child, and he is treated badly and his house is burnt down by the 'Ku Klux Klan', (KKK), which was a white supremacist hate group, whose prime target was black African Americans. But thankfully, good triumphs over bad and the father is acquitted.'

'Thanks Clodagh, that's an excellent summary.'

Hazel was amused to see that Clodagh was actually delighted when praised, as she pretended to be tough, but she had a soft side, and like everyone she enjoyed praise.

'It was very brave of 'Grisham' to tackle such a hot topic, as it touched upon two very sensitive subjects; 'Rape' and 'Whites vs. Blacks' in America.'

'That's the wonderful thing about writing, whether it's 'Fiction' or 'Non-Fiction', you can tackle any injustice in the world, by highlighting any issues.'

'Writing is a wonderful tool, so use it well, and enjoy the gift you have,' Hazel said proudly.

'Would you believe, the day after 'Grisham' finished writing, '*A Time to Kill*', he began working on another novel?'

'It was the wonderful, story of a young attorney, lured to what seemed to be a prestigious, perfect law firm, but he soon discovers a dark sinister side to the firm.'

'Does anyone know the name of the book?' Hazel asked.

Patricia said; 'Yes, it's 'The Firm', and I would highly recommend the book and the movie to everyone.'

'Thanks Patricia, I thoroughly agree with your recommendation,' Hazel said.

'Grisham' writes for the ordinary person, and his writing is very clear and concise, and you don't need a law degree to understand his books. You won't get lost or confused, and unlike some authors, you won't find yourself having to re-read passages to understand the novel,' Hazel said.

'Having observed my three favourite writers 'Binchy', 'Gaiman' and 'Grisham', we see from their three different styles, what suits one person, may not suit another.'

'So please, find your own path, and be brave and believe in yourself. If you want to become a writer, you will become one; it means lots of hard work, research, discipline and dedication, but believe me, you'll find great joy in return.'

'When you see your first short story, or you first novel published, you will experience an amazing sense of achievement.'

'We all aspire to write the best short story, the best play or the best novel, but always remember when writing; 'The type of book readers love, are from writers who write from their heart, and writers whose story is so captivating, that the reader doesn't want to put down the book,' Hazel said excitedly.

'I am really looking forward, to reading all your wonderful, unique short stories,' Hazel said excitedly.

'Yes Ben, did you want to say something?'

'I just wanted to say, I admire 'Oprah Winfrey', and I would like to recommend her latest book; 'The Path Made Clear'.'

'It's about discovering 'Your Life's Direction and Purpose'.'

'It guides, encourages and inspires the reader to discover not only who you are, but who you are meant to be. If you feel unsure of what you want in life, this book helps you discover, and inspires you to find, and live your dream.'

'We have numerous copies in the library, if people are interested in acquiring a copy.'

'Many thanks for that recommendation Ben. I also read Oprah's book, and I would highly recommend it, to you all.'

'Coincidentally, I had intended to discuss '*Oprah Winfrey*' next week, as she is another person who inspired me to write, and made me believe, I was capable of being a writer,' Hazel said.

'We will discuss her now,' Hazel said excitedly as she got her notes ready.

'A reporter once said; 'It's difficult to begin listing the extraordinary accomplishments of 'Oprah Winfrey' without running short of breath.'

'I think that's how most people feel about 'Winfrey', she has accomplished so much in life, and she's a true inspiration to people throughout the world, both female and male.'

'Winfrey' is an amazing woman, who has great belief in herself and in people, and she gives generously of her time, especially to women, sorry guys, 'Girl Power' here.'

'I don't mean to be sexist, but we need people like 'Winfrey' on our side, as unfortunately, women are still not treated equal to men in society.'

'Please indulge me, while I give you a brief outline of Oprah's life. She was born in Mississippi, USA, in 1954, to a teenage single mother, 'Vernita Lee.' Until the age of six, Oprah lived with her grandmother, and then she was sent to live with her father, 'Vernon Winfrey', a coal miner, who lived in Nashville, Tennessee.'

'In my eyes, she's an amazing strong, determined, yet very kind lady, and an inspiration to us all. She was abused and raped throughout her young life, yet she was never bitter, and she never allowed her past dictate, or define who she was. She flourished in school, and she excelled in speech and drama, and she even won a full scholarship to 'Tennessee State University.'

'Her first formal role came in 1985, was her performance as Sofia in 'The Color Purple', *which* won her an Oscar nomination for 'Best Supporting Actress.' She has also appeared in the films, *'Beloved'*, *'The Butler'*, and *'Selma.'*

'Yes Patricia.'

'I think 'Oprah Winfrey' is an inspiration to us all, there is nothing she can't do and she is so kind to everybody, and so modest about her endless talents. When she interviews people, she always gets the best out of them. In my opinion she is the most amazing woman ever.'

'I totally agree with you, she is certainly an inspiration to me too.'

'Winfrey' hosted the highest rated television show in the US, '*The Oprah Winfrey Show,*' for 25 years. She has her own glossy magazine, 'O', 'The Oprah Magazine', and she runs a television network called, 'OWN'.

'Winfrey' is the richest African, American and she is the first and only black multi-billionaire in America. She is also a hugely important humanitarian, and she is regularly referred to, without any exaggeration, as one of the most powerful and influential women in the world.'

'That's an amazing achievement, a wonderful legacy to have, don't you think?' Hazel asked.

'Yes,' Clodagh and Patricia said in unison, and Hazel was glad to see, they smiled at each other.

Patricia said; 'Another area which 'Winfrey' is well known for, is her superb 'Oprah's Book Club.' I believe the endorsement of a book by 'Oprah's Book Club' can actually send it straight to the bestsellers list, which is a wonderful achievement for the author, and for the book club. In our book club, we always check the 'Oprah's Book Club' suggestions and recommendations, and we always enjoy the books they recommend.'

'Thanks Patricia that's great, I would encourage you all to follow 'Oprah's Book Club' recommendations.'

'Here are some quotes from 'the great lady herself,' which coincidently, I had compiled for next week's class, but we can enjoy them now.'

Rebecca, would you please, pass them around.'

'Yes, certainly,' said Rebecca, loving the fact that she was the chosen one.

Marissa smiled, as she knew Rebecca loved being the centre of attention, just as much, as Marissa avoided it.

'Now, let's have a look at some of Oprah's quotes:

'Embrace your uniqueness. You are different, your gift is special, own it and unapologetically share it with the world.'

- Oprah Winfrey

'My idea was to tell stories that affected the human spirit, stories people could see themselves in.'

- Oprah Winfrey

But my favourite inspirational quote from the great lady is;

'With every experience, you alone are painting your own canvas, thought by thought, choice by choice.'

- Oprah Winfrey

'If we examine this quote of 'Oprah's, we see that every experience we have is part of our canvas, and if we do positive things, then we are indeed painting a beautiful, peaceful, fulfilling canvas for ourselves as 'Winfrey' emphasised.'

'My advice to you is; 'If you want to write that novel, you alone can make it happen, by the words, thoughts and choices you make in life, you paint your own canvas, as 'Oprah,' stated so eloquently. So start with small steps, and write your short story assignment, and I hope you enjoy writing it,' Hazel said proudly to her diligent students.

Chapter 24

Susan could still vividly remember that dreadful day, the day the letter arrived, which changed her life and her Mum's forever.

She had never seen her Mum so devastated and so out of control, her Mum had always appeared calm, and in control of life.

Susan noticed as her Mum was reading the letter, she had turned whiter than white, and she suddenly screamed loudly, and fell to the kitchen floor.

The tears poured down her face, as if the flood gates of heaven had suddenly opened, and she had lost all control.

Susan was shocked at her Mum's actions, as she had never seen her act so crazy.

'Mum, what's going on?'

'What's happening?'

She tried to uncurl her Mum's fingers from the letter, but they appeared to be stuck like glue to the page.

'Please Mum, you are frightening me.'

'Let me see what's in the letter.'

'Has someone we know died suddenly?'

Finally, her Mum spoke angrily.

'No, but I wish he was dead.'

'What are you talking about Mum?'

'Please, let me read the letter.'

Her Mum was sobbing uncontrollably, as she finally let go of the letter.

'Here read it, yourself,' she said sobbing loudly.

Susan took the letter, and her hands were actually shaking as she began to read, she felt that whatever was in the letter would change her life, and not for the better.

Dear Alma,

I am so sorry, I really wish things didn't have to be this way, but I can't stay in our marriage any longer, believe me it's nothing you did wrong.

I don't want to hurt either you, or Susan, but I've been thinking about this for a long time, and I just cannot continue to live, as I have been doing. I would like a Divorce, and I hope we can do it amiably, for Susan's sake.

I feel, it's time we went our separate ways, I need to be by myself, as I felt I was suffocating.

I am really sorry for the pain I am causing you, and Susan, but believe me; it's not easy for me either.

I thought we would be together forever, but then things changed for me, I have been missing Kate so much lately; I can't cope with the pain.

I now realise, I didn't take enough time to heal after Kate's death, and I rushed into our marriage. I now need time and space alone, to sort out my life.

Please forgive me. You and Susan truly deserve the best in life; I just can't be part of your life anymore.

Please know that I do love you, and Susan, and a part of me always will.

Conor

After the initial shock of Conor's letter, Alma dusted herself off, and tried to get on with life, for Susan's sake. She had known that 'Divorce' was inevitable, but when she saw it in the letter she realised the finality of it, perhaps, part of her had hoped that Conor would return.

She had always tried to look at the positives in life, and felt proud of herself, and her beautiful daughter Susan, as they had survived Conor's abrupt departure, with strength and dignity. They had dealt with all life's traumas like warriors, but Alma recalled the worst situations they had faced was; 'the Divorce letter', and 'the hair incident'.

Alma sadly recalled how Conor had always admired her dark glossy hair, and he loved to run his fingers through it. She had inherited her beautiful, shoulder length, dark, glossy hair from her Mum. It was her pride and joy, and the hairdressers always commented on how beautiful and healthy it looked.

She remembered smiling and saying to Conor, when he had admired her hair.

'I am so lucky to have nice hair; thankfully it's in our genes.'

She wasn't being boastful or cocky; she just appreciated her good hair genes.

'My Mum, and her Mum, and probably her Great Gran have all been blessed with beautiful, glossy, dark hair, and thankfully Susan has too.'

'Ah! go easy on me, my hair isn't that bad.' Conor had said laughingly.

As Susan grew older she still allowed Alma to brush her hair, and they had lovely chats during that special time.

God only knows what would have happened, if Susan hadn't inherited the good hair gene.

Alma now recalled, when Conor had deserted them, the worst part was the loneliness, the sadness, and poor baby Susan felt it too.

Years later, when the 'Divorce' went through, she struggled but she put on a brave face for Susan's benefit. She knew that Susan missed having a Dad, and that she struggled when she was with her friends and their parents.

Then the unthinkable happened, after the Divorce, when Susan began to lose her beautiful dark glossy hair.

At first, it was just small strands of hair on the pillow and on her hairbrush, and then it was larger clumps. Susan was so upset, she didn't want to go to school, she felt embarrassed because of the bald patches.

Alma brought Susan to Dr Morris, and he informed them, that

sometimes shock or trauma can cause hair loss.

Dr Morris asked Alma discreetly; 'Have there been any changes in Susan's life recently?'

Alma didn't feel like explaining to Dr Morris, the extreme trauma and shock which Conor's desertion and divorce had caused poor Susan, who really missed having a Dad.

Alma said very quietly to him;

'Susan's Dad and I got divorced recently, and she's upset.'

Dr Morris, said calmly; 'Trauma like that can cause 'Alopecia', but don't worry it can be cured, it is only temporary.'

'Thankfully, there are cures for almost everything in life,' he said smiling at Susan.

'Not for 'a broken heart', there is 'no cure', Alma felt like saying.

She shrugged her shoulders to lose the self pity, and instead she said rather firmly;

'Well Dr Morris, what do you suggest?'

'What plan do we follow now?' she asked with such positivity and determination that, Susan smiled lovingly at her.

'Well ladies, let's all work together and get this sorted.'

Susan's face lit up immediately, and Alma was delighted to see the glow back, on Susan's pretty face.

'Firstly, I will do a few tests, and then we'll make a plan.'

Dr Morris proceeded to explain, in lay man terms, the type of tests and how the results would determine, the reason for the hair loss.

'I will do a blood test first. A 'blood test' helps to uncover any medical conditions related to hair loss.'

'I will also do 'A Pull' test, where I gently pull dozens of hairs to see how many come out. This will help determine the stage of the shedding process, and I promise I won't hurt you Susan,' he said very gently.

'Then I will do 'A Scalp Biopsy'. I will scrape samples from a few hairs, which I will pluck from the scalp, and I will examine the hair roots.

This will allow me to determine, whether an infection is causing your hair loss.'

'And finally I will do 'A Light Microscopy', in which I will use a special instrument to examine hairs trimmed at their bases. Microscopy will help me uncover any possible disorders of the hair shaft.'

'Are you both agreeable to begin those tests?' he asked.

'That sounds good, Dr Morris,' Alma said looking encouragingly at Susan.

'Is that okay with you Susan?' he asked.

'Yes please, I want to get my hair sorted before it gets any worse.'

'Don't worry we'll sort it out,' Dr Morris said emphatically.

Dr Morris explained; 'I think it's probably, 'Alopecia areata', which is an autoimmune condition. The immune system is the body's natural defence system, which helps protect it from infections caused by bacteria and viruses.'

'I don't understand, why didn't Susan's immune system kill the infection?' Alma asked.

Alma was sorry she asked the question, when she saw Susan's shocked expression.

'Usually, the immune system attacks the cause of an infection, but in the case of 'alopecia areata', unfortunately it damages the hair follicles instead.'

'But the good news is the hair follicles are not permanently damaged, and the hair normally grows back within a few months.'

Tears came to Susan's eyes and she said;

'Will my hair continue to fall out in clumps, or can tablets stop that happening?'

'Will my hair grow back fully and cover the bald patches?'

Susan bent her head, to show Dr Morris, a few small bald patches.

'Don't worry; we will do our best to sort out the problem. Thankfully you have strong, thick, beautiful hair and you also have good genes, therefore we should be very successful in solving the problem.'

'Will I have to take tablets for the rest of my life?' she moaned.

'No, you won't,' Dr Morris smiled kindly.

'Please, try not to worry, as that may slow down the process,' he emphasised.

Alma was so grateful to Dr Morris, for his tactful manner and his kindness to Susan. She had always known he was a true gentleman; he had a very gentle, kind manner to young and old patients. She had never heard anyone say a bad word about him; he most certainly was one of the good guys.

'A little kindness goes a long way on the road to recovery, and after the massive shock of Conor's final departure, Susan deserved lots of kindness,' Alma thought.

Dr Morris continued to explain in lay man's terms, what he thought the problem and the solution would be, without talking down to Alma or Susan.

'If it is 'Alopecia', there is an over the counter medication, which comes as a liquid or a foam which you rub into your scalp every day, to start the hair re-growth.'

'We will discuss the situation further, when all the tests are completed.'

Like all mothers, Alma was now determined to sort out poor Susan's hair loss, as quickly as possible. Since Conor had abandoned them, she had taken on the role of both parents, and she always tried to be brave for Susan's sake. She knew she had to pick up the pieces, and get on with life without Conor.

Alma was determined to put on a brave front for Susan, as she had been through a lot, with her Dad's desertion and divorce, and now her hair loss. She intended to be with her beautiful daughter every step of the way, on the road, to sorting out her hair problem.

True to his word, Dr Morris called Alma with the results.

'As I thought, unfortunately it is 'Alopecia', but we know what to do, and we'll get the problem sorted for Susan. My secretary will text you the details of the over the counter medication, which you can get in your local chemist.'

'I'll see you and Susan here next week, and I'll phone you during the week, to see how things are progressing.'

'Thank you Dr Morris, for all your kindness and support to Susan, I'll get the medication today, and I'll talk to you during the week.'

Susan used the medicine daily, for a few months and eventually her hair stopped falling out. She was so lucky; it actually grew back as thick and as glossy as it always was. Alma was delighted to see, the light come back into Susan's eyes and her confidence begin to grow again.

On their last appointment with Dr Morris, Susan actually gave him a big 'Thank you hug.' Alma knew it was a big deal for Susan, as she wasn't into hugging since her Dad's total abondment.

When Alma was struggling and trying to console Susan when she looked for her Dad, she used good advice, she had overheard at the school gates.

A Mum was holding her son by the hand, and he seemed quite upset, and she bent down and said;

'Son life isn't always fair, but you just have to deal with it. We will get through this together, you are not alone.'

Over the years Alma had used that good advice, when helping Susan stay positive, and while trying to remain strong and positive herself. She totally understood that the woman was encouraging her son, to be strong and positive in life, no matter what people said or did to him. She had reminded him that she would always be there for him, as all wonderful mothers' were.

It had reminded Alma of her Dad's wise words, which she found very helpful throughout her life;

'Sticks and stones will break your bones, but names will never hurt.'

Her Dad had explained to her when she was being bullied in school; 'No matter what people say it can't really hurt you, as they are only silly words.'

'It's physical things like sticks and stones that hurt, not words.'

'He had emphasised to her numerous times; 'You must always rise above it, and ignore the hurtful things people say, as it's usually their insecurities and their problems, and it's nothing to do with you.'

'They are the ones who feel insecure, and you must be strong and let their silly, hurtful words wash over you.'

'Don't let them hurt you, like sticks and stones can hurt.'

Alma knew her Dad's advice was good; he was a very wise man, and she always tried to live by that motto, and she tried her utmost to ensure Susan did too.

Alma had no time for the people who felt;

'Bullying toughens you up for life, and it's good for you'

She felt that by portraying 'bullying' as a positive thing; it then enabled the bullies to always win.

Throughout her life, Alma had seen numerous situations where people were bullied, and had lost their ability to enjoy life. They had lost confidence in themselves and their abilities, because of the bullies' torments, and sometimes it even caused people to commit suicide.

Alma was determined that bullying, would never happen to Susan, as long as she was alive.

When Conor had deserted them, Alma always took time out to chat with Susan. She knew Susan was struggling, and some of her 'so called friends' had been constantly teasing her.

'You don't have a Dad, he disappeared and deserted you, and your Mum.'

Alma had explained to Susan numerous times;

'It's nothing to do with you as a person. It's their own fear of maybe losing their Dad, which makes them say cruel things; it's their problem and their fear of the future.'

'Don't let it get inside your head, brush it off, throw it over your shoulder and stay positive, loving and carefree, like the beautiful person you are.'

'It's their fear and don't forget, it's one less fear you have, as it has already happened to you.'

Susan would smile, feeling comforted and loved and she would say; 'I know you are right Mum, but some days it's hard to listen to their hurtful teasing.'

'Remember, I told you, what your Granda would say,' Alma said.

'Sticks and stones will break your bones, but names will never hurt,' they would say loudly, in unison.

Alma would then hug and tickle Susan and they would giggle, it was their way of dealing with a tough situation. They had become experts at looking at the flip side of life. They stood strongly together, and faced life head on, no matter what happened.

Lots of Alma's friends had turbulent and frustrating relationships with their children. Alma was eternally grateful, that she and Susan bonded so well.

So many things had happened in their life, but they always rallied through, Alma felt they were now invincible.

In the beginning, when Conor left, Alma found sleep impossible, as her mind was racing; trying to figure out what went wrong with her marriage. She told her friend Maeve, who suggested 'Blackout Curtains'. She took her friends advice and she purchased lovely pink and green, cheerful blackout curtains.

Thankfully, Maeve was right, the curtains had improved her quality of sleep, but unfortunately, they weren't a miracle cure. She knew it would take time for her to mind and body to heal, and hopefully she would eventually get a decent night's sleep.

After Conor's desertion, Alma had felt very lethargic in the mornings, and she tried hard to motivate herself. It took a lot of deep breathing, and calming exercises to put her in a positive mood, before she went downstairs to face Susan, and another day without Conor, the man who vowed to be by her side; 'Until death us do part.'

She had vowed to try her utmost to live life to the fullest, even under the dreadful circumstances, and she wouldn't let life slip through her fingers, like grains of sand.

Her late Mum had always reminded her;

'You only get one chance at life so take it with both hands, treasure it, and try to enjoy every second.'

Alma's Mum was a very positive person, and she tried her best, to pass on those lovely qualities to her daughter. Alma appreciated the advice her Mum gave her, and it certainly helped on the tough days, and boy, there were lots of those lately.

Alma's Mum had lived by a wonderful quote; 'Sometimes acceptance can mean; if you find a large boulder blocking your path, and you can't move it or break it up, then you just walk around it and continue your journey. That's usually more effective than standing there staring, and moaning about it.'

When Alma noticed Susan worrying about things, she reminded her of her Mum's wonderful advice, and it usually put a smile on Susan's face. Alma and Susan noticed, they found the solution to their problems quickly, when they stopped panicking and chose a different path, as Alma's Mum had suggested.

Susan often heard her Mum quote in Irish;

'Níl aon tinteán mar do thinteán féin.'

Her Irish wasn't the best, so she asked her Mum what it meant.

She could have used 'Google' search, but she preferred her Mum to explain it, in her own lovely, flowery words.

Susan was so proud of her Mum, and she felt so lucky, they both respected and enjoyed each other's company. Her Mum was an excellent 'Primary School Teacher' and she was fluent in Irish, but she was an all rounder, as she was brilliant at English and Maths too.

Susan thought there was no end to her Mum's amazing talents and knowledge, but what she loved most about her Mum was she was very modest and unassuming, which added to her lovely warm personality.

Unfortunately, not many of Susan's friends had the same good luck, some of her close friends came from abusive backgrounds and years later, they were still attending psychologists. Thankfully they were no longer in their abusive situations, and they were going through the healing process, and moving on with their lives.

Her Mum very patiently explained what the proverb meant;

'There's no fireside like your own fireside.'

'This proverb reminds us of the importance of having a good home, where there is peace and warmth.'

She continued to explain; 'It literally means; 'There's no hearth like your own hearth.'

'Thanks, Mum, I feel ashamed, I have forgotten a lot of lovely the Irish Proverbs.

'I presume you don't mean 'heart', you mean 'hearth'.'

'Exactly, it means the fireside or the hearth of the home, where families come together, to relax.'

It's really saying; 'There's no place like home.'

'That's so true, Mum, I am so lucky to have such a wonderful home,' Susan smilingly agreed.

Alma was the proudest Mum in the world, when Susan graduated from University with 1st Class Honours, and when she later became a 'Family Law Solicitor.'

She felt so lucky to have reared such an amazing, wonderful daughter.

Chapter 25

When Hazel read the second short story assignments, it was quite obvious Paul, Patricia and Susan were describing the same person Conor, who was their Dad, and yet they didn't seem to know each other.

Jim and Grace had also confirmed her fears, and Grace firmly believed that Conor was the same person, and therefore the father of the three students.

'Are you sure, they don't know each other?' Grace asked.

'I am nearly a hundred percent sure, they don't, judging by their body language.'

'I'll have to talk to them individually first, and then as a group,' Hazel said.

Hazel knew she must handle the delicate, remarkable situation, professionally and sensitively.

The secretary gave her Paul, Patricia and Susan's mobile numbers, and she gave each of them an appointment time before class.

She didn't want to upset them so she just said; 'I am just having an informal chat with some of my students,' and thankfully they didn't question it.

After speaking to them all, she would ask if they were willing to meet as a group, after class. She would then show them their assignments, and let them see how alike they were, and how much they all enjoyed their holiday with their Dad, Conor, with the 'Heart Tattoo.'

Hazel wasn't surprised at how shocked Paul, Patricia and Susan were, when she told them individually, what she had discovered. Thankfully, they all agreed to meet her after class, where she produced their assignments as evidence, of 'Conor's triple life', they extremely upset and shocked.

She gave them time to talk and read each other's assignments. When she returned she noticed that Paul was extremely angry, and the girls were very disappointed with Conor, but they didn't seem as angry.

They informed Hazel, that they planned to meet Conor, and confront him as a group, about his secrets and lies, and his triple family life.

Hazel offered them her support, and Patricia thanked her, and said they would keep her informed.

Her newly found extended family had elected Patricia to make the phone call to Conor. She phoned him and asked him if he would meet her Saturday at 11am, for a coffee and a chat, Conor seemed pleased, and said he looked forward to seeing her.

'Thankfully, he doesn't he know what's ahead of him or he would cancel,' Patricia thought with some misgivings.

She was happy he hadn't a clue, what secrets were about to unfold, and unravel in front of his, lying eyes, as the three of them confronted him on Saturday.

On the Friday, they met in a cafe in Dublin, to discuss their strategy, on how to ruin Conor's life, they way he had ruined theirs.

They tried to appear calm, but it was obvious there were lots of mixed feelings, in particular feelings of hurt and anger.

But when it came down to the crunch, it seemed the girls were more forgiving and more lenient towards Conor, and Paul felt rather angry and disappointed.

'What happened, to the original plan we discussed?' he asked angrily.

'That was in the heat of the moment, and maybe we were too harsh,' Patricia said.

'Well, it's easy for you to be so forgiving, you weren't fed lies and secrets like we were,' Paul said angrily.

'We feel the same as Patricia,' Alma and Susan said quietly.

'We had planned to let the media, and Conor's clients know what a liar and cheat, he is. He has lied to us for years, so he's definitely capable of telling lies to his clients also,' Paul said heatedly.

'In hindsight, we feel that it's only fair, to listen to Conor's side of the story first. Then we can decide what measures we want to take,' Patricia said kindly.

'Confucius' said; *'Before you begin on the journey of revenge, dig two graves.'* Patricia said.

'Who the hell is 'Confusion?'

'Stop being silly, it's 'Confucius',' Patricia said. She was beginning to lose patience with Paul, as he was always grumpy.

'I honestly don't know what you are talking about,' Paul said angrily.

'Confucius' was a Chinese Philosopher, who believed human beings were fundamentally good and teachable. He also established ethical, moral, and social standards, which formed the basis of a way of life known as 'Confucianism.'

'He put emphasis on personal and governmental morality, the correctness of social relationships, and justice, kindness, and sincerity.'

'Well, then I rest my case, 'Confusion', sorry, 'Confucius' wouldn't have approved of Conor's abandonment, and his deceitful, secret lifestyle, and insincerity,' Paul emphasised.

'I am not saying that 'Confucius' would have endorsed Conor's way of life, but he certainly wouldn't have recommended or approved of revenge.'

'He thought, by seeking revenge *you* might not only destroy, the person you are revenging, but also yourself. He felt that with forgiveness and time, the hurt would fade.'

'Well, then he's a better man than me,' Paul said angrily, as he hurriedly left the café.

'See you tomorrow, hopefully hearing Conor's side of the story, will help you to forgive and heal,' Patricia said softly.

Chapter 26

Conor needed all his concentration to focus on his driving, because of the dreadful weather conditions.

Oh my God! Met Éireann had been so right, he now wished he had heeded their advice and stayed at home. Foolishly he had gone grocery shopping, which wasn't even urgent, as he had food in the fridge and freezer; he certainly wouldn't have died of starvation, if he had waited until the storm passed.

'Typical me, I am always doing my own thing in life, and I am always pushing the boundaries, and putting myself under pointless pressure.'

'I made this totally unnecessary trip, which could end, in a life or death situation,' he thought irritably.

He tried to see the funny side of things to calm himself, but the only thing that made him happy; was the thoughts of reaching home safely, and hibernating until the storm passed.

It really was a terrible night, the worst driving conditions he could ever remember. As soon as the wipers pushed the rain away, more torrential rain came flooding onto the windscreen. Even the wipers were struggling, and they began to make weird, creaking noises. He found himself leaning forward and squinting to see the road ahead, but all he could see was the pouring rain.

He pressed his face even closer to the windscreen, but he barely saw the road. He was driving so slowly now, he realised he would be quicker walking, but unfortunately he would be drenched in two seconds. He continued driving very slowly, as he knew it would be impossible to walk against the combination of the strong, stormy, wild winds, and the torrential rain.

He noticed a black, blanket of darkness covering the sky and it was becoming more difficult to see, as all the lights were now dimmed by the bucketing rain. He knew he wasn't too far from home, and he was hoping against hope, he would get there safely.

It was the type of weather people stayed indoors, by the fire. Only fools like him risked their lives and other people's lives too, by ignoring the warnings and driving in crazy, wild, scary storm conditions.

He was annoyed with himself, as he was now aware, that if he needed assistance, the 'Rescue Services' would have to risk their lives, to save his.

'I have learnt my lesson, I'll heed the 'Met Éireann' storm warnings, and stay indoors in future,' he said out loud to the Universe.

His mind and his thoughts began racing, and he found himself thinking about the secrets and lies, which had unfortunately become a big part of his life.

'Maybe, I am being punished for my secrets, and my selfish, deceitful, wicked life.'

He tried to control his thoughts, as he needed total concentration, if he was to make it home alive.

Met Éireann had warned; 'Don't travel unless it's necessary.'

'Why, hadn't he taken their advice like most normal people?'

He suddenly realised he was never happy, unless he was breaking the rules, and look where it had lead him.

He knew in his heart and soul his life was a mess, and lately he was always acting, like a spoilt child.

His friend Christopher had recently asked him;

'What is wrong with you?'

'You are always taking what you want out of life, and you never think about other people or the consequences of your actions.'

As usual, Conor had been thinking about himself, and trying to get his own way. He was a bit surprised with Christopher's outburst, and he tried to defend himself, but he realised there was actually a lot of truth, in what he said.

Those words came back to haunt him now;

'You are always taking what you want out of life, and you never think about other people or the consequences of your actions.'

Well, maybe this time he had bitten off more than he could chew. Conor knew he had messed up big time, with his secret lives, and he had hurt a lot of people on the way.

He began to worry that he may not survive the storm, but if he did, perhaps it was time, to make amends, and sort out the mess.

Maybe, this was 'His Saving Grace time', and possibly this harsh reality, could be a sign, of his last chance to put things right.

As Conor declared out loud, to the Universe;

'If you get me home safely, I'll try my best to change and make amends for my selfish ways,' and then he suddenly heard a very loud bang.

The last thing he saw was a car coming directly at him, on the wrong side of the road.

The last thing he heard was an unmerciful crash, as the two cars collided, he heard himself scream loudly;

'I am so sorry.'

Patricia's hands were shaking as she listened to Nurse Gavin, explain that Conor had been in an accident and he was in hospital.

'Sorry to upset you, but I phoned because we noticed on his mobile, that you were his last phone call. He is in the 'Intensive Care Unit', (ICU), and he's unresponsive but in a stable condition.'

'Can I visit tonight?' Patricia asked, trying to keep her composure.

'We would appreciate if you would leave it until tomorrow, but don't worry, if there is any change, we'll phone you.'

When Patricia got off the phone, she was in total shock; she took a few deep breaths and made a cup of tea to gather her thoughts, before she phoned Alma, Susan and Paul.

She always found that a cup of tea was good for any type of shock, and goodness me, she certainly was in total shock.

A short time later, she phoned Alma and Susan and they were very upset to hear about Conor's accident, but when she spoke to Paul, he hid his feelings of course, but Patricia knew he was upset too.

They decided to go to the hospital together, in the morning, and Patricia hoped it was the right decision.

'The shock of hearing us all by his bedside will either cure him, or kill him,' Paul said boldly.'

Patricia knew he was trying to be macho and brave, and pretend he didn't care.

'We won't all be allowed in together, it will be one at a time.'

'I know,' Paul said irritably.

The next morning they met in the hospital café, and they agreed to visit Conor separately and explain to him who they were, and hopefully Conor would respond.

Alas, a few days later there was still no response, Conor was still in a coma.

Patricia remembered that Hazel was expecting an update from her, on their planned meeting with Conor, which of course hadn't taken place. She decided to phone Hazel and tell her about the strange twist in the tale, and explain that Conor was now in a coma.

Hazel was shocked to hear of Conor's accident and sad to hear he was in a coma. Patricia promised Hazel, she would keep in touch.

A few weeks later, Patricia asked Nurse Gavin, who was aware of the three family's situation, could they all visit Conor together, just for a short time.

'Maybe, it will spur him on to respond and come out of the coma, when he hears us all together, as he still doesn't realise, we have all met,' Patricia explained.

Nurse Gavin, checked it out, and informed Patricia that Dr Mc Quoid said, they could all make short visits for the moment, and hopefully in time, the visiting hours could be increased.

Patricia gave the good news to the family, and they were all delighted, even Paul muttered; 'That's good.'

Conor tried to talk, but he couldn't seem to move his lips. He could hear lots of voices, and people talking in whispers.

'Oh my God! What is happening to me?'

'Is this my punishment for all my secrets and lies?' he wondered.

At first, he wasn't sure if he was having a nightmare or whether he was actually dead. He most certainly could hear the voices of all his families, past and present … and crazy as it seemed, they all appeared to be around his bed.

'It must be a nightmare,' he thought.

'How could they all be around his bed, was he in 'Heaven', 'Hell', or 'Purgatory?' he wondered.

'OMG, his three families now together, but they didn't know about each other, so how was that possible?'

It felt like his worst nightmare.

He realised, if they were at his bedside, he must still be on earth, maybe he was in hospital, and perhaps this was his punishment for treating his families so badly.

The weirdest thing was, they were all chatting amiably to each other.

'Could that be possible in the real world?' he pondered.

'How on earth had they discovered each other?'

Conor had so many questions to ask, if only he could speak.

He tried to speak, but no matter how hard he tried, he couldn't utter a word, and then because of his extreme efforts to speak, he became unconscious again.

'How did his three families, find out about each other?'

'Who had discovered his outrageous secrets, and his despicable lies?'

'Was it his lovely 'Heart Tattoo' that finally gave away the secrets; he had hidden for so long?'

'Will my last days on earth, consist of all my family, by my bedside, reminding me how selfish I have been?'

'Is this part of the torture and torment for all my secrets and my selfish life?' he questioned.

Conor felt totally trapped now, in his mind and his body, neither was working properly, and he felt frustrated with his lack of control of the situation. He had always been in total control and life was always on his terms, now the tables had turned, and here he was at the mercy of the people he had betrayed.

He had so many questions to ask, for instance;

'Where am I?'

'Why am I here?'

'What has happened?'

His mind and body were letting him down now; no matter how hard he tried he couldn't get the words out, to ask those important questions.

Conor now tried to talk to God or whoever was in charge, the person, whom he had banished from his life when Kate and Simon died.

He was in excruciating pain now, and his head was aching, he tried to ask for help, but no words would come, no matter how hard he tried.

'God, what do you want from me?' he pleaded.

'Please give me a sign, and let me know, what you expect from me.'

'I am sorry for all the secrets and lies, I inflicted upon my families.'

'How can I redeem myself, or is it too late for redemption?' he begged.

As time passed Conor, felt so frustrated, it was like his worst nightmare, lying in a hospital bed, unable to speak or move. He understand what people were saying, but being unable to speak to them, and hearing his fate being discussed, without being able to determine the outcome, was so upsetting. How things had changed, he normally was the dictator, the one calling all the shots.

Conor couldn't actually see his family, but he could feel their presence, and hear what was happening around him. He also heard the nurses and the Doctors discussing his case, sometimes a bit loud, and sometimes in whispered tones.

Unfortunately for him, he also heard them gossiping about his three families, and commenting on how he had treated them so badly.

He couldn't always hear their whisperings, but he got the gist of it, and it wasn't very complimentary. He was surprised they weren't more discreet, what with privacy laws etc., but he realised he probably didn't deserve their respect, because of the way he had treated his family.

In his defence, to this day Conor was adamant, he had really loved his wife Kate, and he had never recovered from her death, or the death of his son Simon. This had led him to make very selfish and very bad decisions in life. It was no excuse, but he hadn't set out or planned to hurt any of his three families.

He had loved his wives Alma and Helen but in a different way than Kate, his love for them was more selfish.

He loved Paul, Susan and Patricia too, but unfortunately his selfish ways, didn't allow him to make room for all of them, in his life.

Throughout his life he had fallen in love with three women, and each of the women had great qualities, and he loved each one, in his own special way, but he now realised that Kate had been, his first and only true love.

Conor hadn't actually planned to live his life so selfishly and so secretly; it had just happened, but there was absolutely no excuse for his bad behaviour.

Now he knew, he must pay the price for his secrets and his deceitful ways. He was dreading what the price would be, but for once he intended to face his penance, whether it was on earth, or in the next life, he was tired of running away from his responsibilities.

Unfortunately, he heard two nurses discussing him, and he heard them say;

'It probably would be better for him, if he dies. I wouldn't like to be in his shoes, if he survives, there are a lot of people looking for answers, for the way he treated them.'

Another nurse said; 'His son Paul seems extremely angry, and I certainly wouldn't blame him, I don't think he is as forgiving as the rest of the family.'

Conor totally understood people's attitude, but he felt hurt by what they said, if only they knew, he actually did want to die, and leave them all in peace.

But it seemed that 'whoever was in charge' had other plans for him, they were punishing him by torturing him slowly, allowing him to hear to hear Paul's anger, but not allowing him to talk and repent.

He was constantly slipping in and out of a coma.

One day he heard Alma say it was a month since his accident, and that upset and frustrated him more.

'Why didn't God or whoever was in charge, let him slip away quietly, and give his three families the peace they deserved?'

'Please let me die now, and make me pay for my sinful and mean spirited life, in hell or purgatory, but preferably purgatory,' he pleaded.

Conor tried to slip away quietly in death, but he kept waking up from the coma.

He realised that he wasn't been given, the easy way out, he would have to negotiate with 'whoever was in charge.'

He was glad he was privy to hear the good and bad things, his families said about him and their views on his secret lives.

He still didn't understand how they had discovered each other, and he was amazed to hear them talking, as if they had known each other, forever.

At times Conor wondered; 'Would I be better off dead?'

Some days he felt good, when he heard the family speak nicely about him, and when they pleaded; 'Please Conor come back to us; we miss you so much.'

'We have always missed not having you around,' he heard Alma say.

But some days, they were quite angry and he heard them talk amongst themselves.

'How could he have done that to us?'

'How could he have lived with all those secrets and lies, deserting his families, and yet feel no remorse?'

'Maybe, this is his punishment for being so self-centered,' he heard Susan say.

Then he heard Paul, mutter in agreement;

'You are so right; he is a self-centered prat, and a deceitful person.'

At times Conor found it difficult to listen to their anger, but he was glad to have time, to observe and get to know them, while they were totally unaware, he was listening.

At least, he had a base to start on, if he was given a second chance, but the questions he asked himself were;

'Do I really deserve a second chance?'

'Do I actually want a second chance?'

'Do I want to be a burden on my families, if I don't fully recover?'

'Wouldn't it be better for everyone, if I disappeared off the face of the earth?'

'They could all finally witness my demise, and not spend their life worrying, whether I was going to appear, and then disappear again,' he pondered.

Conor closed his eyes very tightly, he tried to stop breathing, he tried to leave them all behind, but unfortunately, it wasn't as easy as he thought.

After a few hours of fitful sleeping and waking, he realised his time wasn't up;

'It seemed, he had been given a second chance,' whether he wanted it or not.

He must now face the people he had wronged. He wasn't looking forward to the road ahead, but he would walk it more bravely, and more honestly than before.

Conor had no intention of wasting his second chance; he would try his utmost to make amends and make up for lost time, with his families. They would now become his first priority in life, and hopefully in time they would be able to forgive him.

Conor now negotiated and promised, whoever was in charge of his destiny;

'I promise, if you decide to let me live, I will face my three families and I will make amends to them.'

'I promise to love and cherish all my families, and I will atone for all my sins.'

'If you let me survive I will start living an honest, decent life, and I'll be less selfish.'

'I will think of the needs of others first, for a change,' he promised faithfully.

Conor felt quite ashamed when he recalled, how Kate, had pleaded with him to look after Paul, and sadly he had broken his promise.

'Please promise me, you will look after Paul,' Kate had pleaded on her death bed.

'I know you find it difficult to get along with Paul, but please try to be there for him always.'

'He will need your love and care when I am gone,' she said.

'He loves you, and I know you love him, but you are so wary of each other, maybe it's because you are so alike, that's why you find it difficult to communicate.'

'Please promise me, you will take good care of our beautiful son,' she pleaded as she was gasping for air.

Conor had promised Kate he would look after Paul, and now he realised on his own death bed, he had completely broken his promise to her.

He hadn't even tried to fulfil Kate's dying wish. He had been so self-centered, all he cared about was his own pain, and he hadn't bothered to think, Paul's pain and sadness.

He now realised Kate must have been so disappointed in him.

He could feel the tears starting to flow, and he tried with all his strength to say;

'Sorry Paul,' but unfortunately, no one heard him.

He kept trying to move his lips, but the oxygen mask was too heavy to move with his mouth, and his poor arms wouldn't move either, no matter how much he willed them too.

He remembered Kate had often said; 'The Past is never Past' – it will always come back to sit with you!'

How right she was, his past had certainly come back to haunt him.

No wonder Paul was angry with him, he must have felt totally deserted and alone, when Kate died.

'Why did I let my only living son, stay with his Gran?' he puzzled.

'Why didn't I keep in contact with Paul, and love him, as I had promised Kate? '

'Why did I feel that material things and finance, was my only role in his life?'

He had no answers to those questions; he knew he had totally messed up his own life, and the lives of his three families.

Now at deaths door, he realised he wanted a second chance, to make amends to his lovely families.

The tears started flowing again as he tried to answer and make sense of the questions.

But the truth was there were no answers, to those questions.

He had abandoned his son, and maybe it was too late, to atone for his secrets and lies and his desertion. He immediately vowed, he would do all in his power, to get to know Paul, and hopefully Paul would give him, 'A second chance.'

Chapter 27

Alma was shocked at how willing she was to forgive Conor, even after all the pain he put had them through, with his desertion and secrets. She was impressed with herself and Susan, and all the extended family, for their willingness and kindness, in putting their pain and hurt aside, to aid Conor's recovery.

She was also proud of herself, and her beautiful, kind daughter, for putting kindness and love … before hate and revenge, even though some days it was a struggle for them.

She knew Susan had, 'a good, kind heart', and her kindness to Conor at this very difficult time was incredible to witness.

Even though Susan worked and lived in Dublin, she phoned Alma daily, and they were still very close. So close that Alma didn't hesitate to accept Susan's offer to stay with her in Dublin, while Conor was ill.

'I have raised a well grounded, wonderful, kind lady,' she thought happily.

At least something good has come out of this rather bizarre situation,' she thought.

As Susan sat beside Alma, at Conor's bedside she recalled the difficult time she went through during her Mum and her Dad's divorce. Even though Conor hadn't been in her life, she still felt she had a Dad, but with divorce on the horizon, that changed things.

Susan had numerous nightmares after hearing the news of the divorce, and in particular the night she drank too much, as she tried to drown her sorrows and lose her anger, with the help of 'the demon drink.'

Oh my goodness! The demon drink had definitely lubricated her tongue that crazy, wild night. She had talked to anyone who would listen, her friends at first, and then she moved on to total strangers, telling them, about her Mum and Dad's divorce. People made the proper comments and noises, and she ranted on and on, there was no stopping her alcohol lubricated tongue phew!

Even to this day, she still felt embarrassment when she thought about that crazy, wild night on the town. She certainly had 'painted the town red' that night, and she had added all the other colours of the rainbow too.

She knew she was a total 'light weight' where the consumption of drink was concerned, but that terrible night she drank, like there was no tomorrow.

After countless glasses of vodka, her friend Tara dropped her home, she struggled into bed, with all her clothes on, she hadn't the energy or the co-ordination to undress.

That same crazy, wild night she had a dream, actually it was more like a bad, scary nightmare. She dreamt that insects had taken over the house, and they were actually eating the ceilings and the walls.

She tried so hard to scream but her voice was silent, and she tried to escape but her legs wouldn't move, it was a terrible nightmare.

The insects kept multiplying, they sounded like mosquitoes but they looked much bigger, and they kept getting bigger and stronger.

The nightmare got weirder, when lots of strangers suddenly appeared in her house, and they tried to fumigate the insects, but it was all in vain. It reminded her of the 'Ghostbuster' movie.

'Who are you going to call? 'Ghostbusters'.'

In the nightmare, someone suggested weed killer, and cans of weed killer suddenly appeared and people immediately sprayed the ceiling and walls, and eventually, the insects stopped multiplying, and they began to die.

When Susan awoke from the nightmare screaming, she found it hard to believe, it wasn't real, as it was still so vivid and clear in her mind.

She was thrilled when she realised, it was only a nightmare, from far too much drink, which was possibly mixed, with too much self pity.

She felt such an enormous relief, as the nightmare had seemed so real, but she still checked the ceiling in her room and other rooms to make sure all was well. Thankfully there was absolutely no sign of any insects, dead or alive.

At that time, Susan felt she had very little peace day or night, due to Conor's desertion and the impending divorce.

The morning after her binge drinking, she had vigorously brushed her teeth, to suppress the taste of the large consumption of vodka, and to distract herself from her dark thoughts.

She actually managed to crack a smile, when she remembered a witty sign, she had seen recently in her dentist's waiting room;

'You don't need to brush all your teeth. Just the ones you want to keep!'

She really enjoyed the wit, so she had memorised it, thankfully even suffering from a hangover, she still maintained her sense of humour.

After that awful, scary episode Susan stopped trying to drown her sorrows in the 'demon drink' instead, she talked to her friends, and her wonderful, caring Mum, if she was having a bad day.

She knew she was very lucky to have such a kind, caring, broad minded Mum.

Her friends always said; 'Your Mum oozes positivity from the top of her head to the soles of her feet.'

She was very proud upon hearing their lovely comments, and she worked hard on getting her own 'positivity mojo' back, which thankfully she did.

Even though her Dad was no longer in her life, she had to reclaim her sunny disposition, and appreciate how lucky she was, to have her wonderful Mum, always there supporting her.

Not many of her friends were as lucky as she was, and she constantly reminded herself of that, especially when she was feeling sad about her Dad's desertion.

Susan often wondered if Conor hadn't had the 'Heart Tattoo', would his three families be sitting around his bedside now, feeling hurt and confused, yet willing him to live.

It was the 'Heart Tattoo' which he loved so much, which unexpectedly, had given away his secret lives.

'Years ago, when Conor got his tattoo, he wasn't to know, that the 'Heart Tattoo' would uncover his secrets and lies,' Susan thought.

'If Hazel hadn't been such a diligent a tutor, Conor's triple life might never have been discovered, and his three families wouldn't have been united,' she realised.

'Life is certainly full of coincidences, but I am happy we are all together at last, hopefully Conor will pull through and we can hear his side of the story.' Susan pondered.

Patricia was delighted, that her new extended families, were actually supporting Conor, especially now in these crazy, weird circumstances, which they found themselves in.

'Oh my goodness! What crazy stories we could tell, yet people probably wouldn't believe us,' Patricia thought.

'What are the chances of three people meeting in a creative writing class, and their tutor realising, they have the same Dad?'

'Nil, to three chances,' she giggled.

'I suppose, it's better to laugh than cry, about my new situation; my Dad in a coma, and two secret families appearing in my life out of the blue,' Patricia pondered, as she tried to see the funny side of things.

She was surprised how open and kind her two new families were, so unlike Conor with his secrets and lies.

She could see a strong resemblance between herself, Susan and Paul, in looks and in mannerisms, and yet she hadn't spotted the similarities, before Hazel spoke.

After their visits with Conor, they usually all went for coffee, Alma included, and they had lots of amazing stories to share.

Patricia was rather shocked and upset to hear that, Alma and Susan had literally been abandoned by Conor.

Yet, they seemed so willing to forgive him, they had such kindness in their hearts and they relentlessly sat by Conor's bedside, talking kindly and softly to him, willing him out of the coma.

Patricia wasn't sure if she would have been as forgiving under the circumstances. She was certainly the lucky one; she hadn't been abandoned by Conor, unlike Paul, Alma and Susan.

Thankfully her story wasn't as sad or as heart breaking as theirs, at times she felt like laughing out loud, at the craziness of it all, it was like something she would read in a novel, it just didn't seem, like real life.

It was truly amazing, how a random creative writing assignment, brought to light, secrets of the 'Heart Tattoo.'

Thanks to Hazel's observation and detective work, the three families were now united.

They were extremely grateful to Hazel for her amazing discovery, and for following her gut instinct and using the second assignment to confirm whether Conor was their Dad.

Patricia pondered; 'Would Conor have got away with his 'Secrets and Lies' forever if they hadn't attended the 'Creative Writing Classes'?'

'Wow! Isn't life so crazy, so weird and just so unpredictable at times?' she questioned.

'Who would have guessed that, three total strangers who met in a creative writing class,' would one day, discover they were actually related?'

'Even more astonishing, they would discover they had the same Dad, Conor, with a 'Heart Tattoo'.'

'Who would believe that this same man Conor, would be involved in a car accident, and end up in a coma?'

'Who would ever believe that in hospital, Conor would be surrounded by his three children and his ex-wife, who bore no malice, and even wished him a full recovery?'

Patricia couldn't help but smile, at the irony and the craziness of the situation.

'Perhaps someday, I will write a book about it all,' she mused.

'Maybe, if and when, Conor recovers, I will write a novel about my new crazy life, nobody will believe, it's actually based on a true story!'

'It would certainly be a best seller, and maybe even an 'Oscar' winning movie,' she mused.

Hazel was shocked, when Patricia phoned to inform her that, Conor had a very bad car accident, and he was in hospital, in a coma.

She explained to Hazel the situation the three families now found themselves in. Hazel felt astonished that Conor, who had messed up so many lives, was now in a coma.

'My goodness, what next?' she thought.

'Who would have believed, that things in the 'Rutlin Families' world, would take another twist?'

'Life can be so unpredictable,' Hazel thought.

She hoped Conor would make a full recovery, and that she would eventually get to meet the man who had led 'a triple secret life.'

She was fascinated by Paul, Patricia and Susan's story, and she was rather pleased when Patricia promised to keep in touch.

Amazingly, this man Conor, with the 'Heart Tattoo', had now brought a new friend into her life.

After their visit with Conor, Patricia would update them on her research on coma patients, in the local café.

She informed them, she had discovered that; 'Most coma patients' can actually hear their visitor's conversations, but unfortunately they are unable to communicate with them.'

She also reminded them, Dr Mc Quoid had emphasised that coma patients can hear what's happening, but they may be physically unable to show any response.

Dr Mc Quid had continually reminded them; 'Keep talking to Conor, as usually a person's hearing is the last thing to go.'

Sometimes, when they were so engrossed in hearing about each other's life; they would talk among themselves, forgetting Conor could hear.

Thankfully, Dr Mc Quoid's advice would always bring them back on track.

Patricia was convinced Conor's brain was still active and alive, and she firmly believed he could hear their conversations, and she was determined to keep talking to Conor, to encourage him back to reality.

Patricia said; 'Some people who emerge from comas claim they don't remember a thing, it's as if they were in a deep sleep. But believe it or not, most comatose patients claim they were conscious the entire time, but they just couldn't communicate with anyone, no matter how hard they tried.'

'I think Conor is in that category, and he knows we are here, and he can hear our conversations. I am sure he is mystified how we all got together, and that alone should spur him on to recovery,' she said smiling.

'I also read that you must have patience and hope because;

'Healing works on its own schedule, not on anyone else's.'

Alma agreed; 'I think that's very true, we just need to keep talking to Conor, and show him love, and forgiveness.'

'I just can't believe what I am hearing,' Paul said angrily.

'How can you all be so forgiving, when all he ever did was abandon us, while he lived a life of deceit?' he asked.

'It's not easy, but we have to put our feelings aside, and help Conor back to a full recovery. When he makes a full recovery, we can then question his motives,' Alma said patiently.

'It's better to lose the anger, and our desire for revenge, and just deal with the present situation,' Susan calmly agreed.

'Well, do what you want.'

'I can't be as forgiving,' Paul muttered.

Alma felt so proud of Susan; she realised she had the most wonderful, caring daughter from her marriage with Conor, and she would be forever grateful, for that amazing miracle.

Chapter 28

Patricia was extremely upset when she accidently overheard one of the team nurses say to her colleague; 'Dr Mc Quoid may soon take 'Conor Rutlin' off the life support machine.'

Patricia was very determined, that wasn't going to happen, not on her watch. She was convinced given more time, Conor would make a full recovery.

She decided she would do more in-depth research online, and she would check the medical journals in her local library, and she would talk to her new family.

She was a member of the library and the staff knew her well. They were always very helpful, and no doubt, they would point her in the right direction, for her extensive research.

That evening she phoned Alma, Susan and Paul and told them what she had overheard.

'I plan to do more intensive research on 'a coma patient's full recovery', and I'll find lots of successful cases, and convince Dr Mc Quoid and his team, to leave Dad on life support,' she said angrily.

'I can't believe they are thinking of taking Conor off the life support machine already.' 'We have all heard of people who recover, after years in a coma,' Alma said disapprovingly.

'You're so right Mum, I have read that many coma patients make a full recovery,' Susan said.

Patricia was pleased they all felt the same; even Paul surprised her and asked if he could help, she quickly accepted his help, in case he changed his mind.

She asked him to do some online research on patients, who had recovered from a coma, after a number of years.

Susan said excitedly; 'I'll also do research on 'coma patients' who have recovered. I will cite cases where people have come out of comas after months and even years.'

'I know from my legal experience by making it personal, and giving the names of people who have recovered, people often take a step back, and reconsider their decision.'

'Let's all get working on it immediately, the more personal cases and information, we have, the better,' Susan emphasised.

'When we complete our research we should meet and discuss our findings, and then I'll compile a final report, on all our findings,' Susan said eagerly.

'That's a great idea, I can see why you're the best solicitor in town,' Patricia said smiling.

'I most certainly have read stories of people in comas, who were diagnosed in a vegetative state, and sometimes condemned as brain dead and beyond recovery, and then they shock the medical profession, by making a full recovery. I will look at that angle of the situation,' Alma said firmly.

'That could even happen to Conor, couldn't it?' Patricia asked.

'Yes, it could happen to Conor, it's far too soon to take him off the life support machine,' Alma said.

'The fact that, Conor was in good shape physically before the accident, and thankfully, no major injuries occurred during the accident, so surely he's a prime candidate for a full recovery,' Patricia said confidently.

'It's easy for the 'Medical Team' to say, 'pull the plug,' but what if it was their Dad, how would they feel?' Patricia asked.

'Even though, we now know, Conor didn't live a truthful life, and he most certainly wasn't perfect, he still deserves a second chance with his three families,' Patricia said.

'We also deserve to hear his side of the story too, and why he deceived us all with his secrets,' Paul mumbled.

'Yes, we do indeed,' they all agreed.

As Patricia left the hospital, she was already planning her research strategy; they certainly would need lots of proof, to prevent the removal of Conor's life support machine.

She wondered again; 'Would the Doctors and nurses be as quick to switch off the life support machine, if it was their relation?'

She knew that financial issues in hospitals and life in general, often made people forget the human side of things.

That evening, Patricia worked tirelessly on her research, and she was overjoyed with the volume of positive evidence she found. The evidence also showed that, some coma patients made a full recovery, even after years in a coma.

She was thrilled to read; 'People should always assume that the person in a coma, can hear what's happening around them, as hearing is usually the last sensory faculty to deteriorate.'

This exciting evidence made her more determined to talk, and to read to Conor every day.

Susan had also been busy doing her research, and thankfully she found numerous positive case results. She had completed a thorough research and she was pleased with the large number of named cases she found, making her research more personal.

She intended to quote the cases to Dr Mc Quoid and his team and also give them a copy of her findings.

She knew from her own experience as a Solicitor that, 'the written word' could not be ignored. Unfortunately, people often paid lip service to phone calls, but not the written word, people had to address it, because it was there in evidence, for all to see.

When they all met at their usual café, they discussed their research results, and Patricia and Susan updated them on their case findings.

Susan told them about 'Brion Wilson', a man who went into a coma, after a simple operation went wrong. She explained to them that; 'Brion's' chances of recovery were rated at 1%, and even less after a few weeks, and his wife was told by the medical team, that there was no hope.'

'Folks, the wonderful news is Brion Wilson made a full recovery and when interviewed he said, at times when he was in the coma, he actually knew what was going on. He couldn't see, but he could feel and hear things, and when the TV was on, he knew what was happening in the news.'

'When he finally awoke from the coma, he could repeat stories, to the Doctors, which had been recounted to his apparently, 'deaf ears',' Susan said smiling.

Susan continued excitedly; 'Brion said when he was in a coma, he felt his wife holding his hand, and talking to him, and he heard her updating him on the children's lives.'

'He said he knew he was on the brink of death and he was determined to make a full recovery, he felt, he alone had the choice, to live or die, and he so wanted to live.'

'Wow! That's great news Susan, and it's really wonderful evidence which will certainly support our case.'

'We must keep talking and reading to Conor. I am certain he will make a full recovery, especially with all our support,' Patricia said enthusiastically.

'I think that's a good plan,' Susan said.

'Would you believe, since his recovery Brion Wilson, now visits other people in comas?' Susan said proudly, as if she knew him.

'You clearly are impressed by this man,' Patricia said smiling.

'Yes he is an amazing man, and he also encourages the family to talk to the person in a coma, and keep them stimulated by updating them on family activities.'

'People are amazed at his kindness, but he just smiles and says, it's his way of 'paying kindness forward', as he appreciates, the miracle of his survival.'

Susan further informed them; 'In several cases, the decision to remove respirators and feeding tubes from patients has been contentious and often, ends up in court.'

Susan proceeded to read a story from her research notes;

'At the age of thirty two, 'Ellie Kearns' suffered injuries in a road accident which left her in a coma. After nearly twenty years in a coma, she suddenly awoke in the clinic, where the doctors were treating her, and she made a full recovery.'

'Her daughter had visited her every day.' She said; 'I never gave up on my Mum, because I always believed that one day, she would come out of the coma.'

Ellie Kearns, Physician was amazement and he said; 'There are very few cases like this recorded, in which a patient recovers, after such a long period of time in a coma.'

'We should always consider these unusual cases, when making our final decision on a coma patient.'

'Wouldn't it be amazing if Conor just suddenly woke up too?' Susan said excitedly.

'It would indeed,' they all chorused.

Susan said; 'I also discovered that each person's case is different, and the outcome depends on the cause and the severity of the coma, and the neurological damaged caused, but the really good news is, that my research shows that many patients do fully recover.'

'I truly feel, with all our help, Conor will regain consciousness soon,' Susan said.

'I feel the same,' Alma said.

'Me too, I know Conor will fight this, and get back on his feet,' Patricia said firmly.

'How do you know for sure, Conor will recover?' Paul asked angrily.

'Just because you did some research on comas, you now think you are all experts.' 'You think you know more than Dr Mc Quoid and his team.'

'He doesn't even know, if Conor will ever recover,' Paul said frustrated.

Paul now recalled how shocked he was, at how forgiving Alma, Susan, and Patricia were, when they discovered Conor was in hospital. All they talked about was visiting him, to see how he was.

'What were they thinking?'

'This was the man who had deceived and deserted them all, and messed up their lives, without a thought for the devastation he had caused.'

It was true Paul, had never felt a connection to Conor, and he was the one who had asked Conor, if he could live with his Gran.

He would try to keep his thoughts to himself, but he certainly wouldn't be falling all over Conor, like the rest of them.

'God, they were such hypocrites!'

He would visit Conor, but he wasn't convinced, he could forgive his Dad, like his siblings did, and he wasn't convinced that Conor would fully recover, like they seemed to think.

During Paul's research he had seen where patients had never regained consciousness, and the family had accepted the medical advice; 'To take them off the life support machine.'

It most certainly wasn't all 'happy endings', like his new families seemed to think.

'We must all work together to help Conor regain consciousness, and let him know, his life is worth living,' Patricia said firmly.

'We must also tell him; 'we forgive him' and we want him in our lives in the future,' Alma said emphatically.

'Paul, we don't think we know more than Dr Mc Quoid or his team, but we do think Conor needs more time to recover,' Susan said gently.

'We will meet with Dr Mc Quoid and his team, and we will bring our wonderful research as evidence, and they'll have to listen to us,' Susan said firmly.

'We must ask Dr Mc Quoid, for more time, before he considers removing Conor's life support machine,' Patricia said emphatically.

'Perhaps, each of us could spend a day, with Conor, reading and talking to him, to let him know we support him, no matter what has happened in the past,' Alma said.

Patricia and Susan agreed with Alma's suggestion, and they each chose a day to visit with Conor.

Paul remained silent, and quite grumpy.

Alma bravely but calmly asked Paul; 'What day suits you?'

Paul still remained silent.

'Nobody is perfect Paul, not even you, you didn't seem to make life easy for Conor either, from what I can gather,' Alma said.

'You must try to put all that behind you now, and be there for Conor.'

'I know you will regret it, if you don't,' Alma said calmly.

'This will be a second chance for us all.' Patricia said softly to Paul.

'I have to go,' Paul muttered as he hurriedly left the café.

'Don't worry, I'll take Paul's turn, and that will cover us for the week,' Patricia said.

Paul ran down the road, he knew he was about to cry, and that really surprised him, as it made him realise; he cared about his Dad, more than he admitted.

Patricia, Susan and Alma, looked at each other knowingly, as Paul rushed out of the café. They knew Paul had built a strong, defensive wall. to protect himself from feeling or thinking about Conor.

They also knew, that one day it would come crashing down, and they would need to protect him.

'It looked like today, was the day.'

For the moment, they would give Paul space, and Patricia would text him with updates on Conor, hopefully in time, he would realise, they loved, and supported him.

Alma said; 'Paul is probably worried that it's too late to make peace, with his Dad;

'Death certainly brings us closer to reality, and forgiveness, and we begin to see things clearer.'

In truth, Paul was shocked, at how sad and upset he felt when Patricia said; 'Dr Mc Quoid and his team are thinking of switching off Conor's life support machine.'

He felt he couldn't breathe, and he just wanted to escape from the hospital, and from his family.

All of a sudden, what was happening had become reality, and he wasn't ready to face the finality of the situation. He had foolishly believed that Conor would eventually pull through, and things would go back to 'normal', well, 'Paul's normal'.

He had been avoiding reality, and he should have known better, things would never be the same, whether Conor, lived or died.

The family had been dealt with totally new cards, and it was now up to them and Paul, how they played them.

Paul had really and truly thought, things would go back to 'normal' for him.

'But who was he fooling?'

Things would never be the same; he now realised, he had a new extended family, and it was his choice to embrace them or not.

'Even if he did deny his new family, like Conor had, wouldn't it be a total contradiction of what he claimed he stood for?' he questioned.

After much deliberation, he vowed, he wouldn't repeat history and act like Conor, he would accept his new family; Patricia, Susan and Alma, and learn to love them. Thankfully he already admired and respected them, as they were amazing people.

He must stop being so childish, accept the past, and move on, and enjoy his new extended family. Like him, they had been badly hurt, but they were willing to forgive Conor, and start over again.

Surely he could make the effort too, and now was a good time to forgive the past, and embrace the new future.

He finally decided he would take some responsibility, and he would embrace Alma's suggestion, to talk and read to Conor.

After all, it was only recently, Paul had discovered that throughout the years, his Dad had actually kept in touch, with his Gran, and Conor hadn't totally deserted him, as he thought.

It seemed, Conor had paid all his school and college fees, and even funded his school and college trips etc.

'It wasn't his Gran who had looked after him financially, it was his Dad, what a shock that discovery had been!'

Paul only recently discovered that, his Gran had foolishly 'erred on the side of caution' by deciding not to give him birthday, and Christmas cards, which his Dad sent.

She felt that any mention of his Dad, seemed to upset him, and cause mood swings, and to protect him, she hid any reminders of his Dad.

When Paul asked his Gran; 'Why didn't you tell me Dad was helping us financially?'

'She said; 'I am So Sorry.'

'At the time, I thought it was the right thing to do, as you always got angry, and upset, at the mention of your Dad.'

There were tears in her eyes, which scared and upset Paul, as he had never seen his Gran cry, he always felt she was the strong, invincible one.

She said sorry, so many times, he decided to let things lie, and not upset her any further.

That new revelation had made his life more complicated and very confusing.

At the time, he chose not to dwell on it, as it made him feel guilty for disliking his Dad so much.

But now with Conor in a coma and at deaths door, he found himself re-examining his own life.

Perhaps, if he had kept in touch with Conor after their wonderful trip to Canada, things might have improved between them. Paul wondered if Conor hadn't the 'Heart Tattoo', which he was so proud of, would Hazel still have discovered that Alma, Susan, Patricia and himself, had the same Dad.

Paul now recalled what Conor had said to Lucas their Canadian tour guide, about his 'Heart Tattoo.'

'When I look at my 'Heart Tattoo', I get a sense of peace and love,' Conor had said rather proudly.

Lucas had admired Conor for wearing the symbol of 'Love', but Paul remembered how Conor had looked guilty talking about the symbol of love, possibly because he had deserted his own son, and now it had come to light, that he had also deserted other members of his family.

Paul decided he would take his turn at Conor's hospital bed, and help him recover, as he needed to know why Conor had deserted his three families. 'Hopefully I haven't inherited that 'desertion gene',' he mused.

But now, that things were back on track with Marissa and himself, perhaps he had missed out on that bad gene after all.

He obviously had a touch of the bad gene when he had his commitment issues, but thankfully those days were behind him now.

He had lost his fear of commitment, and he was ready and willing to face the world again, with Marissa by his side, as she was undeniably his one, and only true love.

Chapter 29

Patricia and Alma were with Conor, when Dr Mc Quoid dropped in, and asked to speak to them privately.

As they walked down the corridor to the private rooms, Patricia could feel her heart beating faster each step she took.

She suspected what lay ahead, after the conversation she had overheard, but she was ready to do battle for Conor's sake, no matter what plans the medical team had devised.

'My team and I would like to discuss Conor's progress, with you all.'

'Would Saturday at 2pm be possible?' Dr Mc Quoid asked.

'Yes, we will arrange that, with the family,' Patricia said.

'What's normally the next procedure?' she asked anxiously.

'Every patient's brain is different, so unfortunately it's incredibly difficult to predict the outcome of a coma patient. Some coma patients recover completely, but some patients have to re-learn how to speak, how to walk, and even how to eat, and of course some never recover,' Dr Mc Quoid said sadly.

'Unfortunately, in Conor's case we haven't seen any progress whatsoever. The next stage usually is, deciding whether to keep the person on the life support machine, or not.'

'You can't possibly be thinking of switching off the life support machine, it's far too soon,' Patricia said angrily.

'Please don't upset yourself; we haven't made the final decision yet.'

'Give us more time, please. I feel my Dad is totally aware that we are at his bedside, but he just can't communicate yet.

I just know, given more time he will recover, as he was in very good health, before the accident.'

'We have already completed lots of research, and we have lots of evidence to show that people do come out of comas, months and even years later,' Patricia said emphatically.

'As, I said, my team I will talk to you all, on Saturday.'

Patricia and Alma phoned Susan and Paul and they all agreed to meet at Patricia's house. They discussed their research findings again, and they elected Susan and Patricia to be their spokespersons.

They had actually seen Susan in action in court, and they knew she was excellent at getting her point across, using her legal language, and quoting cases.

Patricia was very close to Conor, and they elected her to show the human side of the situation.

The day they all dreaded, finally arrived, they were meeting Dr Mc Quoid and his team, to discuss poor Conor's future.

A decision would be made today, and Patricia hoped and prayed, the team would agree with the family, and leave Conor on the life support machine.

Things had been crazy for her, in the last few days, doing research and chatting with her new extended family. Thankfully they had all reached the same conclusion, even Paul; they had all agreed that Conor must remain on life support, for the foreseeable future.

They were convinced Conor was still fighting to live, and that eventually he would regain consciousness, and they most certainly wanted to hear Conor's story, when he recovered!

When Dr Mc Quoid came into ICU, at least fifteen minutes before the agreed meeting time, they knew by his expression, he possibly wasn't the bearer of good news.

'Could you follow me please,' he said rather quietly.

When they were all settled into the family room, Dr Mc Quoid's team joined them.

Dr Mc Quoid said; 'My team and I have discussed Conor's case, at length. We have completed numerous tests, and we have examined the scans, but unfortunately; we see no signs of progress or recovery.'

'Dr Mc Quoid, in your opinion, how long can someone be in a coma and still make a full recovery?' Patricia asked.

'There is no definitive answer to that question, it's in God's hands, and it depends on how healthy the patient is. A patient in a state of coma is actually alive, but unable to move or respond to their environment.'

'My team and I feel, it's time to take Conor off the life support machine, and let him die with dignity. We completed all the tests and scans again, and we saw no signs of recovery, and unfortunately no response from Conor.'

Dr Mc Quoid said rather sadly. 'We have tried all we can, but unfortunately Conor's body seems unable to respond.'

'Like Conor, many comatose patients stay in ICU, where doctors and nurses continually monitor them and keep them as healthy as possible. Coma patients are susceptible to pneumonia and other infections, but Conor has been very lucky, he hasn't any signs of pneumonia or infection,' but unfortunately we see absolutely, no progress either,' Dr Mc Quoid explained.

'Over the last few months, Conor has received physical therapy, to prevent long term muscle damage, but unfortunately there's no sign at all, of muscle movements by Conor. The nurses have been moving him periodically, to prevent bedsores and they have seen absolutely no sign of progress, or movement.'

'Dr Mc Quoid, I truly feel that Dad has been trying to communicate with us, and I have seen signs of small movements, and twitching of his hands,' Patricia emphasised.

'The family, have completed a lot of research into coma patients, and we noted that a person who regains consciousness after a long period of time, is actually fine.'

'We really feel Conor should be given more time, now that his extended family are supporting him, and willing him to make a full recovery.'

'We are convinced he is aware, we are all here together, and that we 'Love' him, no matter what the circumstances,' Patricia said, hoping to clarify the situation, as she knew Dr Mc Quoid and his team were aware of Conor's three families.

Before Dr Mc Quoid got a chance to reply to Patricia, Susan politely but firmly took over the baton from Patricia, as planned.

Susan had set up a tough strategy so that Dr Mc Quoid would have no choice but to listen to Conor's families.

She knew that given half a chance Dr Mc Quoid would talk them into taking Conor off life support, so she was determined to blind him with cases and facts, to change his mind, without him feeling he had lost the battle, and that they had won.

Susan continued politely but firmly; 'We have cited some coma cases here for your attention, I have copies for you, perhaps you would be good enough to read them, before you make your final decision.'

'In all these particular cases the patients have made a full recovery, and some have even come out a coma, years later. We feel you need to give Conor more time, for his body to heal and recover. Thankfully, he was in good health before the accident, so that should help him recover, given more time.'

'Yes, sometimes the cause of a coma can be completely reversed, and the person can regain normal function, but as I said, we have completed numerous scans and tests on Conor, but unfortunately, we see no signs of that happening,' Dr Mc Quoid said firmly.

'There is also a possibility Conor may have some brain damage at this stage of the coma, we don't know.'

'You need to consider; 'What would Conor want'?'

'You also need to check, if Conor has made provisions for circumstances like this.'

'I am really sorry to ask you this;

'But do you know if Conor has made a will?' Dr Mc Quoid asked.

'If Conor has made a will, you need to check, whether he stated in his will that; he would wish to be resuscitated, or whether he wishes to be left on a life support machine, if he's in a vegetative state?'

'Firstly check that out, and then we will have a further discussion next week, to determine what is best for Conor.'

'We will certainly examine your research, and the case studies you have given us,' Dr Mc Quoid said kindly.

Susan felt quite pleased with the meeting, and she profusely thanked Dr Mc Quoid, and his team, on behalf of all the family.

She did some deep breathing, when she heard that Conor wasn't been taking off life support, as her heart was thumping so fast with relief, she feared she would end up, in A&E Department.

Once again the family went for a coffee to discuss the meeting, and Patricia offered to get in touch with Conor's solicitor, to see what provisions were in his will.

They all agreed, it was imperative, that they devote as much time as possible reading and talking to Conor, to help him regain consciousness.

Susan made a very valid point, that the personal touch, was important for Conor and when dealing with Dr Mc Quid, and his team.

'We need to keep reminding the medical staff that Conor is a person, as well as a patient, and perhaps, they won't be as quick to take Conor off life support. Nurse Gavin is an excellent nurse, and she is very dedicated to Conor, so let's keep her on board too, and always thank her for her support.'

Alma and Patricia were delighted to have Susan's 'legal eagle' advice and support, and Paul grudgingly accepted it.

A few days later, Patricia happily informed them, there was nothing in Conor's will about 'Do not resuscitate' or 'Take him off life support'.

They were all so relieved, and now it was up to them to convince the medical profession, that given more time on the life support, Conor would make a full recovery.

Chapter 30

Conor was shocked to hear Alma say, he'd been in a coma for months; the days and weeks had passed in a total haze.

He felt so frustrated, as most days, he could hear the family talking, and he tried so hard to communicate, but they just couldn't hear him.

He was truly thankful to them, for supporting him under the circumstances. He knew he didn't deserve their kindness and their love, but he was so grateful for their love and support.

They were so generous of spirit and they seemed to be forgiving, which spurred him on to recover, and make amends to them.

He was so ashamed and sorry for the selfish life he had lead, and all the heartbreak he had caused.

He felt so proud of them all, especially Paul, as he knew Paul was struggling to forgive him, yet he came to visit quite often.

'If Paul, really hated me, he wouldn't spend his precious time in ICU,' Conor thought.

Conor's heart soared when he realised, he was getting a second chance; to become a decent, kind, honest and caring person.

Conor knew he had let Kate down, by not looking after Paul, but hopefully she was now by his side, as he intended to change, his wicked ways. He guessed that 'God', or 'whoever was in charge', had no intention of making life easy for him, but he was ready to do battle, and get to know his three families.

Hopefully, he would be allowed back to reality real soon, and leave this awful coma world.

'A world full of sleepiness, with brief moments of reality, where past and present were all mixed into one, thus making him feel frustrated and so confused.'

Conor believed it was a punishment for his deceitful life, but he couldn't endure much more of this crazy, coma world.

One minute Conor could hear his family talking, then the next minute, came a sleep so deep, a state of prolonged unconsciousness, which sent him back into a coma. He now appeared to be stuck in limbo; he was neither in 'Hell', nor in 'Purgatory' and certainly not in 'Heaven!'

He continuously tried to speak, but alas no one could hear him, but he persisted, and made a huge effort to say, the most import word; his three families, needed to hear;

'Sorry.'

Every day, Conor unrelenting tried to say; *'Sorry'* to Paul, Alma, Susan and Patricia, but unfortunately, they couldn't hear him. His strong, stubborn streak, wouldn't allow him give in, and he intended to persevere, until they heard him.

His throat was so dry he could barely move his tongue, and his lips felt cracked and sore from the oxygen mask.

He was determined to put up a brave fight and live, and hopefully 'death' who persistently teased him, would eventually let him be, and give him;

'A Second Chance'.

'A chance to redeem himself, and a chance to explain to his family, what he did was totally wrong, and that his secrets and lies, which had caused so much hurt and pain, would now end.

He really hadn't planned to be such a mean, horrible, selfish husband, or Dad; but he was so broken hearted when Kate and Simon died, and unfortunately he had automatically; 'shut his feelings down' to protect himself, from any further pain.

He honestly hadn't planned to marry or to love again, it just happened, and he had been utterly selfish, and cruel to run away from his families, and his responsibilities.

He had been thoughtless and cruel to Alma, and by having another child, (the lovely Susan), when he couldn't even look after his son, Paul.

He really hoped he would get 'a second chance' to make amends for the hurt and pain, his secrets and selfishness had caused.

'If this 'Coma' ends, I will show my entire family, how much I love them,' he promised.

'I will amend my ways, and make atonement for the past, and I will create a good future together with my three families.'

'Please let me have a future with them,' he pleaded.

Chapter 31

When the alarm went off, Patricia couldn't believe it was Thursday already, the week was going too fast. Alma and Susan had kept in touch with her, after their visits to Conor, and they had sadly reported; 'No change in Conor's circumstances.'

They tried to appear upbeat, and said; 'It's still early days,' but they all knew that now, time was of the essence.

Alma confided in Patricia; 'I really enjoyed my day alone with Conor, even after all our years of separation. I guess I never stopped loving him,' she said sadly.

Patricia was in awe of Alma, she was so forgiving and loving towards Conor, and she showed no bitterness, of having to raise Susan alone.

Patricia thought, Susan was a delightful lady, and a testament to the superb job Alma had accomplished, as a single parent.

Paul hadn't been in touch, so Patricia was taking his place at Conor's bedside. She decided to bring a flask of tea, and sandwiches with her, as time was precious now, and she needed to spend as much time as possible with Conor. She was so conscious of Dr Mc Quoid's intention to switch off Conor's life support machine, that she was determined to try her utmost, to bring Conor back to reality.

Patricia was delighted to have a second day alone with Conor, it was so peaceful just reading and talking to him, without the incessant chatter of the others.

Of course she loved her new family, but sometimes they chatted so much to each other, they forgot to include Conor.

They were trying to catch up on lost time, and sometimes they used the hospital visits, to put together the pieces of the puzzle, of all Conor's secrets and lies.

Now that Patricia had Conor all to herself, she decided to tell him the full story, of how his three families had finally, and unexpectedly met.

She guessed he probably heard them nattering together, during their visits. But she felt Conor needed to hear the full story of how his 'Heart Tattoo' had led to the discovery of his three secret families.

She hoped it would help him understand the situation, and make him realise, they were all willing to forgive him, and they so wished him, a full recovery.

'Dad, I have been very lucky to have you in my life, but I believe the rest of the family were abandoned by you,' Patricia said sadly.

'Dad we all need to hear your side of the story, so you must get better' she said softly.

Patricia began to tell Conor how his three families had discovered each other;

'Paul, Susan and I met in a 'Creative Writing Class.'

'What are the chances of something like that happening?' she asked rhetorically.

'One in a million, you would think eh?' she said gently touching Conor's hand.

'Anyway Dad, it wasn't us who discovered, that you were Paul's, Susan's and my Dad, it was the lovely Hazel, our creative writing Tutor.'

'You probably won't be surprised to hear, that the discovery was an absolute fluke.'

'Hazel gave our class an assignment to;'

'Write a short story about a memorable holiday, with a special person, be they real or imaginary.'

'Well, would you believe it, for his short story assignment, Paul chose his holiday in Canada with you, Dad?'

'Susan chose her holiday in India with you.'

'I chose our wonderful holiday together in South Africa.'

'Wasn't that an absolutely amazing coincidence?'

'Even more amazing when Hazel discovered the guy in the three short stories was actually named Conor, as crazy as it seems none of us changed your name in our short stories.'

'We all mentioned your 'Heart Tattoo', which added to Hazel's suspicion; 'that Conor was the same person, in the three short stories'.'

'To verify her suspicions, she needed more information on the person, Conor, so she set up another assignment with that in mind.'

'Hazel asked our class to complete another assignment, and to elaborate on the character from our holiday story, and she even mentioned physical features, and tattoos.'

'She said it was an exercise in building a strong character, to enhance our writing skills. Never in a million years, would we have guessed, she was actually looking for more evidence, before revealing her findings to us.'

'She very cleverly, asked us to elaborate on the person's values and beliefs, their personality and in particular their physical appearance. Of course we all elaborated on the story of your 'Heart Tattoo, not realising the secrets that surrounded it.'

'She also asked us to draw with words a clear picture of the person, and she reminded us that the person could be fiction or non-fiction, just to throw us off the scent.'

'They were very clever tactics, and she hoped to discover if Conor, with the 'Heart Tattoo', was the same person, in all three stories.'

'We now call her 'Ms Sherlock Holmes',' Patricia giggled.

'Whether you like it or not Dad, you touched all our lives in good and bad ways, and we all undeniably treasured our holiday with you.

We won't abandon you, unlike the way you abandoned, some of your family.'

'Your 'Heart Tattoo' was a total giveaway, so you'll need to get rid of that tattoo, if you want to lead a double, or triple life in the future,' she said laughingly, trying her utmost to coax Conor to speak.

'When Hazel read our second short story assignment, it was quite obvious to her, we were all describing the same person, and yet she felt, we didn't actually know each other.'

'She later told us that she conferred with her husband Jim, and her friend Grace, and they confirmed her suspicions.'

Her husband Jim said, without any hesitation; 'Yes, that's the same person in the three assignments.'

'Grace was absolutely convinced Conor was the same person, in the three stories, and she actually asked Hazel.'

'Are you sure, Paul, Susan and Patricia, don't know each other?'

'That's when Hazel realised she needed to talk to us individually first, and then as a group.'

'It was a difficult time for Hazel but she handled it very compassionately, and very professionally.'

'Dad, I must confess, I was quite shocked and very disappointed in you, when Hazel informed me of her incredible discovery. She explained to me the reason for the second assignment, and she showed me the three identical short stories of 'Conor with the Heart Tattoo', written by Paul, Susan and I.'

'She very kindly gave me a copy of their short stories, and I was shocked how alike we all were.'

'Dad, you certainly gave us the travel bug, as we really love to travel and explore our wonderful world. No matter what our life experiences were with you, amazingly, we all enjoyed our holiday, with you.'

'We are willing to forgive you, so please, hurry up and get better.'

'I know life will be different for us all now, but we can get through this together, and hopefully become a united family.'

In hindsight, Patricia was really glad her Mum wasn't alive to witness the pain Conor had caused, with his secrets and lies.

She had heard of people leading a double life, but it was hard to believe Conor had actually succeeded in living 'a triple life' in a very small country, like Ireland.

Her Dad certainly was a very clever man, but unfortunately, she now realised, he had used his brains, in a very deceitful way.

'If Conor had lived in a vast country like America, or Australia or even China, where the population was extremely high, it would be easy to hide in those countries, but to disappear, in little old Ireland, took guts and enormous self importance,' Patricia pondered.

It showed her, how devious Conor was, to have actually succeeded in having three different families, and leading three different lives, in little old Ireland.

On one hand, Patricia admired his brains and his determination, but unfortunately she realised, he took what he wanted out of life, no matter what the consequences.

Patricia recalled how she and Helen worshipped Conor, and the lovely family life the three of them had together, but now, Patricia wondered, was that a part of the big lie too.

She knew, Helen would have been shocked and hurt to realise her relationship with Conor was based on secrets and lies. She would have been totally distraught to learn that Conor had deserted his son Paul, and married Alma, and then deserted her and her daughter Susan.

The more Patricia thought about her Mum's feelings on this crazy discovery; she was glad, her Mum had been spared the pain. Patricia felt betrayed, but she realised in comparison to Paul, Alma and Susan, she had been treated well by Conor, and he had actually shown love and commitment, to her and Helen.

From their chats over coffee, Patricia discovered that Conor hadn't shown Paul any love or affection, after his wife Kate died, which certainly explained Paul's anger.

It seemed that Conor was happy for a short time, with Alma and Susan, but then he cruelly told them, their love was suffocating him, and he had disappeared from their lives.

'How cruel was that?' Patricia questioned, but there were no answers.

She found it hard to believe that 'the stranger', whom her new family were talking about, was also her Dad, whom she loved, and trusted.

Patricia felt disappointed in Conor, but she knew, she would always stand by him, as he was her Dad, and she really loved him.

'He will certainly have a lot of explaining to do, when he recovers,' she thought rather sadly.

Patricia hoped and prayed Conor would recover, and tell his side of the story, and make some atonement for the pain, and hurt he had caused, by leading 'a triple life.'

Patricia didn't envy the road ahead for Conor, and she thought;

'Maybe he is being punished by the Universe for his secrets and lies.'

She recalled a bad karma quote, which she felt was so true of Conor's situation;

'Be careful how you treat people. What you do to others, has a funny way of coming back on you.'

Patricia shrugged her shoulders, as if to shake her dreary thoughts away, and she continued to read her short story assignment to Conor. She was engrossed in reading the last part of her story, when she heard the door open, she looked up, and she was surprised, to see Paul.

He actually smiled, and said a cheerful; 'Hello,' to Patricia and Conor.

'Wow, that's some progress,' Patricia thought happily.

She held her peace, smiled and returned the greeting.

Patricia was so pleased for Conor's sake, that Paul obviously had a change of heart, and was now willing to help Conor regain consciousness.

'How are things?'

'Has there been any change?' he asked hopefully.

'Unfortunately, there's nothing new to report.'

'Would you like to take a break now?' he offered.

'I'd like to finish reading my short story to Conor, and then you can take over.'

'I actually explained to Conor, how we all met in the creative writing class, and how Hazel discovered, that he was our Dad. Hazel gave me a copy of our short story assignments, and I read them to Conor, and perhaps that will encourage him back to reality.'

Patricia was pleasantly surprised when Paul said; 'Hopefully by reading to him, it will jog his memory and he will recover.'

'It will be nice for you and Conor to have time together today, Alma mentioned, she will drop in later,' Patricia said.

Paul sat beside Patricia, as she continued to read her short story. She was reading the second last paragraph, when she thought she heard crying. She looked at Conor, and she couldn't believe her eyes, she saw tears flowing down Conor's face.

She looked again to confirm; just in case it was her imagination running away with her, she stood up and walked closer to Conor, and she was thrilled to see, she hadn't been hallucinating.

Conor actually had tears rolling down his face, and he appeared to be trying to speak. His eyes were still shut, but he was definitely trying his utmost to communicate.

Patricia recalled the article she read during her research; 'People in comas often shed tears, possibly due to memories, both good and bad, or possibly what they hear, while in a coma.'

'A miracle was happening right in front of her eyes,' she was absolutely thrilled.

Patricia shouted at Paul, who actually hadn't noticed what was happening;

'Paul, look Dad is crying. He's actually trying to talk, he knows we are here.'

'Oh my God! He's going to be okay.' Patricia said excitedly.

'Quick, press the bell for the nurse, it's there beside you, please hurry. I just know he's going to recover, he's coming back to us,' she said laughing, and crying at the same time.

Paul just looked at her unenthusiastically, as he pressed the bell.

She stroked her Dad's face and looked at her hand, which was now wet from his tears. She never thought anyone's tears, could bring such joy to her, but the miracle of Conor's tears most certainly did.

She realised that Conor had taken his first step on the road to recovery, and she wanted to shout from the rooftops;

'My Dad is coming out of a coma, it's a miracle, and he is going to make a full recovery.'

She knew by Paul's expression he wasn't as overjoyed as she was, so she held her emotions in check.

Patricia recalled Paul's story of neglect by his Dad, who had sent him to live with his Gran, and hadn't even contacted him on his birthdays or at Christmas.

'Why should she expect Paul, to jump for joy now, when the man, who had deserted him, might now regain consciousness and live, and do the same, all over again?'

Patricia understood Paul's mixed emotions, she had been the lucky one, thankfully, she had experienced a very different side of Conor.

She was lucky; she saw the kind, caring Dad, not the cruel uncaring man, Paul had experienced. Like all human beings, she knew Conor had his faults, but she never realised his life had been so full of secrets, lies and abandonment.

It did trouble her, but nevertheless, she was determined to help him recover, and hopefully he would turn his life around, and make amends to all his families.

Patricia sent a text to the rest of the family, to let them know the current situation, and she hoped they would have a happier reaction, than Paul.

Nurse Gavin rushed into the room. 'Is everything all right?' she asked anxiously. Patricia was very excited, and she tried to explain what happened. She was tripping over her words; she was speaking so fast, and in very speedy outbursts, which were totally incoherent to Nurse Gavin.

'Take a deep breath Patricia, and tell me exactly what happened,' Nurse Gavin said calmly.

Patricia took a deep breath, and tried her utmost to calm down, even though she still spoke excitedly, Nurse Gavin managed to decipher her erratic words.'

'I saw Dad crying … I felt his face … it was wet from his tears … he is trying to communicate with us.'

'Feel his face, it's still wet from his tears … he's coming out of the coma … he's going to be all right.'

'I just know he's … trying to communicate with us.'

Patricia continued to talk nonstop; she was giddy with excitement, and full of hope.

'Nurse Gavin, during my research into comas, I read;

'People who are recovering from a coma often cry … while they are comatose because … their brain is alert … they know what's going on … but they just can't communicate their feelings in words … hence the tears,' she babbled.

'All right Patricia, let me have a look, I will do a few reflex tests on Conor.'

Patricia and Paul watched, as Nurse Gavin did numerous tests, but alas, there was no response from Conor.

He just lay there in that awful vegetative state.

Patricia felt her heart was breaking in pieces. She still believed her Dad was aware of them, and that he was trying his utmost to communicate with them.

Patricia ever the optimist, wasn't giving in, she was convinced that Conor was getting a second chance in life, and nobody would convince her otherwise.

She was determined to help him recover, and she really wanted to be part of the miracle, which in her mind, was going to happen.

She would ensure that Paul, Alma and Susan, would also be part of Conor's recovery programme.

Patricia knew they all needed to hear Conor's side of the story, the story behind his secrets and lies, and she was now convinced, he would recover, and tell them.

Conor needed to explain to them; 'Why he had chosen to desert them,' when he should have loved and cherished them all.

He most certainly needed to make amends, especially to Paul, whom he had managed to hurt so badly.

Patricia's thoughts were racing wildly; she took a few deep 'Mindfulness breaths' to calm herself, and to return to reality.

'I'll do one more test,' Nurse Gavin said.

'Oh please do,' Patricia pleaded.

'I know Conor wants to come back to us,' she said with passion and hope in her voice.

Then suddenly the miracle happened, as Patricia felt it would, and Conor magically opened his eyes, during the intensive test.

Nurse Gavin smiled at Patricia, as she pressed the bell for assistance, and she also paged Dr Mc Quoid, requesting he come to ICU, immediately.

'See, I was right, Conor came back to us,' Yippee! (6).

'Hello Dad, Welcome back,' she said excitedly.

Nurse Gavin smiled and said to Conor;

'Mr Rutlin, Welcome back.'

'I'll just wet your lips, with water. How are you feeling?' she asked softly.

Patricia noticed Conor blinking his eyes.

'Nurse Gavin, I think Conor is telling you he is okay, see he's blinking his eyes.'

'Yes, your Dad is coming back, to you all,' she said trying to include Paul, who had remained silent.

Paul was rather shocked when Conor opened his eyes, after seeing him lying, for months in a vegetative state; he had given up hope on a recovery. He now realised he hadn't actually believed Conor would recover, unlike Patricia who had amazing faith in his recovery.

Now, he had mixed emotions, but mostly, he was rather pleased, but he was also wary, of hearing Conor's side of the story.

He would try to be patient with Conor, and listen to his side of the story, because he now knew, life can be taken away so quickly.

He certainly wouldn't like to be in Conor's shoes, when he explained to his three families his secrets and lies.

Paul was pleased; he was meeting Marissa later, she would be happy to hear Conor had regained consciousness, and he now valued her support, and advice.

Chapter 32

Conor was happy, when he eventually managed to croak, the most important word;

'Sorry!'

Patricia actually heard him.

'How fitting,' he thought.

'I just heard Dad say; 'Sorry,' she said excitedly.

She knew they didn't believe her, but she didn't care, she had definitely heard him say 'Sorry.'

Conor tried again to speak, and this time they all heard him.

'Sorry!'

Nurse Gavin said; 'It's great to have you back, Mr Rutlin.'

'Dad, don't worry, we all love you, no matter what happened in the past,' Patricia said reassuringly.

'Hello Dad,' Paul said softly.

Conor was happy to hear Paul's voice.

On the days of his coma, when he heard them talking, Conor had been shocked at how angry Paul was.

He knew Paul had no time for him, after Kate died, but it still upset him to hear how much Paul seemed to dislike him.

Of course he understood, as Paul felt he had deserted him, after Kate's death, but he hoped with time, Paul would forgive him.

Conor now recalled how his wonderful daughter Patricia, had whispered in his ear, whenever they were alone;

'Dad, please, get better, and we can all make a fresh start.'

It obviously, was God's will to let him live, but also Patricia's kind words had definitely spurred him on to a full recovery.

He now felt hopeful, that his three families would in time, forgive him.

After Conor had croaked, *'Sorry,'* he actually heard Patricia say;

'Shish, Shish, Oh my Goodness!'

'Dad's trying to speak again.'

Conor, kept forcing his voice and eventually, in a very croaky, whisper he uttered, the most important words;

'I am so Sorry.'

Suddenly the tears were flowing, he couldn't stop them, and he struggled to keep his eyes open, as the tears streamed down his face.

When he eventually managed to keep his eyes open, he hazily saw Patricia, Paul, Susan, Alma, and a nurse standing by his bed.

It was a lot to take in, but Conor was so happy to be alive, and to have been given, 'a second chance in life.'

'Hello there,' they softly said.

Conor was thrilled to hear them speak, and he was so glad they weren't angry with him. He felt his body begin to heal a little, as the heavy burden of guilt, and betrayal was lifted from his shoulders.

He was no fool, he knew there was an extremely bumpy road ahead, but he was willing to make a huge effort, and make amends to them all.

Hopefully in time his relationship with Paul would improve, and perhaps they would leave behind the anger, and separation. But Conor wasn't fooling himself he knew reconciliation would be a slow process, he wasn't even sure, if and when, it would happen.

Conor reminded himself to 'be strong' and deal with whatever was ahead, now that his secrets and lies were exposed. He was no fool; he knew his three families would expect answers, in a week or two.

He tried to get his thoughts together, but the pain in his head, and his dry throat would only allow him to say; 'So sorry,' which he kept trying to repeat.

Patricia, his ever loving, gentle daughter, said;

'It's alright Dad, please don't worry about anything now, just concentrate on getting better.

Two weeks later Conor was thrilled, to be surrounded by Patricia, Alma, Susan and Paul, when he was discharged from hospital.

Conor was beaming, when he realised how lucky he was to get 'a second chance' to amend his selfish ways.

He couldn't believe how excited he was, to see them all again, how times had changed for him, he now loved being surrounded by his family, and he didn't feel one bit suffocated.

His near death experience, made him realise how lucky he was to have such a wonderful family.

He knew his 'angel Kate' was minding them all and his 'angel Helen' was protecting them also.

Patricia very kindly invited Conor to her house, until he was back on his feet again. As he was feeling quite weak, he accepted her offer, as he knew, he needed her help, to make a speedy recovery.

'That's great news Dad, I was afraid you wouldn't accept my help,' Patricia said as she hugged him, she loved him unconditionally, and she didn't judge him, for his shady past.

'Well, it's certainly a change, and progress for me, as I don't like being dependent on anyone,' he said, and they both laughed.

He knew he was a very lucky man, to get 'a second chance' to share his life with Patricia, Paul, Alma, and Susan, and he vowed to make every second count.

By getting a second chance it allowed him see more clearly his mistakes, and it made him appreciate his three lovely adult children, and kind Alma. Life would be busier and more exciting for him with his lovely extended family.

Conor now realised, life was precious, and that nice people, like his wonderful family, were rare and precious too. He was happily surprised, how much he actually enjoyed his large families company, and amazingly he didn't feel stifled or suffocated anymore.

Thankfully his beautiful 'Heart Tattoo' had eventually reunited him with his three beautiful families.

A few weeks later, Conor tried to explain to Paul, Alma, Susan, and Patricia why he had abandoned them, and why he had kept so many secrets, and told so many lies.

Conor said; 'I am not trying to make excuses, for my bad behaviour, but a part of me shut down and died, when Simon and Kate died, and that's when I unintentionally, began my life of secrets.'

He explained to Paul, that he reminded him too much of Simon and Kate, and he wanted to escape the pain, and that's why he let him live with his Gran.

'I am so sorry for abandoning you Paul, I hope you can forgive me, and give me another chance,' he said with tears in his eyes.

Paul, took a deep breath and said; 'I have always believed, everyone deserves 'a second chance', so I am willing to give you another chance,' and he actually smiled.

'I appreciate that, son,' Conor said doing, a thumbs up, hoping with time, Paul would eventually accept, a hug.

Conor explained to Alma, that he had rushed into their marriage, while he was still hurting inside from Kate's death.

'I made such of mess of our life together, I thought you and Susan would be better off without me, so I decided to make a clean break and then go for a divorce.'

'I am so sorry, for the pain I caused; hopefully, you will give me another chance.'

'In answer to that Alma and Susan, surprised themselves, and actually gave Conor a big hug, which surprised him also.

Conor continued; 'Patricia, you and Helen were 'my saving grace' in my life of secrets and lies. But when Helen died, I felt I was being punished once again, and I wanted to escape, but thankfully you wouldn't allow it,' he smiled.

'I know, I pestered you Dad, but I couldn't face losing you, after losing my wonderful Mum, so suddenly,' she said hugging Conor tightly.

'I am so sorry for all the hurt I have caused, and for being so selfish.'

'I was actually struggling big time, with my conscience before the accident, but I hadn't the courage to reveal, or sort out my secrets, and lies,' he confessed.

'Because of my accident, and thanks to my lovely 'Heart Tattoo', I can now stop surrounding myself with secrets, and surround myself instead, with my three lovely families,' he smiled.

'I now realise, how selfish and immature I was, I intend to change my ways, and I'll always be there for you all,' he emphasised.

Conor was now determined to make amends for the past, and hopefully in time, Paul, Alma, Susan and Patricia would forgive him.

Now, that the 'Secrets of the Heart Tattoo' had come crashing down, Conor suddenly felt free and alive, and he now looked forward to the future, with his three wonderful families.

He felt very proud when they called him 'Dad'.

He prayed to his darling angels; 'Kate, Simon and Helen', for help on the bumpy journey ahead, and he asked them to love and support, his three families.

Conor appreciated that his beloved *'Heart Tattoo'* ultimately saved his life, his sanity, and reunited him with his three families.

Acknowledgements

'Thank You' to my dear parents Eileen & Lawrence Mc Cormack (RIP).

'Thank You' to all my wonderful sisters and wonderful brothers, those living, and those gone ahead, to pave the way for the rest of us; Maura, Kathleen (RIP), Brid (RIP), Lena, Paddy, Philip, Bernadette and Dolores and to my dear husband George (RIP).

I am so lucky to have such a wonderful family; I know you are always there for me.

To all my sister-in-laws, brother-in-laws, nieces, nephews and all my grandnieces and grandnephews … who bring great joy to my life, where did the years go phew, ha ha yippee!

'Thank You' to my three adopted sisters; Marie, Phyllis and Kathleen (my husband George's sisters), and to George's brothers and their wives; Sean and Hannah, Tommy and Rita and my brother-in-laws, John and George.

'Thank You' to all my superb friends, you bring great joy to my life.

'Thank You' to all my lovely, very kind and supportive neighbours.

'Thank You' to the amazing 'Travel Department' for all my wonderful adventures, and to all my lovely 'Travel Buddies' whom I've met over the years, especially my Christmas buddies.

Thanks to beautiful 'Ireland' and sunny 'Tenerife' for providing me with peace and tranquillity, and a beautiful sunny space to write.

A Message from Margaret Mc Cormack

My gift for writing and storytelling, I got from my Dad. My persistence and appetite for knowledge, I got from my Mum. My sense of humour comes from all the banter over the years, with all my lovely siblings.

Thanks to the superb authors who inspired me; Maeve Binchy, Oscar Wilde, John Grisham, and Neil Gaiman, James Joyce, Oscar Wilde, etc.

I gave a thumbs up to Maeve Binchy in my novel by including a character 'Maeve'.

Thanks also to 'Oprah Winfrey' for her bravery in leading the way for females, with her motivational and inspirational attitude to life; 'Girl Power.'

I included in my novel; 'Cúpla focal as Gaeilge', 'Some words in Irish' and 'Seanfhocail na hÉireann', 'Proverbs in Irish', as a tribute to my Mum and Dad. They loved the Irish language, and my Mum was a fluent Irish speaker.

I also included my favourite uplifting, cheerful word; 'Yippee!' (6 times) … in my novel for my family and friends to find while reading.

To my lovely readers, I hope you can find the cheerful word also; 'Yippee.'

Thanks to my friend 'Google' who enabled me to research lots of Websites.

Please note any mistakes made compiling the information in my novel, they are solely mine.

Finally, Thanks to you, the 'Readers', I hope you found the journey through my first novel, as exciting as I did when writing, and doing research.

I will leave you with this thought;

'Keep on reading, because it's good for the mind, body and soul, and enjoy all the chapters in your life.'
Yippee!

Available worldwide online and from all good bookstores

www.mtp.agency

Printed in Great Britain
by Amazon

72287531R00215